ALISON WEIR is the top-selling female historian (and the fifth-bestselling historian overall) in the United Kingdom, and has sold over three million books worldwide. She has published nineteen history books, including her most recent non-fiction book, *Queens of the Crusades*, the second in her England's Medieval Queens quartet. Alison has also published several historical novels, including *Innocent Traitor* and *The Lady Elizabeth*.

Katharine Parr: The Sixth Wife is Alison Weir's eleventh published novel and the final book in the Six Tudor Queens series about the wives of Henry VIII, which was launched in 2016 to great critical acclaim. All five previous novels in the series were *Sunday Times* bestsellers.

Alison is a fellow of the Royal Society of Arts and an honorary life patron of Historic Royal Palaces.

ALISON WEIR

SIX TUDOR QUEENS

KATHARINE PARR
THE SIXTH WIFE

REVIEW

First published in Great Britain in 2021 by
HEADLINE REVIEW
An imprint of HEADLINE PUBLISHING GROUP

1

Cataloguing in Publication Data is available from the British Library

ISBN 978 1 4722 2782 9 (Hardback)
ISBN 978 1 4722 2783 6 (Trade paperback)

Typeset in Garamond MT by Avon DataSet Ltd, Arden Court, Alcester, Warwickshire

Printed and bound in Great Britain by Clays Ltd, Elcograf S.p.A.

HEADLINE PUBLISHING GROUP
An Hachette UK Company
Carmelite House
50 Victoria Embankment
London EC4Y 0DZ

www.headline.co.uk
www.hachette.co.uk

Six Tudor Queens

Katharine Parr
The Sixth Wife

1543

HOUSE OF TUDOR

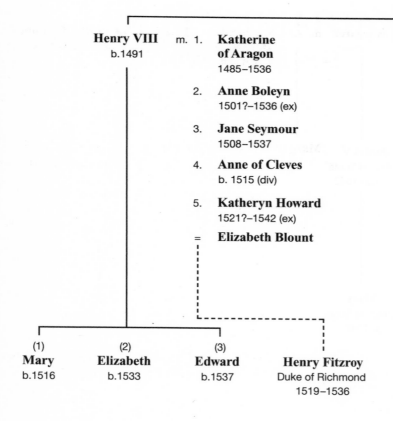

Henry VIII b.1491	m. 1.	**Katherine** **of Aragon** 1485–1536
	2.	**Anne Boleyn** 1501?–1536 (ex)
	3.	**Jane Seymour** 1508–1537
	4.	**Anne of Cleves** b. 1515 (div)
	5.	**Katheryn Howard** 1521?–1542 (ex)
	=	**Elizabeth Blount**

| (1)
Mary
b.1516 | (2)
Elizabeth
b.1533 | (3)
Edward
b.1537 | **Henry Fitzroy**
Duke of Richmond
1519–1536 |

Henry VII m. **Elizabeth of York**

James IV m. 1. **Margaret** m. 2. **Archibald**   **Mary** m. **Charles Brandon**
King of Scots   **Douglas**   Duke of Suffolk
                                                Earl of Angus

James V   **Margaret Douglas**   **Frances** m. **Henry Grey**
King of Scots   b.1515   Marquess of Dorset
1512–1542

Mary   **Lady Jane Grey**
Queen of Scots   b.1536
b.1542

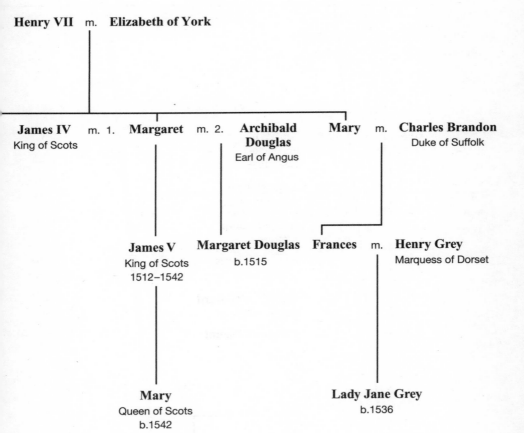

1517

THE PARRS

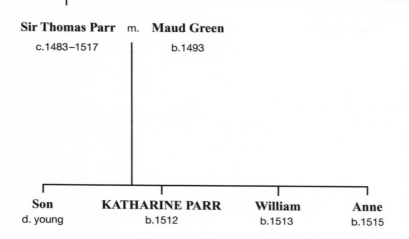

Sir Thomas Parr m. **Maud Green**
c.1483–1517   b.1493

Son   **KATHARINE PARR**   **William**   **Anne**
d. young   b.1512   b.1513   b.1515

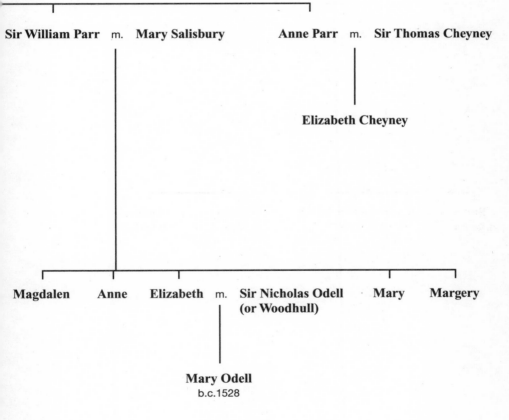

Sir William Parr   m.   Mary Salisbury   Anne Parr   m.   Sir Thomas Cheyney

Elizabeth Cheyney

Magdalen   Anne   Elizabeth   m.   Sir Nicholas Odell · Mary   Margery
                                                   (or Woodhull)

Mary Odell
b.c.1528

Dedicated to the cherished memory of our adored son,
John William James Weir (1982–2020)

and my darling mother,
Doreen Ethel Cullen (1927–2020)

She is a woman, in my judgement, for certain virtue, wisdom and gentleness, most meet for his Highness. And sure I am that his Majesty had never a wife more agreeable to his heart than she is.

Sir Thomas Wriothesley

Considering my miserable life, my heart is of marble, wilful, unreasonable.

Queen Katharine Parr

Part One

'A lively, pleasing appearance'

Chapter 1

Katharine was five when death cast its black shadow over her life. It was a terrible time of fear and grief when the dread plague known as the sweating sickness ravaged London. She squeezed herself into a corner as the house at Blackfriars was boarded up against the pestilence, and shrank at the tolling of the bells of the city's churches and the smell of the herbal medicines made by Mother just in case anyone in the household was struck down. Young as she was, she understood the gravity of the situation. Set to her easy tasks in the still room, she had heard the adults talking in the kitchen beyond, heard them speak of the speed with which the sweat could kill, of people just dropping dead in the street without warning. She learned that even the King had fled from London. She knew, as well as anyone else, the signs of the disease, watched herself in case she felt shivery, or dizzy or thirsty, or developed a headache and other pains. She knew too that, if she lived for a whole day and night with the sweat, she would recover. That would be her only hope.

She was utterly thankful that Mother had returned from serving the Queen. In her calm, reassuring presence, things did not seem as frightening. Mother had taught Katharine and her four-year-old brother William a special prayer: 'Lighten mine eyes, O Lord, lest I sleep the sleep of death.' Each day, they had to confess their little sins to Dr Melton, the chaplain, so that they might always be in a state of grace, ready to meet their Maker. Two-year-old Anne was too young to say meaningful prayers, but Mother made up for that, praying over her youngest every evening as she held her to her swollen belly. Katharine knew there would be another baby brother or sister soon. She was hoping that the horrible sweating sickness would be gone before the child arrived – and that it would be a girl. But the plague raged on, even into November, which was when Father fell ill of the sweat.

Banned from the sickroom for fear of infection, Katharine watched her mother bustling in and out with bowls of steaming water and towels. She watched the front door being unboarded to admit the physician and, two days later, her father's lawyer, both of them with clove-scented linen bound around the lower part of their faces. She was aware of a hush descending on the house and the need to go about quietly.

The next day brought her beloved Uncle William, Father's younger brother, and Father Cuthbert Tunstall, as the children knew him. The priest was placid, wise and gentle, with a clean-shaven face and a crooked nose. He was not only their kinsman, but a great friend to them all and a very important man, for he served King Henry. Katharine adored him as much as she did Uncle William, who was rather portly and had twinkling eyes and a merry round face. Both men were very kind, assuring the children that Father was safe in God's hands and that God could be trusted to do what was right for him. It was a lesson Katharine would always remember. But she did not miss the tear in the eye of her rough-mannered, soldierly uncle.

It was hard to accept that God knew best when, that evening, Mother, bravely stifling her sobs, told them that Father had died and gone to Heaven. The house was draped in black and everyone put on mourning clothes. When Katharine heard the great bell tolling at the nearby Blackfriars monastery, she knew it was for her father. Uncle William told her that it would toll thirty-four times, one for every year of Sir Thomas Parr's life.

The children did not attend the burial in the chapel of St Anne in the Blackfriars, which was where Father had wanted to be buried, next to their older brother, who had died at birth. They watched their mother, her fair hair hidden beneath a nun-like headdress and black veil, walk out of the door, leaning heavily on Uncle William's arm. Little Will was crying, and Katharine was dangerously near tears herself, striving to come to terms with the fact that her father would never wake up and that she would never see him again. She wanted to remember him as he was when he was alive and well.

He had been clever and learned – a great man at the court of King Henry. He had been close to the King, as Mother was close to the Queen, who was Katharine's godmother and took a special interest in her, even though Katharine had never met her. Both her parents had spent much time at court; Mother even had her own chambers there, and Katharine now wondered if she would return to her duties.

It did not matter to her that her father had been rich and important; it was the debonair man with laughter lines about his eyes whom she would remember and grieve for, a good father who had prized and loved his children.

'Do not weep, little ones,' Dr Melton had said kindly as he followed the family out of the house, his missal in his hand. 'Your father has gone to God. We must be happy for him and not question the Lord's will.'

Katharine wished she could be so accepting. She wanted to be like her mother, who was bearing her loss very bravely. But, every time she thought of Father, she could not stop crying.

Agnes, her nurse, put her arms around the children and hugged them, then led them into the parlour where a welcoming fire was crackling on the hearth.

'I will tell you a story,' she said, and proceeded to relate a colourful tale of Robin Hood and Maid Marian. Then she set the children to building a house of cards, and that was how the mourners found them when they returned from the chapel. Mother's eyes were red, but she was smiling as she took Katharine and Will by the hand and led them into the hall, where the funeral meats were laid out. It was a small gathering because of the sweat.

After the meal, the family retired to the parlour and, as the children resumed their building game, the adults settled by the fire.

'I can't believe he's gone,' Mother said, in a broken voice. 'We were granted just nine years together. I never thought to be a widow at twenty-five and having to bring up my children single-handed.'

Katharine watched Uncle William reach across and lay his hand on her mother's. 'You are not alone,' he said.

'No, you are not, Maud,' Father Cuthbert assured her. 'We will look after you. It is what Thomas wanted, and why he named us his executors.'

'You will not be in want,' Uncle William chimed in. 'Will is to succeed his father. The girls have been left marriage portions that will secure them respectable husbands. Not noble ones, but solid matches.'

Mother sighed. 'Yes, and I must be grateful for that, but he left nothing for this little one.' She patted her belly. 'If it is a boy, he will have no inheritance. If a girl, I myself must provide her with a dowry. Thomas was not thinking logically. The illness crazed his brain. Without the income from his offices at court, I will have less money to live on, and I must conserve Will's inheritance. There is nothing for it. I must live modestly.'

'Will you return to the Queen's service?' Father Cuthbert asked.

'When this one is born, I must,' Mother said. 'I thought of going north to Kendal, where I could live more cheaply, but the castle there is derelict, and it is a long way from all my friends.'

'You must not even consider it.' Uncle William was adamant. 'You must close this house up and come to live with me and Mary at Rye House.'

Katharine's ears pricked up. Everything she had ever heard about Rye House had led her to believe it was a wondrous place. Her cousins were there, and it would be a mercy to get away from London and the plague.

Mother's face had lightened. 'William, I cannot tell you what your kindness means to me. I would love to come. It will be good for the children. The air is so healthy there. But I fear I must ask you another favour.'

'You have only to name it,' Uncle William said gallantly.

'I need help with my finances,' she replied, 'and someone to manage our estates in the north, because I will be better placed in the south to secure good futures for my children. I must devote my life to them from now on.'

'You may leave all that safely to me,' Uncle William said.

Mother rose and embraced him. 'No woman ever had a better brother-in-law.'

'Could your own kinsfolk help?' Father Cuthbert enquired.

'The Greens?' Mother shook her head. 'You know that my father died in the Tower under suspicion of treason. I was the last of the line and his heiress. Everything I had, I brought to Thomas. I do have family connections in the north and the Midlands, but . . .'

Katharine had often heard her parents speak of their kinship with noble families – Vauxes, Throckmortons, Nevilles, Dacres, Talbots and Father Cuthbert's family, the Tunstalls, to name a few. These connections were a source of great pride to them all, but it was hard trying to remember their names. She didn't know any of these people and she suspected her mother hadn't had much to do with them either.

'There's no need to worry about them,' Uncle William said, 'not when you have me.'

'And I can help you make the arrangements for your move to Rye House,' Father Cuthbert offered.

'Thank you, my dear friend,' Mother said. 'In truth, I long to be there.'

In the days that followed, they were all busy preparing for the move. The house at Blackfriars was to be shut up and left with a steward in charge. Mother bade Katharine and Will pack their favourite belongings and Katharine filled an iron-bound chest with her dolls, her Book of Hours with its colourful painted borders, the horn book she used to learn her letters and numbers, her spinning top, her ball and cup and her lute. She remembered her copybooks and her box of pens, which were most important, for Mother was teaching her to write in a fine Italian hand, which she practised daily.

On top of them all, she laid her most cherished possession, a fine cloth given to her at her baptism by the Queen, for whom she had been named, and who had herself embroidered on it, within a circle of gold, the initials K.I.P. – which, Mother had explained, stood for 'Katherine, Infanta, Princess' – and the motto *Plus Oultre*. That meant 'Further Beyond', and was the motto of Spain, whence the Queen hailed, but

Mother thought it was apt for Katharine, who, she felt sure, would go further beyond what was expected of her. The cloth had been precious to the Queen because her own mother had made it for her. She must think highly indeed of Mother to give her child such a treasure.

The Queen had also given Katharine beads of German lacquer decorated with gold, which she often wore around her neck. Katharine wished she could meet the good Queen and longed for the day when she was old enough to go to court.

By the time they were ready to leave in December, the sweat had at last run its murderous course and people were out and about in London again.

'I am so glad that life is back to normal,' Mother said, as she pulled on her gloves; and then her face fell. 'Not that anything will ever be normal again.' Katharine knew she was thinking about Father, but she would not let herself be sad for long. 'I was worried about travelling with the contagion still about and would have deferred it if need be. But now we are on our way!' She smiled at her children and picked up chubby little Anne, then led the way through the front door to the waiting litter outside.

Seated beside her mother, snug in furs and with her feet resting on a warmed brick wrapped in felt, Katharine looked back at the house where she had been born, memorising every detail of its timber-framed frontage, the diamond panes of the mullioned windows twinkling in the winter sunshine, the shield above the door bearing the blue-and-white banded arms of the Parrs, and the motto beneath, 'Love with Loyalty'. Life would never be the same as it had been, and she would miss her father, but she was beginning to look forward, for she was embarking on an exciting adventure.

Mother did not wish to be rushed, so they made the journey to Hoddesdon at a leisurely pace, lodging overnight at an inn near Enfield, north of London. Late the following afternoon, they arrived at Rye House, and Katharine was open-mouthed with delight at the sight of it. Rising above a wide moat, and surrounded by a high wall, it looked like a palace out of a fairy tale, with its turrets and battlements. When they passed through the gatehouse, she saw that most of the enclosure was laid with gardens, and that the red-brick manor house was of a modest size. Uncle William led them into a square hall, where Aunt Mary, plump and apple-cheeked, was waiting to greet them with steaming ale and spice cakes. She embraced her husband and Mother, and kissed the children.

'Do come and sit in the parlour,' she bade them, leading them through one of the two doors behind the high table on the dais into a whitewashed room with bright red hangings, where she placed the refreshments on the table. There, waiting demurely in a line, were five little girls, who all bobbed curtseys and stared at Katharine and her siblings.

'You remember your cousins?' Uncle William asked. Katharine nodded, for she had seen the older ones at some long-ago family gathering, but had little recollection of that occasion. 'They will be companions for you all.'

The girls were introduced as Magdalen, Nan, Elizabeth, Mary and Margery, in descending order of age. Magdalen was two years older than Katharine, and Margery was two, of an age with Anne. They were all fair and blue-eyed and very pretty. Despite looking askance at Will, the only boy in the room, they seemed excited to have new playmates. Within an hour, friendships had been struck, and Katharine began to see a new life opening out, banishing the sadness of her old one.

It was a mild winter and the older children were out of doors most days, playing ball, catch or hide-and-seek in the gardens and the vast hunting park, sailing their wooden boats on the River Lea, which fed the moat, or hunting for greenery to make Christmas garlands. They were given ponies and taught how to ride them, and were allowed to accompany the adults when they went hunting or hawking. Katharine loved being out in the fresh, crisp air; she was enthralled by the soaring flights of the falcons, the thrill of the chase and the feeling of freedom being in the saddle gave her. She was fearless, urging her willing pony on to ever greater exploits. Will was happy too. If their cousins had ever been reluctant to admit a boy to their pastimes, they had forgotten it; he was one of them now. Every day, as dusk fell, the children would arrive in the kitchens red-cheeked with their buskins muddy and their hair tousled, and Cook would give them drinks of steaming aleberry.

Not long after Katharine and her family arrived at Rye House, they were joined by a cousin, Elizabeth Cheyney. At twelve, she was much older than the Parr children, but she was pleased to join in their games and tried to mother them, although she got short shrift there. Only the youngest ones suffered her to fuss over them. Katharine felt sorry for Anne, who didn't like being dressed up and pulled about, yet she was grateful to Elizabeth for diverting her. She loved her little sister, and would have spent more time with her, but Anne was too young to enjoy the many exciting distractions at Rye House, not least of which was Katharine's growing friendship with Magdalen Parr. There was a warmth and spirit about the girl that drew her, and soon they were inseparable. And so the busy winter days passed, until the first buds of spring appeared in the gardens.

As the days lengthened, Mother prepared for her confinement. She took from the bottom of her travelling chest the swaddling bands and tiny garments that Katharine, Will and Anne had worn, and had them washed.

A midwife was sent for. The children were shooed away when Mother's pains began, and Elizabeth was ordered to take them out into the park, where they spent a happy day running about.

When they returned, they found Uncle William in the hall, his countenance sombre.

'Your mother is well,' he said, 'but, sadly, the babe was born dead.'

Katharine burst into noisy tears for the sister she would never know. Aunt Mary hastened to comfort her, cuddling her against her warm bosom, as Anne joined in the wailing, not to be left out.

'Can we see Mother?' Will asked.

'When she has rested, child,' Aunt Mary said.

When they did enter Mother's bedchamber, she held out her arms to them. 'God has seen fit to take your sister,' she said in a shaky voice as they climbed up on the bed. 'But He has left me you three dear children. And the little one has gone to be with your father. We must not mourn them too much. They are in Heaven, with God, where we all aspire to be. We will remember them both in our prayers.'

When Mother arose from her lying-in two weeks later, she spent hours closeted with Uncle William and Father Cuthbert, who was visiting Rye House before travelling on to Lincoln, where he was a canon at the cathedral.

'We are drawing up a plan for your education,' she told Katharine one afternoon, when they were all together in the parlour. 'I shall have to return to the Queen's service at some stage, and Uncle William has agreed that you will remain here to be tutored with your cousins. I will be here as often as I can to see you and discover what progress you are making.'

Young as she was, Katharine was aware that her mother was a clever woman who cared passionately about learning. She could speak French and even Latin.

'Your mother has very enlightened ideas,' Uncle William said. 'She has decided that you girls will receive the same education as William. It's all a bit beyond me; I'm just a plain fighting man, so I'm leaving the organising of it to you, Maud.'

'Your mother is following the example of our kinsman, Sir Thomas More,' Father Cuthbert told Katharine. 'He has had his daughters taught on an equal footing with his son. Their learning is renowned. The King and Queen are taking Sir Thomas's advice in educating the Princess Mary.'

'Girls are as intelligent as boys,' Mother declared. 'They are not as weak as some would have us believe.'

'Indeed, they are not!' Father Cuthbert agreed, though Uncle William looked slightly dubious.

'I keep an open mind,' he grinned. 'Who am I to question the wisdom of Sir Thomas More and the King?'

'Oh, go on with you!' Aunt Mary said, giving him a playful buffet.

Katharine had enjoyed the lessons Mother had been giving her for

11

the past year, when she was on leave from the court. She was a good teacher and enjoyed imparting her knowledge to her children. From the way the adults were talking, this new plan for her education sounded exciting.

Uncle William was looking speculatively at Mother. 'It's early days yet, Maud, but you are still young, and some gentleman of the court may offer you marriage. If that happens . . .'

'No,' Mother said firmly, her fair cheeks flushed. 'I do not intend to marry again. I cannot jeopardise Will's inheritance, which I hold in trust for him. No, William, I mean to devote my life to my children. I would see them well educated and well married. And I have a duty to the Queen too.'

'Well, if you change your mind, you know that the children will always have a home here, if need be,' Uncle William smiled.

He told Mother that she could have the smaller parlour behind the dais for a schoolroom. Tables and stools were provided for all the children except the youngest, who were to wait until they were four before they joined the lessons.

The months passed tranquilly. They had been at Rye House a year, eighteen months . . . Every day began with prayers. Mother was a devout woman and desired to instil in her children and those in her charge a deep love of God and obedience to His Word. She found an excellent tutor in Uncle William's household chaplain, Dr Clarke, who taught his pupils about something called the New Learning.

'You know that the Bible contains the Scriptures, which are the Word of God?' he asked them. They all nodded. 'For hundreds of years, the Scriptures have always been in Latin, and priests have sought to explain them to us. Now, scholars are seeking a better understanding of Latin and Greek, so that they can read the Bible for themselves. One day, God willing, we will all be able to read it in English, and it is for that reason, more than any other, that you children must be diligent at your lessons.'

Katharine loved the Bible stories her mother told them. How wonderful it would be to read them for herself. She worked hard at her

Latin lessons and did so well that Dr Clarke taught her some Greek too.

'You have an aptitude for languages, child,' he told her, beaming.

Her mother taught them French, which Katharine picked up easily. Anne did too, when she was old enough to join the older children in the classroom. They were a happy group, the eight of them, fair and auburn heads bent over their books, with the sun streaming in through the latticed window. Their mornings were devoted to lessons and, in the afternoons, they ran free out of doors, playing endless games of ball, chase and make-believe, or building snowmen and gathering holly and ivy in the winter. So happy was Katharine in those heady days of childhood that, after Mother first returned to court, leaving her standing in tears under the gatehouse, watching until the little procession vanished in the distance, she barely missed her. She was lost without Will, though, when, in the spring of 1520, at the age of six, thanks to Mother's influence with the Queen, he was taken as a page in the King's train when his Grace went to France to meet with the French King. When he got home in July, he was full of the wonders he had seen.

'They are calling it the Field of Cloth of Gold,' he related, 'because so many people were wearing their finest clothes. There was wondrous splendour and pageantry, and I have never seen such crowds. The King glittered with jewels! He is a mighty man indeed! When I grow up, Kate, I am going to be a courtier!' Will was never content with his life at Rye House after that.

Uncle William was there more often than Mother was, a constant and affectionate father figure. Katharine knew it was thanks to him that she was enjoying life so much. When she was eight, wanting to tell him how much she loved him and show her gratitude, she decided to give him the Book of Hours she had inherited from her father, and wrote a special dedication in it: *Uncle, when you do on this look, I pray you remember who wrote this in your book. Your loving niece, Katharine Parr.* There were tears in her uncle's eyes when he read it.

Chapter 2

In April, when the world was fresh and green and the trees were bursting with birdsong, Katharine looked at herself in her burnished silver mirror and decided she liked what she saw. She was nearly eleven now, and becoming quite the graceful young lady her mother wanted her to be. Her features were pleasing, her hazel eyes warm and bright. If there was a flaw, it was that her nose was a little too long and turned up, like her brother's. She had grown taller than most girls her age, and she was slender, even with the small breasts budding beneath her bodice.

She hurriedly brushed her long auburn hair and hastened downstairs to join the others in the schoolroom. This morning, they were to study Petrarch's sonnets as an aid to learning Italian, and Cicero. She liked Cicero and agreed with him that a room without books was like a body without a soul. Her younger cousins thought he was boring, and that living with her nose in a book would ruin Katharine's eyesight and make it harder for her to secure a husband, but Magdalen and Anne understood. Neither they nor Katharine were bothered about finding husbands. They were happy as they were. As the wise Cicero said, 'If you have a garden and a library, you have everything you need.' She looked fondly at the books lined up on top of the court cupboard. Precious things indeed!

But before they could get to Petrarch and Cicero, they were to study mathematics. It was Father Cuthbert's idea. A keen mathematician himself, he had once written a treatise on arithmetic. On his frequent visits to Rye House, he liked to see what progress the children had made. Katharine was good with figures and geometry. It was deeply satisfying solving the conundrums they posed.

It was not Dr Clarke who walked into the schoolroom that morning, but Mother, who was home on leave from her duties at court, and Aunt Mary, followed by Elizabeth Cheyney, who, at eighteen, had heavy, well-bred features with a certain demure charm.

'Your good tutor has a megrim,' Mother told them, as they rose from their curtseys and Will from his bow. 'You will have to put up with us for today, girls. Will, Dr Clarke tells me that you have an essay on Julius Caesar to finish, so you will get on with that.'

'And you, young ladies, will accompany me to the still room to make up some physick for the stores,' Aunt Mary told them.

Katharine sighed; she would rather have been at her books. But Mother was ever insistent that girls should be taught to be efficient in running a large household, against the time when they should be married. On certain days, when Will was learning horsemanship, fighting skills and gentlemanly sports, she and Aunt Mary would teach their daughters how to budget and keep accounts, manage the servants, oversee the preparation and service of food, and become familiar with the mysteries of the still room, which included everything from jam-making to distilling scents and mixing medicines. Katharine would much have preferred to be out riding with Will, or even practising fencing with the sergeant-at-arms in the courtyard. How she envied her brother his masculine freedom!

'There is no need to make a face, Katharine,' Mother said. 'Domestic tasks are as important for young ladies as book-learning, and have to be done. There is no point in walking around with a head full of Cicero if your husband is roaring for his dinner! Perhaps you would rather I set you to spinning?'

Katharine caught the twinkle in Mother's eye. She knew her daughter hated spinning. Probably she herself would also have liked nothing better than to be left alone with her books. But, with Mother, duty always came before her personal inclinations.

'Before we get started,' Mother said, 'we have some good news.'

'Elizabeth is to marry the son of Lord Vaux,' Aunt Mary told them. Elizabeth blushed, looking a trifle smug. Lord Vaux was her guardian, and the young couple had been betrothed in infancy; it was an excellent match, for she would one day be a baroness. At fourteen, Thomas was a stolid-featured boy, but old for his age – already, he was studying at Cambridge. He had visited Rye House with his father from time to time over the years, and Katharine had been impressed by his learning and the poems he composed. He and Elizabeth were well suited.

The girls kissed Elizabeth and congratulated her, but Aunt Mary forestalled them, raising her hand. 'It is to be a double wedding,' she said. 'Magdalen, your father has found you a husband too.'

As her sisters gasped, Magdalen went white. She loved her life at Rye House and Katharine knew that she regarded marriage as something that would happen far off in the future.

'Are you struck speechless, child?' Aunt Mary asked.

'I am am-amazed,' Magdalen stuttered.

'Don't you want to know who the lucky bridegroom is?' Mother smiled at her.

'He is Ralph Lane of Orlingbury in Northamptonshire,' Aunt Mary said, without waiting for Magdalen to reply. 'He is fourteen, just a year older than you, and he is set to inherit a fair manor house with twenty rooms.'

Magdalen burst into tears. 'Mother, I do not want to marry anyone, however rich! I don't want to leave you and Father, or Rye House.'

Aunt Mary put comforting arms around her. 'It is natural to feel some reluctance, dear child. You are young and the prospect of marrying must feel strange to you. But you have a careful father, who has made a good match for you, and you will not be leaving immediately. After the wedding you will stay here until you are fourteen. We think you are too young at present to bear the duties of marriage, so you will go to Orlingbury next spring. That will give you time to get used to the idea. And it's not at the ends of the earth – we will be able to visit each other.'

'So I can stay here for another year?' Magdalen raised a tear-streaked face.

'Yes, my chick, you can. And, in that time, we will make you a lovely wardrobe against your becoming a fine lady.'

Magdalen dabbed at her eyes with her handkerchief, sniffing a little.

Katharine felt sorry for her – and for herself, for she knew that she would miss her friend dreadfully when she left for Northamptonshire.

That afternoon, Magdalen went off on her own, striding through the park. She needed time alone to think, she said. When she returned, Katharine and Anne were practising dance steps in the hall as Will strummed his lute. At the sight of Magdalen, they ceased, but she put on a brave smile and bade them continue. Katharine adored dancing, but she could not put any heart into it that day. It was the same with chess and making music, other pastimes she loved – they offered little distraction. Normally, she loved listening to Mother's tales of the court, that fabulous, fascinating place she longed to see, yet, that evening, as Mother chatted with Uncle William and Aunt Mary, she could not concentrate. It had just dawned on her that she too might be found a husband before very long, and that Magdalen might not be the only one who was being torn away against her will from the earthly paradise that was Rye House.

Mother returned to court the following week. When she came home for the weddings, she looked very pleased with herself. Gathering her children about her in the parlour, she embraced Katharine.

'My dear child, I have excellent news!' she said. 'I have found you a husband, a better match than I could ever have expected.'

Katharine suddenly felt sick. It was the news she had feared to hear. She had known it would come, but she had been praying that it would not be soon.

She would not break down, as Magdalen had. She would not dash her mother's hopes for her or spoil her happiness. 'That is marvellous news,' she said, surprised that her voice sounded so steady. 'Who am I to wed?'

'Lord Scrope of Bolton's son!' Mother was triumphant. 'Think of it! He is the heir to a barony. His grandfather, Lord Dacre, who is cousin to your father, himself suggested it. Lord Scrope is his son-in-law. Henry Scrope is thirteen, just the right age for you, and Lord Dacre thinks you will be a good match for him. A marriage between you will strengthen our ties with our noble kinsfolk in the north. I have already written to Lord Scrope. With Lord Dacre's backing, he must agree.'

Katharine relaxed a little. With any luck, Lord Scrope would not agree, for all her mother's excitement. Why should he marry his heir to a knight's daughter with only a modest dowry? And she was but eleven, not yet old enough for marriage, and Mother might decide that she should wait until she was fourteen before going to live with her husband. She might have another three years at Rye House left to her.

'Bolton is a long way away,' she said. 'It would pain me to go so far from you.'

'But it is a great castle,' Mother protested, 'and I dare say Henry Scrope will be often at court, so we will see each other frequently. I will ask the Queen for a place for you when you are married.'

She *could* bear it, Katharine told herself. She *would* bear it. She should be glad that her mother had found her such an eminently suitable husband.

And nothing was settled yet.

May brought the blossom and the weddings, which took place, one after the other, in the chapel at Rye House, with Father Cuthbert officiating. Elizabeth was a happy bride, Magdalen a subdued one. Wearing a new green gown and watching the ceremonies, aware that she might be saying her own vows soon, Katharine thought that the young husbands looked slightly bewildered to find themselves at the altar; probably they would rather be at their books or learning swordplay. Thomas Vaux, especially, seemed nervous. No doubt he was anxious to acquit himself well in the marriage bed. That was something Katharine did not like to think about. She knew something of what was supposed to happen, and it didn't sound very pleasant. In fact, it sounded rather rude.

The wedding feast followed. Uncle William was a hearty host, proud of the good table his wife had provided. There were great joints of meat, raised pies, dishes of peas and new asparagus, and a great sugar subtlety in the shape of the Greek god Hymen, patron of marriage feasts.

Afterwards, there was dancing. The household minstrels struck up a tune and everyone got to their feet. Katharine grabbed Will's hands and soon they were whirling around the floor in a lively *branle*. They danced the evening away until it was time to toast the newly-weds with spiced hippocras wine. Amidst much laughter and merriment, Elizabeth and Thomas were led off by their attendants and, after a decent space, all the guests surged into the chamber where the blushing couple lay next to each other in bed, the sheet pulled up to their chins.

'Do your duty, boy!' roared Lord Vaux, somewhat the worse for drink, as his son shrank visibly.

Father Cuthbert hurriedly blessed the bed, then shooed the company away.

'Let's leave them in peace,' he enjoined, as someone thrust a full goblet into his hand.

'Time for bed, I think,' Mother said.

Katharine went, reluctant to leave the revelry, although the dancing had ended and it was mostly carousing now. She knew her mother had not wanted her to hear the bawdy jests and innuendos. But she *had* heard them and, as she left the room, her cheeks were burning. At the top of the stair, she saw Magdalen, a wraith in her white nightgown, carrying a candle.

'Thank God it's not me,' Magdalen whispered. 'It's bad enough having to suffer what Elizabeth is suffering, without all that vile jesting. At least, when Thomas and I bed, we'll be spared that. But it won't be for ages yet, thank God.'

'Yes, we have a whole year together here still,' Katharine said, a lump in her throat, knowing that Magdalen might not be the first to leave.

A week after the weddings, Mother came hastening into the garden, her face taut with anger. 'Come indoors, Katharine!' she commanded. Katharine stopped dead-heading flowers and ran after her, wondering what she had done wrong.

Mother closed the door to the schoolroom behind them. 'Sit down, child. I have heard from Lord Scrope, and it is not good news.' Katharine's heart soared. What was not good news for her mother might be very good news for her.

Mother began pacing, unable to contain her agitation. 'You are not rich or noble enough for his son, that's the bottom of it. He kept me waiting for ages for a response, then said he would be willing for the betrothal to go ahead, but only if I paid him an atrociously large dowry, a quarter of it due now, with no sureties.'

'But that's outrageous,' Katharine cried, relief subsumed by indignation and the sting of humiliation.

'That's not all!' Mother raged. 'He offered a derisory jointure, then had the barefaced effrontery to say that he would not be returning your dowry if you died before the marriage could be consummated. And he will not enter into any covenants before the marriage takes place, which would leave us in a very precarious position indeed.'

'If his son is anything like him, I wouldn't want to marry him anyway,' Katharine declared.

'Lord Dacre led me to believe that Lord Scrope would welcome this marriage,' Mother fumed.

'Maybe he was just trying to be helpful,' Katharine replied. 'What will you do?'

'I shall swallow my pride and think of a way to retrieve the situation,' Mother declared. It was not what Katharine wanted – or expected – to hear. It was obvious that Lord Scrope was negotiating on sufferance and did not want her as a bride for his son. What was the point of flogging a dead horse? But she said nothing. She knew that Mother cherished fond ambitions for her children, and that the dearest of these was to see them well married.

'I shall have to give the matter more thought,' Mother said, sinking down onto a stool. She reached over and patted Katharine's hand. 'In the meantime, try to forget about this. Go back to your Cicero and your languages, and all the other pastimes you enjoy. Now run along and find the others. Not a word of this to anyone, mind. I would not have it said that we Parrs are not good enough for the likes of the Scropes.'

In July, Mother received another letter from Lord Scrope. She showed it to Katharine as they sat together on a stone bench in the shadow of the garden wall. A light breeze was ruffling the flower beds.

'He wants an answer,' Katharine said. 'Did you not write to him, my lady?'

'I did. I told him I needed time to think about his terms.'

'I suppose he thinks we should be eager to agree to them.'

'See here.' Mother jabbed the letter with her forefinger. 'He is insisting that I pay the first instalment of the dowry by August.' She gave a mirthless laugh. 'As if I could lay my hands on that kind of sum in such a short time. And, even if I could, Lord Scrope has seen to it that he is under no obligation. He could pull out of the agreement, if he so pleases, and ruin me. Katharine, I fear he has no intention of going through with this marriage.'

Katharine nodded, wishing that they could forget all about the project.

Mother rose. 'When I get back to court, I will have one more stab at bringing the match to pass. I will speak to Lord Dacre again. I am sure that he carries some influence with Lord Scrope.'

Katharine wanted to beg her mother to travail no further in the matter, as she was surely doomed to fail. But she said nothing. If the marriage ever went ahead, she would not have Mother thinking that she had never wanted it. She would do her duty, as a loving daughter should, and show the world that she was happy to embrace the future so carefully secured for her.

Soon after Mother returned to court, she wrote to Katharine to explain that Lord Dacre was in the north, but would be in London in a few weeks. Early in the autumn, Katharine received another letter. Lord Dacre was now planning to remain in the north until after Christmas, but had counselled Lord Scrope to be patient and not press for an answer.

Reading that, as she sat at the table in the empty schoolroom, the others having drifted off when lessons ended, Katharine knew that there was little prospect of Mother's hopes being fulfilled. Only a fool would think that she would be happy with such a settlement; it was obvious that Lord Scrope was forcing her to pull out.

She sighed, feeling guilty about being pleased that the matter was coming to naught. As she went about Rye House, she rejoiced that she would soon be free to stay there – for a long time, if she had her way. She had turned eleven in August and was not yet stirred by thoughts of young men or romance. Marriage, she was fast learning, was a hardheaded business, with little account taken of young hearts.

Mother arrived home for Christmas as the baked meats were sizzling in the ovens and the puddings bubbled over the kitchen fire and the house was filled with wonderful aromas. Katharine and her companions had just returned from the woods, their arms full of greenery, in the wake of the men dragging the Yule log that would burn on the fire in the hall throughout the festive season. She found Mother, dressed in her riding cloak, standing by the hearth, holding out her hands to the warmth of the flames. She greeted her children joyously, commenting on how William had grown and how eight-year-old Anne was blossoming into a beauty.

'And you, Katharine,' she said, embracing her elder daughter, 'you are as lovely as ever.'

That evening, when supper was over and they sat in the great parlour making wreaths of holly and ivy, Mother turned to her. 'I have heard from Lord Dacre. He understands my concerns. He has tried his best with Lord Scrope. He reminded him that I am of the good wise stock of the Greens. He even told him that his demands were so outrageous that it was impossible for me ever to agree to them. He suggested that Henry could live here, at my expense, and benefit from our school.' She sighed. Katharine could guess what was coming next. 'But Lord Scrope is adamant. He will not agree to any other terms. He argues that I have had enough time to find the money for the dowry. To be honest, Katharine, I think I can go no further in this matter.'

Uncle William shook his head in agreement. 'You wouldn't want our Katharine to wed into such a family,' he said. 'My advice is to turn down this match.'

'That is my advice too,' Aunt Mary echoed.

'And mine too,' chimed in Will. 'As head of the family, I do not want to see my sister married to a Scrope. There are better fish to fry, I am sure.'

Mother smiled at him indulgently. 'I am sure you are right, my son. I will write to Lord Scrope in the New Year. And now, we can all enjoy a merry Christmas.'

Mother was not fazed by the curt letter she received from Lord Dacre. 'I have offended him by rejecting his grandson,' she said. 'I should not have attempted to gainsay my betters!' Her tone was tart. Katharine did not care that Lord Dacre was affronted. What mattered most was that she did not have to leave Rye House.

Some weeks later, another letter came, bearing the Dacre seal. Mother read it, standing in the hall, as Katharine waited impatiently to know what was in it. She prayed God that Lord Scrope had not changed his mind and offered better terms.

Of late, whenever Mother had spoken of Lord Dacre or Lord Scrope, her tone had been acerbic, but now it softened. 'It seems that your marriage was doomed not to take place anyway,' she said. 'Poor Henry Scrope departed this life last week. A spring fever carried him off, God rest him.'

Katharine felt a deep sadness for the former bridegroom she had never met – a young lad who would never see his fifteenth year.

Soon afterwards, she suffered the real pain of loss, when Magdalen left for Orlingbury. Helping her to pack and prepare for her departure was an ordeal, especially as Magdalen did not want to go and spent much of the time in tears.

'I can't leave you, Mother,' she wept, clinging to Aunt Mary.

'Now stop this nonsense,' Aunt Mary chided, even though her own eyes were glistening. 'You can't go to your husband with a face like that. What will he think, poor man?' She cradled Magdalen in her arms. 'It's normal for a young maid to feel as you do. I did myself, when I had to leave home to marry your father. And I have been happier with him than I ever was in my life before. God willing, you will know the same happiness. You must embrace your future, child, and love your husband. It is your duty, and I hope it will be your pleasure too.'

She released Magdalen and raised her chin. 'You are a Parr, my daughter, and you will do our house proud, I am sure of it.'

Magdalen dried her tears. She was more resigned after that. But, when she hugged Katharine tightly on parting, her composure broke. 'God keep you, dear cousin,' she sobbed. 'I pray we shall see each other again soon.'

When Magdalen had gone, for all the tumbling, chattering presence of her four sisters, Will and Anne, Rye House seemed empty.

Chapter 3

1525–1528

Another summer had come, and Katharine still missed Magdalen, even though she had grown accustomed to her absence. They corresponded frequently, and it was heartening to realise that her cousin was adapting well to her new life, yet sad too, because Katharine knew that she did not need her so much. Her cousin's letters had revealed a new sophistication and there were increasing references to 'dear Ralph'. The most recent ones had been full of excited news about her pregnancy. They had made Katharine realise that it was the one who was left behind who did most of the missing.

When Mother returned from court in late June, she described for them all the magnificent ceremony in which six-year-old Henry Fitzroy had been invested by his royal father with the dukedoms of Richmond and Somerset.

'The Queen was most distressed,' she recounted, as they sat drinking cordial in the garden. 'Poor soul, she mostly hides her feelings, for the King is usually discreet about his amours, but his flaunting of his bastard like that in front of the court, and bestowing on him royal dukedoms, was so humiliating for her, especially since she has given him no son herself. It was as if he was telling her, "See here, Madam, *I* can have sons."'

'How many children has she borne him?' Anne asked.

'Eight, I think, and only one girl living. It's a terrible tragedy.'

'That's why the King and Queen dote on the Princess Mary so much,' Aunt Mary observed.

'Yes, but she is a girl, and a woman cannot rule,' Uncle William declared. 'The King needs a son to succeed him.'

'And the Queen is past the age for childbearing,' Mother said quietly. Katharine could see the impasse. 'So, what is the King to do?'

Mother shifted her stool into the shade. 'The talk at court is that he is preparing Henry Fitzroy for kingship.'

'But a bastard cannot inherit,' Aunt Mary pointed out.

'An Act of Parliament can name anyone the King chooses as his heir,' Uncle William said, 'but getting the people to accept the boy is another matter.'

'I think he means to accustom us to it by degrees,' Mother said. 'The Queen said that he is appointing him a great household, like a second court. It is a pity that it is not to be headed by her own son.'

The very next day, Uncle William received a summons to court and hastened south. Within the week, Aunt Mary came hurrying into the schoolroom where Mother was teaching the younger children French, while Dr Clarke was instructing the older ones in rhetoric.

'Excellent news!' she cried. 'William has been appointed chamberlain to the Duke of Richmond! The Duke is to be president of the Council of the North and take up residence at Sheriff Hutton Castle in Yorkshire. William will preside over his household. It's a high honour, and who knows what benefits it will bring!' She was beside herself with excitement. Katharine knew she was thinking that young Richmond would one day be king – a grateful king who would reward those who had served him well. She herself was thrilled for her uncle and for her family. This was the kind of preferment most people could only dream of.

Mother stood up and embraced Aunt Mary. 'He has well deserved this honour,' she exulted. The younger Parrs were hopping up and down.

'But there is more good news,' Aunt Mary said, showing her the letter. 'William has obtained a place for Will in the Duke's household. He is to be one of the boys appointed as companions for him.'

'God be praised!' Mother cried, flinging her arms around Mary with a passion Katharine had never seen. 'That is the most wonderful news! Dear William, I can never thank him sufficiently. This is such an opportunity for Will; it opens so many chances for preferment. His future is now more assured than I could ever have hoped for.' Tears

26

were running down her cheeks. 'You hear this, my boy?' She let go of Mary and hugged Will, who bore it grinning as the news of his golden future sank in. He was twelve and shooting up in height, but still a rosy-cheeked boy, all angles and mischief.

'In the Duke's household, you will have the best education money can buy,' Mother enthused. 'Your companions will be among the highest-born in the land. I cannot stress how important it will be for you to make friends with them, especially with the Duke. The King loves his son inordinately. Be Richmond's friend, and the world will open up to you.'

Katharine could only think that now Will was to leave Rye House too. She was pleased for him, but could not help feeling a little envious. In a trice, he had been handed a brilliant future. She had always known that Mother's ambitions had centred chiefly on her son, the heir; it was natural. She and Anne, being girls, were of lesser importance in the world. But, she realised, if Will's future was assured, so would theirs be. You could never have high-enough connections. She did wonder, however, how Mother would square her hopes of Richmond becoming king with her devotion to the Queen. She would have to dissemble, of course, but she could not long hide the fact that her son and her brother-in-law were prominent in the young Duke's household. Yet their appointments were not of her making – and the Queen would surely know that.

A few days later, there was further cause for excitement. News arrived that Magdalen had borne a healthy daughter, Laetitia. Then they learned that the Duke of Richmond was to stay at Rye House on his way north. Uncle William wrote that Will would join his household from there. At that, everyone erupted in excitement.

Never had the manor seen such preparations. With only a week to go before the Duke's arrival, the kitchens were working at full stretch and Mother and Aunt Mary were rushed off their feet, striving to get everything ready in time.

The Duke would be bringing a large household.

'Thank the Lord it is summer, and we can sleep people in the barn,'

Aunt Mary sighed, wiping her forehead. 'Now, those sheets for my lord Duke's bed must be aired. And I must send someone to tell the butcher that his delivery is overdue. Did you find the best napkins, Maud?'

'I did,' Mother said. 'And the gold salt cellar, which I've polished myself. Now, where did I put that seating plan?'

They were all having new clothes made. Katharine found herself the proud possessor of a crimson damask gown – it was the most glorious colour she had ever seen. Anne's was pink and Will's gown was a rich black that made him look older than his years.

'You must not outshine the Duke,' Mother said, 'but you do want to proclaim to the world that the Parrs are fit company for a prince.' That was what she called Richmond now. In her mind, he *was* a prince.

On the day the King's son arrived, riding in a splendid litter with Uncle William on horseback by his side at the head of his train, the whole household assembled outside the porch to greet him, bowing and curtseying low at his approach. When she rose, Katharine saw before her a solemn little boy with pinched features, a large nose and fair skin. But he was not solemn for long. She watched him greet the family and won a smile as she curtseyed to him.

Observing him presiding at the high table at the feast, she became aware that this was a child unlike any other, and not because he had royal blood. There was a waywardness about the little Duke, an impulsive tendency that had his hovering tutor constantly murmuring in his ear. His manners left much to be desired and his voice was loud and immoderate. He even scratched himself at table. Mother would never have let her children get away with such behaviour.

But there was Mother, beaming indulgently at the boy, blinded no doubt by the aura of royalty – and looking fondly upon Will, who seemed already to have struck up a rapport with his new master, just as she had hoped. After the feast, their two auburn heads were close together as Will showed Richmond his new lute and Richmond tried to play it. He soon lost interest, so Will fetched his set of wooden soldiers, which found far more favour with their guest.

It had been a successful day. The young Duke had been marvellously entertained and had enjoyed much good cheer. It was with some difficulty that his tutor persuaded him to go to bed.

In the morning, the great retinue reassembled beyond the gatehouse.

'I thank you for your hospitality, Lady Parr,' the Duke said, bowing to Aunt Mary.

'And we thank you, my lord, for gracing our house,' she replied. 'Before your Grace departs, I have something for you.' She nodded to a groom, who led over a grey pony trapped in crimson and gold.

'For me?' In an instant, the budding prince was transformed into an eager boy.

'Of course,' Aunt Mary smiled. 'She is our gift to you.'

Delight filled Richmond's eyes. 'Thank you! Thank you very much.' He paused for a moment. 'I shall call her Bess.' That, Katharine knew, was his mother's name. Bessie Blount had become notorious after it became known that she had borne the King a bastard.

'I shall ride her now,' Richmond announced. 'You may take the litter away.'

'Your Grace, we have some distance to travel,' Uncle William pointed out. 'It would be wiser perhaps to use the litter.'

'I want to ride Bess now!' the boy cried. 'And you shall not stop me!'

If one of his own children had spoken to him like that, Uncle William would have beaten them, but this was a king's son, and much depended on his favour. 'Very well, my lord,' he said in a tight voice. 'It shall be as you wish.'

Richmond mounted his horse. 'Come, Sir William,' he said imperiously, and they rode away. Katharine saw Mother dab her eyes as Will, sitting proudly in the saddle, waved them goodbye.

In the year that followed, Uncle William and Will wrote often from Sheriff Hutton, and it became clear that all was not well in Richmond's household.

'Your uncle complains that Cardinal Wolsey insists on controlling it from London,' Mother explained, shaking her head after reading the latest missive. 'There is little opportunity for William to exert any influence or patronage.'

Katharine had heard a lot about the great Cardinal. Some said he had as much power as the King he served, who relied rather too heavily on him and let him virtually rule England.

'What's patronage?' Anne piped up.

'It is when a person of standing is in a position to obtain favours for people, for a consideration,' Mother explained, sitting down on the schoolroom bench next to her. 'Uncle William had expected to be in that position, and should be, because young Richmond likes him, but it's the Cardinal who wields influence over the Duke's household, not its officers. That isn't all that vexes him. He doesn't approve of the long hours the Duke's tutors make him spend at his lessons.' She paused to tuck tendrils of hair back into her daughter's cap. 'You know your uncle. He believes that boys should prefer sport to book-learning, and that children should be out in the open air as often as possible. But they want to keep Richmond at his books.' She sighed. 'I gather he is a hard child to rule. One tutor has already resigned and the new one cannot control him. Maybe he should have more leisure in which to let off steam.'

Katharine reflected that Richmond would have done very well to be sent to Rye House to be educated under Mother's gentle guidance and the practical wisdom of Uncle William.

Will, however, was thriving at Sheriff Hutton. He grumbled about having to learn Latin and Greek, especially when lessons were disrupted by the mischievous Duke, but he was not as strictly supervised as his young master and could be outdoors more frequently, hunting and hawking with his noble companions. He was thirteen now and sounded quite the young gentleman.

'Soon he will be of age,' Mother said one evening, as they helped to bring in baskets of apples from the orchard, 'and then my task will be done. Before then, I must find him a wife.'

In that, she excelled herself. Learning that Henry Bourchier, the Earl of Essex, had an only daughter, Ann, who would one day inherit his title and his lands, she boldly approached him and spelled out to him the advantages of a marriage between Ann and Will, stressing that Will was in high favour with the Duke of Richmond. No further word was said, Mother recounted later, but two pairs of eyes met in understanding as the Earl took her point. Everyone believed that Richmond would one day be king.

It helped that Mother was friends with the family of the Countess of Essex. It helped – because Essex was deeply in debt – that she promised Ann Bourchier an impressive jointure.

'I dare not think about how much I have had to borrow,' she confessed. Even the King had lent her money, at the Queen's petition. But, no matter what the cost, she was well content. She had bought her son a noble heiress and, in the fullness of time, a title. Will would be my lord the Earl of Essex and live in splendour at Stanstead Hall when he wasn't at court. Mother had good reason to be pleased with herself.

The young couple were married in February 1527 in the chapel at Stanstead Hall, a beautiful red-brick mansion near Bishop's Stortford. The whole Parr family travelled there from Rye House for the occasion, and Uncle William brought Will, having obtained leave from the Duke of Richmond. Katharine had another new dress, a tawny silk one this time, while Mother was resplendent in crimson velvet.

The little bride, a shy girl of nine years, was dressed up in satin and furs, and looked as if she was about to cry when the priest pronounced the blessing. Will, taller than ever and standing proud, played his part to perfection, but Katharine could tell that his heart was not engaged. He wasn't interested in marriage or little girls. But Mother was looking fit to burst with pride.

Of course, Ann was too young to be bedded, so it had been arranged that she should stay with her mother until she was old enough to be a proper wife. Will said goodbye to her without a pang, or so it seemed. If he showed reluctance about anything, it was returning to Sheriff Hutton.

'I want to go out into the world,' he said, as they rode the eighteen miles back to Hoddesdon.

'You are seeing the world, and from the best perspective possible,' Mother replied, tart.

'But I want to be a soldier, like Uncle William,' Will protested. 'And my tutors say I should go to university.'

'If you're to be a soldier, you'll need to spend less time writing music and poetry,' Uncle William said.

'But I love doing that. Surely I can do both?'

'My boy,' Uncle said, 'you can go to university, then go soldiering when you are older.'

'He is going back to Sheriff Hutton!' Mother said, in a voice that brooked no further argument.

When Anne turned thirteen the following year, she left Rye House, for Mother had secured her a position as maid-of-honour to the Queen. It should have been Katharine's, but Katharine had fallen victim to a bad attack of measles when the matter was arranged and, if one of her daughters did not go to court when the Queen needed her, the place would be assigned to someone else, so Mother took Anne with her.

Katharine had always loved her little sister, and they had grown closer since Magdalen's departure. Anne was comely, with wide-set, serious eyes, high cheekbones, full lips and red-gold hair; and she was clever too. She shared with Katharine a love of learning and a special fondness for old Cicero, and of late she had begun corresponding with renowned scholars, who, to her delight, were answering her humble letters. How Katharine would miss her!

Confined to her bed and contagious, she was grieved that she could not hug her sister farewell. They had to content themselves with blowing kisses across the room. When Anne had gone, she buried her face in the pillow and wept.

Yet she did not begrudge Anne the post of maid-of-honour; these days she was of two minds as to whether she herself wanted to go to court. There lay excitement and, hopefully, preferment, and perhaps a rich husband, but Anne's letters revealed a rather different picture. There was little joy in the Queen's household because the King was in ardent pursuit of another of her maids-of-honour, Mistress Anne Boleyn, of whom Mother certainly did not approve. Katharine did not wish to become embroiled in that. Besides, she still loved her life at Rye House. Marriage could wait. She was in no hurry for it.

Part Two

'Brute and beastly'

Chapter 4

1529

Mother was greatly preoccupied. It was well over a year since the King had resolved to have his marriage to the good Queen annulled. It was not entirely on account of his notorious passion for Mistress Anne Boleyn; he needed a male heir and he had convinced himself that his marriage was invalid.

The whole kingdom had rocked with the scandal. Anne Boleyn was hated and lambasted, for public sympathy was with Queen Katherine. Mother felt deeply for her good mistress and offered what emotional support she could when she was at court, but, with the atmosphere so tense there, she said, she would rather be at home.

'I just wish the Pope would rule in her favour,' she said to Katharine as they walked in the gardens on the first warm day of spring.

'I wonder why he doesn't,' Katharine said, her eyes on the green shoots pushing up through the earth.

'Because he is afraid of the Emperor, who is the Queen's nephew and very powerful, but fears to offend the King. But his Holiness shouldn't be swayed by political considerations. He should judge the matter on its merits. To me, it seems that the Queen's case is sound. Her marriage is valid. All the doctors and clerics around her say so.'

'But the King thinks otherwise.'

Mother shook her head. 'Her Grace says that, even if an angel came down from Heaven, he would not be able to shift the King from his opinion. He is mad for this Anne. She queens it over the court. It's not right. When I think of our good mistress, shut away in her apartments, weeping, I could smack him!'

Katharine had to smile, imagining Mother clouting the King. But it was a sad business.

She was sure that something else was going on. Letters with unfamiliar seals kept arriving at Rye House, and Mother was writing more frequently to Uncle William, who was still with Richmond at Sheriff Hutton.

Before March was out, Mother called Katharine into her bedchamber and bade her sit on the bench at the foot of the bed. She seated herself in the high-backed chair by the fire and regarded her daughter.

'Katharine, you are sixteen and ripe for marriage. You will be pleased to know that I have found you a husband. It is an excellent match that might make you a baroness in time. You are to wed Edward, the heir of Sir Thomas Burgh of Gainsborough.'

Katharine had never heard of Gainsborough or the Burgh family. They had not been mentioned among the noble kinsfolk to whom the Parrs were related. But she knew her duty, even though her thoughts had been plunged into a turmoil and her mind was teeming with questions.

'That is very good news, my lady,' she managed to say. 'I am grateful for your care for me. What is he like, this Edward Burgh?'

'By all reports, a promising young man,' her mother said, beaming. 'He is four years older than you. His father has hopes of being granted the barony of Borough. The old lord, who died last year, used the title, although he had no right to it, for the barony borne by his forebears became extinct years ago. But I think he was a little mad.'

Katharine barely heard her. 'Where is Gainsborough?' she wanted to know.

'It's in Lincolnshire.'

'How far away is that?' She needed to hear that it was within visiting distance.

Mother hesitated. 'It is more than a hundred and thirty miles to the north-east, or so my messenger told me.'

At least four days' journey distant. Katharine's heart sank. She felt sick at the thought of leaving her mother and Rye House and going so far away.

36

'I trust Sir Thomas Burgh is eager for this marriage?' She had not forgotten the odious Lord Scrope.

'He is indeed,' Mother assured her. 'He has been active in arranging your betrothal and I am indebted to him for it.' She reached over and picked up her embroidery tambour from the table. 'You need have no concerns, child. The Burghs are an old and respected family, and they have given good service to the Crown over the years. You will like Sir Thomas, I am sure. His first wife was a Tyrwhitt, and therefore distantly related to us, but she died seven years ago, God rest her.' Mother crossed herself. 'She bore about a dozen children, and I imagine that you will be expected to be a good sister to them.'

It was a daunting thought. A dozen children! It might be a chaotic household.

Mother had probably caught the dismay in her face. 'Don't worry, they won't be your responsibility, as Sir Thomas has remarried, and I gather that Lady Alice is an excellent stepmother. And he is often at home. He told me he served as one of the King's bodyguard and was knighted on Flodden Field back in 1513, when we English trounced the Scots, but he has no desire to be a courtier and prefers ruling his own domain. He has had much to do to restore the family fortunes after his father let things deteriorate.' She paused. 'I do hope you are happy at the prospect of this marriage, Katharine. I would not force you into it.'

It wasn't the marriage that had brought the lump to Katharine's throat, but the thought of leaving her mother, which now seemed a worse thing than leaving Rye House. And yet Mother wanted this, saw it as more important than keeping her at home. And Mother had always wanted the best for her.

'I am happy,' she made herself say. 'Thank you, my lady. You have done me proud.'

She was to depart for Gainsborough as soon as all was ready, and found herself plunged into a flurry of preparations. There were gowns to be made, hoods to be fashioned and shoes to be cobbled. Mother bought her a palfrey, since she had grown too tall for her pony, and crimson caparisons for it. But they were taking the litter too, as she could not be in the saddle for the whole journey, and Mother wanted to travel in comfort.

They set off in April. The spring blossom flowered on the trees as they journeyed north. They spent the first night at an inn at Melbourn in Cambridgeshire, and it was here, over the shilling ordinary that they ate in the landlady's otherwise deserted parlour, that Mother laid down her knife and cleared her throat.

'Daughter,' she said, 'I would be failing in my duty if I did not prepare you for your marriage bed.'

Katharine blushed. 'I think I know what to expect,' she said, shrinking at the idea of her devout mother mentioning such matters. 'I have seen mares in foal, and I know that the stallion has been brought to them. I understand it is the same with people.' She did not say that Will had regaled all the girls with talk of the naughty things that went on in great households. She had learned a lot from that.

'Yes, but we human beings are higher than the animals,' Mother said briskly. 'We have souls and consciences. Marriage is a sacrament and to be approached with reverence. It is a wife's duty to submit to her husband in all things.'

'Oh, I will, I will,' Katharine gabbled, eager to move on to a less embarrassing subject.

'It may hurt a little at first,' Mother persisted, 'but that will not last long. And then I hope you will find the joy in each other that Christ ordained.'

Katharine's cheeks were flaming. She could not bring herself to wonder if her parents had found such joy. It was impossible to imagine her pious mother enjoying bed sport, as Will called it.

'This is a good pie,' she said quickly. 'It's full of meat.'

'Yes, this hostelry was recommended to me,' Mother said. 'Your uncle suggested several places we might stay on the way, and he was right about this one. It's clean too.'

The other inns were of a similar standard, so they had a comfortable journey. They stopped in Peterborough to visit the shrine housing the arm of St Oswald in the great abbey. He was the patron saint of soldiers and Katharine knelt and asked him to give her the courage to embrace the future the Almighty had decreed for her. How the dry bone of this long-dead king could help her was a mystery, defying logic, but she inwardly reproved herself for daring to question the holiness of one of God's saints.

When, three days later, they approached Lincoln, they marvelled to see the magnificent cathedral standing majestically high on its hill above the city. They climbed the steep lane that led up to it and made offerings at the shrine of St Hugh. Then they looked at the shops in the Bailgate, where tempting wares were on display, and had dinner at the White Hart Inn, where they stayed that night.

Tomorrow, they would reach Gainsborough, which was less than eighteen miles away. What would Edward Burgh be like? Would it be easy to love him? And would he love her? Katharine was feeling a mounting sense of trepidation, and once or twice had to fight off tears at the prospect of the unknown life ahead of her in these strange and distant parts. Very soon, she would have to bid farewell to her mother and face it alone, which was why she was savouring every last precious moment they were together.

The next day, they donned their best clothes. Katharine had chosen a green gown, for it set off her slender figure and her hair to advantage; she wanted to look her best for her bridegroom. Today, she would ride her palfrey. She had a good seat on a horse, straight-backed and elegant.

They rode past wide fields, marshland and the gentle hills the locals called the Wolds. The people they encountered were mostly humble folk who spoke in an incomprehensible dialect and seemed distrustful of strangers. How different this was from the more populous southern parts of England, where everyone was friendlier and better off.

Gainsborough was surrounded by woodland. The hall abutted orchards and parkland and was an impressive house of red brick and timber. Its spruce exterior and gardens betokened wealth and loving care. As they crossed the moat and entered the gatehouse, a groom ran towards the house, shouting at the top of his voice that they were here.

They alighted by the great entrance door and were shown into a vast hall, where a tall, well-set man with piercing grey eyes and a hawk-like nose bowed and greeted them. There were a good many other people in the room, family and servants, Katharine supposed, but this was the kind of man who drew all eyes.

'My Lady Parr, you are most welcome!' he said, in a refined, confident voice.

'Sir Thomas, it is a pleasure to meet you, and to be here at Gainsborough,' Mother replied.

'May I present my wife?' he said, and a fair-haired lady stepped forward.

'My Lady Burgh,' Mother said, curtseying.

'My Lady Parr.' The woman's voice was a whisper.

'And this is Katharine,' Sir Thomas said, turning to look her up and down as she too curtseyed, then raising her hand and kissing it. 'My son is a lucky young man! Edward!'

A young man stepped forward and Katharine found herself face to face with her future husband. He was an open-faced, nice-looking lad with angular features and a prominent nose, and he was smiling at her. She smiled back. He looked as if he would be easy company and not in the least overbearing. No doubt he had grown up in obedience to his imposing father.

'I am overjoyed to see you, Mistress Katharine,' he said, his voice boyish and warm.

'And I you, Sir,' she replied, making another curtsey.

His brothers and sisters were introduced, all eleven of them, ranging from those of about her own age to little ones. They were well dressed and well behaved, and their manners were faultless. Katharine wondered if they were always so decorous.

'And this is to be your home, Katharine,' Sir Thomas said, waving an arm expansively at the soaring beamed hall with its dais and attractive oriel window. 'Let me show you around.' He led them to the tower through a door in the oriel and up the spiral stairs to a large chamber with a big tester bed and far-reaching views from the windows.

'We keep this room for visiting royalty,' he said proudly. 'King Henry came here early in his reign and' – he lowered his voice –

'King Richard earlier on, but we don't speak of him now.'

The little party descended the stairs and, with Edward walking close to Katharine, trailed behind him through the parlours, the withdrawing room, the great chamber and the gallery, which was hung with family portraits. Mother said later that Sir Thomas must be a wealthy man indeed to be able to afford a gallery, for very few people could bear the cost of these new-fangled additions to great houses. Then they moved on to the west wing, which boasted three floors of lodgings, with a fireplace, beautiful tapestries and a privy in every chamber. Katharine gasped when she walked into one of the ground-floor rooms and saw a canopied bed decked out in chequered velvet and cloth of gold.

'We had this bed made for the King who should not be mentioned,' Sir Thomas told them. He turned to Katharine. 'Now it is to be yours and Edward's. This is your chamber.'

'I chose it especially for us,' Edward said and, as he took Katharine's hand, she knew it would be easy to like this warm, friendly boy. She gazed around the room, at the wide latticed window, the new rush matting, the table laid with a Turkey rug, and the brick hearth. There were nice touches: the flowers in a copper pot on the window ledge, a silver mirror on the table and a little court cupboard, which – she soon discovered – contained piles of fresh bedlinen sprinkled with sweet-smelling herbs.

Later, having helped the maids to unpack and stow away her things, she went to her mother's chamber.

'It's a beautiful house,' she said, 'and I do like Edward. He's been most welcoming and I think he likes me.'

'I think so too,' her mother smiled. 'This is a good family, and I admire Sir Thomas. You will be in safe hands here.'

Katharine agreed. Yet something was nagging at her. She had noticed that Lady Burgh had not opened her mouth when Sir Thomas had shown them around. Maybe she was shy. Or maybe she hadn't been able to get a word in edgeways! She smiled, and then there was a knock on the door and it was time to go down to supper.

* * *

41

The wedding took place a few days later in the ancient parish church of All Saints. Katharine wore an ivory damask gown with a train, and a chaplet of flowers on her head, with her long hair rippling down her back. Edward's brothers, Thomas, William and seven-year-old Henry, escorted her to the church porch, where the ceremony took place, with the younger Burgh girls acting as bridesmaids. Katharine liked Eleanor and Agnes best and had tried to befriend them, to no avail. The six sisters seemed to close in on outsiders, which was how they made her feel. There had been no excitement among them as they all donned their finery and, at the wedding, they smiled prettily, but said little.

When she emerged into the sunlight on the arm of her new husband, she felt as if she had gained status in attaining wifehood and was filled with a sense of elation. She had married into a family that had welcomed her warmly, and she was to live in a beautiful house. God had been good to her. The only cloud on the horizon was the prospect of being parted from her mother, but they would visit each other, certainly. The journey was long, but not arduous.

The wedding feast in the great hall at Gainsborough was lavish, and it felt good to be presiding over it from the high table on the dais. Sir Thomas sat at Katharine's right hand, and Mother was on Edward's left, next to Lady Burgh. All the Burgh children sat at a long table set at right angles to the dais, with relatives and local gentry and clergy seated at the other tables. As dish after dish was brought in, a trumpet sounded and the diners looked up eagerly to see what fresh delights were to tempt their palates.

Katharine was quite calm about her wedding night. With Edward, she was sure it could hold no terrors for her. They had spent time getting to know each other over the past few days and she had discovered that he was a sensitive soul who went in awe of his father and feared he would never live up to his expectations. She could see why. Sir Thomas seemed a genial man, and he had been most kind to her, and to Mother, but his hand was in everything. No one at Gainsborough could be in any doubt as to who was in control. His children were the best-behaved she had ever seen, for he would not brook naughtiness or disobedience. One word or look from him, and they did as they were told. The schoolroom was as quiet as a cloister, as they sat with heads bent over their books. Mother was impressed. She saw it as fatherly care and commendable discipline. She did not realise that, in her own quiet, dignified and loving way, she had ruled her children just as effectively.

Katharine had already worked out that it was best to keep on the right side of Sir Thomas. She had an advantage because he clearly approved of her and was kind to her, as now, when he was proposing another toast in her honour – 'To my son's beautiful bride!'

It was growing dark. Beyond the glow of the candles, she could see the dusk fading outside the oriel window. She did not relish the prospect of the bedding ceremony, but it would soon be over, and then she and Edward would be alone and their married life would begin. She took another sip of her wine, watching the tumblers performing in the open space between the tables. Beneath the cloth, Edward took her hand and squeezed it. She smiled at him.

Presently, Sir Thomas patted her arm. 'It is time, daughter,' he said. Katharine rose, summoned Elinor, the little maid she had been assigned, and nodded to her mother, who left the hall in her wake, followed by Lady Burgh, who had spent much of the evening nervously watching her children and the servants.

In the chamber with the chequered bed, Katharine stood patiently as the women undressed her and drew over her head the fine lawn night-gown she had embroidered in the black-work fashion made popular by the Queen. Mother had taught her how to do it. Then Elinor combed her hair, as Lady Burgh, looking more relaxed now, brought a silver bowl of rose water for the washing of her face and hands, and a cloth to clean her teeth. Mother drew back the counterpane and sheet, and Katharine climbed into bed, seating herself upright against the pillows.

Elinor was then sent down to let Sir Thomas know that they were ready. As they waited, Mother smoothed the sheets and scattered petals on the bed, while Katharine tried to still her thumping heart. Mother gave her an encouraging smile.

When Edward finally arrived, with his father, the priests and all the guests in tow, he looked nervous.

'Well, get into bed, boy!' Sir Thomas said, giving him a little push.

Edward obliged and slid in next to Katharine. Everyone crowded around as the priest stepped forward and raised his hand.

'Merciful Lord and heavenly Father, by whose gracious gift mankind is increased, we beseech Thee assist with Thy blessing this bed and these two persons, that they may be fruitful in procreation of children, and live long together in godly love and honesty, that they may see their children's children unto the third and fourth generation, unto Thy praise and honour: through Jesus Christ, our Lord. Amen.'

Sir Thomas and Lady Burgh handed goblets brimming with spiced wine to Edward and Katharine, from which they drank gratefully, and then Elinor and another maid threw the bride's stockings at the guests to see who would be the next to say vows in the church porch. The couple who were hit – by no accident – grinned at each other; everyone knew they were hoping to wed.

'Do your duty, boy!' Sir Thomas enjoined. And with that the company departed, with whistles and bawdy jokes and laughter, the sound of their voices receding in the direction of the hall, where the revelry would continue.

Edward jumped up and drew the bolt on the door. 'They'll be back in the small hours with more wine to fortify us, and to ask if all went well,' he said. 'But, for now, I don't want anyone playing any pranks.'

He blew out all the candles except one and got back into bed. Katharine lay there, assuming that it was up to Edward to make the first move. After a pause, he reached across and took her hand.

'Are you tired, Katharine?'

'A little,' she said. 'Are you?'

'A little,' he echoed. There was another pause. 'We don't have to do it tonight, if you'd rather wait.'

'I'm happy to do whatever you decide,' she said, realising that he was more nervous than she was.

He put his arms around her and drew her to him, then kissed her on the lips. It was a tentative kiss, not a passionate one. She could feel his ribs beneath her hands. There wasn't much flesh on him.

She waited for him to kiss her again, but he didn't. Instead, he began fumbling under the bedclothes, his movements taking on a regular rhythm. Suddenly, he heaved himself up on top of her and pushed his knee between her thighs. 'I'll try to be gentle,' he breathed. She felt something hard jabbing between her legs and braced herself for him to enter her, but, after some increasingly frantic thrusting, he slumped beside her.

'I'm sorry,' he muttered. 'I must have drunk too much wine. It makes a man useless.'

'No matter,' she said, feeling his humiliation. 'We are both tired. And we have all our lives before us.'

'Bless you,' he said. 'You are the sweetest wife a man could have.'

When the guests returned at two o'clock, banging on the door and demanding to bring in the loving cup, they pretended to be asleep.

In the morning, Edward took Katharine in his arms again and tried once more to make her his wife – but in vain. The same thing happened. He failed at the crucial moment.

'Is there anything I can do?' Katharine asked. She had no idea how to pleasure a man or make his body function properly.

'Just don't tell anyone,' Edward said. 'I feel hung-over. That's the problem. It will be better tonight, I promise.'

She stretched and got out of bed, thinking that Sir Thomas would not be pleased if he knew that the marriage had not been consummated. She realised that, already, she was getting into the habit of worrying about what Sir Thomas would think.

Edward rose and pulled on his nightgown, and they knelt together to say their prayers. At Katharine's summons, Elinor came to help her dress and put her hair up. At this, her first uprising as a married woman, she would cover it with a hood, which she would now wear daily. Never again would she go abroad with her hair loose. Its beauty was her husband's alone to behold.

Mother had provided this first hood. It was in the English gable fashion, in black velvet with long lappets and a black veil.

She was relieved that it was also the custom for a bride to spend the first day of her married life in seclusion, and to be spared the sight of Edward being questioned by his father about the wedding night.

45

'I led him to believe that all had gone well,' he said when he joined her for dinner in their chamber. He looked ashamed, and she wanted to cry out that he had no need, they would succeed tonight! But he changed the subject. 'Everyone sends their best wishes. Some of the guests are leaving today, others tomorrow.' It came to Katharine with a jolt that her mother would be among the latter, and that she would be departing early.

That afternoon, when Edward was out hunting with some of the visitors, there was a tap on the door. It was Mother.

'I came to see that all is well with you,' she said. 'Edward seems to be a little distracted.'

'Come in,' Katharine beckoned, and they sat by the hearth.

'Daughter?' Mother asked. '*Is* all well?'

Katharine hesitated just a little too long, not liking to break her promise to stay silent. 'Everything's all right,' she said brightly.

'Child, you forget that you can't dissimulate with me. Something is amiss. Can you tell me?'

'No, I can't,' she said.

'There is no need to be embarrassed,' Mother smiled, misunderstanding. 'I have been married too. Has Edward hurt you or been unkind to you?'

'Oh, no!' Katharine protested.

'I thought not. I could not believe that of him. But has he done his duty by you?'

She could not lie to her mother. Nor could she betray her husband. So she sat there, saying nothing.

Mother took her hand. 'I understand. You do not want to shame him. But, my dear, these matters are never as you expect them to be. I think it can sometimes take time for a man and wife to become one. Just be patient. All will be well, you'll see.'

Katharine took comfort in that. And, even though she was dreading saying farewell to Mother, when the time came, she kept her composure, as a lady should, and hugged her tightly, smiling all the while.

'I love you, my dearest mother,' she whispered in her ear. 'May God be with you.' She knelt to receive the maternal blessing, then Mother was climbing into her litter and it was trundling through the gatehouse and out of sight. Katharine swallowed, willing the tears not to fall.

Edward guessed that she was struggling not to feel downcast. She hoped he did not think it was because he had again failed to bed her, but she would not let herself worry about that for now. To distract her, he took her up to the attic, where a lot of old furniture and junk was stored. Among it all, she was surprised to see a chair set at a table piled with dusty papers.

'My grandfather used to come up here,' Edward said. 'He was supposed to stay in his chamber, but he wandered at will, not caring what Father said.'

Katharine studied the papers. They were covered with drawings of shields and notes in an untidy scrawl. Here, she realised, were perfect patterns of heraldry, betraying a deep knowledge of the subject.

'How could someone who drew these be mad?' she asked, nonplussed.

'Oh, he was very strange,' Edward said. 'This was the only thing he did that made sense, but he was obsessive about it, which was why my father tried to stop him doing it. Yet he managed to get up here most nights. He'd light candles, and we used to worry that he would set the house on fire.'

'Couldn't he have had the table in his room?'

'Not after he used it to barricade the door and refused to come out for three days.' He paused, looking pained. 'He was filthy when we eventually persuaded him to let us in. Both Father and Mother said never again. Believe me, Katharine, he was strange. He wasn't interested in people. He lived in a world of his own. He didn't care about anyone, didn't understand the grief he caused by his strange behaviour.'

He fell silent again and began sifting aimlessly through an old chest that contained more of his grandfather's papers. 'It's hard to believe that, in his young days, he was at court and jousted for the King. But he became disruptive and had to be placed in the custody of the Lord Chamberlain. He was in the Fleet Prison at one time, and had to borrow money from the old King to buy himself out, but that crippled us financially and it took years of careful management before my father got us out of the mess Grandfather had made. In the end, he was declared insane and had to be kept under restraint. To be honest, it was a relief when he died.'

They descended the attic stairs. 'Some servants won't go up there at night,' Edward went on. 'They say they've heard him up there. I think it's mice or bats.'

Katharine shuddered. She'd have preferred a cranky ghost to bats, and she was glad when they were back on the ground floor, where Lady Burgh found her and said she should come to the kitchens to oversee the preparing of dinner.

An hour later, she emerged, longing to get out into the open air. She thought she would go riding in the park and walked the short distance to the stables, where she called for the groom. Standing in the doorway of the building, she heard a frantic rustling of straw and feared that a horse might be in trouble. One of the mares was in foal, but it was too soon for it to be born. She ran along the passage in front of the stalls, peering into each stable. The rustling had suddenly stopped. The mare was munching hay peacefully. One or two of the horses whickered happily to see her. The end stall was empty. Sir Thomas was out for the day, she remembered, which was perhaps why Lady Burgh had been more talkative.

She heard a slight movement in the empty stable and leaned in. Her eyes could barely process what she saw, still less her brain. For there lay Edward, looking up at her, shocked, with the groom, and both of them had their points unlaced. He sprang up, pulling his hose together. 'Katharine! What are you doing here?'

'I . . . I was going riding,' she faltered. Seized with the urge to get away, she began walking quickly back along the passage.

'Wait!' Edward called after her, but she was running now, desperate to be alone, to try to understand what she had seen and what it meant. She made for the park behind the house, racing through the orchard as if the hounds of Hell were after her. She could hear Edward's voice some way behind her, calling for her to stop. On and on she ran, until the voice had faded and the park was a wide-open vista around her. She was entirely alone. She slowed down, panting heavily, and sank to the ground in the shade of a massive oak, its thick trunk hiding her from anyone coming from the direction of the hall.

Katharine knew that it was forbidden for two men to love each other in the way a man and a woman did. She knew the story of the destruction of Sodom. She had once heard of a priest who had been defrocked for such sinfulness, for the Church took a very severe view of it. But she had never thought to have her life touched by it – or to be married to a man inclined that way.

Why had he married her? The answer was not far to seek. He had done his father's bidding. Had Sir Thomas known of his son's penchant for men? Had he hoped that marriage would set him on the right path, so that he could father heirs? She drew in her breath, trying to stem the tears. What she had seen explained why Edward had failed in bed. He could not love her because he did not desire her – and she might find herself trapped in a barren marriage.

If only Mother were here to counsel her. She dared not write of this in a letter. She contemplated running away to Rye House, but she did not have much money, only sufficient for her 'little necessaries and gewgaws', as Sir Thomas had called them when doling out her allowance. Besides, a woman travelling alone was vulnerable and regarded as not quite respectable. Would Elinor come with her – or would she feel it her loyal duty to warn Sir Thomas of what Katharine was planning? Thinking of explaining herself to him made her realise she could not do it. She could not shame Edward publicly.

But she felt so ashamed herself – so worthless. Why could her husband not want her? How was she lacking? She liked Edward so much; this morning, she had wondered if she was falling in love with him. And she was sure he liked her. But he must like her as a man liked his sister. He might never desire her. Yet she was tied to him and must live with that.

Unable to sit still any longer, she rose and walked further into the park. Had she been mistaken? She did not think so. Was it possible for a man to love both men and women? That was her only hope. But, if they were to have any sort of marriage, Edward must swear to her that he would never lie with a man again. She would insist on it. And she

49

would try with all her might to put the memory of what she had seen today behind her. It was the only way forward.

She heard a horse's hooves approaching. Turning around, she saw that the rider was Edward. She waited for him to reach her. He looked abashed as he dismounted.

'I am so sorry,' he said. 'So very sorry.' He made no attempt to embrace or touch her, but just stood there hanging his head. 'I don't know why God made me the way I am. I can't help it.'

'You must help it,' Katharine said. 'If we are to have a good marriage, you must desist from it. Tell me – tell me truly: do you think you can ever love me, ever get me with child?'

'I do love you, Katharine,' he declared. 'As for the other, I am trying.'

'A true man shouldn't have to try!' she cried, bursting into tears. Never had she felt so alone.

'I am not as other men,' he said sadly.

'Does your father know? Was I bought so that a pretence could be kept up that all was well?' She was beside herself.

Edward looked terrified. 'No, I don't think he knows. I hope not. I would die of shame. I *am* dying of shame. Please forgive me, Katharine. I will do as you ask and avoid the company of men. And I will try to be a proper husband to you. I don't want you to be unhappy.'

He was so full of remorse, so amenable. It was her duty to make the best of things.

'Will you forgive me?' he asked, his eyes pleading.

She hesitated. He had agreed to what she asked, and now she must play her part. 'I forgive you,' she said.

'You won't say anything to my father?'

'Of course not.'

As they walked back to the house, she wondered if fear of her complaining to Sir Thomas was the foremost reason why he had gone along with what she wanted.

It was a hot summer. Katharine took to spending her afternoons in the garden or riding in the park, as she had done at Rye House. In the mornings, she shadowed Lady Burgh, who was teaching her, in her own quiet, nervous way, how to run Gainsborough Hall. There was little to learn, for Mother and Aunt Mary had schooled her well in the management of a large household. Fortunately, Lady Burgh did not overburden her with duties – she seemed anxious to retain control herself and do things just as Sir Thomas liked them to be done – so there was leisure for retreating into her beloved books. Edward spent much time with his father, attending to estate business. Sir Thomas expected it, and valued his assistance. He was always telling Edward that all this would be his one day.

Almost nightly, Katharine suffered the same, familiar ordeal. Edward would strive to last long enough to enter her, but always failed. She would lie there letting him do whatever was needful, praying that they could come together just once. She sensed that Sir Thomas and Lady Burgh were looking for signs of a pregnancy, and soon others would be wondering if all was well.

Mother wrote every week, asking how Katharine was enjoying married life, and sending news from Rye House. Her letters made Katharine weep, she so longed to be back there. Again and again, she was tempted to confide to Mother the truth about her marriage, but always she held back. What could Mother do? She would only worry. And Katharine dared not imagine the furore that would ensue if Sir Thomas found out the truth about his son – or that she had spilled the secret he already knew about.

Uncle William wrote too, disgruntled because he had been dismissed from his post, along with Will, Cardinal Wolsey having closed down the expensive household at Sheriff Hutton. Mother wrote that he had returned home in a morose mood, resentful that he had gained no wealth or influence through his post as chamberlain. Katharine was surprised to hear that, in the end, Will had been sorry to leave. His letters were full of his new friend, Richmond's master of horse, Sir Edward Seymour, who was seven years his senior and, Katharine sensed, everything Will wanted to be. Sir Edward had seen military service in France and been knighted; he had been chosen to accompany Cardinal Wolsey on a diplomatic mission to Paris. He had been familiar with courts from his youth, and now he was going to be a Knight of the Body to the King.

Will clearly hero-worshipped him. He was hoping that he might go to court too, and that Edward Seymour would have a word in the King's ear on his behalf. But, after weeks had gone by and nothing had materialised, Mother made him go up to Cambridge. *He is sixteen now*, she wrote. *He is learned, handsome, charming and sociable. He will do well, I am sure.*

How Katharine missed her siblings. But they had flown the nest and she knew that, if she ever did return to Rye House, it would never be the same.

Chapter 5

1529–1531

Mother's letters were full of the King's divorce – his 'Great Matter', as people were calling it. The Pope had sent a cardinal from Rome to try the case with Cardinal Wolsey, and a court had been set up in the great hall of the Blackfriars, near the Parrs' old house. The Queen was in great trepidation, Mother wrote, because the King was acting as if the verdict were a foregone conclusion and even planning Anne Boleyn's coronation – his Holiness, he was sure, would not deny England's Defender of the Faith his just verdict – but she was being very brave. Fortunately, Mistress Anne had been sent home to await the outcome.

Mother's next letter described how the Queen had come into the court, knelt before the King and made an impassioned appeal, begging him to spare her this ordeal. He had said nothing, just stared past her. She had risen and commended her cause to God – and given the Italian cardinal the pretext he needed to revoke the case to Rome. The King was furious, Cardinal Wolsey was in disgrace and Mistress Anne was back at court, spitting venom. Mother was extremely concerned for Queen Katherine, who was in deep distress. She added that Anne was much affected by it.

The talk at the high table at Gainsborough Hall was dominated by these events. Katharine felt sorry for the poor Queen. But Sir Thomas was of an entirely different opinion. 'She should understand the King's fears for the succession and go gracefully,' he said.

Katharine was shocked, but she knew by now not to cross him or upset his good opinion of her. She had to live under his roof, after all.

'Mistress Anne Boleyn,' he was saying, 'is a true evangelical, a passionate supporter of reform – and God knows the Church is in need of that. Only good can come out of her influence over the King.'

Only scandal, Katharine thought, remembering the poor, devout Queen whom Anne was doing her best to supplant.

But Sir Thomas was warming to his theme and his family sat silent as he held forth. 'You have to buy your way into Heaven these days, while the priests wax wealthy on the money they get for selling indulgences,' he ranted. 'A lot of them are corrupt anyway. Show me a priest's housekeeper, and I'll show you his leman. And don't get me started on the bishops! It's all greed and grab with them, in their gold copes and jewelled mitres and palaces. They live like princes. Yet our Lord, whose example they ought to follow, was a humble carpenter.'

He paused long enough to help himself to more meat. 'What really angers me is that only priests are allowed to interpret the Scriptures. Yet some are unlettered or stupid. It's about time we had a Bible in English, so that we can read and interpret it for ourselves. *And* all those books the Cardinal has banned in the King's name – we should be able to make up our own minds about them too. My friends at court tell me that Mistress Anne reads them with impunity, yea, and even shows them to the King.'

'We don't all enjoy Mistress Anne's immunity, Sir,' Edward murmured.

'We will, boy, we will, once she gets her foot in the stirrup,' his father retorted.

'But is it right to question the Church's doctrines?' Edward persisted, rather bravely, Katharine thought. 'Doesn't that lead to heresy?' His sister Agnes let out a little gasp at his temerity.

Sir Thomas stared at him. 'What is heresy, when Catholics call Lutherans heretics and Luther himself hurls the same accusation at the Catholics? Heresy depends on who's pointing the finger, boy.'

'Then who is to say who is right and who is wrong?'

'Each man must follow his conscience, as Dr Allgood says.' Dr Allgood was the household chaplain, a firebrand of a reformer, and much admired by Sir Thomas. The two enjoyed nothing better than a heated debate on religion.

'But what if the law deems your opinion heresy?' Edward persisted.

'For God's sake, boy!' Sir Thomas roared. 'I am the law here and none shall gainsay me, still less question me.'

Edward subsided. Everyone was suddenly very busy eating. Young Henry choked on his meat and had to be thumped on the back, which proved a welcome diversion.

Much against her will – for she had been brought up to be God-fearing and devout – Katharine had to concede that Sir Thomas had made some pertinent points. How could the poor ever get to Heaven if they had to buy their way in? Why should the bishops live in luxury when many were starving? And why was it wrong to read the Bible in English? And yet the authorities, from the King down, had banned people from doing so. She feared that she might be on the verge of tripping into heresy herself. As for priests, were they not sanctified and set apart from ordinary mortals at their ordination? Were they not eminently qualified to interpret the Scriptures? That was what she had been taught. She wondered what her father-in-law thought about praying to the saints.

She had no idea what Lady Burgh's opinions were, nor did Edward's siblings ever reveal what they thought of their father's views. She had been at Gainsborough long enough now to have seen that no one dared oppose his iron will. He was opinionated and liable to erupt in violent rages at the slightest transgression. His children were plainly scared of him and rendered him absolute obedience. Their good behaviour was the measure of their fear of him.

He was unpredictable; no one knew how he would react. She had seen him send for the tutor and demand to see his children's copybooks. Then he would peruse them with a frown as his sons and daughters stood by, rigid with apprehension, and the tutor visibly trembled. If they were lucky, he would offer a word of praise, which was received as manna from Heaven. More often, he would bark that whichever dolt had written this rubbish deserved a beating – and then he would fetch his whip and administer it. He used that whip often, even for the most minor transgressions, like coming to dinner with uncombed hair or fidgeting in church. It was as if he was watching them all the time, waiting to put them to shame.

So far, Sir Thomas had not shouted at Katharine. She had taken care not to rile him or to draw too much attention to herself, and thought he still had a good opinion of her. But she feared that she too might one day find herself living in fear of his displeasure – especially if she failed in her duty to bear sons. Sir Thomas made no secret of the fact that he was eager for grandchildren to ensure the continuance of his line. She could not tell him why she was not yet with child – it was possible that he really did not know of Edward's inclinations – and so he would blame her. Men always did blame the woman.

As she left the hall for her chamber, to brace herself for another night's embarrassing fumbling with her husband, she sighed wearily. She had been so lucky to have been brought up in a happy and relaxed household, and to have enjoyed its freedoms. How different life had been under the benevolent rule of Uncle William. It was hard to adjust to the domestic tyranny imposed by Sir Thomas.

And now he was calling her back. 'A word, please, Katharine!' His voice rang out.

Dutifully, she retraced her steps and stood before him, as he sat in his high chair on the dais. 'Sir Thomas?' She made herself smile.

He regarded her severely. 'It has come to my notice that you are out riding most afternoons.'

'It has long been my habit, Sir,' she told him uneasily.

'Well, it has to stop,' he said. 'You cannot hope to carry a child if you are sitting in a saddle gallivanting all over the place.'

Indignation rose in her. 'But Sir, I am not with child. If I were, I would stop riding, naturally.' She was aware of his family, staring at her. They would never have dared to argue with him as she was doing.

'Well, you should be with child!' he snarled. 'And there will be no more riding until you have borne one.'

'But Sir—'

Sir Thomas banged the table. 'Be quiet!' He turned to Edward. 'You will make sure that I am obeyed,' he said. She wondered if he was having his revenge on his son for daring to dispute with him about religion.

Edward took her hand and led her towards the door to the west wing.

'Do your duty, boy! Get me a grandson!' Sir Thomas called after them.

When they reached their chamber, Katharine threw herself on the bed and wept. She did not know how she would bear not being able to go out riding. It was one of her greatest pleasures. Of course, she could walk in the park – unless Sir Thomas dreamed up some reason why she should not do that – but it would not afford her the exhilarating enjoyment of being in the saddle, racing across open country with the wind in her hair. It was unjust and unfair. She wished she had never come here. She would have given anything to be back at Rye House with her mother. Never had she felt so homesick.

'I'm so sorry, Katharine, I'm really sorry.' Edward was almost weeping himself. 'This is all my fault.' He pulled her into his arms. Desperate for comfort, she clung to him, and then they were kissing – and then that which she had most desired was finally happening.

Lying in bed afterwards, filled with relief that she was not destined to be stigmatised as a barren wife, and wondering if she was already with child, Katharine rested her head in the crook of Edward's arm.

'I don't know what came over me,' he chuckled, 'but I'm glad it did. Now I can look my father in the face.'

'Do you think he is mad, like your grandfather?' she asked.

'I don't know,' Edward sighed. 'He's not mad in the way my grandfather was. But it seems there's a mad beast in him. He seems to take pleasure in intimidating us all.'

'Well, I'm not letting him intimidate me!' she declared. 'Just let him try. He will find that I have a stout heart.'

'You'll be more than a match for him,' Edward said, squeezing her. 'I'm sorry about the riding, though.'

'I can bear it better now that I know I might have good cause to stop,' she told him.

'I pray you are right!' he said, and kissed her.

There was no baby. And there were no more couplings. Whatever magic had worked for them on that one occasion had deserted them. It was back to fumbling and striving, with no happy endings. As the weeks went by and winter drew in, Katharine feared that people were eyeing her speculatively, hoping to see signs of a pregnancy. Maybe it was her imagination. Pray God Sir Thomas would not question her – that would be mortifying!

But they were all to have some respite. In December, he was summoned to court. At last – at last! – the King had decided to revive the old barony of Borough and wished to invest him with it. At the same time, he was called to sit in the House of Lords as Lord Borough of Gainsborough.

Sir Thomas was exultant. This was what he had hoped and worked for all these years. He strutted around the house like a puffed-up cockerel, insisting that everyone address him as 'my lord'.

'You will inherit my title one day, boy,' he told Edward, clapping him on the back. 'You too will be a peer of the realm, and your son after you.' He flashed him a pointed look.

'It is you I am proud of, Sir,' Edward said, ignoring the jibe.

Everyone breathed a collective sigh of relief when the new Lord Borough departed for London. 'Don't expect me back for Christmas,' he said to his lady as she handed him the stirrup cup when he left. 'I know not how long this Parliament will sit for, and I mind to see something of the revelry at court.'

After he had ridden away, the oppressive atmosphere in the hall lightened. They had a wonderful Christmas. As the Yule log crackled on the hearth, and the garlands of evergreens gave off their festive scent, the family feasted, revelled, sang, danced and made merry. There were games of blind man's buff, hide-and-seek and snapdragon, and they rode out hunting on St Stephen's Day, Katharine defying Lord Borough's ban in doing so. The children laughed and romped as they never did normally, and even Lady Borough joined in the fun, looking so much more relaxed.

Twelfth Night was the culmination of the celebrations. There was to be the traditional great cake, baked with a pea and a bean, and all the young people were excitedly praying that they would be given a slice containing a favour, so that they could be king or queen for the evening and hold sway over the revellers. Edward's brother Henry and his sister Agnes won the prizes, but Henry's rule dominated the evening. He laid down forfeits, daring everyone to do the silliest things. Katharine had to stand as still as a statue for five minutes, with all the company watching to see if she moved. She didn't. Then it was Edward's turn, and he had to get down under each table and crawl the length of it. He made sure he tickled the toes of everyone seated there, prompting giggles and squeals.

Then Henry beckoned the steward over and bade him kiss the fairest lady in the room. The poor man looked abashed for, in the normal way of things, the ladies of the family were beyond his aspirations. But Edward's sisters were all giving him the eye, for he was a handsome fellow, and even Lady Burgh was giggling. After a pause, he walked around the back of the high table, bent down and kissed her lustily on the mouth. She went pink with astonishment, as everyone heaved with laughter – until they became aware of Lord Borough, cloaked and booted, standing in the doorway watching them, his expression thunderous.

'What's this, Madam?' he roared. The steward had turned pale, but Lady Burgh was ashen. Her husband stalked over and grabbed her by the wrist, pulling her up from her chair.

'My lord!' she faltered. 'I pray you . . .'

'It was just a bit of fun, Sir,' Edward cried out. 'We were playing forfeits. Henry is king of the pea and he ordered our good steward to kiss the fairest lady in the room. Naturally, he chose Mother. There was no harm in it.'

Surely, Katharine thought, Lord Borough had been witnessing this kind of festive horseplay all his life? From what she had heard from Mother, things were no less riotous at court. He must have known that it was, indeed, harmless tomfoolery, and that his wife was blameless, but, being him, he was making something sinister of it. Still holding poor Lady Burgh's wrist in his iron grip, and ignoring her cries, he dragged her out of the hall. They could hear his shouts and her screams fading into the distance.

Everyone sat in stunned silence. The minstrels had stopped playing. Some of the girls – and Henry – were crying. The steward, red-faced, hurriedly summoned the servants to clear the boards. No one attempted to continue with the revels.

Lord Borough's groom pushed open the door and addressed Edward. 'Sir, the master wishes you, Mistress Katharine and all the young gentlemen and ladies to attend him in the great chamber without delay.'

As one, Lord Borough's children rose to do their father's bidding, trooping dutifully, if apprehensively, to the great chamber. For a mad moment, Katharine wondered how he would react if she refused to go with them, for she feared there was some nastiness afoot, but she had lived at Gainsborough long enough to know that there would, for certain, be unpleasant consequences.

She was horrified, when she entered the great chamber, to see poor Lady Burgh kneeling at a prayer desk, tears streaming down her cheeks, and Sir Thomas, still in a rage, flexing his riding whip. There was a collective gasp from his children.

'Gentlemen, ladies,' he barked, 'I have summoned you here so that you may witness how a husband corrects a wife who has shamed him by her wanton behaviour. Watch – and profit morally from it, you boys who must learn how to rule a wife, and you girls who must remember that a wife has to be above suspicion.'

As he roughly pulled up his wife's skirts and raised the whip, Katharine looked away, burning with indignation. She had never known it was in her to feel such fury. It took all her willpower not to step forward and wrest the whip from her father-in-law's hand. She would not give him the satisfaction of seeing her watching him beat his poor wife. She kept her eyes downcast, flinching at the sound of Lady Burgh's cries and whimpers. Twelve times the brute brought the whip down on her flesh, immodestly exposed to the appalled gaze of her children. Had he no respect for his wife? How did he think she would exercise her maternal authority after this?

At last, it was over, and Lady Burgh slumped, weeping, over the prayer desk. Lord Borough stalked out of the room as Annie and Marget, the eldest girls, hastened to comfort their mother and help her to bed.

'If we've learned anything tonight,' Katharine muttered to Edward, 'it's that your father is a cruel bully.'

Edward was shaking. 'I remember he did this to her before, when we were small. He had no cause then.'

'He has no cause now!' she retorted angrily, as they followed the subdued young Burghs and their mother from the room.

Edward closed their chamber door behind them and sank down by the fire. 'You didn't realise, then? We all knew. Mother and the steward . . . It's been going on for some time. No one blames her. We've been pleased for her, for we know how hard her life has been with our father. He knew too. That's why he made an example of her. He doesn't love her; she's just his property, and no man lays hands on that.'

'I had not known,' Katharine said, thinking how well Lady Burgh had concealed the affair. 'Are they actually lovers?'

'I don't think so. She's a timid soul and wouldn't take the risk.'

'I wish someone would stand up to him!' Katharine fumed.

'I can understand that you are tempted – but don't!' Edward enjoined.

'I don't want to live under his roof,' she told him.

Edward shook his head. 'Nor do I. But he does own other houses. It would be good for us to have our own establishment. It might help us, you know . . .'

'It will be good for you to be away from your father's controlling influence,' she said. 'Will you ask him?'

'When things have calmed down, I will.'

'Promise me!' she demanded. 'I don't want to live here a moment longer than I have to.'

The answer was no. Still in a bad mood, which meant that the whole household was living under a cloud, Lord Borough asked why he should waste money on setting his son up in a separate household when he could continue to live at the hall in comfort. What did he lack for?

Edward had not the bottle to tell him exactly why he wanted his own home, but he kept asking – and was repeatedly denied.

'He thinks you are putting me up to it,' he told Katharine, as they walked the dogs in the park.

'I am!' she said. 'Do you think you can wear him down?'

'It's never been done before,' he admitted. But he tried, as often as he dared, all through that fraught spring, and always to no effect.

'We have to try a new tactic,' Katharine said.

She wrote to Mother, telling her everything – even, God forgive her, about Edward's problem – and begging her to help. She said she feared that Lord Borough might be violent. He had broken his wife's spirit and his children were cowed. She would not have frightened her mother for the world, but she needed her calm strength now more than she had ever done.

She did not have to wait long for a reply. *I am coming to visit you,* Mother wrote. *I have written to Lord Borough to tell him. I did not say anything about the matters you have confided to me. Nothing could induce me to stay under his roof, but my manor of Maltby is about eighteen miles away, and I shall lodge there. If need be, you and Edward can accompany me, but I hope it will not come to that.*

Katharine could not wait for her mother to arrive. It was many months since she had seen her, and she still missed her very much. She was counting down the days to her visit.

In the meantime, she and Edward rode over to Stallingborough, taking the litter, for it was a day's journey away. One of Lord Borough's many friends in the county was Sir William Askew, who was in the King's service as a tax collector. For all his unpopularity in that respect, he was a genial man and had invited Edward to bring Katharine to his fine manor house. 'My children would love to meet you,' he said.

So they went, and were pleased to find that the younger Askews were as pleasant and welcoming as their father. Over a delicious dinner, Sir William talked of his visits to court and, when drawn by his guests, spoke of the King, although he was guarded in what he said and Katharine gathered that he had little love for his sovereign.

Of his five delightful children, Katharine liked nine-year-old Anne best. She was an intelligent girl who seemed eager for knowledge and enjoyed asking questions. Katharine would dearly have loved to have Anne Askew join the schoolroom at Gainsborough. She would certainly liven things up. Even Lord Borough would be impressed. (There she went again, thinking of her father-in-law's opinion!)

Lying in the guest bedchamber that night, Katharine had a nightmare. All she could see was Anne's face, her mouth open in a silent scream, her hair in flames about her. It was so horrific that it woke her and she shot bolt upright, crying out.

'What is it, sweetheart?' Edward mumbled, springing up beside her.

'I had a nightmare,' she faltered, shuddering at the memory. 'Oh, God . . .'

'What was it about?' he asked, squeezing her tightly. 'And don't say nothing, because you're clearly upset.'

She described it to him, embarrassed to reveal just what her mind was capable of, and could sense him tensing in the darkness.

'She looked older in the dream, but it was definitely her. Oh, I pray it isn't a portent. She's such a lovely child. I would hate anything awful to happen to her.'

'It's just a bad dream,' Edward soothed. 'Only superstitious fools see omens in dreams. Put it out of your mind.'

Good advice, but impossible to follow. The Askews must have wondered what was amiss with her when she bade them farewell and hugged Anne tightly, fighting off tears. And the nightmare remained with her for days afterwards. She could not stop thinking about it.

It was June when Mother arrived, looking every inch the great lady in damask and jewels. Her manner when she greeted Lord Borough at the outer door was imperious, as befitted one who served the Queen. But Mother did not know that he despised Queen Katherine and knew that she was out of favour at court. He behaved towards Mother as if he was humouring her. Katharine ignored him. She was just thankful to be held in her mother's embrace again and to bask in her serene, comforting presence. Mother would put things right, she knew it.

The cordialities were observed. Lord Borough hosted a superb dinner in the great hall and had even hired a consort of musicians from Lincoln for Mother's enjoyment. The talk at the high table was confined to pleasantries, news of the court – wisely, everyone avoided talking about the Great Matter – and the problems of managing large estates. Only when the last of the fruit and the loving cup were being carried away did Mother turn to Lord Borough. 'Would it be possible to talk in private?' she smiled. Katharine and Edward exchanged covert glances.

How Mother did it, they never knew, for she said afterwards that there was no need to tell them. But, a good hour later, she and Lord Borough emerged from the little parlour and he told Katharine and Edward, quite pleasantly, that, on Lady Parr's advice, he had decided they should set up their own household. He had not long since been offered the joint office of steward of the manor of Kirton in Lindsey for himself and Edward, and had at his disposal a modest house, as he described it.

Katharine wanted to fling her arms around her mother, but restrained herself and thanked her father-in-law, as prettily as she could, for his kindness and generosity. Edward looked happier than he had in months, and for that she was deeply grateful. God willing, once they were on their own, they would be able to have a true marriage. And it would be wonderful to be mistress of her own household. She knew she was equal to the task. She was nearly eighteen and she had learned a lot from her mother and Lady Burgh.

'Kirton is a fine manor house,' Edward said. He was familiar with all the family properties, for his father had involved him in the management of the estates.

'I know I shall love it,' Katharine said, exulting in her good fortune. 'Is it far from here?' She meant to say, is Lord Borough likely to be on the doorstep every few days?

'It's about twenty miles north, in the Wolds,' Edward told her, with barely the hint of a conspiratorial smile.

'We have to complete the legal formalities,' Lord Borough said, 'and the house is in a sorry state inside. I shall send in carpenters and painters to repair and refurbish it. The gardens need attention too. Katharine, you and Edward may take some furniture from here, and I will give you some money so that you may buy what you lack.'

Heavens, Mother *had* done her work well! She was standing there, beaming benevolently. Again, Katharine wanted to throw her arms around her.

She did not mind so much now when Mother went home, or that she had to live at the hall while the repairs were being carried out at Kirton, for they would be departing when their house was ready, for a new life. She did feel a pang at leaving Lady Burgh and the children, but maybe, after Mother's intervention, Lord Borough would be kinder. Certainly, in those final few weeks at Gainsborough, he was as amiable as he had showed himself before her marriage.

They rode north to Kirton on a fine day in October, the baggage carts loaded with household stuff trundling in their wake. The road was winding and rutted where the sun had baked the mud, and it would probably be impassable in winter, but if that kept Lord Borough away, so much the better. They did not mind the demands of the ride. Their hearts were high, they were heady with expectation – and they were not disappointed. When they crested the gentle hill overlooking the Wolds at Kirton, and Katharine first set eyes on the manor house, she was open-mouthed with delight. The pale stone crenellated hall with its pitched brick roof had gabled wings at either end and tall pointed windows. Green lawns and mature trees surrounded it. Hurriedly dismounting and beckoning to a waiting groom to look to their horses, they raced inside and ran about the house like two excited children, exclaiming at its spaciousness and admiring the freshly whitewashed walls, the polished wood floors and the wide fireplaces. In the bedchamber, they hugged each other.

'This is a new beginning for us, Katharine!' Edward said, kissing her. 'I promise to be a better husband from now on.'

And he was. Away from his overbearing father and the tensions at Gainsborough, he was able to relax and, once more, they achieved physical union. Katharine dared to hope that the cradle she had optim-istically brought from the hall would soon be occupied by Edward's heir. How pleased Lord Borough would be. No, she admonished herself, she must stop thinking always in terms of pleasing her father-in-law!

She had missed two courses and was beginning to wonder if God had answered her prayers at last. Heaven knew, she had pleaded with Him often enough. There was no chapel at Kirton, only a prayer desk, so she often betook herself to the parish church, where she had become a familiar sight, kneeling on the tiles before the altar. The villagers praised her to her face for her devotion and her charity. She had been among them for just over a year, and they had taken her and Edward to their hearts.

She knelt down in the empty nave, fixing her eyes on the statue of the Virgin and Child that stood on the altar, next to the crucifix.

'Holy Mother,' she murmured, 'please intercede for me, that I might bear a child.'

It suddenly struck her that praying direct to God might be more effective. Did one really need the intervention of His Mother or one of the saints? Communion with God should be a simple thing – but it wasn't. Lay people had to rely on their priests and a whole hierarchy of clergy to interpret the Scriptures for them. And the Scriptures were in Latin, making them unintelligible to most. It seemed that the Church had put up barriers between individuals and God – and who was she, a simple young woman, to question that? Yet she was one of His children, with a soul to safeguard, and the certainties of her youth were crumbling to the extent that she was no longer sure that she was on the right path to salvation.

Troubled, she returned to her prayers, daring to beseech her Maker Himself for the thing she desired most, and hoping that He would not be angered with her.

Relations with Lord Borough were much better now that they were conducted at a distance. The manor house was a domestic haven. If Edward seemed not quite at home in their marriage, Katharine was not complaining. They liked each other and were good friends. It was infinitely better than the kind of union Lady Burgh endured. But a baby would crown everyone's happiness.

If she worried about anything, it was her mother, who had chosen to remain in the service of the Queen with Anne, even after her Grace had been banished from court last summer. Now Queen Katherine was living in Cardinal Wolsey's former house, the More, in Hertfordshire, royally served, but those who attended her were regarded by the King with suspicion and lived under a cloud. Katharine could only applaud her mother's loyalty, yet she would have preferred it if she had distanced herself. Surely Uncle William could secure her a place at court with the Lady Anne? He had helped Edward Seymour to obtain one for Will after he graduated, and both he and Will were now in high favour with the King. Thank goodness Mother's stubborn loyalty to the Queen had not prejudiced that. But you never knew. The King had a mercurial temper these days, she had heard, and his favour might be withdrawn on a whim. Oh, why didn't Mother and Anne just go home to Rye House? But maybe, Katharine reproved herself, she ought to trust her mother to do what was morally right.

Early in December, as she was making her pleasant preparations for their second Christmas at Kirton, a letter arrived, addressed in Anne's elegant handwriting.

Dear Sister, it began, *I have heavy news*. Katharine read on, disbelieving. Mother was dead. What had begun as a cold had affected her lungs, and no one, not even the Queen's own physician, had been able to save her.

She was gone, irrevocably gone. Her life in this world was a closed book. She had been thirty-nine, far too young to die. Katharine could not take it in; the reality of it kept hitting her painfully. She knew that Mother was now with God and that she should rejoice for her, but how was she going to live without her; how would she fill that vast empty space where she had been?

She sank to her knees amidst the jumble of festive gifts. 'Holy Mary, Mother of God, pray for us sinners now, and at the hour of our death,' she intoned. 'O Lord, grant unto her eternal rest. Merciful Father, hear our prayers and console us.' Tears were streaming down her cheeks.

'Oh, Mother!' she cried aloud. And that was how Edward found her when he came running.

When she was calmer again, she re-read Anne's letter. Her sister had written that Queen Katherine was being very kind to her and had said that she could remain with her for as long as she wanted. Anne was clearly appreciative of her goodness, yet she confessed to having a yearning to be away from the More. It was too sad a household, doubly so now that Mother wasn't there. She would have liked to go to court to serve the Lady Anne, but felt she was being disloyal to the Queen, and to Mother's memory, in wanting this. Poor Anne. At sixteen, it was natural for her to seek some gaiety in her life. She saw precious little of it in the banished Queen's service.

Will and Uncle William attended the funeral. Mother was buried beside Father in the chapel of St Anne at Blackfriars. Katharine spent the day in church, praying for her mother's soul. Soon afterwards, Uncle William sent her a package. Inside, she found the Queen's baptismal cloth and seventeen pieces of jewellery, which Mother had left her in her will. As they tumbled out of a velvet pouch, she recognised with a pang the ring with a pointed diamond set with black enamel that had been Mother's favourite piece. There were pendants, a pair of bracelets set with garnets, and miniature pictures of the King and Queen, beautiful things that anyone would be glad to own, but Katharine would have given anything to have her mother back instead.

Uncle William had written that Mother had left money for the founding of schools and for dowries for the poorer maidens among her many kinsfolk. That was typical of her goodness. She had also bequeathed a few jewels to her daughter-in-law, Ann Bourchier, but they were only to be delivered to her when her marriage to Will had been consummated. Katharine raised her eyebrows at that. Ann must be fourteen now, surely of an age to bed with her husband? But, apparently, they had not begun living together. Will never mentioned her in his letters, and Katharine had the strong impression that he was happy to be distanced from her. He seemed so far away, as did the household at Rye House. How she wished she could be with her brother and her uncle at this sad time. It would be such a comfort. But the roads were atrocious at this time of year and a journey would be hazardous.

She longed to see her sister too. Anne had written to say that the King had made her a royal ward and was now her legal guardian. It would be to her advantage, and his, for she could look to him to arrange a good marriage for her, but she would rather have had Uncle William, who was far less frightening than the King. Anne's news brought home to Katharine yet again how young women were at the mercy of powerful men.

Edward was a marvel. He did not reproach her for crying too much, unlike the priest at the church. He was always there when she needed to talk and distracted her with endless games of cards and dice. The tragedy had brought them closer, and Katharine thanked God daily for sending her such a husband.

But all that grieving took its toll. The tiny hope that had been burgeoning in her body was overwhelmed by her suffering and passed from her in an ordeal of blood and pain. Edward had not even known that she was with child – she had been just about to tell him – and he was shocked.

'There will be another babe, you'll see,' he soothed, cradling her in his arms. 'We'll make another.' And he tried, in his usual diligent way, and did his duty well, but nothing happened. God evidently did not intend for Katharine to have that kind of consolation. Was He angry at her boldness in approaching Him direct? Or was it that He knew what was best for her? She must not question His will.

Chapter 6

1533

Edward had been really pleased when he was appointed a Justice of the Peace. It was thanks to his father's influence, of course, yet he meant to deserve the office on his own merits. He was twenty-five now and gaining in stature in the county.

He had attended the quarter sessions in Lincoln at Epiphany, and did so again at Easter, wearing a new black gown of fine wool and a cap with a brooch on the brim. He looked grave in manner and handsome, for his face and body had filled out in recent years. Katharine waved him off, hoping he would not be gone long. She would miss him, for he had become very dear to her.

He was back within a week, lying pale and feverish in a litter loaned by a fellow judge. Katharine helped him into the house and up to bed. She sat beside him as he lay there listlessly, mopping his hot brow with a damp cloth.

'Don't die! Please don't die!' she prayed. 'Merciful God, spare him to me!'

She had wasted no time in summoning a physician from Scunthorpe. While waiting for him to arrive, she prepared an infusion of betony and sage and made Edward drink it. Soon afterwards, when his breathing became shallow and fitful, and he barely knew her, she knew she must send for Lord and Lady Borough and dispatched a messenger on the fastest horse in the stables. Then she summoned the priest and returned to keep vigil beside Edward, holding his hand and willing him to live. Surely God would not be so cruel as to take him from her too? She had lost her mother and her unborn child, and still grieved deeply for them.

The physician arrived, examined Edward and shook his head. 'It will take a miracle,' he said, resting a kindly hand on Katharine's shoulder. 'You must prepare yourself, Mistress.'

She felt nothing but fear and bewilderment. This could not be happening.

The priest performed the last rites as Edward lay unheeding, his breathing laboured, his face grey and his lips blue. Katharine knelt beside the bed, praying harder than she had ever prayed before. When she looked up, he gave a croaking gasp and fell silent.

She rose, numb with bewilderment. There was no emotion, just a strong sense of disbelief.

Lord Borough took charge when he and his wife arrived later that day. Lady Burgh's grief was pitiful to see. He was made of sterner stuff, although Katharine could see that he was struggling to control his emotions. He had lost his firstborn son. It was a hard blow for any man to take.

His chaplain did his best to comfort them all, exhorting them not to question God's will, but to give thanks for Edward's life and pray for the passage of his soul through Purgatory. As he spoke, Katharine realised she did not really believe that there was such a place as Purgatory – and was shocked at herself.

Standing with the Burgh family by the open family vault in Holy Trinity Church at Gainsborough, she could only think that, not two weeks ago, Edward had been looking forward to his trip to Lincoln, and they had been lovers the night before he left. Her courses had arrived as usual, so there wasn't even any hope of a baby. Edward's brother Thomas was the heir now.

She still had not wept. She had done as the chaplain had enjoined and tried not to grieve, for it was sinful to question God's wisdom. Edward had attained eternal life and they would be reunited in Christ one day.

As she returned to Gainsborough in a litter with Lady Burgh and Elizabeth Owen, Thomas's wife, and joined the family and their guests for the funeral meats, she felt some comfort in being, at not quite twenty-one, a widow of means. It meant that she was independent and her own mistress. She was hoping that Lord Borough would inform her of the financial arrangements that had been made for her. She did not have long to wait. When the mourners had departed, he sat down with her at high table.

'I have ordered that your dower be transferred to you,' he said. 'You will receive the manors of Oxted and Allington in Kent, and Westcliff in Essex. Beyond that, I have also assigned you the income of two of my manors in Surrey and one in Kent. My solicitor will send you the documents and the keys to the manor houses.'

'Thank you, my lord,' she said, glad to be free of her obligation to this man. 'You have been more than generous.'

'I am going to court soon,' he said. 'You will have heard that the Lady Anne has been proclaimed queen?'

Katharine stared at him, amazed. She had been so busy and preoccupied that news from the world beyond Kirton had passed her by. 'Has the Pope granted a divorce?'

'I'm assuming so. The King married her in secret. There is a lot of speculation as to when, for she is clearly with child. The important thing is, we have a reforming queen, and I, for one, am glad to be serving her. I have been appointed her chamberlain.'

That was such a high honour. Doubtless the King, or the Lady Anne, had heard of Lord Borough's zeal for reform. Even so, Katharine spared a thought for the poor old queen, exiled from court and put away against her will. How sad Mother would have been. It was a blessing that she had not lived to see this.

'I am pleased for you, my lord,' she said.

He inclined his head. 'This marriage may be the answer to all our prayers. Let us hope that England will soon have the prince she needs.' His eyes narrowed. 'Where will you go?' he asked.

With a jolt, she realised that he was expecting her to leave Kirton. She had intended to stay there and had made no alternative plans. Suddenly, it was plain to her that she was no longer wanted by the Burghs. Without children to anchor her to the family, she was redundant.

'I have not thought yet,' she faltered. 'When do you want me to leave?'

'There is no hurry,' he said, 'but we would like the house to be made available to Thomas and his wife as soon as is convenient.'

'Then I will make other arrangements as soon as I can,' she told him.

'And I will make sure my solicitor gets the deeds to you quickly,' he said.

Part Three

'A very painful and dangerous time'

Chapter 7

1533–1534

Back at Kirton, and finding the place so empty, Katharine thought about what she should do. Uncle William had written to say that she was most welcome to return to Rye House. Aunt Mary was there and their youngest daughter, Margery, was still unwed and at home. But Rye House would not be the same as it had been in the days when it teemed with young Parrs and dear Mother was alive. She thought about moving to one of her dower manors, where she could live independently, yet she knew no one in Kent or Essex or Surrey and did not relish living in isolation. But she did have relations in the north.

Father Cuthbert had been appointed bishop of Durham three years ago and was also serving as president of the Council of the North. They had corresponded from time to time; his letters were full of news, although she noticed that he never referred to the King's Great Matter. Knowing him well, she suspected that he was keeping his head down, and his distance, so as not to get involved or incur the King's displeasure. Now, when she wrote to him of her plight, he suggested that she go to stay with a distant cousin of both hers and Edward's.

Lady Strickland has been thrice widowed, he informed Katharine. *She was first married to Sir Walter Strickland, your kinsman, who died five years ago. Then she was married to the old Lord Borough's younger son, Henry, but he died within a year of their marriage, and her third husband, who I think was called Darcy, passed away last year. I saw her recently when I had occasion to travel to Kendal. She lives nearby at Sizergh Castle in Westmorland and, during our conversation, she confided that she is lonely. You would be perfect company for each other. Would you like me to write to her, suggesting that you go to stay with her for a time? Sizergh is a beautiful house with pleasant gardens, and Lady Strickland is a most delightful person. I am sure that this would be a healing experience for you.*

The more Katharine thought about it, the more the idea of going to Sizergh appealed to her. Lady Strickland sounded ideal company, and there would be no painful memories there. She wrote to Father Cuthbert to accept his kind offer and was pleased when a warm letter arrived from Lady Strickland herself, saying how happy she would be to have Katharine come to stay with her. She would make her most welcome.

With a lighter heart, Katharine ordered the packing of her belongings. Her only sadness was that she would be leaving Elinor behind; Lord Borough had commandeered her for Elizabeth Owen. On the day the litter drew up to take her away from Kirton for the last time, she walked around the house, remembering Edward in every chamber, and finally shedding tears for him. It was hard having to consign him to the past and let him go, but she had to look to the future.

The journey took a week. Katharine and her escort travelled through Yorkshire and across the Pennine Hills into wilder, more sparsely populated country with broad skies and a sweeping, majestic landscape.

Sizergh Castle stood solidly on flat ground surrounded by gently undulating fells. Its four-storey square tower and adjoining hall were built of ancient grey stone, much weathered. It was larger and more imposing than Gainsborough Hall or Rye House. Katharine was thrilled to see that it was surrounded by beautiful gardens. She would feel very grand staying here.

Lady Strickland came out to greet her. She was a pretty woman in her mid-thirties with frizzy golden hair that kept escaping from her French hood. Her black gown was of good cloth and she wore a *memento mori* cameo with a skull. But she was anything but mournful.

'Mistress Burgh, my dear, it is so good to see you. Welcome to Sizergh!'

Katharine alighted from the litter and embraced her hostess, who kissed her on the cheek and led her through the porch and into the castle hall. There, waiting in a row, were her children. Katharine counted nine of them, three boys and six girls, all looking restive and mischievous. There was none of the unnatural composure of the Burgh children. Once the introductions had been made, and Lady Strickland told them they could go and play, they scampered off, laughing and jostling each other. Then their mother invited Katharine to sit with her at the polished table and the steward brought them wine and little cakes. Before long, Katharine found herself liking her hostess very much. She had sympathy, wit and wisdom, and was one of those rare people to whom you felt you could confide anything.

After they had eaten, Lady Strickland led Katharine up the tower stairs to the chamber that had been prepared for her. 'The castle is old – about two hundred years, I think. I'm holding it in trust until my eldest, Walter, comes of age next year, but we have agreed that I will go on living here. Fortunately, all my husbands left money for our daughters' dowries, although finding suitable matches is a challenge, I can tell you. Still, there is no hurry. Here we are.'

She opened a heavy oak door and Katharine stepped into a large, light room with three trefoil-shaped windows set in an alcove. There was an oak tester bed with green damask hangings, a Turkey rug on the floorboards and a high-backed chair by the fireplace. A maid appeared with a basin and ewer for washing and a towel of Holland cloth, which she laid on a chest beneath the window.

'The privy is through there,' Lady Strickland said, pointing at a door in the corner. 'If you need anything, ring that bell.' A little handbell stood on the mantelpiece.

'It's perfect,' Katharine said. 'You are so kind.'

'You can stay as long as you please,' Lady Strickland smiled. 'I shall be glad of your company.'

It was a pleasant existence. Katharine had hours of leisure for reading her hostess's books. She liked to spend time pottering in the still room, making perfumes and preserves. Lady Strickland – Kat, as she now called her – kept pressing her to stay on. In gratitude, she spent time teaching the daughters of the house, remembering her mother's precepts about the importance of educating girls. The boys, Walter, Thomas and Roger, had a tutor, but he was against their sisters joining them for lessons. Katharine had no good opinion of him, for he insisted on a lot of boring learning by rote. By contrast, Elizabeth, Anne, Mary and Agnes Strickland all enjoyed their lessons. The younger girls, Anne Burgh and Frances Darcy, were too young to be taught with them, but were always included when the girls were at play. It was a happy household and evoked for Katharine sweet, poignant memories of Rye House.

Anne wrote from court to say that, thanks to Uncle William's influence, she had been appointed a maid-of-honour to Queen Anne. The old Queen had let her go with her blessing, doubtless understanding why her family were keen for Anne to dissociate herself from her.

Anne's next letter was full of the new Queen's coronation and the beautiful gowns the maids had been given. *I felt like a queen myself,* she wrote. *I saw your dreadful Lord Borough in the procession, bearing her Grace's train. He was wearing a surcoat and mantle of white cloth of tissue and ermine, and looked as royal as she did.*

Father Cuthbert had also attended the coronation, but was less enthusiastic. *The crowds were silent as we passed and I could sense a certain hostility. Some commented on the incongruity of a woman six months gone with child wearing virginal white. I saw Lord Borough, who thinks very highly of himself. The word at court is that the King gave him a stinging rebuke for appropriating the former Queen's barge and burning off her coat of arms.* Katharine could well imagine Lord Borough doing that.

It was clear that Anne was a stout admirer of the new Queen and had become an ardent supporter of religious reform. Katharine did not discuss this with Kat, because Kat held to the old ways. The high-beamed chapel at Sizergh would never see an English Bible if she could help it. So it was best to steer clear of debates on religion. For Kat, there was no debate – but Katharine, having had her eyes opened by Lord Borough, of all people, was beginning to wonder if the old ways were the right ways after all. Then, always, she would rebuke herself for entertaining so sacrilegious a notion.

The months went by swiftly, as they do when you are enjoying life. The two women rode out every day. Sometimes they went hawking. One summer afternoon, they visited nearby Kendal Castle, Katharine's ancestral home, which stood on a high drumlin overlooking the town. It was a stout fortress with thick walls intersected with towers, but it looked abandoned, and ivy was reclaiming the stonework. They climbed the hill as Katharine wanted to go inside, but the doors were locked.

'To think that I could have been born here, or grown up here,' she mused. It was a far cry from Blackfriars, which Will now used as a town house.

'I'd rather not go in,' Kat said, pulling a face. 'It's probably derelict and creepy.'

'All the better!' Katharine laughed, then ran down the hill. It was so good to be young, unattached and carefree, and to be able to enjoy her freedom.

They untethered their horses and rode into Kendal, where they looked at the goods on sale in the shops and visited the parish church to see the chapel where Katharine's grandfather, Sir William Parr, and some of her ancestors lay buried. Then they made their way back to Sizergh for supper with the children and a peaceful evening spent embroidering and chatting.

Winter was approaching. Chill winds were blowing in from the nearby ocean and there were autumn mists on the fells. It rained daily.

Katharine had been at Sizergh for five months when the letter from Father Cuthbert arrived. He wanted to know if she had any thoughts about remarrying, because he knew a gentleman who might find favour with her. It was her father's second cousin, John Neville, Baron Latimer, one of the members of the Council of the North. After their last meeting, Lord Latimer had confided that he was looking for a wife.

He told me that he needs companionship for himself and a mother for his children, since he is often away, either attending Parliament or the Council here, Father Cuthbert wrote. *He is forty years old and kin to yourself and Lady Strickland. His seat is at Snape Castle in the North Riding of Yorkshire, and he is of the great house of Neville. You could do a lot worse, my child. My Lord Latimer is an upright man and I am happy to commend him to you, if you are willing.*

Katharine sat down, staring at the letter, thinking hard. She was torn. Did she want to be married again? She would rather stay here. But for how long could she presume on Kat's hospitality? There might come a time when she had outstayed her welcome, hard though that was to believe right now. And there were other considerations to be taken into account. She had realised by now that the income from her dower was ample for one who was lodging as another's guest, yet it would not support such a good standard of living if she had to take herself to one of her dower manors and face life alone, which did not appeal to her.

Yet now, here was this lord – a baron of standing who was almost twice her age, but was offering her a new life in which she would be mistress of a castle and live in comfort and esteem all her days. Oh, what should she do?

After pondering a long time, she resolved to ask for Kat's opinion and showed her Father Cuthbert's letter.

'I know him,' Kat said, smiling. 'A good man, and diligent. It would be a worthy match. I should be sad to see you go, Katharine, but I would not stand in the way of your making such an advantageous marriage.'

Katharine wondered if Kat had ever envisaged her stay at Sizergh as permanent. Yet she believed she had her interests at heart.

'I'm not sure,' she said.

'Why don't you write to the Bishop and tell him that you might be interested, but that you would like to meet Lord Latimer before deciding. Tell him that I should be glad to welcome him as my guest to Sizergh. Snape can't be much more than fifty miles away.'

'Thank you,' Katharine said. 'That's by far the best course.'

She wrote, not only to Father Cuthbert, but also to Uncle William, who sent an enthusiastic reply. *The Nevilles are the oldest, most powerful and illustrious family in the north,* he wrote. *They have always been good lords to the Parrs. But now, while they represent a long tradition of service, we are the new men. I urge you seriously to consider this marriage.*

When Lord Latimer arrived at Sizergh on a freezing day in November, Katharine and Kat were waiting in the porch to receive him. Katharine was still wearing black in memory of poor Edward, but her gown was of velvet and her hood lined with pearls.

His lordship greeted them in a bluff manner, his flat, weather-tanned features creasing in a smile. He spoke with a broad northern accent. Dignity sat well on him, as did his riding clothes, which were not showy, but of excellent quality.

Kat had ordered a good dinner of venison and hare. As they talked, Katharine found Lord Latimer to be a plain-spoken Yorkshireman. You knew where you stood with him; there was no artifice about the man.

'I don't like the court,' he told her. 'I like living a quiet life in Yorkshire, God's own country. I keep myself to myself, managing my estates and looking to my tenants. I have no truck with these new-fangled religious notions; I worship as my forefathers did. That's good enough for me.'

It was as if he was laying his cards on the table. This is what I am. Take me or leave me.

'I have never been to court,' Katharine said, 'but I have family serving there. I am quite content with country life.'

'She's never happier than when she is on a horse,' Kat put in, signalling to the steward to serve more wine.

Lord Latimer smiled. 'A woman after my own heart! I've been to the court. I served the King as a gentleman-pensioner, one of his personal guard. You don't get accepted unless you're as tall as I am. When I was just twenty, I was with the King's army when he took Tournai. He knighted me afterwards. He's a bluff man, King Hal, and I liked him, but when this Great Matter of his marriage came about, I decided I liked Yorkshire better. I've rarely been at court since. Didn't want to get embroiled. When they asked me to put my name to a petition to the Pope, asking him to grant the King an annulment, I just signed.'

'It was probably the wisest course,' Kat said.

'And the safest.' He helped himself to more venison. 'I don't hold with Lutheranism and I'm no evangelical, but I've seen a lot of super-stitious nonsense. Have you ever heard of the Holy Maid of Leominster? No? Well, Cardinal Wolsey asked me to investigate. The woman was living in the rood loft above the chancel at the priory of

Leominster. She'd been there for years, for the Prior was convinced that God had sent her. People claimed she was so holy that she needed neither food nor drink. All she ate was angels' food, as she called it – the wafers used in Mass. And we had reports that the wafers would fly up to her from the altar during the service. The old Cardinal, rest his soul, was determined to discover if she was genuinely holy. He ordered us to search the rood loft. And what do you think we found?' He looked from Kat to Katharine. 'Meat bones hidden under the bed and a thread long enough to reach the altar, dangling from a loose floorboard.'

'What happened to her?' Katharine asked.

'She was ordered to leave the priory. It turned out that the Prior had been keeping her as his leman. They were both sentenced to perform public penance.'

'I often wonder if the miracles that are said to take place at shrines are genuine,' Katharine said.

'Oh, I'm sure they are, or most of them,' Lord Latimer said. 'Just because one is proved a fraud, it doesn't mean that the rest are. That's why old Wolsey was keen to root it out.'

A large apple pie was served, which Lord Latimer praised to the skies. After finishing dinner, the three of them sat by the fire as dusk fell, chatting, and Katharine found herself warming to their visitor. He wasn't a handsome man, but he had a kind face and there was an integrity to him.

Presently, Kat stood up. 'I'm just going to arrange some supper. Please help yourselves to more wine.' She indicated the flagon on the hearthstone then left the room. Katharine suspected that she was giving them some privacy. She sat there, waiting for Lord Latimer to say something. After all, they both knew why he had come.

'Bishop Tunstall told you that I'm twice a widower?' he asked.

'He did,' Katharine smiled.

'My first wife was the sister of the Earl of Oxford. She gave me two children, John, my heir, who is thirteen, and Margaret, who is eight. My lady died six years ago, and I won't say I haven't missed her. My second wife was a good woman, but she passed away not two years after we were wed. I've been on my own these past three years, and my children need a mother. But that's not the only reason why I wish to marry. I'm lonely. I want a companion and helpmeet. I liked the sound of you when Bishop Tunstall sang your praises, and now, having talked with you, I see you are calm and sensible, with a welcoming manner, and a woman of spirit. Will you wed me, Mistress Burgh?'

The proposal did not take her by surprise, even if it was precipitous. She was ready with her answer. With a mental apology to the shade of Edward, who had been dead just six months, she smiled at her suitor. 'As soon as I am out of mourning, my lord, I should be delighted to accept.'

For answer, he stood up, pulled her to her feet and kissed her, startling her. It was a man's kiss, and it took her unawares, making her realise in a few moments how young and inexperienced – and unin-clined – Edward had been.

When he broke away, Lord Latimer took her hands and they stood there, looking at each other. 'Ours will be a good marriage,' he said.

Chapter 8

Katharine insisted that they wait until a year of mourning had passed before arranging the wedding. It was to take place at Snape, and Kat had very warmly insisted that Katharine stay with her until then.

'I shall miss you,' she said. 'I am so enjoying your company.' It was heartening to know that, and that she was not outstaying her welcome. She would be glad to remain at Sizergh for a little longer. She could think of far worse places to while away the months of her mourning.

When the spring came, she laid away her black gowns, those tangible reminders of Edward, and took pleasure in wearing colours again. She had kept up a correspondence with Lord Latimer, and now she wrote to tell him that she would be happy if he would begin preparations for their marriage. All she had to do was order a wedding gown from Kat's tailor. She chose her favourite crimson colour in a light fabric of silver tissue.

Kat was coming to Snape to act as her attendant at the wedding. A capable aunt was brought in to take charge of the children in her absence. Early in June, the two women set out on the fifty-mile journey across the Pennines to Snape Castle. Their route took them through the glorious vistas of Lakeland fells and Yorkshire's moors and dales, and so into Richmondshire. On the way, Katharine reflected on the past chapters of her life and their different settings – Blackfriars, Rye House, Gainsborough, Kirton and Sizergh. Now she was beginning another – and she was not yet twenty-two.

Her eyes widened when she saw Snape Castle nestling in its peaceful green valley. She had not expected it to be so imposing or stately. It was bigger than all the houses she had lived in, even Sizergh, although it was built in a similar grey stone with crenellations, and she surmised that it was not as old. The Nevilles had money, and in past times they had built great fortresses to guard and control the north. Yet Snape was a noble house, not a stronghold. This was a peaceful place with sheep grazing contentedly in the surrounding fields.

Lord Latimer greeted them warmly, kissing Katharine on the mouth in the old way of greeting.

'Welcome, Mistress Burgh! I am right glad to see you – and you, Lady Strickland! May I present my children? This is John, although we call him Jack.' He nudged forward a sullen-looking boy with a shock of unruly black hair, who made the sketchiest of bows and did not smile. Katharine did her best to be gracious. It could not be easy having a new stepmother invade your life, especially if the boy had loved his mother.

She turned to his sister Margaret, a fey child with wispy golden curls and winsome, angelic features. Margaret was almost dancing with excitement at meeting her and impulsively threw her arms around Katharine when she bent down to kiss her cheek. This child would be easy to love.

Lord Latimer showed them around the castle. Listening to him talking in his plain way, and again aware of the calm strength of the man, Katharine felt drawn to him, as before, and was grateful to Father Cuthbert for having found her such a fine husband. Soon, she would be Baroness Latimer, a member of the aristocracy. She had done rather well, she reflected. Mother would be proud.

Lord Latimer pointed to some little coloured tiles set into the plasterwork over an arched doorway. 'These are very old. A gardener found them while he was digging outside. There's a whole floor of them down there, but it's much broken. We salvaged these and had them put here. There were some old pots and a statue down there too. Our chaplain thinks they might date back to the time of the Romans. For all I know, he may be right.' He led them up a twisting staircase. 'There has probably been a habitation on this site for centuries. We Nevilles got Snape through marriage.'

They ascended to the top of the tower. Katharine was looking around her, thinking that the whole place needed a woman's touch. She exchanged glances with Kat at the sight of a layer of dust on a cupboard.

But it was a beautiful house and could be brought to life without too much effort. When Lord Latimer led her to the window of the tower room, she looked out on a well-wooded hunting park and magnificent scenery stretching far beyond. This was a glorious place. She was itching to restore it to what it should be.

When they returned to the great parlour and the servants brought in a hearty meat pie and a great joint of beef, Lord Latimer insisted that Katharine sit at the opposite end of the table to him, as the future mistress of the house.

'I'm glad to see you here, lass,' he said. 'And mind you call me John from now on.'

Katharine and John were married the next day in the castle chapel. It was a simple ceremony, with the two children, a few of the local gentry and the household in attendance. The bride's gown looked iridescent in the sunshine streaming through the high windows. After much pleading, Margaret had been allowed to act as bridesmaid, although Jack remained mute and unsmiling.

When the priest had pronounced the final blessing, John kissed Katharine and again there was that frisson between them. Holding her hand high, he led her downstairs to the hall as everyone clapped and the servants hastened away to fetch the wedding fare. The feasting lasted all afternoon and then the guests went home. John had made it very clear that there was to be no bedding ceremony. When they were at last alone in the great bedchamber, he served them both wine and sat with Katharine by the hearth, reminiscing on the day.

'And a rare sight you looked in your fine gown,' he complimented her. 'Well, wife, finish your drink. It's time for bed.' He stood up and held out his hand.

It was so different with him. There was no hesitancy, no frantic efforts to maintain a hardness, no tentativeness. He was lusty and he wasted no time. Later in the night, they enjoyed a more leisurely coupling, and Katharine fell asleep thinking that she must surely be with child after this. In the morning, John claimed her again. There was an easiness between them now, and a mutual pleasure at being one.

This, she thought, was how marriage should be, and she spared a thought for poor Edward, who had not really been fitted for it.

It gave her great satisfaction to hear herself addressed as 'my lady' or 'my Lady Latimer'. It was gratifying to have a title and be living in a castle, with a husband of standing who gave her a free hand in its running. There was much to be done. Her first task was to dismiss the steward for his slackness. In his place, she appointed John's comptroller, Walter Rawlinson, a burly, loyal giant of a man. Briskly, with his help and that of his wife Bess, she rallied the servants, who she feared had grown rather lazy, lacking a mistress. There was a flurry of dusting, polishing, brushing, sweeping, scrubbing, washing and beating of rugs. Katharine herself donned an apron and joined in, as did Kat and young Margaret, who were eager to help. Soon, every surface and ornament gleamed, the castle was fragrant with the smell of beeswax, dried petals and fresh garden flowers, and the kitchens were spotless. The standard of meals improved, and the service of them.

John was impressed. 'Never seen the old place looking so good. You're a marvel, Kate. And you too, Lady Strickland. I thank you for your help.'

'I've learned a lot about managing a household from Kat,' Katharine smiled. 'You've seen Sizergh and how well it is run. I've taken example from that.'

She was sad when, a month after the wedding, Kat left. They had become like sisters. 'We must write to each other,' they promised, and Katharine shed a tear as she watched the litter trundle away.

She had feared that she would be isolated at Snape and that life would be too quiet, so she was surprised to find herself at the centre of a busy social scene. She had kinsfolk within easy riding distance, and they came to visit, and invited her back. John was on friendly terms with most of the gentry thereabouts, who also called or played host. There was feasting and hunting aplenty, and the broad beauty of the Yorkshire Dales afforded plenty of opportunities to indulge her passion for riding. The city of Ripon was just ten miles away, and Katharine rode there regularly to shop and to say prayers in the ancient cathedral. Sometimes, John took her to York, which was a day's ride distant, and they stayed in his house there. She loved the old city with its fine minster, its bustle and its proud civic buildings, and was gratified to be treated with such respect by the leading citizens.

She would have liked to meet John's numerous siblings, but they were all married and living in far-off parts of the kingdom. She had the impression that they were not a close-knit family and that there had been quarrels and tensions, but did not like to pry. However, John spoke often of his brother Marmaduke, who resided in Essex, and it was clear that there was affection between them.

With John's blessing, Katharine took responsibility for Margaret's education, wishing to instil a love of learning in her stepdaughter and look to her religious instruction. While an unwilling Jack struggled with the lessons set him by his tutor, a severe-faced man who was never averse to beating knowledge into him, Margaret flowered, and it was a joy to see her excel at her studies. She was a happy, willing child, her sunny nature embracing all that was good in life. Biddable and eager to please, she took pleasure in everything. It was soon clear that she adored Katharine, for she was never far from her side.

Jack was another matter entirely. He was sullen, touchy, dishonest and given to outbursts of violent rage. Katharine had never had to deal with such a difficult child – although, in truth, at fourteen, this one looked to be on the verge of manhood. You never knew where you stood with him. He resisted all her attempts to rule him or woo him. She put it down to the loss of his mother when he was young. She understood that he regarded her as an interloper. She also suspected he knew that Margaret was her favourite. Yet Margaret was so easy to love. She would love Jack too, if he would let her. She would not give up on him.

She and John had been married for five months when he asked her to accompany him to London. 'I ought to show my face in Parliament,' he said. 'It would be politic.'

News had reached Snape that the King had broken with the Pope and been proclaimed Supreme Head of the Church of England under Christ. John didn't approve and he had been most unhappy when he heard it bruited that everyone, when required, was to swear an oath acknowledging the King's new title and the little Princess Elizabeth, who had not been the hoped-for male heir, as his successor.

'It's not right,' he had growled, riding out with Katharine to inspect the estate farms. 'Only the Pope can be head of the Church, as our Lord ordained.'

'But you will swear the oath, if asked?' Katharine urged. 'It would be the wisest course.'

John reached across and patted her hand. 'I'm not a fool,' he said. 'I will swear.'

'God will know what is in your heart,' she said.

She knew he would keep his word. He had good cause to retain the King's favour, as she discovered one day when she found in the castle library a printed book called *The Castle of Pleasure*, written by one William Neville. Happy to get her hands on any book, she read it. In verse, it told the strange tale of a man called Desire, who was led by Morpheus, the god of dreams, to a wondrous castle where, in the garden of perfection, he met a lady called Beauty and expressed his love for her. Awaking from this idyllic realm, he lamented the inconstancy of human affairs.

That evening, she asked John if he had read the book.

'That one!' he said. 'No, I've never read it. I've no time for such flights of fancy. My fool brother William wrote it, and much good it did him. He has a mind full of fantasies.' He hesitated. 'Kate, there is something I should have told you. The year before last, William was accused of treason.'

Katharine gasped. 'Why?'

'He was said to have consulted three magicians who predicted the King's death – and mine.' He shrugged at the absurdity of it. 'God knows what madness visited him. I can understand that he wants my inheritance, although it grieves me to think he might murder me for it. Plotting fratricide is bad enough, but compassing the King's death is lunacy.' He shook his head. 'But maybe he *was* mad, because it turned out that he wanted to be earl of Warwick, for some reason I cannot fathom. Then, as if this was not enough to hang him, he dabbled in magic. He even tried to make himself a cloak of invisibility. His own chaplain attested to it. I myself was questioned by the Privy Council, although I knew nothing of his doings. They examined our brothers George and Christopher too. Not that my heart was bleeding for them – would you believe they took me to court after our father died? They said I had appropriated property that was rightfully theirs. It wasn't, but that was not the point. So much for brotherly love.'

He rose and poured himself a goblet of wine. 'Anyway, by God's providence, I did not come under suspicion and William was released, since they could not prove anything against him and suspected malice on the part of his accusers. But I wonder. He's stupid enough to have done such things. It ruined him, of course. He impoverished himself paying lawyers' bills – and him with a family to support.' He sighed, exasperated.

'Why didn't you tell me?'

He gave her a wry look. 'Because I thought it might put you off. I'm sorry, I should have been honest.' He regarded her for a moment. 'Would it have made a difference?'

She shook her head. 'Not at all.' It touched her to see him looking so grateful.

It was a long journey down to London and Katharine was utterly relieved when they finally reached John's town house in Charterhouse Square. She was weary of inns and monastic guest houses, and being jolted on the road all day, with a cold wind blowing through the leather curtains of the litter. At least the children had not been subjected to such rigours; they had been sent to stay with Kat at Sizergh. And Katharine and John had been able to visit Rye House on the way and see Aunt Mary, who had made them very welcome. The house seemed small after Sizergh and Snape, but it was good to be back, despite the poignant memories of the happy years there that could never be recreated.

John's residence stood not far from St Giles' Church in Cripplegate and the old London wall and barbican. He had leased it two years before from the Abbot of Pershore. It was a handsome residence that formed part of a quadrangle of buildings overlooking a large, well-kept expanse of lawn. Just across the square stood a monastery of Carthusian monks, the London Charterhouse.

'That lawn covers a plague pit from the time of the Black Death,' John told her.

'I'd rather not have known that.' Katharine made a face.

'Don't look so worried – the bodies are buried deep and there is no possible risk of contagion.'

Some servants had been sent ahead with strict instructions from Katharine to have the house made ready to the high standard that now prevailed at Snape. As she walked around her new domain, she was pleased to see that her orders had been obeyed. She admired the linenfold-panelled reception rooms, the pleasant dining room over-looking the square, and the large kitchen, which boasted a fireplace about eighteen feet wide. Lifting her skirts, she descended to a vaulted brick basement where barrels of wine were stored.

'Houses around here are in demand,' John said, as they sat down to a dinner of partridge and pork. 'Many officers of the court live nearby. Master Leland, the King's Antiquary, lives next door. It's under an hour's walk to Whitehall Palace.'

'It's a lovely house,' Katharine enthused, 'and it's not far from Will's place at Blackfriars. We must visit him as soon as he can get time off from his duties at court, and I'd like to invite him and Uncle William to dine.'

'You invite whoever you want, lass,' John said.

It was good to be back amidst the lively bustle of London, which she remembered from childhood. Even the noise and the smells could not dent her pleasure in being in the city. When John was at the Parliament House or at court, she liked to wander around the streets and markets, or browse in the goldsmiths' shops along Cheapside, or walk around the vast expanse of St Paul's Cathedral, admiring the monuments and looking for bargains in the stalls along the nave. She was happy at home too, taking pleasure in the fine furnishings and liking to pour an afternoon cup of wine in the cosy chamber she had chosen as her parlour, and sip it, lost in a good book.

John was not so happy. Listening to him complain about the King's ministers and their policies, the impossibility of securing an audience with his Majesty, and the general cut-and-thrust of court life, Katharine gained the impression that he enjoyed little influence and had few friends at Whitehall. The only noble who seemed to be friendly was a fellow Yorkshireman, Sir William FitzWilliam, who was related to the Nevilles. If John were to gain the King's favour, and perhaps win some preferment, Sir William was a good ally to have, for he was close to the King, and to Sir Thomas Cromwell, who was all-powerful, having long since replaced Cardinal Wolsey as chief minister.

As time went by and these hopes were not fulfilled, Katharine began to see her husband in a new light. She realised that he was indecisive and that his judgement was too unreliable for high office. He would avoid confrontations if he could and make compromises that pleased nobody, least of all himself.

When Uncle William came to supper, and they had enjoyed a happy reunion, she confided her concerns to him while John was showing Will his cellar. It was wonderful to see them both again after so many years apart. Uncle William looked the same as ever, and Will, at twenty-one, was now a tall, broad-shouldered man with a red beard, whose courtly finery sat on him elegantly. She imagined that he was popular with the ladies and noticed that he never referred to his wife, from which she inferred that they were still not living together. It was all rather strange, she mused. Yet she was more concerned about John.

'I was not unaware of the problem,' her uncle said, mopping up gravy with his manchet bread. 'I've seen him and spoken with him from time to time, and asked how he's been getting on, but I don't really think he knows himself what he wants.'

'He wants to be in favour with the King, after what happened with his brother.' She knew how he fretted that he had incurred his Grace's displeasure.

'Yes, but for that you need to be zealous for the Royal Supremacy and demonstrate unquestioning loyalty and obedience to his Majesty. If it's a court or public office John's after, he needs to show strong leadership. He has many good qualities, but I fear he doesn't have that in him. Tell me, is he here in London because he wants to be, or because he thinks he ought to be? Because I'm getting the strong impression that he'd rather be up north managing his estates, far away from the court. And I think his constant complaints reflect his awareness that this is not his natural habitat. My advice would be to see this Parliament through to its prorogation, then go home and enjoy life. I dare say the King has long forgotten about William Neville.'

It was sensible advice, but when Uncle William tried tactfully to put it to John, John shook his head.

'I need to know where I stand with the King,' he said.

Katharine laid a hand on his arm. 'You should not worry about that, husband.'

Her words made no difference. When John wasn't sitting in Parliament, he was haunting the court, waiting with the crowds of other petitioners who were craning to catch the royal eye as the King came forth in procession to Mass each morning. And, in the end, he got the reassurance he had been waiting for.

'The King smiled upon me!' he called, crashing through the front door. 'He turned his head and looked directly at me, and he smiled.'

Katharine expected him to continue, to say that he had been granted an audience and some great favour, but that was it. All he had got was a smile, which had cost the King nothing. And yet it was enough. John was happy. He could go home and get on with his life, knowing that his sovereign had smiled benevolently on him and held no rancour on account of the dangerous idiocy of his brother. He was safe now.

Having been brought up in a family driven by ambition, Katharine was surprised at her husband's lack of it. Yet he was a good man, a king in his own kingdom, and he was kind to her. She could have done a lot worse. And she understood why a smile was enough, in a way that Uncle William and Will never could.

Shortly before they left London, she received a letter from Father Cuthbert. *I had hoped to see you in London, but I fear I have offended the King by questioning the Royal Supremacy, and he has commanded me to remain in the north. Do not worry. I have tried to redeem myself by showing a willingness to explain to the Princess Dowager the grounds on which her marriage to the King was annulled, and I will take the Oath of Supremacy when I am asked. So far, there is no word of my being stripped of my bishopric and my offices. But do not be concerned for me, my child. I have had my say, for the discharge of my conscience, and I hope the King realises that I am loyal to him at heart.*

Yes, Katharine reflected, but a man cannot serve two masters. People were having to make a choice between king and pope. For some, it must be a dreadful moral dilemma, one that might jeopardise the salvation of their souls. For others, like John, Uncle William, Will and Father Cuthbert, it was a matter of pragmatism. She, being a woman, was unlikely to be asked to take the oath, yet she would do so if required. She had heard too much about the Church needing reform to accept its tenets unquestioningly, as she had in childhood and youth. She found herself astride the fence, as it were, unable to shake off the faith Mother had instilled in her, yet fascinated by new ideas she was hearing at every turn. You could pick up any number of tracts at the booksellers' stalls by St Paul's, and John came home from court daily, grumbling about the latest outrage against the old religion.

'Some would like to see the statues of saints removed from the churches, condemning them as graven images and false idols,' he ranted. 'Some even see crucifixes as idolatry. This is what happens when people read the Scriptures for themselves. It's Queen Anne's fault. She encourages it, even though it is banned. And none dare gainsay her. She has the King under her thumb.'

Secretly, Katharine would very much have liked to have debated religion with Queen Anne. She suspected there might be a lot of common ground between them. John would have been aghast at the notion!

'We'll be away from it all soon,' she said soothingly.

'Aye, but this wickedness will go on until it engulfs the whole kingdom,' he sighed.

'The court's reach doesn't extend too far north,' she said. 'What happens in London does not always affect the kingdom as a whole. And the Queen's influence may not endure if she fails to give the King a son.'

'Hush!' John looked alarmed. 'That's as good as speaking treason!' He glanced nervously about him. 'I hope none of the servants heard.'

'There's no one about,' she said, hoping it was true and wishing the words unsaid.

In truth, she was growing weary of London – or, rather, of being in

London with John. He was a duck out of water. She found herself looking forward to returning to the peace of Yorkshire.

Back at Snape, Katharine resolved to make an effort with Jack. She had written to Kat asking for her advice, and Kat had urged her to confront the problem. She realised it was time to pay proper attention to her stepson's education, give him some moral guidance and correct his faults. His father and his tutor, she knew, would have beaten him for them, so she shielded him as often as she could.

'Jack, look at me!' she said, after catching him lying in a haystack when he was meant to be writing an essay, and dragging him back to the castle. 'You must pay attention to your studies. They are the key to living a successful and fulfilled life. You've had all afternoon to write that essay. You could have done it by now and be out enjoying yourself.' She sighed, seeing she was getting nowhere. 'Well?'

'I was going to do it this evening,' he muttered. 'I've written some of it.'

'I'd like to see it,' she said.

'You can't make me!' he flared. 'You can't push me about. You're not my mother!'

Be patient, she counselled herself. 'No, and I could never expect to take her place, but I do have your interests at heart and, as we live under the same roof, it would be better for both of us if we tried to be friends.'

All she got was a shrug.

'You haven't written anything, have you?' she challenged as they entered the castle.

He wouldn't meet her eye.

'Go and do it now. You don't want to risk another beating. And Jack – stop telling lies. It's not clever and the truth will always out.'

'Go fuck yourself!' he snarled, picking up a vase of the flowers she had picked and dashing it to the stone floor, where it splintered into little shards that scattered everywhere. She stared at it, shocked at the obscenity and his violence.

'What's happened?' John asked, hurrying into the hall.

'It's nothing,' she said. 'Jack was just telling me about the essay he's been set, and I managed to knock the vase over. Silly me!'

'I'll call a groom,' John said, hastening away.

Jack was staring at her, his cheeks flushed.

'Don't you dare do anything like that again, or swear at me,' she hissed.

'No,' he mumbled. 'Sorry.'

She left it at that.

That evening, John joined her in her parlour to share a nightcap of steaming aleberry.

'Did you really knock over that vase?' he asked.

'Why, yes.' It sounded like the lie it was.

'You don't fool me, Kate. You see, I know my son. He won't do the work set him, and I doubt he would ever want to talk about it with you. My guess is that you told him off for his tardiness and he smashed the vase in retaliation. Am I right?'

'I'm sorry, I was just trying to protect him and show him that I care about him,' she admitted.

John grunted, leaning his head back against the chair. 'He gives me headaches, that boy. I don't know what to do with him. He's touchy, takes everything the wrong way, grudges any praise I give him and seems to exult in defying me. He thinks it holy to commit sin and, if I reprove him, he says his friends get away with worse. And he lashes out without thinking. Punishment seems to make no difference.'

'I think the answer is to treat him with kindness,' Katharine said, 'and that is what I intend to do. He may never love me, but I am determined that he will respect me.'

'Well, I wish you luck!' John said. He sounded as if he had almost given up on his son.

'He's only fourteen, young enough for me to mould him and instil some sense of responsibility in him.'

Her gentle approach seemed to work. She preferred the carrot to the stick. Constantly, she encouraged both children to love learning and to excel. If she had to administer a reprimand, she did it privately, respecting their dignity, and never raised a hand to them. And she continued to protect Jack from his worse self, even when she caught him pinning a terrified serving maid to the wall and trying to kiss her. She wrenched him off, then took him away and gave him a sharp lecture on how gentlemen should treat women. She remained aware that there was the potential for violence in him and wondered if she was placating him because she was frightened of him, but her methods seemed to be having results. Whatever the means, she had moved him to behave better. Everyone noticed the change in him, and John was amazed, and very grateful.

That Christmas, they celebrated Margaret's betrothal to Ralph Bigod. John was elated to have secured for her the son of his near neighbour, Sir Francis Bigod. It had cost him more than he could afford, but he was happy to make the sacrifice. Margaret, in her usual joyous way, professed herself delighted – she was but nine and did not fully grasp what marriage would mean. The wedding would not be taking place for at least five years, and that was an eternity to a child of her age. Katharine was pleased about the betrothal and intended to see that Margaret was well prepared when the time came, as her mother had prepared her. Sir Francis was a powerful advocate for religious reform, which Katharine was coming to see as essential. Men like him might make all the difference to society at large.

News of another coming wedding arrived early in the new year. That spring of 1535, Katharine and John travelled to Thornton Bridge, east of Ripon, to see Kat married to her fourth husband, William Knyvett, whom Katharine took to immediately. It did her heart good to see her friend so happily married. Thornton Bridge was not far away, and they would be able to visit. Kat and William came to Snape three times that year and Katharine and John joined them for Christmas at Thornton Bridge Hall.

In some ways, it had been a grim year, with the King executing Sir Thomas More, Bishop Fisher of Rochester and others for opposing his marriage and his reforms. At Snape, however, life was good, with few clouds on the horizon. Katharine prayed that it would stay that way.

Chapter 9

1536–1537

After Epiphany, they went back to London, as Parliament was again in session and John felt bound to attend. He was often in a black mood when he came home in the evenings, grumbling about Queen Anne's pernicious influence, the illegality of the Royal Supremacy and the King's plans to close down smaller monasteries and convents.

'He has declared himself Supreme Head because he wants to get his hands on the Church's wealth,' he seethed. 'The people will not stand for it, you'll see. No one wants to see the faith they grew up with overthrown, or the monasteries.'

'Shh!' Katharine hissed, gesturing furiously. 'What you're saying might be treason!'

John subsided, glowering. 'I just wish,' he said, lowering his voice, 'that we could go back to the old ways and that the King would forget this nonsense. It's all the fault of that whore.'

'You mustn't call her that.'

'She seduced him with her witchery and her dangerous ideas. She's split the kingdom. And there's talk about her at court. People are saying she's no better than she should be.'

'You should not speak disrespectfully of her. Someone might hear and report you.'

'So we're all silenced and she gets away with so-called reforms.'

Katharine got up and put her arms around her husband, feeling the tension in his shoulders. 'There's nothing we can do about it,' she murmured in his ear, 'so why waste time fretting? We just have to get used to the changes that are being made.'

'You don't have to sit in Parliament and keep your mouth shut against your better instincts,' John retorted, yet he put his hand up and clasped hers. 'Sometimes, I think I'd be better off staying away from the House. The good people of my shire rely on me to represent them; Yorkshire folk like to stick to the old ways, as is right, but I can do nothing for them.'

There was no easy answer to that. And Katharine too was finding it difficult to keep her mouth shut.

In March, John came home in a foul mood. 'They've passed the Ten Articles,' he growled. 'This is the King's plan for the Church of England. I can't believe it's happened.'

'Sit down, husband,' Katharine bade him, bending to rake up the fire. 'Tell me what this means.'

'The King wants to *purify* the Church,' he snorted. 'He wants to rid it of superstition, as he calls it. There will be no celebrations of saints' days, no pilgrimages, and no praying to statues. His Majesty has graciously retained the Mass and the Real Presence, and we are still to be justified by faith *and* good works. At least he has not embraced Martin Luther's doctrine that we can attain Heaven by faith alone.'

'So the King remains at heart a true Catholic,' Katharine observed thoughtfully.

'I suppose we must be grateful for small mercies,' John conceded grudgingly. 'But the visitations of the monasteries have begun. Ostensibly, this is to assess their moral rectitude and their financial viability, but, mark my words, Cromwell will use it as a pretext to close them down. Katharine, I've had enough. When Parliament goes into recess for the summer, we should return home. I am needed by the Council of the North.'

She would have preferred to stay in London and keep abreast of the exciting developments in Parliament, but her place was with her husband, and she would go home with him without protest, for she did not want to give him any cause to suspect that her views were growing increasingly apart from his.

* * *

It was May when they got back to Snape, where letters from Anne, Will and Uncle William were waiting for them.

'Merciful Heaven – the Queen has been executed!' Katharine exclaimed, looking at John, aghast.

'What?'

Katharine scanned Uncle William's letter. 'She was accused of adultery with five men – one was her own *brother* – and of plotting the King's death. I . . . I can't quite take it in.'

John read the letter. 'I did hear things, at court and in the Parliament House. Someone said she had a bad reputation, another that she was free with her favours. But I put it down to malicious talk; there was enough of that about her. Maybe the Papists made an occasion to get rid of her – and good riddance.'

Katharine had never heard of a queen of England being executed. It was appalling. If only she knew what to believe.

She opened Anne's letter. Her sister sounded very upset. She had liked the Queen and shared her zeal for reform, and now, Katharine thought, she would lose her place at court. But no. When she read on, she learned that Anne had been told, in confidence, that she was to stay on at court to serve a new queen. *We all know who it will be*, she had written. *For some time, the King has been pursuing Mistress Jane Seymour, who has served as maid-of-honour alongside me. If rumour be true, she served the King as well as the Queen. She is a devout Catholic and I fear we will see a halt to reform. It is my belief that the conservatives at court invented those charges against the Queen to put the Seymour in her place. Burn this, dear sister, as soon as you have read it.*

With a heavy heart, Katharine showed John the letter then threw it into the fire. She burned Will's too, for he had also expressed his gloom at the bitter blow Anne Boleyn's fall had dealt the cause of reform.

The news of the Queen's death, speedily followed by tidings of the King's marriage to Jane Seymour, was the talk of every great house Katharine visited. She heard people gossiping about it in the market at Ripon and even overheard the cathedral canons disputing as to whether the charges were trumped up or not.

John was in no doubt that the hand of God was in this. 'Now we have a Catholic queen, and may God bless her.' Almost everyone agreed with him. He was right. The new ways were not popular in the north.

They returned to London in June so that John could attend Parliament. He was hopeful of seeing the recent reforms swept aside, in the wake of recent events, but his buoyant mood did not last.

'Nothing has changed,' he grumbled as he walked into the house and threw his cap on the hall seat. 'They're pressing ahead with their ungodly business, come what may.'

Katharine poured him some wine and handed him the goblet. 'Maybe Queen Jane doesn't have the influence that Queen Anne did.'

'I'm sure you're right. People say the King chose her because she's the exact opposite of Anne. By all accounts, she's a little milksop. It'll be *yes, Henry* and *no, Henry* – whatever his Majesty says.'

Katharine wondered. When he'd visited them two nights ago, Will had said that, when the ambitious Seymour family had united with Cromwell and others to bring Anne down, Jane had been involved in the conspiracy. How deeply involved no one could say. It had made Katharine wonder what lay behind the new Queen's quiet exterior. Perhaps she was playing a long game. She must care about the religion she was reputed to hold dear. Maybe she knew that with a son in her arms she would be in a strong position to influence the King.

Katharine sighed inwardly as she hung John's gown on the peg by the door. Two years they had been wed, and there was no sign of a child, although not for the want of their coming together. John was as satisfactory a lover as ever. Unlike the King, he did not lack an heir, but it would have been fulfilling to have children together. The subject was never mentioned, and she often wondered if he was inwardly disappointed in her barrenness.

To ease his tension, she kneaded his shoulders as he sat in his chair. 'The King has only been wed for a few weeks. Give it time.'

But John was still brooding on his grievances. 'I've had enough,' he said. 'I'm sick of all those lords rabbiting on about how wonderful the King's reforms are, and me standing by with my mouth shut. I think we should go home. The Act of Succession has been passed, settling the throne on Queen Jane's issue. The late Queen's daughter is now a bastard in law, like the Lady Mary.'

Katharine spared a thought for little Elizabeth who was only, what, two years old? How dreadful to be punished so severely for her mother's crimes, poor little mite.

'Yes, we should go home,' she said, suddenly wanting to be as far from the court as possible.

No one could have failed to observe that the north was seething with unrest. At the inns and manor houses where John and Katharine lodged on the way, people were angry. They saw gatherings in churchyards and marketplaces, and firebrands fuelling the discontent with inflammatory speeches. Everyone they met had an opinion. Like John, folk had been hoping that things would now be as they had been before the King broke with Rome. The changes he had wrought struck at the fundament of their daily lives. It had got to the stage where no one knew if they were allowed to pray to the saints or whether they could go on pilgrimage – or even which sacraments were to be observed.

'We need certainty,' John declared, as he sat at the head of the family table at Snape on their first night back there. 'The King has undermined the natural order of things. People are worried about the safety of their souls.'

Katharine had no answer. She did not think the King would ever lose face by returning to the Roman fold and, secretly, she supported his resolve to rid the English Church of superstitious practices and abuses. Why would you pray to a saint to intercede for you if you could pray direct to God Himself? She did not mourn the disappearance of holy statues from some churches. The Lord had commanded, 'Thou shalt not make unto thee any graven image', so she was at one with the King on that. Yet, in most of the churches round about, the priests and the people had clung on to their images.

The groundswell of discontent became increasingly louder. John heard it all the time when he met with their neighbours and tenants.

'They are all loyal subjects,' he said. 'No one wants to see the King overthrown. They just want the old faith restored, the monasteries spared and evil ministers like Cromwell removed. Without his pernicious influence, his Grace might pay more heed to his people. But they are feeding him with lies, these reformists . . .' He stumped off to wash before dinner.

To Katharine, though, the King's measures seemed wise – and right. She could not imagine any ruler welcoming criticism for acting on the advice of learned and conscientious men; no wonder it was being said that his Grace was excessively touchy these days, not least because he was grieving for his son, poor young Richmond, who, Will had informed her, had died suddenly at the end of July. By all accounts, the King was an intelligent man, well educated and soundly versed in theology. She was in no doubt that he was qualified to make sound decisions about religion. But she kept her thoughts to herself.

Towards the end of September, John returned from Ripon in a state of agitation.

'It's not just the monasteries they are dissolving,' he told Katharine. 'They are planning to close the churches too. My friends on the city council have heard that royal commissioners will be carrying out visitations at all the churches in the north. By God!' He banged his fist on the table. 'This King is the Antichrist. He'll do away with religion entirely and send us all to Hell!'

'Do you know for certain what the commissioners' purpose is?' Katharine asked, finding it incredible. 'Maybe they are coming to ensure that the new laws are being observed in the churches.'

'Yes, just like they did in the monasteries.' He rounded on her. 'And now they are closing them down, one by one. Just the smaller houses, we're told, but mark me, they'll take them all in the end. The King will have their wealth.'

Katharine had not shown John the letter in which Will had written of his Grace's fears that the monasteries were hotbeds of Popery. She had no idea if such fears were well founded, yet it stood to reason that the monks were clinging to the old order.

John was pacing up and down on the flagstones. 'Once the monasteries are closed, we'll see monks and nuns on the streets. Who will succour the poor, or heal the sick, or run schools? Who will preserve all that book-learning you hold so dear? Kate, this has to be stopped! People up here want an end to it. There's talk of rebellion in the air.'

'And who will do the stopping?' she asked. 'Are you willing to rise against the King? Will you risk being arrested for treason? Think of what they do to traitors, John! Think of your children, who could be dispossessed. Think of me!' She realised she was actually wringing her hands in supplication.

He paused. He had his back to her, so she could not read his face.

'Think of your tenants and all who depend on you, John. You're a good lord to them. They could never have a better one. Please consider carefully before you do anything rash. Do you really think you are of the stuff of which martyrs are made?'

He turned to her, frowning. 'Do you care for your faith, Kate?' he asked. 'Would you see it overthrown and these new ways imposed on us?'

She was taken aback. Dare she tell him that she was with the King when it came to religion? 'Of course I care,' she said. 'My faith is everything to me – but you are too, and I would not have you put yourself at risk, especially as we don't know if these rumours about the commissioners are true. No, John, what people should be doing is petitioning the King, out of his fatherly mercy, to heed their concerns.'

'Since when did Henry Tudor ever listen to anyone?' John flung back. 'He'll go his own selfish way and leave the rest of us to shift as best we can!'

She left it there and went to tell Cook that dinner could now be served. The atmosphere at table was strained. John looked like a bull about to charge, Jack sat there mute and even Margaret's sunny prattle subsided. Katharine attempted to start a conversation, but no one responded. She was glad to get up and retire to her parlour. John did not join her. She had never known him to be in such a bad mood.

October was a week old when they received a visit from Lord Redmayne of Harewood Castle, a good friend of John's whose seat was not thirty miles south of Snape.

'Greetings!' he said. 'I am on my way to Middleham Castle and other places to raise the alert. Have you heard that there is a rising in Lincolnshire?'

Katharine and John stared at him.

'Good God, I'm surprised you didn't hear the church bells ringing from here,' he said. 'It started in Louth, when some vicar called for the restoration of the old religion and urged his flock to rise up in protest. They did, and soon all the towns nearby were in an uproar. A petition was sent to the King. It got short shrift. Within ten minutes, or so it seemed, a royal army led by the Duke of Suffolk had marched into Lincolnshire. The rebellion was all over in two weeks.'

John whistled in disgust. Katharine could not look at him. She knew she would read the words *I told you so* in his face.

'You see, Kate, what comes of sending the King petitions!' he said. Lord Redmayne looked at her curiously, but said nothing. They gave him some wine and then he was on his way.

'Listen to me in future,' John said, more tenderly, as they came in from the porch.

She nodded. 'You were right.' She wanted things to be well between them again.

Will had marched north under Suffolk's command and sent a letter telling Katharine what had transpired. *We trounced them*, he wrote. *They were ill-prepared. I've been in Louth and Horncastle, overseeing the hangings. There has been a great harvesting of misguided souls. I think people will think twice about rebelling against the King in future.*

Three days later, they were woken at night by Walter Rawlinson, John's steward. 'I beg pardon, my lord, but the Abbot of Jervaulx is here, insisting he see you.'

'What the devil does he want?' John grunted as he got up and pulled on his night robe.

'He says it is urgent, my lord.'

When the men had gone downstairs, Katharine leapt out of bed and threw on her own robe. She had to know what was going on. She raced after John and found him with a tall monk, cloaked and hooded, in the hall.

'My lord, I crave sanctuary here,' the Abbot asked, sounding slightly out of breath. 'There are hundreds of armed men at the gates of Jervaulx Abbey. They came an hour ago, demanding that we rise with them in defence of the old religion and the monasteries. Some of my monks were eager, as they fear closure, although it has not yet come to that. But I am loath to defy the King. I had the gatehouse door barred against them and made my escape through a postern gate by the stables. I have ridden here like the wind. May God forgive me, I have left my brethren behind and it will look as if I have abandoned them, but I had to seek help. Those men mean business. I am afraid they will come after me.'

'Do not fear, Father Abbot,' John said, without hesitation. 'I have a grange not far from here. My steward will escort you there. It is out in the wilds and no one will look to find you in those parts. You must take some food.'

'I will see to it,' Katharine said, hastening to the kitchens, where she packed a basket of cold meats, slices of pigeon pie, apples, bread, cheese and wine. They were doing the right thing. Violence and intimidation never solved anything. In sheltering a man who was fearful of being made to rise against the King, they could only meet with royal approval.

The Abbot took the basket gratefully. 'Bless you, my lady, and you, my lord. I will not forget your kindness. At least, if they come here, you will be prepared.'

They watched as he and Walter mounted their horses and rode away into the night.

'What will we do if they do come?' Katharine asked. It seemed inevitable that they would.

'We too will bar our door to them, lass,' John said grimly. ''Tis one advantage of living in a castle.'

She could not get back to sleep or relax. She lay there, alert for the sounds of hooves or voices. But all remained quiet. The next day, she went about her daily tasks with half an eye on the windows, her ears straining to hear any untoward noises.

At midday, when they had just finished dinner, a young monk was shown in.

'My lord, my lady,' he said in a broad Yorkshire burr, 'I beg pardon for disturbing you, but did our Abbot come your way? We need him to come back to the abbey. The rebels say they'll burn it down if he doesn't, and they look as if they mean it. They are insisting he swear an oath to support their cause. Please help, my lord!'

John hesitated. 'I think I know where he might be.' He rattled off directions and sent the monk on his way.

'Let him persuade his Abbot,' he said. 'God knows, I'm as keen to see the old ways restored as those rebels, but rising against the King is sheer stupidity. Look at what happened in Lincolnshire.'

'I pray they won't come here,' Katharine said fervently.

They heard no more of the Abbot, or of the burning of Jervaulx, so they assumed that he had gone back and sworn the oath.

When three days had passed without incident, John went into Ripon on business and took Katharine with him. In the bustle of the market, she became aware of an undercurrent of chatter. People were talking excitedly or warily, and it was there that she first heard the name of Robert Aske – several times. When she met up with John at the inn where their horses were stabled, she asked if he had heard of the man.

'All too often today,' he said. 'It seems he is raising all Yorkshire for the old faith. But it is to be a peaceful protest. They are calling it the Pilgrimage of Grace.'

'It's a rebellion, whatever they call it,' Katharine said, mounting her palfrey and following John out of the yard.

'Aye, that's how the King will see it.'

'And that rabble at Jervaulx weren't engaged in a peaceful protest. Pilgrimage indeed!'

When they returned to Snape, Walter was waiting for them. 'My lord, there is word from Jervaulx. The Abbot did go back, but those bastards roughed him up and forced him to take the oath.'

'At least he can tell the King he had no choice,' John observed, crossing himself.

'My lord,' Walter continued, 'some gentlemen arrived not long since. They are all wounded and came begging shelter. I didn't turn them away, because one of them says he is known to you, my lady, and that he is a royal tax collector.'

'I do believe it might be Sir William Askew,' Katharine said, recalling her visit to Stallingborough six years ago, when she had had that ghastly nightmare. 'John, you'll remember my telling you that he was a friend of Lord Borough and had a prodigy of a daughter.' She turned back to Walter. 'What has befallen these gentlemen?'

'I think they will tell you, my lady.'

It was indeed Sir William, and three of his clerks. She greeted him warmly and presented him to John, who called for wine. 'You all look as if you need it,' he observed. It was true: their clothes were bloodstained and covered in dust, and they all had bruises or black eyes. One was missing a tooth, while another had a broken nose. Katharine sent Margaret for hot water and towels and called for her two maids to clean the wounds. As they did so, the men talked.

'We were set upon as we went about our duties,' Sir William told them. 'Those ruffians said they weren't paying taxes to uphold the King's religious policies. They beat us, stole the tax money we had on us and ran off. We could have been dead, for all they cared. My lord, I pray you will forgive our coming here, but I remember Lady Latimer with great affection, and I fear I have rather presumed upon that.'

'You are most welcome, Sir William,' John smiled, pouring more wine.

'It is good to see you, even in these circumstances,' Katharine said. 'How is your family?'

A shadow crossed Sir William's face. 'Our eldest girl, Martha, died not long since, God rest her. It was a bitter blow. She was to have been married to a local gentleman, a Master Thomas Kyme. Now Anne, her sister, is to marry him instead.' He frowned. 'She's just turned fifteen.'

'Is she happy to take Martha's place?' Katharine asked, sensing that something was amiss.

There was a pause. 'She understands that this marriage will help me financially, since Martha's dowry was not returnable. But I had to do a lot of persuading.'

She wondered what form that persuasion had taken. 'But she is amenable now?'

'Aye, my lady. I think so.'

'Have you been at court of late, Sir William?' John asked.

'I served as a juror at Queen Anne's trial,' he told them.

'What did you make of the evidence?' Katharine asked, avid for information.

'There's no doubt that she was as guilty as Hell,' he replied. 'The case against her was detailed and thorough.'

Katharine still wondered why a queen who had been so zealous for reform, and who was making such amazing progress in her quest for it, would have conducted her private life in such a reckless way. It did not make sense.

'Queen Jane is a gracious lady,' Sir William was saying. 'Such a contrast to that other. The Lady Mary was saying as much when I visited her in the summer.'

To be in favour with the Lady Mary, and to revere Queen Jane, Sir William must be of the Catholic persuasion, Katharine gathered.

'You've heard of Robert Aske?' he asked, turning to John.

'Aye, more than I'd have liked to.' John's mouth set in a grim line. 'He's a kinsman of mine, although I've never met him, but I'll be making sure to keep my distance now. The man's a fool, and dangerous.'

'The problem is, he's a pious fool, and they're the worst,' John opined. 'He can't see that, while he's motivated by principle, he's opening the floodgates to all kinds of malcontents.'

'You'd do well not to get involved,' Sir William said, as his fellows muttered their agreement. Then he rose. 'We must thank you for your kindness and be on our way.'

'Do stay the night and rest,' Katharine urged.

'Thank you, dear lady, but I want to get back to Lincolnshire before any rebellion blows up here.'

John returned from a visit to a neighbour, Sir William Ingleby, at Ripley Castle looking worried.

'Ingleby may be a stripling, but he's very well informed. He told me that, two days ago, Robert Aske entered York at the head of ten thousand men. After Mass in the Minster, he made them all take this oath he's devised, the Oath of the Honourable Men, as he calls it, and they came flocking to swear it. It binds them to maintain the Catholic Church, to preserve his Majesty and his heirs, to banish evil counsellors, and to restore true religion and the monasteries. Kate, it'll end in civil war. They are to march under a banner of the Five Wounds of Christ.'

He began pacing up and down. 'God knows I don't want to see the old ways overthrown, but this is rebellion, no less, and I am not sure if I should support it.'

Katharine shivered. She could never tell John her personal views on the matter; after all, she owed him fidelity and obedience. Moreover, she loved him and wanted to keep him safe, which meant ensuring that he did not support the rebels in their treasonous enterprise, which might be a blow to the cause of reform.

'Stay out of it, husband,' she urged. 'Look how ruthlessly the rising in Lincolnshire was put down. These men are putting their lives and their livelihoods in jeopardy.'

John looked troubled. 'Yes, Kate, but this matter touches the safety of our souls and our way of life.'

She was vehement. 'You look to the safety of *your* soul, and let those fools go to destruction their own way. I beg you, John, stay out of it. You could lose everything, and then where would I and the children be?'

'I may not have a choice, Kate,' he muttered, downing a goblet of wine in one gulp. 'Ingleby tells me that the "pilgrims", as they call themselves, have surprised a great many gentlemen in their own homes, just like they surprised the Abbot at Jervaulx, and demanded that they join them.'

'If they came here, they'd have me to contend with!' she declared, with more confidence than she felt – and realising that, of the two of them, her inner strength was probably the greater. Her greatest fear was that, if the rebels did come, John would capitulate because he supported their cause. It was a question of whether that was more important to him than her, his children, his title, his property – and even his life. He had once said that the salvation of his soul mattered more than any earthly considerations – yet how strong was that conviction? She hoped he would never be put to the test.

A few days later, when the russet leaves lay like a carpet on the ground and a cold wind blew from the east, the rebels came to Snape. There was no gatehouse, no moat, nothing to stop them. They were a motley band about fifteen strong, mostly farm workers by their dress, with a couple who looked like clerks, but they all bore on their sleeves felt badges embroidered with the Five Wounds of Christ, and all were armed, some with daggers, some with spears and some with pitchforks.

Katharine saw them arrive from the window of her little study, heard the rap of the iron knocker on the oak front door. She saw Walter hastening towards the door and hurried after him into the hall. John was already there. She could tell from his face that he had seen their visitors too.

'It's a rebel band,' he said.

'Shall I open up?' Walter asked, his face grim.

'Call out and ask them what their business is.'

'Say my lord is away,' Katharine urged, her heart thudding. 'Don't let them in. There's no knowing what they will do. They threatened violence to the Abbot, remember!' She was trembling.

'Hush, lass,' John said. 'Just ask them what they want, Walter.'

The door knocker sounded again, more insistent this time.

'Who are you and what do you want?' Walter called.

'We be pilgrims in the Lord's cause, and we want to speak to Lord Latimer.'

'His lordship isn't here!' Katharine shrilled. 'He has gone to London.'

'That ain't what we've been told,' a man shouted.

'Nay! Nay!' the others chimed in. 'Let him show hisself!'

At that moment, Jack and Margaret appeared, white-faced, at the bottom of the stairs.

'What's going on?' Jack asked.

'I'm frightened!' Margaret said, seeking comfort in Katharine's embrace.

'It's the rebels. They want your father to join them,' she explained, putting a finger to her lips and lowering her voice. 'I've told them he is in London.'

Jack looked at her with something like respect.

There was a flurry of blows on the door.

'Open up! Show yourself, Lord Latimer!'

'Go away!' Katharine put all her authority into her voice. She was Lady Latimer and she would not be intimidated by a bunch of yokels!

'We're staying right here until his lordship appears and joins us in our righteous cause. He's of the old religion, like us. He should be supporting us. We need leaders like him.'

'You are all fools!' Katharine cried. 'The King will not stand for your defiance. You cannot hope to win. You will ruin yourselves and the rest of us. Now, stop harassing women and children and go away.'

'We know his lordship's in there,' a man yelled. 'Is he such a coward that he must hide behind a woman's skirts?'

John's hand went to his dagger.

'Don't open the door, Father!' Margaret squealed, prompting a further volley of banging. Katharine put a hand over the child's mouth, but it was too late.

'Now we know you're in there! Open up, my lord, or we'll burn the house down around you!'

'You can escape out of the service wing and use the postern gate, my lord,' Walter said, keeping his voice down.

'And have them burn the castle anyway? No, I must face them,' John said. 'Open the door.'

'No!' Katharine and Margaret cried at once, and some servants who had gathered in the hall to see what all the commotion was about fled back to the service wing. Jack too looked to be on the verge of fleeing.

'Jack, take Margaret upstairs and stay there,' John ordered, and Margaret was dragged away crying.

'It will be all right,' Katharine called after her, then chided herself for misleading the child because, of course, it would not be all right. But she must gather her inner resources and stay strong.

At John's nod, Walter opened the door.

'That was a quick journey back from London!' one of the farm hands jeered.

John straightened and glared at him. 'If your wife had begged you, with sound arguments, not to answer to your people, you would have done the same, my good man.'

'Immortal souls are at stake, my lord!' retorted a man with a mop of black hair who had done most of the shouting and seemed to be the leader. 'What sound arguments can there be against the saving of them? We are rising in a holy cause—'

'Using unholy methods and intimidation!' John barked.

'Some might say the end justifies the means,' one of the clerks chimed in.

'I won't mince words with you, my Lord Latimer,' the black-haired man said. 'You are to come with us. Master Aske needs leaders like you. Other lords have joined us – there's Darcys, Constables, Percys and Nevilles in our forces, most of them kin to you, I believe.'

'No,' John said. 'I will not join you.'

'Seems you don't have a choice,' the leader said, fingering his dagger, then raking his eyes up and down Katharine as she stood behind John in the porch. She froze, petrified of what she feared he had in mind. 'If you resist, we can try a little persuasion. Or you can come quietly and join the cause. It's up to you.'

John must also have seen the man ogling her. 'There is no need for persuasion,' he said. 'I will come. Just give me a space to pack some things. Walter, see that my horse is saddled and my saddlebags filled with provisions.'

Katharine was trying not to weep. She would not have them think her a weak woman. But she was terrified for John, who was being dragged off God knew where in a dangerous venture.

He turned to her. 'If aught should happen to me, remember that I died for my faith. But tell anyone who asks that I did not seek to be involved in this rebellion and was constrained with threats against my will and my better judgement.'

'Get a move on,' the pilgrim leader muttered.

John went upstairs. They even sent a man with him to ensure that he did not give them the slip. Katharine waited in the porch, stony-faced, determined to remain on her dignity. Inside, she was in turmoil, convinced that this would have no happy outcome.

John came down presently, took her hand and kissed her. 'Look after Snape and the children for me,' he said. 'May God bless and keep you.'

'And you too,' she said, clinging to him for one last embrace on parting. 'Come back to me as soon as you can. And please, don't take any risks.' She felt she could count on him not to, for he often waxed vocal on young men who indulged in heroics.

Calling the children downstairs, she stood with them and watched him ride off with the rebels, trying to still her raging sense of foreboding and clenching her fists as she kept control of her emotions. Would she ever see him again? Beside her, Margaret sobbed uncontrollably.

Hours later, after a messenger had delivered a letter from Thornton Bridge, Katharine too was weeping. Kat was dead. William sounded distraught, as well he might, for he had lost his bride of just eighteen months. Her son Walter's betrothed had hanged herself, for reasons no one knew, and all Kat's joy in her new marriage had turned to terrible grief. She had succumbed, all too easily, to a fever.

Katharine could hardly believe it. She knelt in the chapel and prayed as she had not prayed in a long time. The Church might teach that suicides were mortal sinners who would never attain Heaven, but she liked to think that a merciful God would reunite those two tragic women for eternity.

It was awful not knowing where John was or what was happening. After a few days, Katharine ventured into Ripon to see if she could pick up any news. No one could tell her anything.

She wrote to Father Cuthbert, informing him what had happened and asking him to keep an ear open for any word of John. It was a week before she heard back, but there was no news because Father Cuthbert had shut himself up in his castle at Norham in the far north, for fear that the rebels would force him too to join them. *The King has commanded me south*, he wrote, *but I have made the decision to stay here and risk his displeasure. He can have no idea of what the situation is like in Durham and Yorkshire.*

Katharine was going mad with anxiety when – at last! – she received a letter from John. They had taken him to Pontefract Castle, which Robert Aske and Lord Darcy had commandeered as their headquarters. Unlike John, Lord Darcy had apparently had no qualms about rising in rebellion. Under his eagle eye, John and his brothers, who had also been taken by the pilgrims, had been made to swear the Oath of the Honourable Men. *These people will have me lead them in the rebellion*, he had written. *I had no choice, for they said they would kill me if I refused. I have openly stated that I did not seek or start this rising. I want it to be common knowledge that I was constrained to join it.*

He went on to say that the rebel forces gathered at Pontefract now numbered forty thousand men, and that he had been given command of the men of Richmondshire and Durham. *We are about to march on London to petition the King. The leaders here think that his Majesty will dismiss his evil counsellors and abandon his reforms, poor, gullible fools. But I pray God we will succeed in our aims, because to fail would be fatal. May He have mercy on us all!*

Were these men mad or foolish? Katharine wondered. Did they not know this King? Were they really about to take on the man who had defied the Pope and founded his own Church? The man who had sent Sir Thomas More and the saintly Bishop Fisher to the block for refusing to take the Oath of Supremacy? This King surely would not look kindly on anyone who defied him. They must be insane.

A week later, she received a worrying letter from Uncle William. *It is known at court that your husband has gone over to the rebels*, he informed her. *He and the lords with him are spoken of as traitors. The King's Highness is bent on revenge; he says he will not be dictated to by his subjects. He has sent the Duke of Norfolk north with an army. Will is with them. All resistance is to be crushed.*

Katharine's worst nightmare was coming true. She could not stop trembling. There was no doubt in her mind that John would be taken for a traitor and suffer the fate meted out to those who committed treason. She had never seen it happen – she was squeamish about executions – but Will had and, while he had not gone too much into gory detail, he had said enough to enable her to imagine, shuddering, the awful choking sensation of being hanged until you were near dead, the agonising rip of the knife in your belly, the unimaginable pain of having your vitals drawn out of your body and, if you were a man . . . Dear God, that could not happen to John, dear John, who had been a good husband and father and had never wanted to commit treason.

She went about the castle like a wraith, dreading the arrival of a messenger or, worse still, armed men. If the dead could haunt the living, her ghost would walk these rooms one day, wringing its hands, as she was doing now.

Would they arrest her too, thinking her complicit? Walter could vouch for her innocence, surely, but would they believe him? It was all she could do to keep calm for Margaret, who was missing her father and fretting about him. Jack had retreated into his usual resentful moodiness, yet this time she knew it was because he was worried. He was sixteen now, nearly a man. Thank God the rebels had not taken him too.

She burned with hatred for them and resentment against the faith they were defending. Would Christ condone their threatening behaviour, their refusal to understand that His way was not violence? This rebellion was meant to be a peaceful protest, but, so far, it had looked anything but. More and more, she was beginning to see the light. Religion *must* be reformed. Why defend an old order that was rotten to the core? A good start had been made. Why try to turn the clock back?

She sought refuge in prayer and in her Book of Hours. God, she feared, might grow weary of her importuning. How she wished she could read the Bible for herself, in English. Her Latin was good enough for her to understand the services in the chapel, but what of all those poor ignorant folk who had little idea of what the priest was saying? For them, religion was a mystery indeed! And yet these rebels wanted them kept in ignorance. It was beyond belief.

* * *

When another letter from John arrived, Katharine almost sank to her knees in relief. He wanted, above all, to know if she and the children were safe. He was well and had been chosen by the rebels as their spokesman at a parley with the Duke of Norfolk at Doncaster. *I have a passing acquaintance with him*, John had written, *and did think him a martinet with few finer feelings, but he understood that I was acting against my will, for he took me aside afterwards and told me that he would speak up for me to the King. In truth, I had been a poor advocate for the rebels, for I was all too aware that the Duke's army was encamped before Pontefract. Yet he was conciliatory. He promised that the pilgrims' demands would be considered by the King and that, whether he agreed to them or not, we would all receive pardons, for his Majesty knew we were sincere in our concerns and wanted to avoid an effusion of blood. Thus, we agreed a truce and Master Aske said we must all disband and go home. I shall be with you very soon. May God keep you until then.*

The letter left Katharine much disquieted. It was widely at variance with what Uncle William had written. Was it possible that the King had had a change of heart? Or did he know himself to be outnumbered, for all his fine army? She wanted to believe that John would receive a pardon, but something told her that it had been obtained too easily.

On the first day of November, she was sitting at her table by the window, looking over Walter's accounts, when she heard the clop of horse's hooves. Rising, she could see John and his squire riding up to the house. She flew downstairs, shouting for Jack and Margaret, wrenched open the front door and raced to embrace him as he swung himself down from his mount.

'Oh, husband, I am glad to see you!' she cried. Margaret was dancing around her father, waiting for a kiss. Even Jack was grinning. Between them, they pulled John into the hall and sat him down at a trestle table. Katharine took his cloak and cap and called for hot spiced wine. As he sipped it, he recounted the events that had happened since he had been taken by the rebels. At length, Margaret got fed up with talk of oaths and truces and ran off to play. Jack, who had been listening avidly, turned to his father.

'If you have to rejoin the rebels, Sir, I want to go with you.' The light of battle was in his eyes.

'No,' John said firmly. 'I will not have my son jeopardising his future by rebelling against the King.'

'But the pilgrims are not rebelling against the King, only against his evil ministers and the changes they have made. You told us that the King is ready to listen to their pleas. He has promised you pardons.'

John hesitated.

'Which means that there will be no need for the pilgrims to gather again,' Katharine said quickly.

'But, if they do, I want to go with you, Father!' Jack was getting angry; his cheeks were flushed.

'I said no!' John barked. 'That's an end to the matter.'

'I will go. I'll run away! I won't have you treating me like a child,' Jack stormed.

'Then stop behaving like one,' John called after his son as he stomped off.

'He'll get over it,' Katharine sighed. 'He was very worried about you while you were away.' Inwardly, she was relieved that they were alone and could talk unguardedly. She filled their goblets. 'I was surprised that you were offered pardons so quickly,' she ventured.

'If they materialise, which I doubt,' John replied, turning her blood to ice. 'It was impossible for the Duke to give battle or retreat, as he had no cavalry and we had the flower of the north. Norfolk must have been aware that their weakness was exposed. Hence the offer of pardons, to get us to disband. Kate, they are playing for time. This isn't the end of the rebellion. There will be a reckoning. I hope the Duke will speak for me, as he promised, for I would not have the King thinking me guilty of treason. Yet there is no getting away from the fact that I joined the pilgrims, acted as their spokesman and have, effectively, opposed my sovereign.'

It was exactly what Katharine had been thinking. It nagged at her, that Norfolk had glibly promised pardons, probably so that he could fight another day. It gave the King time to raise more forces.

To her amazement, John's pardon, signed and sealed by the King, arrived within a fortnight. The wording, however, was ominous.

'He accuses me of contributing to the ruin of the kingdom and the advancement of our ancient enemies, the Scots, who might have taken advantage of the rebellion to raid over the border,' John read. 'In truth, the King sounds mightily aggrieved. And he warns that he will deal with any further insurrection in person, and will bring an army to repress the malice of his rebels, to their utter confusion.'

'Oh, John, you must be careful!' Katharine cried.

'You think I am not mindful of my own skin?' he replied, and hugged her.

He had not been home three weeks when Robert Aske wrote, urging him to join the pilgrim leaders for a conference in York. They had heard from the King and matters needed to be debated.

'Don't go!' Katharine pleaded. 'Don't get involved again. You were lucky to be pardoned last time. You may not be so lucky in future.'

John's face was grey. 'I have no choice,' he said. 'I was warned that there would be reprisals if I abandoned them.'

'There will be reprisals if you don't!' she flew at him.

'This is not a new rebellion, lass, just a conference. I'd rather hear what the King's thinking is. Know thine enemy!'

Ignoring her protests, he rode off, leaving her racked with foreboding. Every day, she was on her knees for hours, praying for his return or for news of him. When his messenger came, she snatched the letter and tore it open. Her heart almost failed her as she read it.

It seemed that the King deeply regretted having pardoned the pilgrims. He had sent to tell them that he took it marvellously unkindly that they, being his subjects and having long experience of his clemency and his readiness to hear the petitions of all and redress grievances, would attempt a rebellion rather than sue to him. *His Grace calls into question our sanity and marvels at the ingratitude shown him in this insurrection, especially by men of nobility like me,* John had written, as if the King had aimed his displeasure directly at him. *He wonders at his nobles suffering such a villain as Master Aske to be privy to our affairs and says that he and his lords at court consider our honour greatly tarnished by our folly.* Katharine could imagine John's reaction when he heard that. *There is much confusion here as to how to respond. They have called another meeting for next week, in Pontefract. I will stay in York until then.*

'No!' Katharine said out loud. 'Come home!'

'Are you all right, my lady?' asked Bess, Walter's wife, as she entered the hall with a brace of rabbits for supper.

Katharine mentally shook herself. One must never show weakness in front of servants. 'I am perfectly well,' she smiled.

She did not see John again until Yuletide was almost upon them. In the meantime, he had written to tell her that a settlement seemed to be in sight, and that she must not worry. She did, of course.

He arrived back as the servants and the children were putting up evergreens in the hall and the castle smelt of Christmas spices, roast meat and fruit puddings.

'Father!' Margaret cried, running to him and throwing her arms around him.

'John!' Katharine dropped the wreath she was making and hastened into his arms. 'Tell me, is all well?'

He smiled at her. 'The King has agreed to everything!'

'Oh, my goodness . . .' She was at a loss for words. It was the last thing she had expected. 'Tell me.'

They extricated John from Margaret and retreated to the closet he used for estate business, which was well away from the excited chatter in the hall.

'Well?' Katharine asked, desperate to hear his news. 'Oh, forgive me, I should send for some refreshment for you.'

'It can wait.' He placed his hand on hers. 'When we met at Pontefract, Master Aske had us draw up a list of our grievances. All the things you would expect. A return to Rome, the monasteries spared, the Lady Mary declared legitimate, the clergy relieved of heavy taxes, Cromwell and other subverters of the laws of the realm and maintainers of heretics to be dismissed and punished – and we asked that a Parliament be held at York and that the Queen be crowned there. I voiced the opinion that none of these would be pleasing to the King and that he would be angered by them, but Aske sent the articles to the Duke of Norfolk all the same. I was worried that we were dicing with fate, so I wanted to know where we stood morally and legally. I knew that Archbishop Lee was in York. He's a king's man through and through. We had invited him to the meeting, but he did not come. I said we should ask him if there were any circumstances in which subjects might lawfully move against their prince, and Master Aske said *I* should go and put that question to him in church the next morning. So I went.'

'Oh, John,' Katharine breathed, 'you didn't?'

'I wanted an answer,' he said bluntly.

'But you could have been accused of inciting treason!'

'That's water under the bridge now, lass. As it happened, the Archbishop would not speak to me, so I left him a note explaining why I had come. But, when he was in his pulpit, he declared that no true subject could take up arms without the King's permission. Some pilgrims in the church with me started shouting at him, so the clergy made him take refuge in the vestry and locked the door.'

Katharine was horrified. When news of this reached the King . . .

John touched her cheek. 'There's no need to look so worried, lass, not now. This week, the Duke of Norfolk summoned us to Doncaster and said he had been instructed by the King to issue a new free pardon and to inform us that a Parliament *will* be held in York to debate their demands, *and* the Queen's coronation, at Whitsuntide. I went with Master Aske to receive the general pardon from the Duke, and we expressed our gratitude on behalf of all the pilgrims. Then Norfolk told us to go to our homes and bade Master Aske ride south to London, for the King had invited him to spend Christmas at court as his guest.'

Katharine tried to look pleased, but her heart was racing. The King had not acceded to their demands; he had said only that Parliament would consider them. In appearing to grant what they wanted, he had cunningly got them to disperse. In her view, John was far too trusting.

'The danger is passed,' he said, 'and we can get on with our lives. Being among the pilgrims was a very painful and dangerous time for me, but it is over now, I thank God.'

She wished she could believe him. He had brought them close to disaster in challenging the Archbishop. As she left him to order food while he changed out of his riding clothes, she tried to suppress her inner turmoil and braced herself to put on a brave front over Christmas, for the children's sake.

Throughout the festivities, which were very merry because John had said they had cause to make much good cheer, she kept worrying about the future. She could not rid herself of her fears, could not stop imagining John being butchered on a scaffold, or herself and the children being cast out from Snape, grief-stricken and homeless, their future eternally blighted by her husband's treason.

John *must* be made to distance himself from the rebels, or people would begin to think that he had not acted under duress. Maybe Uncle William or Will, who had marched against them, could be persuaded to put in a good word on his behalf with the King. His Grace had no cause at all to doubt their loyalty. Both had heartily embraced the recent reforms and Uncle William had been entrusted with overseeing the closure of monasteries in Northamptonshire. But a personal appeal by John himself would probably be the best course. It was essential to make the King understand that he had not acted of his own volition.

When they were finally abed on Twelfth Night, and John was mellow with wine, she turned to him and found herself crying and her fears spilling out.

He was kind. 'I understand, Kate,' he said, cradling her in his arms. 'You speak sense. I will go to London and make all right with the King.'

He left in January, and Katharine resigned herself to weeks of anxiety as she waited to hear from him.

A fortnight later, she received a letter. He was at Stamford, on his way back to Yorkshire, and would be attending to business in Malton before riding home. He would be with her ere long.

That was fast work, she said to herself, sitting down on the hall settle to digest the rest of the letter.

He had not seen the King. He had got as far as Hertfordshire, where a royal messenger had found him and informed him that he was ordered north to do his Majesty service on the Scottish marches, for it was feared that the Scots would take advantage of the recent disturbances and invade. He was to report to the Lord Warden as soon as possible. *It is good news*, he wrote. *It means his Grace still trusts me. When I lodged in an inn at Stamford, I received a letter from Sir William FitzWilliam. He had made a good report of me to the King, of my being among the pilgrims against my will.*

May God bless Sir William FitzWilliam, Katharine thought, rising to complete her daily tasks. Maybe they had heard the last of this whole sorry business.

Chapter 10

1537

Dinner was finished and the children had disappeared to their chambers. Katharine reached for her book and settled down to enjoy a few snatched moments. The wind was roaring outside and she was grateful to be sitting in the cosy parlour with the fire crackling in the grate.

She had not been there ten minutes when she heard shouts from outside. Jumping up and peering through the window, she caught her breath as she saw that a crowd of about twenty men had gathered outside the castle. By the look of them, they were in an ugly mood.

'Come out, traitor!' they shouted. 'Traitor! Turncoat! Show yourself!' Some were shaking their fists, others brandishing weapons and farming implements.

Trembling in fright, she hastened to the hall, where she saw Jack and Margaret running down the stairs.

'Go back up and stay there!' she said, in the firmest voice she could muster.

'Stepmother,' Jack said, 'in my father's absence, I am the master here. I will deal with them.' For all his bravado, there was a tremor in his voice.

'Your father would never forgive me if I let you,' she said, but he just stood there, as the clamour outside grew louder. The servants were crowding into the hall, some bullish, some clearly terrified, and they were all looking to her for directions. She was so frightened that she could barely speak, but somehow God gave her the courage.

'Open the door,' she instructed Walter. He stared at her.

'Open it, please,' she repeated.

'Aye, do as my lady says,' Jack ordered.

The bolts squealed as they were wrenched back, and Katharine found herself confronting the angry, baying mob. She realised with a shock that she knew some of them; she had passed the time of day with them in the market or been served by them in neighbouring houses.

'Why are you harassing women and children?' she cried above the hubbub.

'It's not you we want, lady,' growled a big man with a shock of red hair. 'It's Lord Latimer, the traitor!'

'He is not here,' she said. 'And why do you call him traitor?'

'We be pilgrims. He has betrayed us.'

'Aye,' another man yelled. 'We know he's been to London wi' his tail atween his legs to curry favour with the King.'

'Lord Latimer had legitimate business in London,' Katharine cried. 'The King has granted what you asked for. How can my lord have betrayed you?'

They all began talking at once, in aggrieved tones. Someone had told them that John was desperate to regain the King's favour.

'Please go away,' she urged them. 'He is not here. I do not know where he is. When he returns, I will tell him of your concerns, and I am sure that he will put your minds at rest.'

'Yes, go!' Jack echoed. 'You have no business coming here and scaring everyone.'

'We were told that his lordship was here,' barked Red Hair.

'Well, he isn't, I promise you,' Katharine declared, praying that they would leave. 'If you must, you may come in to satisfy yourselves of that.'

She had not thought that they would be so bold, but no sooner had she spoken than they surged into the castle, almost knocking her down and ignoring Jack's outraged protests.

'Shut up, boy,' one said. 'You should be hanging your head in shame at what your father has done.'

'It's you who should be ashamed,' Jack retorted, but was silenced with a blow to the mouth. Blood dripped from his cut lip. Katharine hastened to him, but he waved her away. Around them, the rebels were toppling over benches and stools, ransacking chests and racing through to other parts of the castle. They weren't just looking for John; they seemed to be intent on vengeance and destruction. She could hear loud crashes from the direction of the kitchens. Merciful God, where would they stop?

Margaret must be terrified. Shaking in rage and terror, Katharine flew upstairs and found her stepdaughter cowering, whimpering, under a table, with the cloth pulled well down to conceal her. Her eyes widened in fright as Katharine lifted it up.

'Stay there!' Katharine said. 'I will not let them harm you. They seek only your father. Thank God he is not here.'

She left Margaret's room, closed the door and watched stonily as the intruders poured into the bedchambers, making short and noisy work of their search and emerging with armfuls of stuff – good hangings they had ripped from the walls, a silver reliquary and various treasures that the Latimers had cherished for generations. She thanked Heaven that her jewels were in a secret compartment in her marriage chest. They would never guess that it had a false bottom.

She held her breath when they thrust themselves into Margaret's chamber. She could hear them banging about and prayed that the child would not make a noise. She sagged with relief when they came out, but her anger flared when she saw that one of them had Margaret's doll in his hand. It was a fine doll, bought in York.

'You wouldn't steal from a child?' she challenged. 'How would you feel if someone took your child's toy?'

The man, an oafish fellow built like a barrel, looked at her mutinously, as if weighing the cost of opposing her. She knew she wasn't in any position to bargain with him.

'Please,' she said, softening her voice. 'My stepdaughter is distressed enough.' She held out her hand for the doll. To her great surprise, the man gave it to her.

'I'm not a monster,' he said. 'Pilgrims be honest men.'

She was about to say that honest men did not ransack and loot houses, but thought better of it. Instead, she laid the doll on the bed and followed the men down to the hall, thanking God that Margaret had not been discovered.

She seethed when she saw that one of the rebels was grasping a gold salt cellar. It was one of John's prized possessions because King Henry VII had given it to his father in reward for loyal service. Broken furniture was lying around the hall and the armorial glass in one of the windows had been smashed. Such wanton vandalism shocked her.

'So, are you satisfied that my lord is not here?' she asked Red Hair, in the most scathing voice she could command. 'Did your men have to do so much damage while looking for him?'

He glared at her. 'Traitors get what they deserve.'

'My father is no traitor!' Jack hissed. Katharine silenced him with a look.

'Now, will you please leave,' she said to the rebels.

'Not until we are sure of Lord Latimer,' Red Hair told her. 'Our orders are to wait here for him. He has been sent for and warned, in no uncertain terms, that we will destroy this castle if he does not return directly.'

Katharine was so appalled that she could barely speak. 'You will do no such thing! I will not have a gaggle of thieves living under my roof. Just leave, now.'

'You don't have a choice in the matter, lady,' said a skeletally thin, dour-looking man who seemed to be Red Hair's second in command. 'We mean to hold you and his lordship's children hostage until he shows himself loyal to us again.'

Outrage and fear welled up in her. Her heart was racing and she felt faint. 'This is all so unnecessary! The King has granted your requests. What more do you want?'

'Lady, do you really think this King will keep his word? Strikes me we've been fobbed off with empty promises. Everywhere you go, there is unrest. The people are worried, and they are angry. We're in need of our leaders, and Lord Latimer should remember the oath he took.'

'We pilgrims don't hurt women and children,' Red Hair said. 'Ours is a holy cause and we are devout men. We will trouble you as least we can. You are free to go about your daily business, so long as you stay in the castle.'

Katharine was seething. How dare they tell her what she could and couldn't do in her own house!

'So long as you haven't destroyed it!' she retorted. 'So much for not hurting women and children!'

'That would be down to Lord Latimer,' the Skeleton said. 'If he cares for you—'

'We'll sleep in our cloaks in here, on the rushes,' Red Hair interrupted, 'as I don't expect my lady will be offering us the best bedchambers. Matthew, did you check the supplies?'

'Aye, Master,' said a puny youth with crooked teeth. 'There's plenty for all.'

'Those supplies have to last all winter,' Katharine protested.

'Well, lady, you'll just have to tighten your belts like poor folks do,' sneered the Skeleton.

She realised they had bested her. There was nothing she could do.

'Come, Jack,' she said, and retreated upstairs.

'Listen well,' she muttered, pulling him into her bedchamber. 'I know you're angry, but don't provoke them. Think of me and Margaret. I'm not sure that we can count on these rebels to act devoutly all the time. So far, they've not acted devoutly at all. Being women, your sister and I are especially vulnerable.' She shuddered, envisaging what they might do to her. 'Promise me you will hold your tongue and stay out of sight as much as possible. I will be keeping to my room and making sure that Margaret does too, with the door bolted.'

Jack frowned. 'I was going to slip away and fetch Father.'

'No! It would only make things worse for us. Now promise me, please!'

'All right.' He shrugged resentfully and slunk away.

She had resolved to stay in her bedchamber, but she was restless there. Dusk was falling and it would soon be time for supper. She really ought to go and give instructions to the kitchen servants, who would be wondering what they should be doing. After all, why should she not order her own house?

She opened the door quietly and crept to the top of the stairs. From there, she could see that the men had put the battered benches and stools back in their places and piled up the broken bits of furniture in a corner. They were sitting around, huddled in groups, cloaked against the cold, for a chill wind was blowing through the broken window.

'For God's sake, stuff that with cloth,' Red Hair snarled at them. He was seated at a trestle table with the Skeleton and two other men, and one of his cronies was writing what looked like a letter – with *her* quill pen and *her* ink, if you please! 'And fetch young Matthew. He can take this to Lord Latimer.'

'What have you said to him?' the Skeleton enquired.

'I've bidden him come home without delay, and said we are holding his lady and his children as sureties, in case he decides to hare off to London again. I've reminded him where his duty should lie. Matthew can explain more, can't you, lad? Put the fear of God into him!'

They all laughed, for it was impossible to imagine the undersized boy taking on anyone. The laughter died on their faces as they saw Katharine descending the stairs. She walked past them in silence, burning with fury, and on to the kitchens. She was further enraged to see the destruction the rebels had wrought in every chamber. It would take days to set the castle to rights. She could have wept, but she would not let them think her weak.

Five days passed, six, seven, with no sign of John. They had settled into an uneasy routine, with Katharine avoiding the trespassers as much as possible and ensuring that they received only meagre rations. She was no longer frightened of them – if they were going to force their attentions on her and Margaret, they would surely have done so by now – but she fiercely resented their presence and just wanted them gone. The hall stank like a byre. These were men who rarely washed and thought nothing of pissing in the fireplace or a corner. Walter kept offering to see them off, but there were too many of them, so she warned him not to confront them. He wasn't pleased, but she made him understand that it was not worth the risk.

The rebels were growing restive, angrier by the day as John failed to appear. From her vantage point on the landing, Katharine listened to them talking, staying in the shadows and stealing silently away if she heard one of them stir in the direction of the stairs.

'Perchance Matthew missed him on the road,' one man suggested.

'He could have taken another way.'

'Everyone coming up here uses the Great North Road.' That was the Skeleton.

'What if his lordship fell ill and is holed up in some hostelry?'

'Then Matthew would surely have got word to us,' snapped Red Hair. 'I'm giving him till tomorrow.'

Katharine drew in her breath. Where was John?

That day, a letter arrived for her.

'Is it from Lord Latimer?' Red Hair barked, grabbing it from the messenger as she went to take it.

'Yes,' she said tersely, recognising the writing and the seal.

He handed it to her. 'You'd better open it then and tell us what he says.'

Recoiling from the sour odour of him, she took the letter, broke the seal and read it.

'My lord is at Malton, where he had planned to be,' she said. 'He says that all is well and that he will finish his business and be home soon.'

'No word of Matthew?'

'No. You can read it for yourself.'

Red Hair shook his head. 'I can't read. Sounds as if Matthew missed him, the numbskull.'

'Excuse me,' Katharine said, and went upstairs. She had made it her policy to say as little as possible to the rebels. But what she heard next stopped her in her tracks.

'Cold bitch, ain't she?'

'Needs a good seeing-to.'

'Nah, not worth it. These high-born ladies are no good in bed. Don't feel pleasure like normal women. Give me a whore any day!'

There was a crude burst of laughter.

Katharine felt her cheeks flame with indignation. How dare they insult her thus? How ignorant they were. For men like these, the marriage act was clearly no better than a rut in the hay.

She was about to disappear into her chamber, not wanting to hear more, when she heard Red Hair's voice; his tone was not jocular.

'You forget what we are here for!' He banged his fist on the table. 'I'm sending to Lord Latimer at Malton, to say that he must return at once and look to his loyalties and his obligations, or we will put his wife and children to death.'

Katharine gasped, frozen with terror. It was a bluff, surely. They would never go so far . . .

There was a sudden silence in the hall.

'He'll know it's no empty threat,' Red Hair said, his voice like steel. 'He will come.'

What should she do? She was shaking with fright. She must get word to John, and fast. She cast her mind about frantically, wondering which of the servants was up to the task. Then it came to her. Jack could go. He had been moping in his room all week, not venturing out, and sulking because he felt he was being treated like a child. He would not be missed, surely. She would have food sent up for him, just as usual.

She tapped quietly at his door. He was sitting by the fire, whittling arrows. He looked up at her resentfully, but his expression changed when she told him what she wanted him to do. 'You must impress upon your father that he must come home. These men will stop at nothing.'

'I'll go,' he said, jumping up.

'I knew you would, but we have to think of a way to smuggle you out,' she whispered.

'Easy. Look.' He led her to the window, which overlooked the kitchen gardens and the stables, and pointed to a small door in the brick wall. 'Those fools haven't bothered to check that there's a postern gate. No one's guarding it. I can go through there. I'll ask one of the grooms to exercise my horse and tell him to meet me a mile up the road.'

It did seem easy. Too easy.

'We'll have to get you to the kitchens without them noticing anything unusual.' To do that, they must descend the stairs and cross the hall, in full view of Red Hair and his men.

'You go to your room,' he said. 'I'll wait a while and go down. I don't need to explain myself to that rabble. If they ask, I'll say I'm going to get a book.'

'Very well.' She was still shaking. 'And Jack – Godspeed!'

She waited with her door ajar, tense in case she heard an altercation. She was willing Jack to get away safely. He *must* get away – for all their sakes.

There was no audible confrontation. After two hours, she began to relax and believe that he had succeeded. He was a good horseman, a gentleman trained to make better speed than a labourer on a farm horse. How far was it from here to Malton? Forty miles? Three days' ride at most, there and back?

The rebels apparently never noticed that Jack had gone. Katharine went about her daily business, tense and alert for any activity outside. Pray God John would hasten home soon.

Two days passed. Then, on the third morning, there came the sound of approaching riders. Katharine flew to the window of her bedchamber and saw John reining in his horse below, with Jack and his squire in his wake. He looked bedraggled and exhausted. She ran downstairs and would have pulled the front door open, but Red Hair and the Skeleton were barring her way.

'We have unfinished business with his lordship,' they told her. 'That has to be settled before anything else.' They opened the door.

John strode in, his face flushed with fury. 'What is the meaning of this?' he demanded of them. 'Why are you here, occupying my castle? Why has my son had to come and fetch me as a matter of urgency?'

Katharine had never seen him so magnificent, so much the aristocrat. Even the rebels were looking at him, awestruck.

'Well?' he barked.

Red Hair was the first to speak. 'We was told that your lordship had turned from us and gone to London to seek favour with the King. We was angry that you had abandoned us, when you'd taken your sworn oath.'

'So you decided to come here and terrorise my wife and children! You stupid oafs. I am not obliged to explain myself to inferior persons, but I see that I shall have to. I have business interests in London, which I needed to attend to. I have kept my oath to you and supported you to the best of my ability because I share your concerns and your love for true religion. The King has promised to redress your grievances. My friends at court think he will keep his word. But he will not be pleased to hear that, having been commanded to help guard the border marches against the Scots, I have had to come back here, out of my way, to deal with your threats, which will do our cause no good. So, what quarrel do you have with me? What reason to camp in here' – he wrinkled his nose – 'eat up my victuals and intimidate my family? Is this the way to treat a fellow pilgrim? Is this the way pilgrims are supposed to behave?'

Katharine could see from the rebels' faces that they were wavering, wondering if they had made a grave miscalculation.

'It seems we have been misinformed,' Red Hair said at length.

'Very much so!' John retorted. 'Now, will you kindly leave my house?'

Katharine held her breath as the men looked at each other.

'Come, lads,' Red Hair said, and walked across the threshold without another word. The rest followed, looking sheepish. Katharine shut the door behind them and exhaled in relief. John folded her in his arms.

'My God, Katharine, I did not know what I would find here. Snape burned to the ground, you and Margaret . . .' His voice broke.

'It's thanks to the courage of Jack here that you were able to get back so quickly,' she said, rejoicing to have John back and utterly glad to have those men out of the house.

Jack had leapt onto one of the benches in the hall to peer out of the window. 'They've gone.'

After Margaret had come dancing downstairs to greet her father, her former gaiety restored, Katharine led John through the battered chambers. He was appalled to see the damage that had been wrought. 'Those bastards! The devils! Don't worry, Kate, we'll have the masons and carpenters in, and all will be set right.'

He summoned the servants and ordered them to clean and freshen the hall. 'My lady and I will take dinner in the parlour,' he said.

It was so good to be sitting at table with John again, with the children between them.

'You made good time,' Katharine marvelled.

'I hastened back as fast as I could. We spent the night in the ruins of an old manor where I used to get up to mischief as a child. It was freezing and I was worried sick for you. Jack told me what they had threatened. I never saw their messenger, or I'd have made haste to come sooner.'

'Is it true that people at court think the King will grant the rebels' demands?' Katharine asked.

John gave her a rueful smile. 'No, it isn't. And, of course, those fools do not know that I never reached London. After I received my commission, I wrote to Sir William FitzWilliam, telling him that I was ready to do the King's bidding. I asked him if he thought his Grace was angry with me. I said that, if it were his pleasure that I live in the south, I would leave the north. I told him I have but small power here, and that no house is strong enough to withstand the rebels.'

As Katharine's heart leapt at the prospect of moving permanently to London, he regarded her with concern.

'You must have been petrified,' he said.

'*I* was very brave,' Margaret piped up.

'Of course you were, sweetheart. And Jack was heroic. You must be very saddle-sore, my boy.'

Jack flushed. 'I'm all right.'

'I admit, I was scared,' Katharine said, aware that John would be horrified if she told him that she would always be wary of Papists now, and that her reformist leanings had been strengthened over the past few days.

'I would that I was not going to the border,' John said. 'I'd far rather be off to London. I still need to know where I stand with the King. I wish I could see him and assure him that I did not willingly commit treason.'

'Don't worry!' Katharine admonished. 'Your actions today are proof enough of your loyalty.'

'Aye, maybe you're right, lass.'

John left for the northern marches before sunrise the next morning, cloaked and muffled against the freezing weather.

'Stay safe for me!' Katharine urged as she stood in the darkness to see him off. She was praying that he would not meet with other bands of rebels.

He steadied his horse. 'Well, lass, this is farewell for now. God keep you.'

'And you!' she said fervently.

Before very long, she received a visit from Lord Redmayne.

'Bigod's risen against the King,' he said, as soon as he had seated himself by the fire and been served wine.

'Sir Francis?'

'Aye, the very same.'

'But he was against the Pilgrimage of Grace.'

'Not any more, my lady. I have it on good authority that he dared to say publicly that no one should be supporting the Royal Supremacy, and that the King would renege on his promises. He's come out in support of the rebels and is raising his tenantry in arms.'

'Will this never end?' Katharine cried, and told her guest about the rebels occupying the castle.

'They should have been hanged,' he declared, 'or horsewhipped at the very least.'

'I can't believe this of Sir Francis Bigod,' she said. 'His son is betrothed to my stepdaughter. He seemed such an upright man.'

'I think you can forget about the betrothal now,' Lord Redmayne said grimly.

He stayed to dinner, then went on his way to Middleham to warn his friend, the royal constable, of the rising. And Katharine found herself fretting once more.

* * *

Bad news travelled fast. In late February, wayfarers stopping at the castle to beg refreshment brought tidings that the Duke of Norfolk had marched north again at the head of a great army, her uncle and Will were of the company, she later learned. This time, there was no nonsense about being conciliatory. Martial law was declared, and a curfew imposed. Mercilessly and efficiently, Bigod's rebels and anyone else whose loyalty to the Crown was suspect were rounded up and hanged. Robert Aske was taken, and Lord Darcy, even though, word had it, they had denounced Bigod. Like trusting children, they had remained confident that the King would keep his promises. But March came and went, and there was no Parliament in York and no crowning of the Queen. Instead, the King seemed bent on punishing all who had opposed him.

All that spring, the slaughter went on. Rotting bodies hung from trees and gibbets throughout Yorkshire. Katharine stopped taking Margaret to Ripon for fear of what they might see. Daily, she thanked God that John was far away on the border, but she had nasty moments when Anne wrote from the court to say that his brother Marmaduke had been imprisoned in the Tower for having joined the pilgrims, and when Uncle William informed her that the Privy Council suspected Walter Rawlinson of having been involved in the rebellion. Fortunately, John's other brothers had escaped arrest, but he would be worried if he learned about Marmaduke. As for Walter . . .

'That's nonsense!' she said aloud, and dashed off a reply to her uncle, declaring that she knew for a fact that Walter was innocent; she would vouch for him with her life.

In May, John came home. Norfolk, who was moving through the north to execute his terrible vengeance, had summoned him to Durham.

'What for?' Katharine faltered. Was it to assist in the suppression of the rebels, or was he too to be punished?

'I don't know,' he said, his face set in grim lines. 'But I must go. I had to come here first to warn you.' She was both touched by that – he had made a long detour – and fearful because he clearly thought the summons was ominous.

She wanted to beg him to stay, to flee to Scotland or Ireland, to go overseas – anything to keep him safe – but that would be to admit guilt.

'I don't like this,' she said. 'Let me come with you.'

'This is not women's business, Kate.'

'Anything that touches my husband is my business.' She did not need to say that, if he was adjudged a traitor, his estates would be forfeit and she and the children would be penniless. The words lay unsaid between them.

'Very well,' he said. 'I shall be glad of your company.' He hadn't argued the point, and she suspected that he really wanted her with him.

'Walter and his wife will take charge of the children for us,' she said, wishing that Kat was still here, for she would readily have taken them.

Durham was spectacular, with its massive castle and cathedral towering above it on high cliffs. This was where Father Cuthbert held sway as prince-bishop. Katharine would have given much to see him, but he was away in Sheriff Hutton, attending the Council of the North.

As they entered the city, they were assailed by the sight and smell of decaying corpses swinging from gibbets, left there as warning to any who might contemplate rising against their sovereign. Holding her handkerchief to her nose and keeping her eyes fixed on the cobbles, Katharine allowed John to guide her palfrey along the streets, keeping as far as possible from the bodies.

They found an inn with a vacant room, left their horses to be stabled and ordered some food, but neither of them had much appetite. Katharine was praying that, after they had seen the Duke of Norfolk, they would soon be back here enjoying a celebratory drink, and that all their fears would have been for nothing.

In the afternoon, they went, as directed, to the castle to see the Duke, and were shown into a massive hall. A table had been set up at one end, at which three men were seated. Two were wearing the black garb of clerks; the man in the middle was Norfolk. His furred gown, satin doublet and fine leather boots bespoke nobility.

John bowed and Katharine curtseyed. The Duke raised his eyebrows at the sight of her. He had a flat, dour face with a prominent nose, thin lips and world-weary, heavy-lidded eyes.

'My Lord Latimer,' he said, his voice gruff. 'And your good lady, I believe.'

'Your Grace, I brought my wife to see you, as she can tell you what we have suffered because of the rebels.'

The Duke indicated two chairs. 'Pray be seated. Well, my lady?'

'Your Grace,' Katharine said, determined to show herself a brave, loyal subject, 'when my lord was away on the King's business, a band of rebels came to our castle and occupied it.' She related the whole appalling tale, stressing that John had been forced to join the rising in the first place, and how terrified she had been when the pilgrims had threatened to kill her and the children if he abandoned them.

Norfolk listened, his impassive face giving little away. 'And they left without protest when you demanded it?' he asked John.

'Yes, your Grace. But they've since been putting tales about that my steward, Walter Rawlinson, joined them of his own accord, which is a lie. I've known him and his family all my life and there is not a treacherous soul among them.'

Norfolk nodded.

'Walter was very angry when they forced their way in,' Katharine said.

The Duke shifted some papers on the table and picked up a letter.

'I heed what you both say, but I've been hearing things about you, Latimer. His Majesty and Master Cromwell want me to establish whether you were a prisoner of the rebels last year, or if you joined them willingly.'

'He was forced! I saw it,' Katharine leapt in. John laid his hand on her arm.

'My wife speaks truth,' he told the Duke. 'I had no intention of joining them. My first loyalty is to the King, whose favour means much to me.'

'And yet,' Norfolk said, steepling his fingers in front of his face, 'you cling to the old ways in religion.'

John hesitated. 'I have sworn the Oath of Supremacy.'

The Duke leaned forward. 'Listen, man, you and I are of one accord in these matters. I like the old ways too. In my view, there are those who want to push things too far, like our friend Master Cromwell. Don't think I don't sympathise with those wretches I've had to punish. But ours is not to question what the King decrees. We must be obedient subjects. I don't hold with all this book-learning that leads people to challenge Holy Writ, but that's another matter. The question is, what is to be done about you?'

'All I ask is to establish my unwavering loyalty to his Majesty and his laws,' John declared.

'Very well. Know, then, that the King has instructed me to ask you to condemn that villain Aske and submit to his Grace's clemency.'

'Condemn?' John echoed. 'Surely he is judged by now?'

'A public condemnation by you will go a long way towards settling the King's mind.'

Do it, Katharine was praying. *Do it. Aske knows you were constrained, and nothing can help him now.*

John did not pause. 'I will do it. I do condemn him. He rose unlawfully against the King and incited his Majesty's subjects to rebel against him.'

'Write that down,' Norfolk instructed a clerk. When the man had finished, John signed the document.

'Now, my lord,' the Duke said. 'You shall go to London to explain yourself to the King. I have little doubt that he will receive you back into favour, for I shall write to Master Cromwell and tell him that I cannot discover any evidence against you other than that you were forced and that no man could have been in more danger of losing his life.' His long face broke at last into a smile.

'Thank you, your Grace!' John exclaimed, rising and bowing low.

'Thank you,' Katharine echoed, and swept a deep curtsey.

The moment they were outside in the open air, she linked her arm in John's and squeezed it. 'He's not such a martinet as he looks,' she said. 'There's a good heart in there somewhere. He believed you.'

'More to the point, he believed *you*. But we're not out of the woods yet, lass. I've yet to see the King.'

'I don't think you'll have any problem with the King,' she told him. 'Don't forget, we have friends at court who will help us. The priority now is to get to London as soon as possible.'

'We could go directly south from here,' John said. 'We have changes of raiment in the York house; we can take those. I'll send a groom to Snape to tell them what we're doing.'

'I'm sure they'll manage without us for a while,' Katharine said, eager to be away to London.

On the way south, she thought about what she could do to ease John's path to the King's forgiveness. Norfolk's report would hopefully predispose his Majesty to mercy. Will was still in the north, but Uncle William was back at court and in high favour, and he would surely be in a position to speak for John. Sir William FitzWilliam might also be willing to intervene.

When they approached the barbican at Bootham Bar, the northern gateway to York, a sentry held up his hand.

'Your business here, my Lord Latimer?' There was hostility in his tone. He was probably a supporter of the pilgrims and, naturally, would see John as a rebel.

Katharine could sense her husband bristling. 'I am for London, on my lord of Norfolk's business. We are lodging here tonight, in my own house.'

The sentry grunted and waved them through. Katharine was sickened to see that, here too, there were bodies hanging from trees.

'Oh, my God,' John muttered as they turned their horses into Stonegate. 'It's Jonas the bookseller. And that's the sexton from Holy Trinity. Good men, both of them. Such a waste of life.'

It was the same in other places on the Great North Road. There was no escaping the gruesome sights. Katharine was relieved when they were past Lincolnshire and travelling through shires untouched by the rising.

At Peterborough, they stopped a while, so that she could visit the abbey and the tomb of old Queen Katherine, who had died last year. Mother would have wanted Katharine to pay her respects. As she knelt by the sepulchre, she reflected sadly on how the Queen had died alone, exiled from the court, far from the husband and daughter she adored. It pained her to read the epitaph, which described her as the Princess Dowager. Even in death, they would not call her queen.

Leaving the abbey to join John, who was waiting on the green outside, she overheard some monks talking about Queen Jane being with child. It was a ray of sunlight in a world overcast by strife and tragedy. Katharine offered up a silent prayer that the child would be a prince. Perhaps the King, in his joy, would be a kinder father to his subjects.

When they neared London, she began to feel some trepidation. What if John was walking into a trap, or was under surveillance? She had heard it bruited that Cromwell had an army of spies. She resolved to be vigilant, just in case. She held her breath when they entered the City of London by the Barbican, but they were not challenged.

No one responded to John's request for an audience with the King. He kept going to the court and haunted its galleries with crowds of other petitioners, hoping that his Majesty would notice him while walking past in procession, but he waited in vain. Uncle William was away on his estates and John could not find Sir William FitzWilliam anywhere. He fretted that he had become invisible and grew daily more disheartened. Most people he spoke to urged him to go home, or abroad, for safety's sake.

They had been at Charterhouse Square for an anxious month when he began seriously to consider this. Then, to his and Katharine's surprise, Will was announced. It was so good to see him again.

'But I thought you were in the north?' Katharine cried, hugging him.

'I got back two days ago, sister,' he said, as they plied him with drinks and sweetmeats. 'I'll have to go back at some stage to sit on the commissions trying the rebels. But I'm relishing this furlough.'

'You will stay to dinner?' she urged.

'Nothing could give me greater pleasure. To be honest, I had thought to find you gone.'

Katharine shivered. 'We were thinking of leaving. You must have heard that John is under suspicion of treason.'

Will's smile faded. 'There was talk of it up north among the rebels we arrested.'

'They think him a traitor to them,' Katharine explained.

'They told me that the King was displeased with him. He too may think him a traitor. That's why I hastened back after witnessing the executions of Master Aske and Sir Robert Constable. Master Cromwell has commended me for that, so I am in good credit with him and can probably help you. I stopped at Rye House on my way south to alert Uncle William, who is on his way to London now.' He reached out and took Kate's hand, his eyes full of sympathy. 'Believe me, sister, he and I have several times made suit to the King for John, and others have spoken up for him too. I will try to see Master Cromwell tomorrow. Sir William FitzWilliam should be at court later this week. He will assuredly help.'

This all sounded very encouraging.

'His Grace of Norfolk said he would inform his Majesty that John had committed no crime,' Katharine said.

'And I am hoping to see the King soon, so that I can explain what happened,' John added.

'Then you have nothing to worry about, I am sure,' Will smiled.

Katharine could see John visibly relaxing and resolved to set her fears aside and enjoy the dinner.

Over their meat, they spoke of family matters. Katharine thought it odder than ever that Will did not mention his wife. As far as she knew, they had still not begun living together. It was now ten years since their wedding, and Ann Bourchier must be twenty, more than old enough to be bedded.

'How is Ann?' she asked tentatively.

'Well, I suppose. I haven't seen her for ages,' Will said. He did not sound particularly interested.

'You never speak of her,' she said gently, patting his arm. 'She is your wife.'

'Tell her that,' he retorted, his voice bitter. 'She bursts into tears every time someone says we should start living together. Her father keeps insisting, but she knows how to wheedle her way around him.

I've said that I'll give her until next year, when I'm done in the north. If she still makes a fuss, I will be applying for an annulment. A man needs an heir. I'm twenty-four and don't want to waste time.'

'I'm sorry to hear this,' Katharine said. 'What's wrong with her? Have you tried wooing her with kindness?'

'I have! Flowers and gifts and sweet words . . . I've tried them all. I'm beginning to think that she just doesn't like men or the duties of marriage.'

'Go and see her again, Will. Talk to her. Be patient and ask her why she is reluctant. Say you want to help her. Go gently.'

He smiled ruefully. 'All right, Kate. I'll do as you suggest.'

'My wife is not to be gainsaid,' John grinned. They all laughed.

As they talked, it became plain that Will knew how to negotiate the quagmire of intrigue that was the court. He seemed to have many friends there, which was understandable given his easy charm and amiability. The cut and quality of his clothing and his appreciation of fine food and wine proclaimed him a man of taste. He was cultivated too, numbering among his friends Sir Thomas Wyatt and Norfolk's son, the Earl of Surrey, both notable poets.

'You should invite them to supper,' he said. 'I can assure you of good company. There is never a dull moment with Surrey, and Wyatt is more his amusing self now, after getting over the events of last year.'

'Last year?' Katharine and John looked at each other blankly.

'The fall of the Queen. He loved her, you know. He and the King were rivals for her in the early days. He never got over her. He was a mess when it happened. They put him in the Tower too, but here's a strange thing. Cromwell immediately wrote to tell his father that he would be set free – and he was. So was Sir Richard Page. Yet the other men were executed. It seems to me that their arrest and release was a sham intended to convince people that the others were really guilty.'

Katharine had long wondered about that. 'But they were, surely?'

'Some think that they, and the Queen, were innocent.'

'Surely the King would not knowingly send six guiltless people to their deaths?' John asked incredulously.

'Wyatt has his own theory about that; don't forget, he is friends with

Cromwell. He thinks the King did believe them to be guilty. All I will say is that Master Cromwell is a clever and determined man. Ruthless too.'

Katharine felt a chill run down her spine. That a minister could be so audacious, unscrupulous – and cruel! It brought home to her, like a punch, how dangerous a place the court could be.

'But why?'

Will laid down his knife and took a swig from his goblet. 'The Queen was out to bring Cromwell down, so he pre-empted her and got rid of those who would have supported her too.'

'Queen Jane ought to be shaking in her shoes, if this is what can happen to queens in our time.'

Will frowned. 'I think she was involved in the conspiracy against the Queen. She had the most to gain. And now she is with child, and no one, not even our friend Cromwell, can touch her, especially if she bears the King a son.'

'Hearing all this makes me glad not to be a courtier,' Katharine said. 'Is there anyone of integrity and honesty among them?'

'The higher you go, the less evident those virtues are,' John observed.

John never got to see the King, but he received his pardon, thanks to the combined efforts of the three Williams. Yet it came at a high price.

'I am forgiven, but it seems I am still under suspicion, and I fear I always will be,' he muttered, when he showed Katharine the document signed and sealed by the King.

'Why?' she asked, nonplussed. A pardon was a pardon, wasn't it?

'I was summoned to see Master Cromwell,' he said, stumping through to the parlour. 'I am dismissed from the Council of the North. And I am to pay Cromwell an annual consideration – in reward for his part in securing my pardon, he says. It's extortion, pure and simple, and I will have to sell some property to meet the cost. I'll have to lease out this house for a start. Kate, it looks as if, from now on, I am to live my life always looking over my shoulder. I will be watched, make no bones about it. I will always be looking at my servants and my friends and wondering who has been ordered to spy on me.'

She went to him and hugged him, pressing her cheek against his. 'Count your blessings, John. You still have Snape and other estates. And you are alive and free of the fear of prosecution! That's more important than anything. And, really, it won't be hard to live the upright, normal life you have always lived. Soon, any spy will see that and realise they are watching you in vain, and Master Cromwell might conclude that it just isn't worth the money to have you under surveillance. If he really intends to do that.'

'Oh, I'm sure of it. He's a slippery, blackmailing upstart.'

'Forget about him. Let us get on with our lives.'

It was unjust, unlawful and plain wrong, she raged inwardly, although she kept a smile on her face for John's sake. There were worse things, she reflected later, as she sat in her bedchamber and her maid combed her hair. Only that morning, she had received a pleading letter from Sir Thomas Burgh's wife Elizabeth. She had borne him a son and heir, but the appalling Lord Borough had taken one look at the child's sallow complexion and declared that it could not possibly be of his blood. As soon as Elizabeth had risen from childbed, he ordered her out of his house, raging that she was a whore and an adulteress. In vain had her husband tried to keep her, but his father had been implacable.

Please help me, dear sister, Elizabeth had written. *I am living in a nunnery that is soon to be closed down.*

Katharine decided to send her some money. Before she went to bed, she scribbled words of comfort in a letter, adding, with a mischievous grimace, *I do urge you to appeal to Master Cromwell.* If Elizabeth took her advice, Lord Borough was going to have some explaining to do!

After leasing the Charterhouse Square house to Lord Russell, John and Katharine left London to stay at his brother William's manor of Wyke, near Pershore in Worcestershire, John being reluctant to return to Snape until the last rumblings of rebellion and retribution had died down in the north. But he felt uncomfortable at Wyke, since William was as strange and unpredictable as ever, so they moved to a manor house at Stowe Nine Churches, not far from Northampton, which

John had inherited on the death of one of his Neville great-aunts. Before too long, Walter escorted the children south to join them.

Katharine enjoyed creating a comfortable home at Stowe. She loved the rolling Northamptonshire hills that surrounded the village, the mellow stone cottages and the church with a high square tower that local folk told her had been built before William the Conqueror invaded England. The climate here was kinder than in Yorkshire. But the best thing about Stowe was that less than a day's ride away was Burton Latimer, where John had another manor house. This was in close proximity to Orlingbury Hall, where Katharine's cousin, Magdalen Parr, Lady Lane, lived, and Harrowden, the residence of Elizabeth Cheyney, Lady Vaux. Katharine and Margaret rode over to Burton one fine September day and stayed for a week, during which time they made surprise calls on Magdalen and Elizabeth, and enjoyed very happy reunions and long discussions about religious reform.

It was as well that Katharine had friends in the area, because John was often away on the King's service. Always, he thought he was being tested. He was frequently sent back to do military service on the border, and he also had to meet his obligations as a justice of the peace, serving on many commissions and presiding over quarterly assizes. In between times, he visited Snape, attending to estate business, and made occasional forays to York to check that his house was being kept in good order in his absence.

Katharine soon decided that she preferred living at Stowe; Snape held too many bad memories for her. The rebels' occupation of the castle had affected her more than she had thought possible. In truth, she still feared that they would exact some retribution, for she had twice accompanied John to York when he had been required to mete out justice to those who had hitherto evaded capture, and the mood in the city seemed hostile. She felt much safer in Northamptonshire.

She was there when, in October, she received a letter from her sister, telling her that the Queen had borne a prince, named in honour of St Edward the Confessor. London, Anne wrote, was celebrating with bonfires, processions, free wine and street parties. Everyone was going mad with joy – and she, Anne, was to attend the christening!

John was away, but Katharine rose to the occasion. She had her cooks baking and roasting for a whole day; she bought large quantities of ale from the local innkeeper and summoned her minstrels. Late in the afternoon, she opened her hall to the villagers and bade them sup heartily and toast the Prince with her. When they had eaten their fill, there was dancing, with Walter leading her out to the floor first, and Jack and Margaret following. She had not had so much fun in years.

Her pleasure was crowned when she learned that Will had been knighted. *My lord of Norfolk and Master Cromwell recommended me to his Majesty*, he wrote. *And, thanks to Uncle William's recommendations, the King has appointed me a gentleman of his privy chamber.*

That *was* good news. The gentlemen of the privy chamber spent their days attending the King. They were his closest friends and associates — and they had his ear. No one was better placed to exercise patronage. Will would assuredly become wealthy from the gifts, inducements and bribes given him by hopeful petitioners and clients. It was reprehensible, but it was the way the court functioned. What mattered was how high her family had risen and how well they now stood in the King's favour. If only John could too.

The trees were nearly bare and autumn winds were blowing across the hills when Anne's next letter arrived from Hampton Court. Queen Jane was dead, lost in childbed. Anne and the Queen's other ladies and maids were keeping constant vigil by their late mistress's bier and were to follow her coffin when it went in procession to Windsor for burial. Katharine said a prayer for the Queen's soul, thinking of that poor, motherless infant in his grand nursery at Hampton Court Palace.

Anne sounded very upset. She had served three queens in succession and was now without a post. She wrote that Uncle William had said she was welcome to go to Rye House, but she didn't want that. *I have grown used to life at court*, Katharine read. *I do not want to rusticate in the country. But there will be no places for any ladies at court now that there is no queen.*

Katharine replied at once, inviting Anne to come to Stowe and stay with her while she contemplated her future. Anne accepted with alacrity. It was wonderful to see her again, and to witness her getting on so well with Magdalen and Elizabeth. Those were happy weeks spent visiting, hunting, hawking, debating religion and then preparing for Christmas.

One day, as they sat together at the parlour table, sticking cloves in oranges, Anne confided that the main reason she had been reluctant to leave court was that she had a suitor.

'I knew you weren't telling me everything,' Katharine ribbed her.

'I couldn't keep it to myself any longer,' Anne confessed. 'Uncle William knows about it and is discussing it with the gentleman.' Her voice betrayed her eagerness for the match.

'So, who is he?' Katharine could barely contain herself.

Anne looked torn. 'Promise you'll tell no one. It's William Herbert, an Esquire of the Body to the King. He is the grandson of the old Earl of Pembroke, who fought in the War of the Two Roses.'

'And stands to inherit the title?' Katharine was agog. Her sister, a countess? That would be a feather in the family cap.

Anne hesitated. 'That is his hope. Although his father was the old Earl's bastard, he himself is in high favour at court and can look for great things.'

'Wasn't his grandfather executed for treason?'

'Yes. That's why the earldom fell into abeyance. But the King may revive it.'

Privately, Katharine had reservations. A bastard could not inherit a title. Anne's expectations were built on a hope that might never be fulfilled. But she said nothing. Uncle William evidently approved, and he was a shrewd man.

Katharine didn't want Anne ever to leave. In her sister, she had found a kindred spirit, for Anne was even more avid for religious reform than she and her friends were. John got on well with her and Margaret was so sweet with her that Katharine almost felt jealous. It was one of the merriest Christmases in years.

Chapter 11

Katharine's advice to Will had borne fruit. He made an effort and paid court to Ann as if he were an eager suitor rather than a husband who wanted his rights. Gradually, he won her over and they began living together in the court lodging he had been assigned when he was appointed to the privy chamber. It comprised just two rooms and a privy, yet such apartments were the most sought-after in the royal palaces, those nearest the King's lodgings being especially prized. Ann should be delighted to be at court and living in such prestigious accommodation. All would be well for the young couple, Katharine felt sure.

But, within a month, she had a letter from an exasperated Will. Dismayed, she handed it to Anne. 'Ann does not want to live at court,' she related. 'She says she hates it there and has taken herself off to Blackfriars. What must it look like to the King and his courtiers?'

Anne frowned. 'I've met her twice. She's a country bumpkin and a whiner. I gather that her parents dote on her as their only child and gratify her every whim, but they neglected her education. She doesn't dance, doesn't sing, doesn't play an instrument – no wonder she wants to go back to the country.' She laid the letter on the table. 'To be honest, she is no wife for Will. A man making his way in the world needs a helpmeet, not a millstone around his neck.'

'I'd like to shake her,' Katharine muttered. 'He's a good catch, handsome and willing to please her. She could do a lot worse.'

They wrote a joint letter to Ann, pleading with her to make more of an effort for Will and offering to help in any way they could. There was no reply.

* * *

Anne remained at Stowe until February, when the Parrs journeyed the ninety-odd miles to Herefordshire for her wedding to William Herbert. Ewyas Harold was a remote village set in glorious rolling countryside, but its castle, the Herberts' seat, set on a high mound, was more of a fortress than a noble residence. Nevertheless, Lady Herbert, William's mother, had done her best to make it welcoming for her guests. When they arrived with Anne, Jack and Margaret on the day before the wedding, John and Katharine were conducted to a large chamber with thick stone walls hung with vivid tapestries and furnished with an oak tester bed made up with snowy linen. A warm fire crackled on the hearth, dispelling some of the draughts from the narrow windows. It had been a long journey and Katharine was glad to lie down for a while. John joined her, and soon they were making love. As ever, she wondered why her womb had not quickened during these past four years. It seemed that God did not mean her to be a mother.

As she lay with her head in the crook of his arm, John pulled the counterpane over them both.

'I'm sorry I haven't given you a son,' she whispered.

He kissed the top of her head. 'No matter, lass. No man ever had a better or more plucky wife. Look at how you dealt with those rebels! Besides, I have a son, although he needs teaching a few lessons. God knows how well he will look after Margaret when I'm gone.'

Katharine stiffened. 'You're only forty-five!'

'Aye, lass, but a man can be called to meet his Maker at any time. It's best to be prepared. I'm thinking of buying some monastic land to give Margaret an income when the time comes. There are estates near York for sale, at Hamerton and Nun Monkton. I'll offer for them when we get back to Stowe.'

'It will mean you going to York again.' He was away so often.

'Things are quieter there now. You should come with me.'

She smiled up at him. 'Do you know, I think I will.'

They met William Herbert that evening. A tall, rangy man in his mid-thirties, he filled the room with his large presence. He had close-cropped black hair, which hopefully explained why they had heard a guest referring to him as 'Black Will Herbert'. At supper, Sir Roger, a garrulous local priest, whose healthy appetite and round belly reminded Katharine of Friar Tuck, enlightened them further.

'He's a good fellow, but choleric,' he said. 'In fact, he's a mad fighting fellow and loves nothing more than a punch-up.' He leaned forward confidentially, and Katharine wondered what was coming next. 'You've heard of that business in Bristol?'

Katharine and John looked at each other blankly. 'No.'

The priest leaned in closer. They could smell his bad breath. 'There was an affray between some watchmen and some of Mr Herbert's Welshmen. He killed a mercer and had to fly to France to escape the King's justice. He took service under the French King and gained a fine reputation as a soldier. On the French King's say-so, King Harry welcomed him back with open arms. Black Will's never looked back. He's been in the King's household ever since and has earned many rewards and marks of favour.'

Katharine was horrified. This was the man her beloved sister – her refined, learned and gentle sister – was marrying? He was no better than a thug, for all his noble blood. Yet there was Anne, smiling lovingly at him at the centre of the top table, and there was Uncle William, slapping him on the back as they shared a jest.

She threw a sideways look at John, but he had begun a conversation with the lady on his left. She smiled across the table at the priest and turned to Will, who was seated at her right. 'Did you hear that?' she murmured in his ear.

He smiled. 'All long in the past. I like Herbert. He'll make Anne a good husband.'

'But what of his temper?'

'Quick to flare, quick to subside. I've told her to let it go over her head. Not that she has any reservations. She's mad for him.'

Katharine watched them together. She had to admit that there was something very attractive about Herbert, with his raven hair and lean looks. And he was clearly taken with Anne. You could see it in the way he looked at her.

John, questioned further in bed that night, merely shrugged off

Katharine's concerns that Herbert was not the right man for her sister.

'Go to sleep. He's a sound man and they love each other. Reformed rakes make the best husbands.' Soon, he was snoring.

The next day, before the wedding went ahead, everyone gathered in the castle hall to witness the signing of the marriage contract. Katharine noticed that Herbert used a stamp and was astonished to realise that he couldn't write. How would Anne, literate and well read, stand being married to him? But Anne was smiling, radiant in her pink bridal gown of silver tissue with her hair loose beneath a chaplet of flowers. Well, if she was not concerned – and, at twenty-two, she was old enough to know her own mind – then Katharine should not be either. She ought to be pleased to see her sister so happy.

It was a joyous wedding, and she so enjoyed seeing Will, who had come from York, and Uncle William and Aunt Mary. Magdalen Lane had come, and several northern cousins, as well as a host of Herbert relations. There was great merriment when the remnants of the wedding feast were cleared. The wine flowed freely and everyone got into the spirit of blind man's buff and hide-and-seek. It made Katharine feel like a girl again.

Even if John had not won back the King's favour, he had at least, through hard work and diligent attention to the many duties heaped on him, been able to put some money by, and, early in 1539, he leased the mansion at Charterhouse again. Although he had to visit the north from time to time, his commissions and his attendances in Parliament often brought him to London these days, and Katharine always seized the opportunity of accompanying him. He sat in the House of Lords almost every day that spring and early summer, but, one morning, just as he was about to leave, he flung his cap on the settle and sat down.

'John?' Katharine asked. There was something wrong. She had suspected it for days.

'I'm not going to Parliament today,' he said.

'But aren't you due there?'

'I can hardly represent the views of my countrymen in voting for the passing of the posthumous Bill of Attainder against Lord Darcy,' he said. 'I respected him as a man of principle.'

'Your absence will be noticed,' she felt bound to say.

'Let it be!' He had never spoken to her so tersely before. 'I have played their game for too long. I'll be in my study. If anyone asks for me, I'm ill.' He got up and stumped off.

When there was a knock on the front door a couple of hours later, Katharine froze. It might be Lord Cromwell's men, come for John. But no. The steward showed in a young girl of extraordinary beauty with a bright, determined look on her familiar face. It took a moment for Katharine to recognise her.

'Mistress Anne Askew!' she cried. 'How lovely to see you. And how grown up you are!'

'Lady Latimer, I am so pleased to see you. Forgive my turning up unannounced, but I need help and I thought you could advise me.'

'Of course,' Katharine said, wondering what this could be about. 'Do sit down. What are you doing in London? Is your husband with you?'

'No,' Anne Askew said. 'I've left him.'

'Left him?' Katharine was shocked. No woman left her husband unless she had a very compelling reason. For a start, everything she owned was his, and she would have nothing on which to support herself.

'We did not get on,' her visitor said. It sounded unconvincing, for countless couples did not get on. 'Lady Latimer, I well remember that, when you visited us all those years ago, you talked with me and I realised you had an open, tolerant mind.'

'You were perceptive for so young a person,' Katharine smiled, a little warily, wondering if Anne was going to confess to having run off with a lover.

'I just knew. You were so warm and kind. And I need your kindness now. You see, I have embraced the new religion. I am a Protestant.'

Katharine drew in her breath. Didn't Anne know how dangerous it was to be a Protestant, as the followers of Martin Luther were now calling themselves? In England, it was considered heresy, and was illegal. Those who refused to recant were burned at the stake. This was why she herself had held back from embracing Protestant beliefs, even though she was drawn to them, and why she told herself that all she wanted was to see the Church reformed. With a shiver of horror, she remembered that awful dream she had had in Anne's father's house.

'Dear girl, you should be careful,' she warned. 'For all you know, my servants might have overheard you just now, or I myself might think fit to report you to the authorities. I would never do that, of course, but you must be more circumspect.' A terrible thought struck her. 'What if people assumed that we were having a secret prayer meeting? I too might be in danger.'

'I would not bring any harm to you,' Anne protested. 'But God's Word must be known and His warriors and handmaidens must gird their loins. Some years ago, an old priest in Lincolnshire gave me a copy of William Tyndale's translation of the New Testament in English.'

'That book is banned,' Katharine said, alarmed at what she was hearing and thinking that she ought to ask Anne to leave.

'I have studied it, over and over again,' Anne was saying. 'I have learned a lot of it by heart. If it has taught me one thing, it is that the Catholic doctrine of transubstantiation is false.'

'That is heresy,' Katharine pointed out, really worried now. 'People have been burned for saying it.'

'But listen!' Anne was seemingly oblivious to the danger. 'How can the bread and the wine become the actual body and blood of our Lord during the Mass?'

'Because a miracle takes place when the Host is elevated at the altar,' Katharine countered automatically, wondering if she still believed it.

'There is no miracle!' Anne's eyes were shining. 'The bread and the wine are purely symbolic of Christ's sacrifice. The rest is Papist superstition.'

'Many devout people believe in the Real Presence,' Katharine said.

'Then let me ask you something,' Anne cried. 'What if a piece of the consecrated bread falls to the floor and a mouse eats it? Does the mouse then receive the Blessed Body of Christ? Is he saved?'

Katharine had seen this question posed in theological books. It was a popular one in these days of reform. 'St Bonaventure tells us that the

156

bread remains the Body of Christ only as long as it is still being used as a sacrament.'

'It's pure sophistry!' Anne retorted. 'No amount of elevating can make bread and wine the Body of Christ in the first place.'

'Please keep your voice down!' Katharine spoke sharply. 'You must not say such things openly, especially in my house.'

'Oh, but I do, Lady Latimer! I have openly debated the matter in churches and marketplaces in Lincolnshire. The church authorities do not like it, and they have moved me on, but they have not molested me.'

'Then you have been very lucky indeed. Tell me, what is a young woman like you doing this for? You are, what, seventeen, eighteen?'

'Yes, but I was called to spread the truth.' She spoke with such certainty and zeal, and the dogmatism of the young, that Katharine realised there would be no moving her.

'So why are you here?'

'My husband threw me out. He is a Catholic, and he supported the late rebellion.'

Katharine's sympathies tended towards Thomas Kyme. She too did not want to harbour in her house one who might be accused of heresy.

'He never loved me,' Anne elaborated. 'He used to beat me if I argued with him. He said I was a bad influence on our children.'

'You have children?'

'Yes, two.' Anne's voice grew wistful. 'I miss them, but I could not go on living a lie. I was already thinking of divorcing him. I wanted the freedom to preach the Gospel.'

Katharine's head was reeling. Divorce? It was virtually unheard of, and then strictly for the rich, for it could only be granted by Parliament. As for preaching the Gospel, that was for priests. The Church would give short shrift to a lay person, especially a woman, who tried to subvert its teachings. Yet she instinctively knew that it would be futile to argue with Anne or try to dissuade her from rushing headlong to destruction.

'So how did you get to London?' she asked, deciding not to quiz the girl on her sweeping statements.

'Others of like mind gave me money and helped me,' Anne told her.

'I wanted to come here. There are many Protestants in London and I can make more difference as a gospeller. I have connections with the court, you know. My brother is the King's cupbearer and I have a half-brother in the privy chamber. My plan is to spread the Word at court.'

Katharine was seriously beginning to think that the young woman before her was mad. That was what she would say if anyone asked her about Anne, for both their sakes. 'So how do you think I can help you?' she asked reluctantly.

'Could I stay here?' Anne asked. As brazen as that.

Katharine recoiled – not too visibly, she hoped. 'I'm afraid that won't be possible. We have guests here just now, and we will be leaving for Northamptonshire soon, for the harvest.' Only the latter was true.

'Oh.' Anne looked crestfallen. She seemed unaware of the enormity of her request and the things she had just told Katharine.

Katharine would not let herself feel guilty. Anne had imposed herself on her; she was not her problem. Yet she could not leave the girl to spend the night out in the open, aprey to London's pimps and thieves. 'Look, Anne, I will give you some money. Use it to get yourself home to your father. The streets of London are not paved with gold – or full of Protestants. If you start preaching here, you really will be in danger.'

'I don't want money, my lady. And I intend to stay here in London.'

'Then I'm afraid I can't help you,' said Katharine, rising. 'I bid you good day.'

When Anne had gone, Katharine sank into her chair, relieved to be rid of her. What was it with these people – Lord Borough, Robert Aske, Anne Askew – that they were utterly convinced they were right and could see no other point of view? People should always be open to other views and new ideas. There was much sense in what the Protestants believed, but Anne was the last person to be their advocate. She was guaranteed to put people's backs up with her tunnel vision and complete unawareness of the effect she was having.

Katharine stood up and went through to the still room to make some quince jelly, one of John's favourite preserves. She could not shake off the fear Anne's visit had engendered in her. That nightmare still haunted her. Had their conversation been overheard? Had she said anything she shouldn't have said? She even thought of summoning her servants and telling them that she had just got rid of an unwanted visitor who was a little crazed, and that anything odd they had heard should be put down to the ravings of a madwoman. No. Least said, soonest mended: wise words her mother had often repeated. She wouldn't even tell John.

Her sister Anne was flourishing. William Herbert was proving an excellent husband. When Anne bore her first baby in the autumn, called Henry after the King, Katharine and John went to visit her at Whitehall Palace, in Herbert's cramped, but coveted, courtier lodging overlooking the River Thames. They admired the child, a lusty little bruiser who much resembled his father, and gave it a silver rattle that Katharine had ordered from a goldsmith in Cheapside.

When Henry finally stopped bawling and fell asleep in his cradle, and the men had retired to the outer chamber for a celebratory toast, Anne sat up in bed and turned to Katharine. 'You know the King is to marry again?'

'No!' This *was* a surprise. It was two years since Queen Jane had died and Katharine, like most people, had assumed that his Grace, now having a son, would not venture on the perilous seas of wedlock again.

'It was announced this week. He's marrying a German princess called Anne of Cleves. And I am to be a lady-in-waiting!'

'That's marvellous news,' Katharine smiled. 'But what about young Henry?'

Anne's face clouded over. 'We can't keep a child here, obviously. Before I learned of the appointment, I was going to live with him at Ewyas, but now I will have to send him there with a wet nurse. My Lady Suffolk has recommended a good, clean woman. It's not what I want, but it's best for Henry.'

Katharine thought that being nursed by his mother was best for Henry and wondered what she would do if she were in Anne's position. But, she thought sadly, she was never likely to be, and shouldn't judge others.

'You will miss him,' she said.

'I know – desperately. But, with this new preferment, I can give him a better life.' Her voice was brisk.

Seeing her sister looking distressed, Katharine told her about Anne Askew's visit.

'I've heard of her,' Anne revealed. 'She preaches quite openly and has been reprimanded for it, but she carries on undaunted.'

'I fear she is heading for a fall,' Katharine said. 'Don't have anything to do with her – she's dangerous.'

'I'm not that stupid.' Anne made a face. 'I don't want to get roasted!' She leaned over the cradle to gaze at her son. 'Changing the subject, I've noticed that Will isn't happy.'

'I know.' Ever since he and Ann had begun living together, he had lost his customary bonhomie.

'She's a strange girl,' Anne said. 'He brought her here to see the baby and she hardly said a word. She's been appointed a gentlewoman of the privy chamber to the new Queen, but she hates the court. The King is hosting a banquet later this month, and all the Queen's ladies are invited, but Ann said she doesn't want to go. She has no idea of the honour being done to her!'

'She must go,' Katharine said, incredulous. 'Will must make her. But I'm concerned about him.'

Anne took a sip of cordial. 'She doesn't seem to have any feelings for him, and there's no spark between them.'

'Poor Will. He deserves so much better.'

It galled Katharine to see him so needlessly unhappy. When he brought Ann to supper at Charterhouse Square soon afterwards, she braced herself for a tense evening, but Will had good news.

'I have brought some fine wine because we are celebrating tonight,' he announced, placing a silver flagon on the hall table. 'I am to be elevated to the nobility, as Baron Parr! It's in recognition of my services to the King in the late rebellion.'

Even as she was flinging her arms around him and John was clapping him on the back, Katharine was aware of Ann, standing there impassively, failing to share their joy. What was wrong with the girl?

Anger welled up in her. Disengaging from Will, she turned to her sister-in-law. 'Isn't this wonderful news?' she asked her.

'Of course,' Ann said. 'It's a step up. But, when my father dies, he will be an earl.'

It went against all the rules of courtesy to be rude to a guest under your roof. Yet that rule applied in reverse too, and Ann, in belittling Will's achievement, had been insulting and unkind. Katharine could not stop herself. She would not have his exultation deflated. 'It's far more meritorious to have earned one's preferment than to inherit it!' she declared. 'It's what you do in this life, rather than who you are, that matters.'

Ann's pale face flushed, but she said nothing. Katharine turned back to Will and squeezed his arm. 'I, for one, am delighted for you, brother. You deserve this mark of honour. Now, shall we go to the parlour? Supper is about to be served.'

After that, it was a fraught meal. Ann barely said a word. Even John, who hadn't much time for female moods, noticed how distanced from them she was.

'Did you enjoy the King's banquet, Ann?' he asked. He knew that she had not wanted to attend.

'It was well enough,' she replied, toying with her roast beef, which she had hardly touched. 'But I do not like the court. I much prefer country life.'

'Well, we shall go down to the country for Christmas,' Will said resignedly. Katharine guessed that he would rather have stayed for the lavish festivities at court.

'You could spend Christmas here with us,' she said, smiling at him.

'Yes, you would be very welcome,' John told them.

'Thank you, but we will be going to the country,' Ann said coldly.

'Is that what *you* want, Will?' Katharine asked.

He nodded. 'If it makes Ann happy.'

There was nothing more she could do. People chose to go to Hell in their own ways.

Chapter 12

1540

After the King's wedding in January, Katharine found herself visiting the court more and more frequently. Anne and Will were always inviting her there. She was either going downstream to Greenwich or upstream to Whitehall, and sometimes, as spring approached, further afield to Hampton Court.

Had she ever thought she lived in luxury? It was nothing compared to the splendour of the royal residences, with their vast chambers, brilliant, gilded décor, sumptuous tapestries and rich furnishings – and the pleasure gardens filled with fragrant flowers and glorious walks. She adored flowers and she and Anne spent many happy hours outdoors, identifying various blooms and sneaking the odd clipping for Katharine's small garden at Charterhouse Square. Everywhere around them, the courtiers were taking their recreation. There were tennis plays, bowling alleys, archery butts, tiltyards and fishponds, all dedicated to their pleasure. She spent many an afternoon competing with Will at the butts. At Hampton Court, they went hawking in the great park, or took a boat along the Thames as far as the abandoned Syon Abbey and back.

She had thought herself well dressed, but could not compete with the courtiers' rich velvets and damasks, their costly furs and gorgeous jewels. She found herself looking at her wardrobe afresh and planning improvements. It was a necessity, if she was not to look out of place in the royal palaces.

She got to know several of William's friends, young men who were as eager for advancement as he was, and Anne introduced her to some of the ladies who served the Queen. Even the young and very pretty

Duchess of Suffolk condescended to be friendly towards her. She was an elegant woman with wide-set eyes and a retroussé nose. Her half-Spanish blood showed in her dark good looks; her mother had been Katharine of Aragon's favourite lady-in-waiting.

Anne admired her very much and had told Katharine a lot about her. She was much younger than her husband, the Duke. She had been betrothed to his son, but when Suffolk's first wife, the King's sister Mary, had died, he had himself married Catherine Willoughby, as she then was. She had been fourteen. Now she was a spirited twenty-one-year-old, exuding vivacity and wit. Beneath it all, Katharine knew, she was learned and devout, but never a bigot or a sobersides. No one spent even ten minutes in her company without being impressed by her zest for life.

Only to Anne did Katharine confide her leanings towards reform.

'We'll make a gospeller of you yet!' Anne said. They were alone in her lodging, but Katharine flinched.

'Shh!'

Anne shrugged. 'No one can hear us. These walls are very thick. You know that my lady of Suffolk shares our zeal for reform?'

'I wondered about that.'

Now Anne did whisper. 'I think she favours the new religion.'

'Then she had best be careful,' Katharine said, unsurprised.

While they were walking in the gardens one day, Katharine met the King. He was approaching along the path, leaning heavily on his cane, surrounded by laughing courtiers who seemed to be hanging on his every word. She had seen portraits of him, and knew him to be a big, hearty man with a broad chest and a commanding presence, but she was unprepared for the reality. He was very fat – two men could easily have got inside his doublet – and he looked old. There was grey in his red hair and he walked with a bad limp. She could make out the bulge of bandages beneath his white hose. Fortunately, she saw him before he saw her, and was able to collect herself and put on an expression of awe as she and Anne sank into deep curtseys.

'Mrs Herbert!' the King exclaimed. 'What a pleasant sight to grace this lovely garden. And who is this lady with you?'

When he gestured to her to rise, Katharine was filled with trepidation.

'Your Majesty, may I present my sister, Lady Latimer?'

Now he would remember who her husband was. She began to tremble.

His shrewd blue eyes appraised her. 'Latimer, eh? Your husband has done us good service in the north, Madam, and I gather that you too dealt effectively with our rebels! You are most welcome here.' He made her a slight courtly bow.

'Your Majesty is very kind,' she replied, overwhelmed with thankfulness to hear his praise of John.

'I will leave you ladies to make the most of this unseasonably good weather,' he said, and walked on, as she and Anne curtseyed again.

'You must be relieved,' Anne said, when he was out of earshot.

'I am!' Katharine replied. 'I can't wait to tell John what the King said. It will be the greatest comfort to him.'

They sat down on a shaded bench by the river. There was no one nearby, but still she lowered her voice. 'His Grace is not a well man,' she muttered. 'I feel sorry for him – and I liked him.'

'People do like him,' Anne said. 'It's that charming, friendly way he has – the common touch. It makes them forget what he's capable of. And yet sometimes I think that, if life had been kinder to him, if he'd been vouchsafed an heir much earlier on, if the Pope hadn't denied him an annulment, if Anne Boleyn had been faithful, and if people hadn't opposed him . . . well, I think he would have been a different man today.'

The breeze blew a strand of hair across Katharine's face. She tucked it back under her hood. 'I admire him for reforming the Church. It was a brave thing to break with Rome.'

'But it was the right thing to do. The Papacy is corrupt and encourages superstition.'

'That's true. I am all for reform, but sometimes I find myself thinking that it's only a short step from being a reformist to being a Protestant. A step that makes all the difference legally.'

Anne's eyes met hers. 'I have taken that step.'

Katharine turned to her sister, open-mouthed.

Anne smiled at her. 'Yes, I have. Herbert too.' It was her wont to call her husband by his family name. 'And Will. But, dear sister, do not breathe a word of this to anyone.'

Katharine already knew that Will was an ardent reformist, like Uncle William, and she had long wondered if he had thought about following Luther.

'My lips are sealed,' she said.

'I think you want to take that step too,' Anne said, regarding her searchingly.

Katharine lowered her voice. 'In my heart, I think I *have* taken it. I know it is a dangerous step, and John would be appalled, but I have felt called to make it for a long time.'

Anne squeezed her hand. 'I am so happy for you, sister. These are sad times, when people cannot follow their own consciences, but God knows the secrets of our hearts. It is through our faith alone that we will be justified. One day, I pray, we will have the freedom to worship openly.'

A broad smile lit up John's face when Katharine told him what the King had said. It was like the sun coming out.

'All those petitions, all that waiting around in palace galleries, desperate for reassurance, and you bump into him by chance and get it immediately,' he said. 'Kate, you're a wonder!'

'I'm pleased to have been of service,' she told him, as he caught her in his arms and kissed her. 'Mmm, that's nice. Now you can relax and enjoy life. We have much for which to be thankful.'

'We do indeed!' he said. 'And the thing I thank God most for is you!'

It was hard practising her new faith in secret. She had to make an outward show of following religious custom, for she was too fearful of reprisals if she betrayed her true beliefs. At Mass, when she took the bread and the wine, she thought of them as symbols commemorating

Christ's sacrifice, not His Real Presence. She spent many hours at her private devotions or reading books on divinity, believing that the way to achieve salvation was to forge a prayerful relationship with God. She liked the idea of coming close to Him herself without having to rely on the intervention of a priest. She was eternally thankful that the King had ordered that a copy of the English translation of the Bible be placed in every church, so that all could read the Scriptures. She bought herself one from a bookseller at Paul's churchyard, and cherished it. It was a marvel to have her own copy of the Word of God. John also had purchased a New Testament, for even he believed that everyone should be able to read the Word of God.

It was a heady feeling, being able to interpret the Bible for herself, rather than blindly accepting what the Church of Rome taught. The Scriptures were the key to entering into communion with God and achieving Heaven, and in them were to be found the standards against which all morality was to be measured.

She would have liked to have taken down the statues of saints that John kept around the house, but dared not. She had, some time since, ceased seeking the intervention of the Virgin Mary and the saints. Where in the Bible was that recommended?

Yes, it was hard, keeping the faith when she had to stay silent. It was too dangerous to do otherwise and she was not the stuff of which martyrs were made. But she was happy; she felt fulfilled spiritually. She had found her path.

March had turned cold again when Will turned up unannounced at Charterhouse Square one evening.

'My father-in-law is dead, God rest him,' he announced. 'He took a fall from his horse and broke his neck. I am now earl of Essex in Ann's right. Ann is very upset. She wants to go home to Stanstead Hall, which is ours now, but I really ought to stay at court until the King confirms me in the earldom.'

'You should,' Katharine said. 'Ann must understand that.'

'I've said we'll go as soon as I hear from the King. It's just a formality and I doubt I'll be kept waiting long.'

But he was. By the middle of April, the King still had not spoken, and Ann put her foot down and insisted that they leave for Essex. Katharine hastened to court to remonstrate with her. She found her alone in the lodging she shared with Will, writing a letter in untidy, ill-formed handwriting.

As soon as Katharine walked in, Ann jumped up and turned it face down on the table, looking as if she had been caught out doing something she shouldn't. But Katharine had other things on her mind.

'Good day, Ann,' she smiled. 'I hear from Will that you are hoping to go to Stanstead Hall.'

'We *are* going to Stanstead Hall,' Ann said, in a tone that brooked no argument.

'May I sit down?' Katharine asked.

'Yes, of course,' Ann replied grudgingly.

Katharine did so. 'Ann, I know you hate the court and you want to get away, but it is crucial that you stay here until Will is confirmed in the earldom. I'm sure it won't be very long—'

She looked up as Will crashed into the room. 'By God!' he seethed. 'I'd like to kill that varlet Cromwell!' He was beside himself, almost in tears; she was amazed to see it, for Will never cried.

'Why? What has he done?' Katharine and Ann asked at the same time.

'He's stolen my earldom, which is mine by all the laws of inheritance!'

'He can't do that,' Ann shrieked. Katharine had never seen her so animated. 'It's mine by right!'

'Not any more,' Will spat. 'His Majesty has declared the earldom extinct and has recreated it for Cromwell – just because Cromwell wanted it. To think that that jumped-up blacksmith's son, that dog, now holds one of the oldest and greatest earldoms in England – well, it doesn't bear thinking about.' He was pacing up and down, beating his fist into his other hand.

'It's appalling,' Katharine breathed, thinking of how Cromwell had extorted money out of John over the past five years, for no other reason than that he could. He was unspeakable.

The door opened again, and there was Uncle William. 'I heard the news and had to come,' he said darkly. 'My boy, this is an outrage. Cromwell has gone too far this time—'

'Pardon me, Uncle, but I am going right now to protest to the King in the strongest possible terms,' Will interrupted, grabbing the feathered bonnet he had thrown down.

'Wait!' Uncle William held up a hand. 'I was about to say that I think it strange that his Majesty has elevated Cromwell at this time. The talk is that Cromwell is finished. He's been finished since he arranged the Cleves marriage and the King decided he did not like the lady. It is only a matter of time until he suffers the same fate he has brought on so many others.'

'But why would the King give him an earldom?' Will asked, looking unconvinced.

'He has been known to show favour to those he means to destroy. And Cromwell has many enemies, who are doubtless dripping poison in his Grace's ear. Norfolk, for one, would love to see him brought down, and Bishop Gardiner of Winchester, who hates all reformers. So, Will, I urge you to bide your time.'

'But the earldom's mine!' Ann protested, in tears.

'Hush, girl,' Uncle William said. 'We have to play a long game here.'

'It's not right,' Will muttered, although less vehemently. Katharine knew he would take their uncle's advice.

'So you will stay here at court?' she asked, rising and making ready to leave.

'We must,' William said emphatically, and Ann, who had opened her mouth to protest, took one look at him and shut it again.

As Katharine hastened along the galleries of Whitehall towards the landing stage where the boatmen waited for fares, she was still shaking with indignation at Cromwell's theft of Will's earldom and going over in her mind what Uncle William had said. Anne had told her that the King rarely visited the Queen, even though the Queen was a very pleasant lady and a kind mistress. She had heard gossip that the royal marriage hadn't even been consummated. It all chimed with what she had heard today.

Seated in a boat, she marvelled, as always, at the great houses of the nobility as she was rowed below the Strand. At Baynard's Castle, an old royal palace rising directly from the water, she alighted. From there, it was a short walk to Charterhouse Square. As she passed by St Paul's Cathedral, she paused to look at the booksellers' stalls, as she often did. There was a tract against Popery that she quite fancied, and Sir Thomas Malory's *Morte d'Arthur*, which she thought Margaret, and even Jack, would like. She bought the books and went on her way, unable to banish Will's predicament from her mind. He had been dealt a great injury and she felt so bitter on his behalf.

She had become aware that the court was splitting into factions, both trying to control the King. The reformers were led by Cromwell, Archbishop Cranmer and Queen Jane's brother, Will's old friend, Edward Seymour, Earl of Hertford; and supported by Will and Uncle William, among many others. The Catholics were led by Norfolk and the eagle-eyed Stephen Gardiner, Bishop of Winchester, who wanted a return to the old faith. Would the Catholics succeed in bringing down Cromwell? It was not often that she was in sympathy with them, but she fervently hoped so!

Weeks went by, and nothing happened. Will was climbing the walls with fury and frustration. And then, nearly two weeks into June, the word was all around the court and the City. Cromwell had been arrested – for treason and heresy! Cromwell was in the Tower!

People thought it incredible that so mighty a lord had fallen. He had been the King's right-hand man. Yet he had overreached himself, and ridden roughshod over others' rights, as Katharine had good reason to know.

John was jubilant. 'This means I won't have to pay that protection money any more! Thank God we are rid of the bastard!'

Will was eagerly hoping for clarification of the position regarding the earldom of Essex, and wasted no time in presenting a petition to the King.

'He said he cannot consider anything until the legal process against Cromwell is concluded,' he told Katharine, when she next visited him at court.

'Have patience, boy,' Uncle William counselled. 'Unravelling Cromwell's affairs will be a gargantuan task and the only one capable of doing it efficiently, although I hate to say it, is Cromwell.'

'Well, he can do it from Hell!' Will growled.

The next news that had all England buzzing was that the King was divorcing the Queen. Katharine had only seen Anne of Cleves once, from afar, at a tournament on May Day. Their Majesties had been watching from the oriel window above the Holbein Gate at Whitehall, while Katharine and John had been lucky to get seats in the stands that lined the street below. The Queen had displayed a regal bearing, but looked to be no beauty. Katharine felt sorry for her. How dreadful to be so publicly discarded after just six months of marriage.

The divorce was accomplished within a matter of weeks – a lot faster than the years it had taken for the King to rid himself of Queen Katherine. The word at court was that Queen Anne had been most accommodating and was secretly pleased to be a free woman. Certainly, she had done well out of it, for the King, to show his gratitude, had showered her with great houses and riches.

No sooner had the hubbub over the divorce died down than it was announced that his Majesty had remarried. The bride was Norfolk's niece, Katheryn Howard. She had served alongside Anne in the former Queen's household, and Anne told Katharine that she was pretty and kind, but not very bright – *and* she was thirty years younger than her bridegroom.

'How many more wives will the king have?' Katharine wondered. 'That's five so far!' She was standing at the parlour table at Charterhouse Square, arranging flowers. The August day was hot and she had pulled off her hood and her oversleeves.

'Maybe he wants more heirs,' John observed, from behind the estate map he was studying. She glanced at him, praying that was not a veiled reproach, but he did not look at all reproving. He laid down the map.

'It's more good news, Kate. The Catholics are back in the saddle.' It was not good news for her, but it certainly was for him. There had been no demand for the payment due at midsummer; Cromwell was dead, butchered with three strokes of the axe on the King's wedding day, and they were free of his sharp practices. But the King was still finding plenty for John to do.

He rose and poured wine into two goblets. 'With Cromwell gone, and a Catholic queen in the King's bed, we might see some return to the old ways.'

'The reformists will fight it,' Katharine observed.

'It's about time the Catholics had their say,' John said. 'We've been out in the cold and ignored for too long!'

Chapter 13

1541–1542

'Ann's left me,' William said, striding into the hall at Charterhouse Square one balmy night in June, tense with anger.

'What?' Katharine cried. 'Sit down and tell us what's happened.'

'How can she have left you?' John asked, incredulous. In his book, wives didn't do such things.

'She has run away with her lover – some bastard monk called John Lyngfield, who was the Prior of Tandridge before they dissolved it.'

Katharine looked at John, shaking her head. If men in holy orders behaved like that, small wonder that the King had closed down the monasteries.

Will sat down heavily by the fire, still wearing his cloak. 'In some ways, it's a relief. She's never been a proper wife to me. But I'm furious that she has shamed me. I don't know how long it's been going on.'

Katharine would have wagered that it had been going on last spring, when Ann had covered up the letter she was writing. 'The shame is all hers,' she said.

'They have fourteen pounds a year to live on,' Will snorted. 'We shall see how long love's sweet dream will last on that.'

'And you knew nothing about it?' Katharine asked.

'Looking back, there were signs, but I wasn't interested enough to care. She told me herself, quite brazenly. Good riddance to her, I say! Now I can enjoy life without a millstone around my neck.'

'Amen to that,' Katharine said. 'I never liked her.'

'Will you apply to have the marriage annulled?' John asked, getting up and calling for some wine.

'It can wait. I'm in no hurry to remarry,' Will said. 'I'd like an heir one day, but I can't think about that now.'

Soon, they were flushed with good Rhenish and Will was in better spirits.

'I wish that varlet joy of her,' he slurred. 'He's welcome to her.'

When Katharine visited the Herberts at court a fortnight later, Anne told her that Will was pursuing Dorothy Bray, one of Queen Katheryn's gentlewomen.

'He's a dark horse,' Katharine observed. 'He never told me about that.'

'It's causing a scandal,' her sister said disapprovingly, as they hastened through the gardens, Anne being late to join the Queen at the archery butts, having spent time chatting to Katharine. 'They don't seem to care what people think. That's her there.' She indicated a dark-haired woman with beautiful, chiselled features at the edge of the group of young women surrounding the auburn-haired little Queen, among whom the Duchess of Suffolk was holding forth animatedly. There was a sultriness about Dorothy's looks that would appeal mightily to men. You could have said the same about the Queen.

'Your Majesty, please pardon my tardiness,' Anne panted, sinking into a deep curtsey and pulling Katharine down with her. 'My sister here, Lady Latimer, arrived, which caused the delay.'

The Queen smiled sweetly. She was indeed very pretty and looked so young. Katharine felt a pang for her; it could not be easy, being married to the obese, ageing King.

'No matter, dear Anne,' Katheryn said. 'Lady Latimer, it is a pleasure to see you.' She held out her hand to be kissed. 'Now you must take your turn with the rest of us.'

'Oh, but your Majesty, I am not very good at archery,' Katharine protested.

'Neither am I!' the Queen smiled, and handed her a bow and some arrows.

Nervously – they were all watching her – Katharine fitted an arrow to the bow, positioned herself in front of the butts and took aim. Whoosh! The arrow fled through the air and embedded itself just inside the bull's eye. She stared at it in disbelief. Everyone clapped.

'You're not very good at archery?' the Queen giggled. 'You could have fooled me.

'I've never done that before!' Katharine cried.

'Bravo, my Lady Latimer!' said a familiar voice behind her. Suddenly understanding why the Queen and the other ladies were sinking into deep reverences, she turned and hurriedly followed suit. The King and his gentlemen were gazing admiringly at the target. 'You have hidden talents, my lady.' He smiled at her. 'Doesn't she, my love?' He took the Queen's hand and kissed it devotedly, while she stood on tiptoe and kissed his cheek.

'It was pure luck, your Majesty,' Katharine said. 'But I have heard, Sir, that you are highly skilled at archery.'

He beamed at that. 'I will show you,' he said. He took the bow from her and aimed. The arrow sped almost invisibly through the air and split hers in two. The ladies burst into applause as the King flushed with pleasure. 'There's life in the old lion yet,' he told his gentlemen, grinning. 'And Katheryn can vouch for that!'

Katheryn blushed becomingly. But maybe she saw in him what attracted Katharine herself – a reassuring authority, kindly courtesy and loving devotion. Many wives survived on far less.

The King stayed with them for a while, telling them about the great progress to the north on which the court would soon be embarking. 'It will be an opportunity to receive the submission of those who were against us in the late rising,' he said, his arm around Katheryn's waist; clearly, he could not keep his hands from her. Katharine kept her eyes lowered, remembering John's part in the events of four years ago. She was glad when the King moved on, bidding farewell to the Queen with a hearty kiss.

Katharine and John went to Stowe when the court left for the progress. That autumn, Magdalen Lane's husband died unexpectedly after a short illness, and Katharine spent a lot of time at Orlingbury comforting her cousin and taking charge of their ten distressed children. Seeing Magdalen, clad in black and drawn with grief, made her realise how far they had all come since those spacious days at Rye House. She herself would be thirty next year, quite middle-aged. It did not seem possible. But Magdalen at least had the consolation of three boys and seven girls, who ranged in age from Laetitia, who was sixteen, to the baby in the cradle. And she had been left comfortably off. When Katharine's visit came to an end, she knew she could leave the running of the household safely in Laetitia's capable hands, while her mother took time to mourn; Magdalen had instructed her daughters well.

As she rode home, she wondered yet again why God had seen fit to send her cousin an abundance of children while she herself was blessed with none. What had she done to displease Him, that He would withhold that precious gift from her? She had been a good wife to two husbands, she had lived a godly life and she had been unfailing in her devotions to Him. But she had been married to John for seven years now with no sign of a child, and she was not getting any younger. Maybe she had some unknown ailment that prevented her from conceiving. She could only thank God that John had never reproached her for her barrenness.

At least she had Margaret, who was as close to her as a daughter. And she was getting on better with Jack. They were growing up quickly – he was twenty and Margaret fifteen. It was time, surely, to be nudging John to think about betrothals, yet she held back, for she did not want to lose Margaret just yet.

In November, Katharine was delighted to hear that Will had been appointed captain of the Gentlemen Pensioners, the King's elite personal guard to which John had once belonged. She went to court to see him march at the head of his troop along the gallery that led to the royal apartments at Hampton Court. He looked very tall and imposing, carrying his poleaxe and wearing his wine-coloured doublet and his gold medallion of office. He had asked Master Holbein, the King's painter, to take his portrait, for which he would be wearing his insignia. Katharine, standing with Uncle William among the throng that lined the gallery, felt deeply proud of her brother. Dorothy Bray was there too; Katharine saw the look that passed between them as he went by, and was glad that he had found love.

Will told them later that the King had not come forth that day into his presence chamber. The Gentlemen Pensioners had kept watch in an empty room. Katharine learned why when Anne came running to catch up with her as she walked to the jetty to hail a boat.

'Kate! The Queen has been arrested.' Anne was out of breath, her eyes wild. 'She is shut up in her apartments and all her women are being questioned. I've already told the Council that I know nothing.'

Katharine had spun around. 'Why has she been arrested?'

'She has been accused of misconduct before her marriage.'

'But that's not a crime.'

Anne lowered her voice. 'No, but I think that the reformists who arrested her – those same councillors who examined me – are out to ruin her and bring down the Catholics, and are working on the premise that there is more to tell.'

'What do you mean?' Katharine's whisper was almost carried away on the breeze.

'I fear they hope to find evidence of misconduct after her marriage too.'

'But that would be treason!'

Anne shivered. 'It would. And the penalty would be death, as it was for Anne Boleyn.'

Katharine stood there, holding on to her hood against the wind. 'I cannot believe that the Queen would have taken such a stupid risk, with Anne's example before her.'

'Maybe, like Anne, she was desperate to present the King with a son.' Anne bent forward and spoke in Katharine's ear, although there was no one about and the boatmen were yards away. 'The word is that the King lacks vigour in bed.'

Katharine could believe it, given his weight and his ill health. 'But he adores her; it's plain to see. He would not abandon her, surely?'

Anne's expression was grim. 'Kate, I have served all five of his wives, and I know him well enough to say that his pride in himself and his kingship is greater than his love for anyone else. He will not tolerate infidelity. But he is deeply grieved and has shut himself up in his apartments. I saw Will just before I came here, and he said that his Grace is a broken man.'

'It's a dreadful situation,' Katharine said, thinking of that poor young girl. 'The Queen must be terrified.'

'She's been weeping and wailing ever since they arrested her.' Anne paused, then lowered her voice again. 'I feel sorry for her, and I would never wish harm to her, but this might see the Catholic party brought down for good. In which case, the reformists would again be in the ascendant, which can only be good news.'

'But not for the Queen,' Katharine said. 'Yet one must ask, as Cicero did, what is the highest good?'

'St Thomas Aquinas would say that the highest good is to live the life of the righteous in communion with God. There can be no arguing with that. But I will do or say nothing to the Queen's prejudice. I would not have that on my conscience.'

'Nor I. What should I do? Go home?'

'Yes,' Anne urged. 'Would that I could come with you, but I dare not, lest something sinister is made of it.'

They kissed farewell and Katharine hailed a boat, fearing that the cause of reform might ride on the shedding of a young girl's blood.

In the depths of winter, the Queen was sent to Syon Abbey. Evidence of adultery had been found, which came as no surprise to Katharine. Whether it was genuine or not was another matter; Anne had heard that her fallen mistress had denied everything. Katharine and John speculated at length as to what would happen to the Queen, until Uncle William arrived late one evening and informed them that she was to be attainted in Parliament in the new year.

Katharine, John, Anne and Herbert were sitting at table in the parlour with the remains of their supper before them.

'There will be no trial,' Uncle William told them. 'Parliament will draw up a Bill of Attainder and examine the evidence. Then there will be three readings of the Bill. If the lords and commons vote it through each time, it will become an Act enshrined in law.'

'And what will that mean for the Queen?' Katharine asked.

'Those attainted of treason are sentenced to forfeit their lives and their property to the Crown. She will die, poor soul.'

They sat in silence for a moment.

'May God comfort her,' John said at length, crossing himself. 'What she has sown, she has reaped through her own foolishness.'

And the determination of her enemies, Katharine would have said, but was aware of the need to be circumspect. She felt ashamed that those who claimed to be the champions of reform had hounded a naïve girl to her death.

Anne looked as if she was fighting back tears. She had lost her position when the Queen's household was dismissed. She was still living at court, sharing Herbert's lodging, and had been entrusted with the safe-keeping of the Queen's jewels. They were locked away in a strong-box under the floorboards of the Latimers' bedchamber. When Anne had brought them to Charterhouse Square, she and Katharine had opened the large casket and exclaimed over the magnificent pieces twinkling and glittering inside. Anne had wept.

'I just know she will never wear them again,' she sobbed. 'She wasn't allowed to take any with her to Syon, only her hoods edged with pearls and plain black gowns.'

Katharine had not been able to get the image of the pretty little Queen out of her mind. She could only imagine the mental torture the girl was going through, shut away from the world, not knowing her fate.

Anne had been questioned several times. Mercifully, she had known nothing. Looking at her sister across the table, Katharine thanked God that she had escaped unscathed. Others had not been so lucky. Several maids-of-honour and chamberers had been arrested, while many of the Howards and their dependents were in the Tower. Norfolk, that wily old fox, had managed to remain at liberty, but he had lost the King's favour, and the conservatives had suffered a severe setback. Gratified though she was that the reformists were back in control, Katharine's heart still bled for the Queen.

'Have you seen the King?' she asked.

'He is still in seclusion,' Will said. 'Very few have access to him. We gentlemen spend our days in the privy chamber at cards and dice.'

'He will have to get a grip soon,' Uncle William said, frowning. 'The business of the kingdom must go on.'

'He was in seclusion after Queen Jane's death,' Anne recalled. 'He got over that.'

'I just pray he will be merciful,' Katharine said.

That seemed unlikely. The following week, the Queen's lovers were executed. Some of Katharine's servants went to watch and came back sickened at the butchery they had witnessed. When she had cause to pass under London Bridge on her frequent boat trips along the Thames, she kept her eyes lowered for fear of seeing the rotting heads of those two wretches on spikes high above her.

At her urging, she and John went to Stowe for Christmas, which was bleak because the children were at Snape. But John had to be back in London in January to attend a new session of Parliament. Anne and Herbert had gone to Ewyas and Will had accompanied them, for there was no merrymaking at court.

John was fretting because Parliament was pushing through the Queen's attainder.

'The radicals are bent on it,' he seethed, arriving home grim-faced, unhappy to see the Catholic party brought so low. 'They are even having a stamp of the King's signature made, to save him the pain of assenting to the Queen's death.'

'Maybe he will spare her,' Katharine said hopefully.

John looked thoughtful. 'There is a rumour going around the Parliament House that he means to have her imprisoned for life.'

'Do you think that will happen?'

'Not if the reformists have anything to do with it!'

It seemed that they held sway, having driven this affair from the very beginning. John returned one day stone-faced and told her that the Bill had been passed.

'Then she will die,' she whispered.

'I fear so,' he said.

'What a terrible world we live in.' She took his cloak, her hands trembling. She had heard of people being executed before – Sir Thomas More, Anne Boleyn and Robert Aske, to name a few – but none of their tragedies had affected her as much as this one. To condemn a young girl to die violently was a dreadful thing. And, ultimately, it was the King who was responsible. He could have stopped it. Instead, he remained shut up, wallowing in his own misery and the blow to his manly pride. He had gone down in her estimation, by a long way. How could she have thought him a kindly and amiable man? It just went to prove that charm was only surface deep!

On the day of the execution, which was to take place privately in the Tower, she stayed at home and prayed for the Queen, shuddering at the thought of what was happening not two miles away. Uncle William had said that, when Anne Boleyn had been beheaded, a cannon had been fired from Tower Wharf, but Katharine never heard any. They had not even accorded Katheryn Howard that dignity. She had been erased from history in silence.

A fortnight later, Anne arrived at Charterhouse Square and announced that she was with child again. Suppressing her envy, Katharine hugged her.

'Congratulations!' she cried. 'I am so pleased for you both.'

'Herbert is delighted!' Anne said. 'Come to court and we can celebrate properly. The King has come out of seclusion and is to host three banquets: one for the lords of his Council, one for lawyers and one for ladies. I can secure you a place if you want to accompany me.'

Katharine was appalled. 'He is throwing banquets so soon after his wife's execution? He ought to be ashamed!'

'I know, I know! But don't forget – he is the injured party in this tragedy. That is how everyone at court sees it. And Will says his Grace has adopted a new rule of life. He wants to put the past behind him. I saw him the other day; he was walking in a gallery with Master Holbein. He looks very old and grey and I swear he has put on more weight. Katharine, we should remember that he was touched deeply by the tragedy of the Queen. Of your charity, do not think ill of him.'

'You are suddenly very sympathetic!' Katharine rounded on her sister.

'I know him, Kate. I know he can be cruel and that he has not always treated his wives well. But he adored the late Queen. I saw them together many times and he could not stop caressing her. This time, the fault was not his.'

'So it's not his fault that she is buried in the Tower chapel with her neck severed?' Katharine's tone was tart.

'She was guilty of treason.'

'Was she? Will saw her written testimony and that of Thomas Culpeper. Both denied that they had committed adultery.'

'Katharine, they had secret meetings in her privy! Uncle William told me that, even if they did not do the act, the intention was there. And that is treason.'

'I won't argue with you, Anne.' Katharine realised it was cold in the hall and walked through to the parlour. 'But I don't wish to go to the banquet.'

'What banquet?' John asked, looking up from his accounts. The papers were spread all over the table. He rose. 'Hello, Anne.'

Anne wasted no time in telling him about the banquets.

'You should go, Kate,' he enjoined. 'It will cheer you up and it is politic to show support to the King at a time like this.'

She stared at him. 'Are you ordering me to go?' He had never been an overbearing husband and had always allowed her to make her own decisions.

'No, I just think it is wise. Sometimes we have to set aside our finer feelings in favour of what is expedient, as I well know.'

There was no arguing with that. She capitulated, and Anne insisted on looking through her gowns to see which would serve best for the occasion. Katharine was now pleased that she had outlaid a tidy sum on a sumptuous one of green velvet edged with pearls and a crimson damask kirtle to wear beneath it. She had thought twice about paying so much, but told herself that it was a wise investment. Lavish display at court was everything. And it would show off her jewels to perfection.

The palace was ablaze with candles and the tables in the watching chamber were laden with tempting sweetmeats, artistically prepared and presented by the King's French cook and his assistants. A servant in livery offered them goblets of wine as they arrived. The room was full of ladies in gorgeous gowns, their jewels winking in the candlelight, and there was a hubbub of excited female voices.

'His Majesty himself ordered and inspected the lodgings of the ladies who are staying at court tonight,' Anne said. 'He should be here soon.'

As if on cue, there was a fanfare of trumpets and there he was, advancing into the room and greeting his guests. He was the only man present, apart from the guards and servants, and the ladies clustered around him like bees to a honeypot as he made them hearty good cheer and spoke to each one as familiarly as if he had come to see her alone. He was practised at this, Katharine saw. It was how he reeled people in and made them forget what he was capable of. How he must be enjoying all this female adulation; what balm it must be to his pride, after being so publicly cuckolded.

As she stood with Anne and her friends by the fireplace watching the King making his way around the room amidst much laughter and gaiety, with the ranks of ladies moving to allow him through as the Red Sea must have parted for Moses, Katharine bent to Anne's ear.

'Has this been arranged so that he can find a new bride?'

'Heavens, no! The King enjoys feasting ladies. He's done it several times. He likes female company.' Anne lowered her voice. 'But I doubt any of these ladies are in a hurry to marry him, not now that this new law has been passed.'

John had told Katharine about Queen Katheryn's Act of Attainder requiring any lady whom the King might decide to marry in the future to declare, on pain of death, any misconduct in her past. She looked at the women around her, remembering what Anne had said about some of them. 'I imagine that rather narrows the field,' she murmured.

Anne smiled. 'Few nowadays would aspire to such an honour. Would *you* marry him, if you were free?'

'Not for all the money in the treasury,' Katharine retorted, keeping her voice low. 'You'd have to be a fool to marry a man who either puts away or kills his wives. You would need nerves of iron!' She glanced around nervously, realising that her words could be construed as seditious, even treasonous, but their companions were talking to others and all eyes were on the King.

The Duchess of Suffolk joined them. 'Watch out, his Majesty is coming this way,' she muttered. 'Look busy.'

Katharine stifled a smile. 'What will your Grace do now that there is no queen to wait on?' she asked.

'Oh, go home and have lots of babies, I suppose,' the Duchess grinned. 'Well, that's what my lord would like me to do, but I've produced the requisite heir and a spare and do not fancy being a brood mare again.'

Anne patted her belly. 'I have no choice!' she laughed. 'This little imp is due in the summer.'

'You'll have a nursery-full at this rate,' Katharine smiled.

'And very commendable too!' the Duchess said. 'Speaking of children, my belief is that the King *will* marry again. The future of his dynasty depends on the life of one small child.' She leaned in, lowering her voice. 'I can only say I am heartily glad that I am already married!'

Anne's eyes widened. 'Has he shown an interest in you?'

'In the past, before . . .' There was a pause, then the Duchess's eyes twinkled. 'I heard that the ambassador of Cleves made the Lady Anne move closer to London to be ready for the King's summons. Her brother is pressing his Grace to take her back.'

'That will never happen,' Anne said. 'He gets on well with her these days, but I don't think he ever fancied her as a man should fancy a woman.'

'His part is not to fancy her, but to get heirs!' the Duchess said crisply. 'He's the King! Bedding his wife is a matter of state.'

'With respect, your Grace, you should lower your voice,' Katharine murmured. 'The King approaches.'

He had been chatting with a circle of ladies about two yards away. Now he loomed over them, a massive figure of a man, but he was leaning heavily on his stick as he bade them rise from their curtseys. 'I trust you are enjoying our little banquet, my ladies,' he said. 'Would you like more wine?' He signalled to a servant, who hastened over and refilled their cups.

'We are having a wonderful evening, your Majesty,' the Duchess said.

'The food is fabulous, Sir,' Anne added.

Katharine was looking at the King, still wondering how he could have sent his young wife to her death. But, of course, he hadn't! It had been done for him with that wooden stamp. Yet he must have authorised its use.

'Are you enjoying yourself, Lady Latimer?' He had picked up on her silence. His piercing blue eyes were boring into her. They were warm, but she imagined that they would turn icy if she displeased him.

She made herself smile. 'Very much, Sir. I confess I am overwhelmed by it all. This is the first time I have attended a court banquet.'

He looked mollified. 'I hope it will not be the last, Madam.' He turned to Anne. 'I imagine that you will be retiring to the country soon, Mrs Herbert.'

'Yes, Sir. We are hoping for a brother for Henry. If it is a boy, we mean to call him Edward, after the Prince.'

The King beamed at that. 'I wish you as goodly a child as he is.'

'How is the Prince, Sir?' Lady Suffolk asked.

'He's four now, and thriving,' the King said, his face becoming animated. 'He knows his letters too, and he loves nothing better than to watch a joust.'

'I can see that he is already taking after his father,' the Duchess observed.

Katharine could only feel sorry for the little boy, deprived of another stepmother. But she kept the smile on her face. 'He sounds very toward, Sir.'

'He is a prince of whom England will have cause to be glad,' the King said loftily. 'Now, my ladies, I must move on and speak to more of my guests. I wish you all a pleasant evening. By the way, Lady Latimer, that is a beautiful gown.' He bowed and limped away, joining another cluster of simpering women.

'Poor little Edward,' the Duchess said. 'No wonder he's a prodigy. Those who have charge of him are forever exhorting him to emulate his father. It's a heavy burden to place on a child.'

'It's easy to see that the King dotes on him, though,' Anne said.

'He doesn't see him very often. But, yes, he is proud of him.'

They talked until the trumpets sounded again and his Majesty bade them all farewell and left. It was the signal for everyone else to depart. As the servants came forward to clear the tables, Katharine watched the King disappearing down the gallery, probably desperate to sit down and take his ease. Glittering, all-powerful and cruel he might be, but he was still a mere mortal, and an ailing one at that.

Will remained besotted with Dorothy Bray. Katharine had had them both to dinner at Charterhouse Square, and had found herself liking Dorothy, who paid less heed to her reputation than she should, but was just what Will needed at this time. It was plain that her brother had got over the desertion of his wife. She herself rarely gave a thought to Ann Bourchier these days. Doubtless Ann was still living in sin and penury with her prior.

She was surprised, therefore, when Will turned up at Charterhouse Square in a foul temper one afternoon in June.

'Whatever is the matter?' she asked, rising to her feet. She had been about to doze off, having eaten a hearty dinner.

He shrugged off his wet cloak and laid it across a chair. It was teeming outside.

'It's Ann!' he exploded. 'She's had a son by that bastard, and do you know what? Legally, it's mine! I've taken advice on this. She could try to make me support it.'

'Will, calm down.' Katharine was shocked, and still trying to gather her wits. 'It's a year since she left you; the child cannot possibly be yours.'

'I will not own it!' he shouted.

She took his arm and led him to the settle. 'Listen. No court would make you. She has been living with a monk for the past year, cause enough in itself for scandal. We can testify to that. So could others.'

Will was breathing heavily. 'She could easily say that we met and coupled during that time. It would be my word against hers.'

'Has she actually said she expects you to support the child?'

Will snorted. 'That bastard Lyngfield wrote to me. Thought I should know about the child. They are giving it my name. *My name!*'

'What did your lawyer advise?'

'A pre-emptive strike. I am applying for a legal separation on the grounds of her desertion and adultery.'

'That's very sensible. I'm sure you will be granted one.'

'He's drawing up the papers now, as we speak. But if that bitch says that our marriage was never valid and tries to have it annulled, I could lose the earldom of Essex.'

'I hardly think so, Will,' Katharine said. 'You're not seeking an annulment. It's a true marriage and the earldom should come to you as her husband.'

'I hope you're right.' He sighed and buried his face in his hands. 'I'm sorry, Kate. I shouldn't burden you with my troubles.'

'You need to talk to someone, so why not me? And it's always good to see you, even if you just come and shout for a bit. John's just gone up north again; he's had another summons to do military service on the border. I pray it's not as wet there as it is here, for it will be miserable for him. Anyway, I'm glad you've come because I've had sad news from Anne. She lost the baby.'

'Oh, no,' Will replied, shocked. 'That's really sad. And here am I, complaining about my own woes.'

'My heart bleeds for her,' Katharine said, letting the ever-ready tears fall. 'But at least she has one son to console her.'

Will put his arms around her. 'She's done better than we have, Kate.'

She winced. 'Don't go there. I would give much to have a child, but God has seen fit to withhold that blessing.'

'You're not over the hill yet,' Will reminded her. 'There's still plenty of time.'

'I keep telling myself that. Anyway, enough of my woes. Will you stay for some supper?'

The relentless rain continued. Katharine missed John, but it was easier to practise her religion while he was away, and not have to follow the Catholic observances. He wrote that he was in good health, which was a miracle considering that he was cold and wet most of the time. He would be home in August, his tour of duty done. For Katharine, it was not a moment too soon. She fretted constantly about his continuing exposure to the dreadful weather.

Everywhere, even in the London markets, there was a dearth. The harvest had been ruined. By September, the rain had given way to unseasonably cold winds, so that it felt like winter. There had been no word from John for a while. Katharine had been looking for his return daily and was getting worried. He should be home by now.

When he walked through the door at the end of the first week of September, she could have wept with relief – until she saw his face. He looked grey and old, washed out – definitely not himself.

'Where have you been?' she cried, throwing her arms around him. 'I've been desperately worried.'

'The roads were flooded, lass,' he said wearily, 'and I couldn't get a letter to you. It would have taken as long as I did.' He coughed.

'You're ill,' she said, appalled. 'Sit down by the fire. I'll make you a hot posset.'

When she returned with it, he was coughing again. He sipped the drink gratefully, but refused the little cakes she had made against his hoped-for return. 'I'm not hungry, lass, but this is a fair warming drink. By God, it was biting cold up on the border.'

'It's been cold here too. Oh, it is good to have you home.'

'Aye, it's good to be home, Kate.' He sounded as drained as he looked.

'How long have you had this cough?' she asked anxiously.

'I was coughing a bit on the way up north. Then it got worse.'

'It must have been the weather. It's not good for anyone to be constantly exposed to rain and cold. A few days in the warm will work wonders for you.'

'Aye, lass,' John said, sipping the posset, then setting the cup on the hearth. 'How are things here?'

'Will has been granted a legal separation, John and Margaret are well – they will be home soon from the shops at Cheapside – and Anne's boy is thriving. She grows bored at Ewyas.'

'The sheep won't be as stimulating company as the courtiers,' he grinned.

187

'Did you stop at Snape?'

'Aye. Walter sends his duty to you.' He yawned.

'Would you like to rest before supper?' she asked, then realised that he had suddenly fallen asleep. Gently, she lifted his head and placed a cushion under it. She hated to see him so poorly. It had been foolish of him to make the long journey in his condition, but, she supposed, he had wanted to get home as much as she had longed to see him. Well, he was in the best place now. She would nurse him and get him well. She would start by making a herbal remedy for a cough. She left him snoring and went to her still room. Presently, she heard John and Margaret returning and hurried to greet them, warning them to delay welcoming their father until he had awoken from his nap.

The herbal remedy made no difference. John was still coughing three days later and feeling unwell. He was spending the mornings in bed and eating very little.

'Please try some pottage, for me,' Katharine pleaded.

'Stop fussing, woman,' he grunted, but he did take a few spoonfuls.

Margaret was upset to see her father so ill.

'You just have to give him time,' Katharine soothed her. 'He'll be better in a week or so.' To divert her stepdaughter, she ordered them both new gowns, her own of scarlet and Margaret's of yellow. At seventeen, Margaret was quite the young woman, fair and very slender, yet she had never lost her joyous outlook on life. She adored her father and was content to sit for hours reading to him as he sat in his chair by the fire.

Jack did not seem as worried. He was better behaved these days and helping to run the Latimer estates in the Midlands, so he was not often in London, but he was as self-centred as ever and Katharine feared that he was impatient to step into John's shoes. There had been some discussion about his residing at Snape to manage the northern lands, but of late he had resisted the idea. No, she thought, you want to be here when the moment comes. *Well, it will not. I will nurse your father back to health if it's the last thing I do!*

But, as the weeks went by, she began to feel less confident, and even found herself treating Jack with greater consideration, aware that he might soon be master here. No! She fended off the thought, yet it had to be faced: John was failing. As the bitter, frosty winter set in, his cough grew harsher and he began to lose weight. His grey complexion alarmed her, as did his terrible night sweats. This was no mere cough that was going to get better with physick and rest. It was something else, she realised with dread, something sinister.

It was John who sent for the physician. 'I know I'm not getting any better, lass,' he said, as he dragged himself out of bed on a snowy December morning.

'You should stay there and rest,' she urged.

'If I take to my bed, I'll never get out of it,' he muttered, pulling on his hose with immense effort.

'Don't say that!' she begged.

He ignored her. 'You'll be all right when I'm gone, lass, and Margaret. I've made my will.'

'You're not going anywhere,' she said briskly.

The doctor stood there in his long black gown and cap and held the bottle up to the weak light coming through the window. 'Hmm,' he said.

You don't really know what's wrong, Katharine thought, impatient with his humming and hawing.

He put his ear to John's breast, then took his pulse again.

'Do you have any pain in your chest?' he asked.

'Yes,' John answered.

'And have you coughed up any blood?'

'No.'

'That's good. Well, I will bleed you to balance the humours of the body. Then you should start to feel better.'

Katharine was a little dubious about the blood-letting, for John was in a weakened state already, but she bowed to the doctor's greater wisdom and the leeches were set to do their work.

Her visits to court had ceased. Her life had narrowed down to these four walls. All her hopes were focused on John. She loved him. It had never been a grand passion, but they enjoyed an easy relationship and he treated her as an equal, which she liked. If she lost him, she would be cast adrift, emotionally and physically, for she could not see herself being made welcome in Jack's household. There had been a truce between them, nothing more, and she knew that his respect for her was grudging. As for Margaret, she did not like to think of the impact John's death would have.

Snow fell daily and the ground underfoot was treacherous with ice or filthy with slush. The hard winter was having its effect. Katharine's servants made forays to buy food and other necessities and reported that there was barely any firewood to be had anywhere, while what few provisions were on sale were being sold at an extortionate price, especially the fish at Billingsgate market.

Will and Uncle William visited regularly, bringing news from a world that now felt so distant. The King of Scots was dead of a broken heart after being trounced by the English in battle at Solway Moss.

'Scotland is in chaos,' Uncle William related, eyeing John with concern. Katharine had told him that it was two weeks since the doctor had been, and that still there was no improvement. 'King James left only a daughter, born a week before. The Scots now have a little queen called Mary.'

'King Henry is jubilant,' Will said. 'Scotland can no longer pose a threat to England's security. Their nobles will be too busy fighting each other for power to make war on us. The Queen Regent will have all to do to control them.'

'I'd have fought at Solway Moss if I'd been on the marches,' John said.

'Thank God you weren't,' said Katharine.

'But it would have been good to be there at the victory,' he replied.

'Well, there won't be many opportunities for fighting now, unless we make war on the French,' Uncle William said.

After a night of being kept awake by John's coughing attacks, Katharine awoke to see blood on his pillow. Just a few spots, but enough to alarm her. She insisted on calling back the physician.

His face was grave after he had examined John. 'This is a consumption, I fear.'

'That's me done for,' John muttered. Katharine reached for his hand and squeezed it. She was trembling, aware of the implications of what the doctor had just said. John was dying. No amount of treatment could cure him.

'You must rest, my lord,' the doctor ordered. 'Conserve your strength. Eat a good diet.'

'He eats barely anything,' she said.

'Then he must have plenty to drink. Keep warm, Sir, and take what exercise you can. Walk around the room, but don't go out of doors as it is freezing.'

'How long have I got?' John asked.

There was a dreadful silence. 'Not long,' the doctor said. 'I am very sorry.'

Katharine fought back tears and went to put her arms around John, offering what comfort she could.

'Madam, I would advise you not to go too near your husband,' the physician warned. 'This disease is contagious. You should sleep in another room.'

'No!' she cried. It was cruel to deprive them both of the closeness they desperately needed at this time.

'It is for your own sake,' he insisted.

'Yes, Kate,' John said, in a surprisingly strong voice. 'I need you to be here for Margaret when I am gone.'

There was no answer to that. 'I wanted to give you comfort,' she said.

'It will be more of a comfort to me to know that Margaret will be looked after.'

It grieved her to have to keep her distance. If she or Margaret sat with John, reading to him, it had to be several feet away. Her laundress had to boil-wash the sheets and she herself cast the bloody rags John used as handkerchiefs into the fire.

Christmas was a dismal affair. She went to church, but could not pray, her mind was so disturbed. Jack was distant; she could not tell if he was mute with sorrow or shutting her out. Margaret, who had guessed the worst, went around red-eyed and wan.

Uncle William and Will joined them for Christmas dinner. Katharine and Margaret had gathered what evergreens they could to make the house look festive for what they were sure would be John's last Christmas, but in London there was little to be found. They had a great joint of beef, though, and a Christmas pie. John managed to sit at the head of the table in the parlour, a little apart from them all, and bade Jack stand up to carve the meat. But he could not stay at table long. After a few mouthfuls, he retired to rest.

Uncle William shook his grizzled head. He himself had aged these past months. 'You should prepare yourselves. He's not got long.'

Margaret looked as if she was going to cry. Uncle William noticed and changed the subject. 'I saw the Prince the other day,' he said. 'He's five now, and a proper little boy with good manners. He has been schooled well in behaviour.'

'He's fair, like his mother, but favours the King in looks, and he is forward for his age,' Will added. 'The King means to marry him to the Queen of Scots and unite the two kingdoms under English rule.'

'The Scots won't take that kindly,' Jack said, spearing another slice of beef on his knife.

Uncle William raised his napkin to his lips. 'They won't have much choice, not now that his Majesty has concluded a new alliance with the Emperor and plans to invade France, which is allied to Scotland. The French will have all to do to repel the joint forces of England and the Empire. They won't be able to come to Scotland's aid.'

Their talk washed over Katharine's head. Presently, she rose and went to check on John, who was asleep, his forehead glistening with perspiration. There were fresh streaks of blood on the pillow. She gazed at him for a long time, drinking in the sight of him, knowing that soon she would be able to look upon his face no more. She felt so helpless. Was there nothing anyone could do? Was it really God's will that they should part? How would she live without him?

Chapter 14

1543

In the third week of January, Will urged Katharine to visit him at court. Her first instinct was to say she could not leave John, but John himself insisted.

'You deserve a bit of life, lass,' he told her, sitting wrapped in furs by the fire, where he now spent his days. He had not been well enough to attend Parliament when it resumed a week ago, and he was eating barely enough to keep a bird alive. 'You go. I'll be all right. Margaret here is doing a grand job of entertaining me.' She had read aloud to him almost every book in the house.

'I'll get you some more books on my way home,' Katharine said. She felt guilty for being glad of the respite and for looking forward to visiting the court. She had been confined to this sad house for weeks now. It would do her good to have just a little break. She wasn't being selfish, surely?

Sitting in the boat that was taking her to Whitehall, she realised she had come to accept that John was not long for this world. She had been praying constantly for him, that his sufferings would be eased and his passing gentle.

She was worrying about what was to become of her. She was thirty, and there was a lot of life in her yet. She could always move to one of her dower properties, but she would be a stranger there. She doubted that her income would support her renting a house in London. And there was Margaret to think of . . .

The boat was nearing Greenwich. There stood the sprawling palace with the rolling heights of the hunting park behind it. She alighted at the stairs, paid the boatman and told the guard at the gatehouse that she was visiting Lord Parr.

Will's lodging overlooked a cobbled courtyard that was, as always, milling with people. When he opened the door to admit her, she saw that he was not alone. Two men, who had been sitting by the small fireplace, rose to greet her. One she recognised – it was the sombre, habitually black-clad figure of Edward Seymour, Earl of Hertford, brother to the late Queen Jane and uncle to the Prince. He made a small bow. 'Your servant, Madam.'

She turned to the other, taller man and barely stifled a gasp, for he was arrestingly good-looking with a stately bearing, lean features, heavy-lidded, twinkling eyes, close-cropped auburn hair and a luxuriant beard.

'Kate, may I present Lord Hertford's brother, Sir Thomas Seymour,' Will said. 'He is lately returned from an embassy to Nuremberg.'

Katharine felt herself blushing like a green girl. 'It's a pleasure to meet you, Sir Thomas,' she replied.

'The pleasure is all mine,' he replied, raising her hand and kissing it. As he did so, their eyes met and there was a sense of recognition. She felt as if she had been winded. She could not take her eyes from him.

He was every inch the courtier, a contrast to his brother in his scarlet and yellow attire.

'How is John?' Will asked. 'Lady Latimer's husband is very ill,' he told the Seymour brothers.

'He grows weaker by the day,' she said.

'I will pray for him,' Hertford said stiffly.

'Is there anything I can do?' Sir Thomas asked. The warmth in his eyes made her feel quite emotional.

'No, but it's very kind of you to offer.' She felt she should be saying something more weighty to express the gravity of John's malady, but she was finding it hard to collect her thoughts in the presence of this charming, beautiful man.

To her disappointment, the Seymour brothers soon made their excuses and left, so that she could talk to Will alone. Brother and sister settled by the fire and he gave her a goblet of the warm aleberry he had fetched earlier from the palace servery. She told him how John's strength was declining daily, and he said how sorry he was to hear it.

'I miss Anne,' she said. 'It would be good to have her support at this time. Jack is useless. He makes himself scarce most of the time and leaves the ordering of the house and the doctors to me. Margaret's very good with John, but she keeps bursting into tears. I fear I needed this short respite.'

'You are always welcome here,' Will told her.

'I liked Sir Thomas Seymour,' she said.

'All the ladies like Sir Thomas! And Sir Thomas likes Sir Thomas. He's full of himself.'

'He seemed very pleasant to me,' she said.

'You met him for five minutes, Kate! I serve with him in the privy chamber most days. He can turn on the charm at will, which is why he is popular. The King likes him too. But be warned. He is hardy, wise and liberal, and fierce in courage, but somewhat empty in matter. He acts without thinking and he burns with jealousy of his brother. There is no love lost between them. It galls Tom that he is the fourth son of his father and not the oldest.'

'Is he married?'

Will gave her a shrewd look. 'No. He's thirty-five and no woman has as yet managed to snare him. There was talk of his marrying Norfolk's daughter, the Duchess of Richmond, but that came to nothing. I've heard that he once took a mistress and ruined her reputation, but that was some time ago. He's ambitious. He'll be looking high for a bride.'

For a mad moment, Katharine looked ahead to when she would be free, a widow with something material to offer, and was shocked at herself. How could she be contemplating remarrying when her dearest John was still alive?

To her amazement, Sir Thomas was waiting for her when she left Will's lodging and emerged into the courtyard.

'My Lady Latimer!' he said, bowing flamboyantly. 'I felt I had not sufficiently expressed my concern for your poor husband.'

She was much taken aback. 'That's very kind,' she faltered, aware of how near to her he was standing. She could smell the new leather of his boots.

'Will you walk with me?' he asked.

'I should go home,' she said, desperately wanting to stay, yet knowing that a lady should never appear too eager for a man's company.

'Of course. But shall we have a stroll in the gardens first?'

She was unable to resist. 'Very well, a short stroll to the jetty.' He offered her his arm and she took it, thrilling at the physical contact. No man had ever made her feel like this.

As they walked along the gravelled paths that led between bare railed flower beds with green-and-white striped poles at each corner, she told him about John's illness.

'I am sick with dread with every day that dawns, thinking it will be his last,' she confided, thinking how easy it was to talk to this handsome stranger. 'That is why I must leave soon.'

'That is a pity, but I understand,' he told her. 'I do hope that I may have the pleasure of your company again, Lady Latimer.'

'I don't know when that will be,' she said, envisaging death, mourning and seclusion.

'I am always at your service.' They had reached the landing stage, where he kissed her hand and bowed.

As she sat in the boat, huddled in her cloak, and watched his tall, elegant figure recede into the distance, her mind was in turmoil and her heart racing.

The next morning, when she went in to see John, he was lying in the tester bed looking drained of colour.

'I think I will spend the day here, lass,' he said feebly, coughing and wheezing badly. As she helped him to sit up, plumping his pillows, she noticed how painfully thin he was.

'Should I send for the doctor?' she asked.

'Nay, Kate. There's nothing he can do. I'll just have a quiet doze.'

She left him and sat down to her correspondence, rising to check on him every so often. Looking on his gaunt, sleeping face, she felt guilt for being attracted to Thomas Seymour, and resolved not to think of him. Her husband deserved her whole attention.

At half past eleven, she carried in a dish of very costly fish in a white sauce the cook had prepared. John managed six mouthfuls of it, then laid down the spoon wearily. She fed him four more.

'You've done well.' She smiled and wiped his mouth with a napkin. She went to the court cupboard to fetch some ale, but he had fallen asleep by the time she returned. She ate her own dinner with Margaret in the parlour. When Margaret said she would sit with her father and read to herself, Katharine grabbed the opportunity of taking a short nap.

Loud raps on the front door woke her. It was near dark outside. She must have slept for hours. Disorientated, she sat up straight, smoothed her hair and adjusted her hood, just in time for Gregory, their London steward, to announce the arrival of Sir Thomas Seymour.

She was instantly awake. Goodness, he was bold to pursue her like this! She heard his voice booming magnificently in the hall, and then he was striding into the parlour, filling up the room with his brilliance.

'Sir Thomas, what a lovely surprise,' she greeted him.

'Lady Latimer, forgive the intrusion, but I had to come. A friend in the privy chamber recommended this physick for your husband.' He held out a small bottle. 'He swears by it for coughs.'

Katharine took the bottle, her eyes meeting his. There was no mistaking what they read there.

'Thank you, Sir Thomas. How very kind.'

She bade him sit down and called for wine and cakes. Then she looked briefly in on John and rejoined her visitor.

'I will give him your medicine later,' she said. 'He is sleeping now.'

They talked. The conversation flowed. He told her about his childhood at his family home, Wulfhall, in Wiltshire, and about his late father and his loving mother and his many brothers and sisters.

'We were all cock-a-hoop when Jane married the King. We've never looked back since. It was the beginning of our family's greatness.'

She had realised by now that he had a tendency to brag. He had already told her that he had a fine reputation as a jouster. Listening to him, it sounded as if he was one of the most debonair gallants at court.

But he was good-natured and lively company, and clearly interested in her. She told him about her own life, the halcyon days at Rye House, her marriages and the Pilgrimage of Grace. His eyebrows rose in admiration when she told him how she had coped with the rebels.

'It's a wonder the experience hasn't made you hot for reform,' he grinned.

'Well, I do lean that way,' she admitted with a smile.

'So do I. You'll have heard that the Seymours are of the gospelling persuasion, especially my brother.' There was a faint sneer in his voice as he said the word. 'Martin Luther has nothing on him! Not that Ned would sanction heresy,' he added quickly.

As they talked and she learned more about Thomas, she discovered that he was well educated and well off, for many rewards and preferments had come his way. He had been at court since his youth and, later on, had served on various diplomatic embassies abroad. But his real passion was for the sea. He was clearly a man of action who found it hard to be confined within four walls. He had sailed the Channel with the King's fleet, patrolling it lest the French dare attempt a raid. She sensed that he would have loved it if they had. Yes, he was dashing, but he seemed also to be honest, witty and kind – and he wrote poetry. Bad poetry, he'd said, chuckling.

'I wonder why I have not seen you around the court,' she said.

'I've been at the French and Imperial courts for most of the last five years. But I did take part in the jousts at Whitehall a couple of years ago. Were you there?'

She recalled sitting in the stands with John – he had been in health then, she recalled with a pang. 'Yes.'

'I was the defender in white velvet.'

'Of course!' She remembered thinking how magnificent he looked. He had had his visor down, so she wouldn't have known who he was. 'Your side won.'

'Naturally!' He was irrepressible.

'Tell me about your work abroad,' she asked.

'Where do I start?' he grinned, his eyes raking her. 'I was in Vienna for some time, although I doubt you'd want to hear about Hungary's defences against the Turks! I came back via Nuremberg, recruiting mercenaries for the King on my way, although I had to let them go in the end because his Majesty thought their price too dear.' He grimaced. 'Nuremberg is a beautiful city. I spent Christmas there.'

'I suppose you will have another mission soon,' Katharine said, realising with a shock that she felt sad at the prospect of his being away.

'The King is always finding ways of keeping me out of mischief!'

There was a tap on the door. It was Adam, the cook.

'Madam, are you ready for me to serve supper?'

'Oh, goodness, is it that time already?' she cried, realising that she had sat here alone with Thomas Seymour for far longer than was seemly – and she had forgotten to look in on John for some time. Guilt washed over her. And yet, for the last couple of hours, she had felt more alive than she had in years – or ever, perhaps.

She stood up. 'I must go to my husband. Sir Thomas, would you do me the honour of staying to supper?' She stole a furtive glance at the waiting Adam to see if she could detect any hint of disapproval, but his face remained impassive.

'Thank you,' Thomas said. 'The honour will be all mine.'

'It will be poor fare,' she warned him, 'but excellently prepared.' She smiled at Adam. 'This dearth is affecting everyone. Even the Lord Mayor is restricting himself to one course at each meal.'

'I will be grateful for the smallest morsel,' he grinned.

John was sleeping when she crept into his bedchamber. He looked so ill. In her heart, she had already been unfaithful to him, but he would never know that. And she had her future to think of. She loved him, but he was leaving her. She wished with all her might that it could have been otherwise. She would never have entertained taking a lover.

All through dinner, which they ate with Jack and Margaret in the parlour, with hailstones rattling on the windows, her mind was working furiously. She knew she was not mistaken. There was a tangible attraction between her and Thomas. She could not stop looking at him, he was so beautiful. He drew her in with his wit and his warmth and his physical presence. What must it be like to be bedded by such a man?

She kept catching him looking at her. Was his interest purely amorous? She could believe that. He could never have lacked for female company, which was possibly all he sought from women. Did the idea of seducing her pique his fancy? He might think her desperate for the sensual pleasures her husband could no longer give her. Or did he anticipate that she would soon be a rich widow? If so, he was going to be disappointed. John would be leaving her comfortably off, but by no means wealthy enough to attract a fortune-hunter. Yet, somehow, she could not believe that Thomas was just after her money.

If she were free, they would be well matched. He was just five years her senior; they came from similar backgrounds; both were drawn to the court – and there was this powerful enchantment between them. She was sure he felt the same. Was this love, the love of which the poets wrote, the kind of love that had made King Henry turn the world upside down so that he could have Anne Boleyn?

She pulled herself up. It was ridiculous to be fantasising about love and marriage when she hardly knew the man – and it was wrong, with her husband yet living. She banished such thoughts from her mind and joined in the conversation.

When Thomas took his leave, he kissed her hand. 'May I call again?' he asked.

She thought of what John's children might think, and the servants.

'If my lord remains stable, I may visit my brother at court this Saturday afternoon. You would be welcome to join us at his lodging, I'm sure, at about three o'clock. If I'm not there, you will know that it is because my husband is poorly.'

She had made the right response, she was sure. Not too eager. Circumspect, but accommodating. And, if Will was present when she and Thomas next met, there could be no impropriety.

'I will be there,' he said, and disappeared into the snow.

Over the following days, she agonised over whether she should be encouraging Thomas's friendship. The angel on one shoulder told her she should not, but the devil on the other assured her that it could do no harm. Her conscience told her that it was wrong to put personal inclination before moral duty. Oh, God, was that what John had become, a moral duty? No, she loved him – except she had never wanted him as she wanted Thomas.

She went to court. She told herself there was no reason why she should not visit her brother. Margaret was keeping John company.

Thomas was at Will's lodging before her. He rose quickly and bowed as her brother greeted her. The conversation was animated and Will was liberal with the wine. Dorothy Bray joined them and soon they were very merry. And, all the while, Thomas's avid eyes were on her as he sought continually to draw her on her opinions. It was clear that he was interested in her for herself, as well as for her modest charms.

When Thomas disappeared into the privy, Will turned to her, his face flushed from drinking. 'He likes you, Kate. It's wise to keep in with the Seymours. When the Prince is king, they will be in power. You could do a lot worse.'

'Will!' Katharine and Dorothy chorused. Dorothy slapped him lightly. 'You are incorrigible! In a breath, you have committed treason and encouraged adultery.'

Will's flush deepened. 'Sorry. I did not mean it to sound like that. But, Kate, if you play your cards aright . . .'

'She doesn't need to play any cards! He's hot for her. But he can't say anything because her husband still lives.'

'What could he say?' Katharine asked. 'We've known each other for such a short time.'

'Many marriages have been made in less,' Will told her.

'I am not sure he is thinking in terms of marriage.'

He smiled. 'Oh, I think he is.'

They fell silent as Thomas rejoined them. 'Was it something I said?' he joked.

She left before he did. She did not want to go, but it was unwise to appear too eager. She walked through the frosted palace gardens, hugging her secret happiness to her. Will thought Thomas's intentions were serious, and that was all she needed to know. She could wait. John must come first while he needed her.

Somehow, she got lost among the box hedges and the brick walls.

She had taken a wrong turning. She found a gap in a hedge and pushed her way through, to find herself in a beautiful knot garden like a cloister garth with a covered walkway along two sides. Gilded heraldic beasts on striped posts stood sentinel over the formal flower beds. There was a little square stone pleasure house in the far corner. Someone was sitting in it. She could hear sobbing.

She ought not to be here, intruding on this very private moment. She turned back to the gap in the hedge. As she bent to go through it, she stepped on a twig. Crack!

The person in the pleasure house rose and stepped out. She would have recognised that mighty figure anywhere.

'My Lady Latimer?' the King said, looking as appalled as she felt.

'Your Majesty, forgive me! I got lost and there was this gap in the hedge . . .' She sank belatedly into a curtsey, trembling. 'I beg your pardon for the intrusion.'

'No matter,' he said, his voice hoarse. 'I was praying for something to lighten my mood, and here you are. A serendipitous coincidence. Rise, please.'

She sagged with relief and nearly fell over, recovering her balance just in time. 'I am glad to have been inadvertently of service. I will leave your Majesty in peace now.'

'No, don't go,' he said. When she dared to glance at his face, she saw that it was ravaged with age and sadness. He looked even older than he had when she had last seen him, when he had feasted her and the other ladies. 'Stay a while and comfort a lonely old man.'

She had thought him cruel and his charm superficial. Now, seeing him broken before her, she could only feel compassion – and astonishment that he was still mourning his little Queen.

'How can I be of service, Sir?' she asked.

'You can keep me company for a space,' he said and, to her amazement, he took her hand and led her to the pleasure house. It had plush bench seats around the walls and a table, on which stood a silver ewer and a wine glass of Venetian work. A small brazier glowed in a gap between the benches.

'Be seated, pray,' the King invited, and sat down heavily opposite. 'I like to come here when I have leisure and enjoy some private time, because I am rarely alone otherwise. Would you like some wine?'

She accepted the glass reluctantly, aware that she had already had a lot to drink. But the muzzy feeling seemed to have been banished by this strange encounter.

'I trust you are well, my lady,' he said. 'I miss seeing your sister at court, but your brother is always good company, and your uncle is one of the best men I have ever met.'

She smiled. 'I am well, Sir, but my lord is not long for this world. That is why I have hardly been at court.'

'I am sorry,' the King said mournfully. 'Death gathers all those we cherish. If you love, you invite pain.'

'I would rather know pain than never know love,' she said.

He drew a deep breath and wiped away a tear with a massive hand laden with rings. 'It is a year today,' he said, 'and I cannot forget her.'

'Time will heal you, Sir.'

'Forgive me,' he said. 'Sometimes, I think I will go mad. Half of me hates her for betraying me; the other half just wants her, desperately. I'm sorry, Madam, I should not be troubling you with my woes.' He made an effort to smile.

'It is no trouble at all, Sir,' Katharine assured him, thinking that this was all rather unreal. And then, probably because of the wine in her, she did something extraordinary. She reached across and pressed her hand on his. 'You *will* feel better. Just give yourself time.'

He did not withdraw his hand, but sat there gazing at her with those intense blue eyes. 'You're a good woman, Lady Latimer, and a comely one too. If I were ten years younger, I'd have been pursuing you. Alas, what would you see in me now?' He gave her a rueful grin.

'I see a very sad man who needs cheering up,' she replied, withdrawing her hand.

'And will you be the one to do it?' he asked, grasping it back.

'I think, Sir, that you have the strength of mind to do it yourself. It must be very lonely sometimes, having to make impossible decisions that you know will affect you adversely. Your Grace should find comfort in knowing that you did what you thought was right.'

He sighed. 'She committed treason and endangered the succession. Worst of all, she betrayed me. But I would not have executed her had it been left to me. I was persuaded that she should die, told that I could not show leniency when others had suffered death for less, that I could not let my personal feelings sway me; that would have been to show weakness, and a king must always be strong. So I was strong. But it does not stop me from having regrets.'

She was stunned. She had thought him the kind of man who never had regrets, still less expressed them. That he should be sitting here, confiding his inmost thoughts to her, was extraordinary. It was even more extraordinary that she was beginning to see things from his point of view.

'I am so sorry that your Grace was plunged into that terrible dilemma, and one not of your own making. I saw you with the Queen. It was easy to perceive how much you loved her. She did a terrible thing when she betrayed that love. It beggars belief.'

'My fool says she asked for what happened to her.'

'Your fool?'

He smiled. 'Yes, Will Somers. He knows all the secrets of my heart. He doesn't mince words with me. He keeps me grounded.'

Jesters, she knew, could get away with much that would have brought down wrath upon others.

'I do not like being a widower, Lady Latimer,' Henry said. 'Being married feels to me a natural state for a man. It has been God's will that I should suffer so many mishaps in my marriages – and there were others to blame, of course. For all that, I am still convinced that, one day, I will find true happiness in wedlock with a lady who will love me and not have it in her to betray me. Someone like my Jane.' His face clouded over briefly. 'And I will choose her myself, not take someone pushed into my path by the factions that blight my court.'

Remembering what Lady Suffolk had said about women not exactly queuing up to be queen, Katharine chose her words very carefully. 'Your Grace is deserving of such a rare person. I pray that you will find her.'

'It will not be easy.' He gave her a grim smile. 'I will take no one who does not support my religious policies: no stiff Catholics nor anyone who has drifted too far towards heresy.' Her heart missed a beat at that. 'But,' the King went on, 'I am not averse to a good theological debate, although few women are learned enough to take part, and some are too opinionated.'

He paused, frowning a little. Katharine suspected he might be thinking of the first Queen Anne; she doubted that any of the wives who had followed her would have been able, or sufficiently interested, to debate religious issues. Given the parameters he had imposed, he was looking for a paragon.

'Do godly matters interest you, Lady Latimer?' the King asked.

She froze. But it was probably just a polite question. She had been so careful. How could he know anything about her great secret?

'I do enjoy a friendly argument,' she said.

'And you like to discuss religious doctrine?' Was there a reason for his probing? Please God, surely he was not thinking . . .

'I do when I wish to have a point clarified to me,' she said, gathering her wits. 'I am a great advocate of your Majesty's reforms. I admire you for breaking with the Pope. He is a greater persecutor of all true Christians than ever the Pharaoh of the Children of Israel was.'

The King was staring at her in open admiration. 'By God, my lady, you have the sow by the right ear!'

She relaxed. He could have no doubts about her now.

She realised she had grown cold; the coals on the brazier had burned to embers. She shivered. Dusk had long since fallen and she ought to get home.

'Your Grace, by your leave, I should return to my husband.'

'Of course,' he said, clambering awkwardly to his feet, as she hurriedly rose too. 'Such wifely devotion is commendable.' He raised her hand to his lips and kissed it. 'It has been a physick to me, talking to you. I hope I may have the pleasure again soon.' His blue eyes had taken on a sudden warmth.

'It will be *my* pleasure, Sir. I'm glad that I was able to help.'

He gave her directions to the jetty and she slipped through the hedge, then hurried to the boat. As she sat, her teeth chattering, being rowed to Blackfriars Stairs, she reflected on what a remarkable afternoon it had been. First, Thomas's growing interest in her, and then that remarkable meeting with the King. Her heart was pounding, her thoughts racing. Thomas wanted her enough to marry her! It was love that was flourishing between them; she did not need even to wonder about that. And the King had shown her extraordinary favour, which augured well for the future. If things went awry after John died, she sensed that she would have a friend and protector in him.

Chapter 15

1543

She was losing John. He lay listlessly, hating to be handled by anyone other than her, so it was she who performed the intimate tasks that kept him clean and comfortable, she who fed him mashed morsels with a spoon and held a cup to his parched lips. He could no longer concentrate on the books Margaret read him, but would stare unseeing at the window. There was life in his cough, though. It racked his wasted body and left him convulsed.

'Will he die soon?' Margaret whispered nervously, as she met Katharine on the landing outside John's bedchamber.

'I think so.' Katharine embraced her. 'You must be glad for him. He is going to God. And I will be here for you.'

'My lady!' The steward's voice floated up the stairs. 'Sir Thomas Seymour is here to see you.'

She flushed. She had told him not to come! But she suspected that he rarely did as he was told.

'Please sit with your father a little longer,' she bade Margaret. She had been about to take over that duty.

Still wearing her apron, she hurried downstairs and found Thomas waiting in the hall, doffing a hat with a large, showy feather.

'Sir Thomas, welcome. I fear you find me at a disadvantage.'

'It does not matter,' he said, kissing her hand for just a few dizzying moments too long. 'I just wanted to see you and assure myself that you are in health.'

'I am, I thank you, but my husband is not. I fear he will not see out the week.' Tears welled, which she fought back.

Thomas took her hand. 'I am so very sorry,' he said, his booming voice now gentle. 'I should not have intruded. But, if there is anything I can do, just say the word.'

She looked into his eyes, which were filled with kindness, and knew that she loved him, that she would never love anyone else in this way. She knew now that love *could* be sudden and overwhelming – and be none the less for that. She longed to be in his arms, to lay her face against that brushed leather jerkin and be comforted. She was sick of having to stay strong for those who depended on her.

'Would you like to sit down?' he asked.

'I should get back to my lord,' she protested, with some reluctance.

'There is something I would like to say to you,' he said. 'I will not keep you long.'

She felt the heat flooding her cheeks. What could he have to say to her?

'Come through,' she said, walking ahead into the parlour, hoping he could not sense the excitement coursing through her. What a wicked woman she was, feeling like this when her poor husband was dying upstairs!

She turned suddenly to tell him to go, but her body collided with his and all at once she was in his arms and he was kissing her, and every moral and social consideration flew out of the window.

'My dear lady!' he murmured, releasing her lips at length. 'Oh, my lady. I know it, you feel the same!'

She could not speak. This was happening to her, staid, dutiful Katharine Parr, who had never dreamed of looking at a man outside wedlock.

'I knew!' he said, gazing down at her jubilantly. 'I knew when I first saw you that you were special and that I wanted you.'

'I knew it too,' she breathed. 'I have thought of you constantly since. But, Thomas, this is wrong. I cannot betray my lord.' She broke away.

'He is dying,' he said, taking her hand. 'And you will be a widow soon.'

'I am not a widow yet.'

'All I want from you is an understanding,' he pleaded. 'I will not ask you formally now, but if I can hope . . .'

She hesitated only for a moment. How could she resist him? He was offering her everything she wanted – and the assurance of a happy future.

'Yes, you may hope,' she said, wondering how it was possible to feel such joy at a time of great sadness.

In the middle of February, a messenger in the royal livery arrived at the house.

'These are from the King's Majesty. I am commanded to present them to my Lady Latimer,' Katharine heard him say as she hurried down to the hall from John's bedchamber, where she had seen the man's approach from the window.

It was a large, heavy parcel, wrapped in silk tissue, valuable in itself. What was this, and why had it been sent to her?

She had to help the steward carry it to the hall table. When she pulled apart the layers of tissue, she gasped. Inside lay a pile of the most exquisite garments. There were four fabulous gowns in the French, Venetian and Dutch styles, in plush velvets and damasks, as well as sleeves, buckram underskirts and even generous lengths of the finest linen for making smocks. She shook them out, one by one, speechless, as Margaret danced around her, crying, 'Oh, look!' and 'How wonderful!'

In the end, Katharine had to sit down. She stared at all the finery spread over the table and tried to collect her thoughts. No gentleman sent such gifts to a lady unless he had serious intentions towards her or was bent on seduction. And no lady accepted them if she valued her honour. But then she saw the letter that had dropped to the floor. She stooped to retrieve it and broke the seal bearing the lions and lilies of England. He had written: *My Lady Latimer, please accept these tokens of my gratitude for your kindness to me. I am greatly indebted to you. This world now seems to me a better place, containing as it does a lady filled with such goodness as you are. I trust that we shall meet again very soon. You know where to find me. Your brother can tell me when you are coming and, if you wish, he may be present. Your servant, Henry R.*

She caught her breath. This was not a man bent on seduction. And his mention of Will being present rang a bell. It was something Anne had said, long ago. Yes, she remembered now. Her sister had told her that, when the King had been courting Jane Seymour, he had visited her in the presence of her relatives to protect her reputation.

Merciful God! He was not seriously thinking of pursuing her with a view to marriage? Her heart was Thomas's, given already, and they had that understanding between them. And she had a husband in bed upstairs!

This could not be happening. She liked the King, but marrying him? No. She could not, ever. He was too old, too fat, too unwell, too terrifyingly powerful. Imagining going to bed with him was impossible. And he had been married five times already. He had beheaded two wives, divorced two others and lost one in childbed – not to mention all the suffering that had been inflicted on those five unfortunate souls. Maybe some had deserved what they got, but Katharine had learned enough of court politics now to know that there were factions poised to bring down a queen they disapproved of and shove another in her place. And she herself was already vulnerable because of her secret beliefs – and her secret love. How could she keep these things hidden in palaces where nothing stayed concealed for long and in which the very walls had ears?

She could sit still no longer, she was so agitated. She stood up and fingered the gorgeous gowns – gowns fit for a queen. Dare she return them? No, she could not. It would be a grave insult, implying that the King's motives were less than honourable.

With Margaret helping, she carried the clothes to her bedchamber and laid them carefully in the chest at the foot of the bed. She could not wear them, not with John so ill, and soon she would be in mourning. If ever the time came that she needed a gown for the court . . . But she knew what that would mean. It would convey a coded message to the King. These gowns were intended to be worn at court, and by a woman marked for queenship.

She would not respond to his Grace's invitation. She would not meet with him again. She would behave as if the gift was purely a token of gratitude.

But then, a week later, Will turned up, out of breath and very excited. 'The King is asking for you, Kate! I am to bring you to the royal library after dinner. Make haste, put on your best gown.'

'Will!' she cried, appalled. 'Stop there.'

'No, Kate, you stop there.' They stared at each other. It was the first time they had raised their voices to each other since childhood. 'The King is interested in you. I don't know how this came about, but he has been praising you to the skies. I've not seen him so animated since he was with the last Queen. You must capitalise on this.'

'How can you be so mercenary?' she cried. 'He has showed me favour, that is all. I entered his garden by mistake. We talked. He has sent me gifts, tokens of esteem.' She showed Will the letter.

'By God!' Will exclaimed. 'I do believe his intentions are serious.'

'But he hardly knows me.'

'He has heard a lot about you from Uncle William and me. And, when he wants something, he goes the whole way. He made up his mind very quickly about Katheryn Howard.'

'Will, stop! Listen,' she pleaded. 'I do not want to marry him. I do not want to be his mistress.' She paused, debating with herself whether she should tell him the truth, aware that she wanted to proclaim it to the whole world. She took a deep breath. 'I am in love with Sir Thomas Seymour and we have an understanding that we will marry in the future.'

'What?' Will sank down on the bench, shaking his head. 'Tom Seymour? He's a dark horse! And you? You kept this quiet.'

'That is because John, who I love and respect, still lives. But my heart is set. You encouraged it, remember? "It's wise to keep in with the Seymours." You must accept my decision.'

Will stared at her as if she had taken leave of her senses. 'Kate, listen to me. A match with the Seymours would indeed have been advantageous – but this is the King! You could be a queen. Just think of the benefits that would come to our family – and to the cause of reform!'

'No,' she said. 'I will not even contemplate it.'

'You're mad!' he said, shaking his head again.

'No. I do not want to be queen. And we are doing nicely enough. I know the King hasn't granted you the earldom of Essex yet, but I am sure he will, in time.'

'I doubt it, if you refuse him.' Will's tone was bitter. 'What am I going to tell him? He's expecting you at two o'clock.'

She stood up. 'I shall go, never fear. I shall be charming and witty company. But I will make it clear that it is to be friendship only. What else could it be, since I have a husband living?'

She dressed carefully, in a black damask gown with a crimson underskirt, one of those sent her by the King, and a new French hood trimmed with garnets. She and Will said nothing as they sat in the boat, wrapped in furs against the late-February cold. At the palace, he led her to the King's lodgings, through the great watching chamber and the presence chamber, where he bowed to the empty throne, and to the privy chamber beyond. Guards raised their halberds as they passed. One greeted Will cheerily.

Katharine had had in her head a vague image of the privy chamber as a large room. In fact, it comprised a warren of them, mostly small closets.

'The King likes his privacy,' Will explained, breaking the silence, 'and he likes to be warm.'

He led Katharine through a door that led to a larger chamber with a gilded and battened ceiling, furnished with desks and lecterns, the shelves underneath piled with books. The King, looking splendid in green velvet and hatless, his greying hair cropped close to his head, was sitting at a desk at the far end, an open volume before him in which he was writing marginal notes. He put his pen in the inkwell and rose to greet her.

'My Lady Latimer!' He limped towards her with hands outstretched and she sank into a deep curtsey. When he bade her rise, she saw that Will had gone.

'Your Majesty, this is a great honour,' she said.

'The honour is mine,' he said. 'I have been looking forward to seeing you again, and methought we should meet somewhere warmer. This is my library.'

She had never seen so many books.

'Sir,' she said, a little breathlessly, 'I should like to thank you for your wonderful gifts. They seem so great a reward for so small a service.'

'Not at all,' he said, beaming at her. 'You helped me to turn a corner. That was the more precious gift, for which I can never thank you sufficiently. Now . . .' He waved a hand in the direction of the desks. 'I know you enjoy reading, and I thought you might like to see some of my treasures here.'

For the next half-hour, he showed her exquisitely illuminated manuscripts and printed books, many of them from France and Italy. All were bound in velvet or gilded leather and embossed with the royal arms. He had scrawled notes and questions in many of the margins, revealing how deeply he thought about the contents.

'These are Froissart's chronicles,' he said, picking up a large tome. 'I inherited it from my grandmother.'

The library was a treasure house. Forgetting her reluctance to be here, Katharine leafed avidly through the volumes he handed her: Bibles and devotional books, works by the Church Fathers and the classical authors of Greece and Rome, and books of romance and chivalry.

'Have you read Aristotle?' the King asked eagerly.

'I have, Sir, but I prefer Cicero,' Katharine said, picking up one of her favourites.

'Ah! The great republican! There is much to admire about him. But Aristotle is without peer as a philosopher. He was a true polymath.'

'I must bow to your Majesty's greater wisdom.'

'I am impressed by your breadth of knowledge,' he said, turning to look at her appreciatively.

'My mother was determined that I should be well educated,' she told him. 'I owe her a lot. She did not subscribe to the old-fashioned view that literate women would waste their skill writing love letters.'

'Your mother was a wise woman,' he observed. 'I always admired her. I had both my daughters educated and have never regretted it.'

More relaxed with him now, and relieved that he was not trying to show her any more than friendship, she walked over to a large table by the wall on which piles of manuscripts were heaped untidily. 'What are these, Sir?'

'They have come from the monasteries,' he told her. 'I wish to preserve our ancient learning.' A lot had been destroyed, she had heard. She wondered now if it was true.

'Are all the monasteries closed now, Sir?' she ventured.

'Yes, all. Their lands are in the possession of those who uphold my reforms. There has been much support for the Dissolution.' He sighed. 'Yet there are some who would push me too far. I will *never* tolerate Lutheranism in my realm. Mine is, and always will be, a Catholic church. The gospellers want the Mass in English, but I am determined that it will stay in Latin. They also think I should permit the clergy to wed, but I will not brook that. And those who deny the Real Presence of Christ in the Mass are just plain heretics.'

She felt a frisson of fear, although she could not think that he had any reason to suspect her. She was dismayed that he seemed to be harking back towards Roman practices. Like all good reformers, she too had been praying that he would promulgate more radical policies.

She resolved not to answer a meek yes to everything he said. There was more to her than that, and he should know it. But she diplomatically chose to contest the least controversial of the issues he had raised. 'Sir, might I ask why the clergy should be celibate? I have always thought it unnatural for people to deny themselves the comforts of marriage. And a married priest could perhaps better understand the concerns of his parishioners.'

The King's eyes lit up. This was his *métier*. 'My lady, they emulate our Lord, who never married. As He said, they have freely renounced marriage for the sake of the Kingdom of Heaven. They consecrate themselves to God with an undivided heart. No one forces them to be ordained. It is voluntary.'

'Yet many more might answer that calling if they were not required to give up the flesh.'

'Quite so, my lady. But one might argue that they do not have a perfect vocation.'

They talked on, and she realised that she was enjoying his company.

It irked her a little that he always had to be right, but that was natural, she supposed. Not only was he the King, and constantly deferred to, but his knowledge was breathtaking. His learning far exceeded hers.

Dusk was falling. She had been watching the ornate clock on his desk.

'Do you need to go, my lady?' he asked.

'I hate to break up such an enjoyable visit, Sir, but I do not like to leave my lord for long. I do not think he is long for this world.'

The King rose stiffly to his feet. 'Then you must go to him. And I shall hope to see you again soon.' He took her hand and kissed it. There was a warmth in his eyes that alarmed her.

She curtseyed and left, then sped to Will's lodging, needing to talk to someone. He gaped at her in astonishment as she burst in.

'I cannot see him again,' she declared. 'To do so would be to encourage him and give him hope, where no hope can be.'

'Has he behaved improperly to you?' Will asked.

'Not at all. He was friendly and kind and interested. But he wants to see me again, and I don't want him to fall for me.'

To her annoyance, Will was looking pleased. 'Kate, think about it. He is doing everything honourably. His intentions are serious. He wants to make you queen!'

Before she could round on him, a voice boomed behind her. 'What?'

'Sir Thomas!' She stared at him as he stood framed in the open doorway.

'Is it true?' he demanded, his dark eyes blazing. 'The King is pursuing you?'

'I fear so,' she said, thinking how wonderful it was that he had arrived at this very moment. 'And I am trying to tell my brother here that I am not interested.'

'She says she has an understanding with you,' Will growled.

Thomas slammed down the pack of cards he had been carrying on the table. 'She does indeed, although we will not be discussing it further until Lord Latimer has been called to his reward.'

'You would not stand in the way of her marrying the King, surely?' Will flared.

Thomas shrugged. 'If she tells me that is what she wants, I will withdraw my suit. A widow is free to make her own choice. And she has made it plain what that choice is, so I suggest you respect it.'

Will looked fit to boil. 'This is not just about Katharine's personal wishes. It affects our whole family.'

'So I am to be just a stepping stone to your preferment?' Katharine asked. 'You're doing very nicely without me. You've reached the privy chamber; you have the King's ear; you are in line for an earldom. What more can you want? As for the rest of the family, they seem content with their lot.'

'Uncle William thinks you should marry the King.'

'He is entitled to his opinion, but this touches *me* closest of all. *I* will decide my future – and it lies with Sir Thomas here.' She reached out her hand to him and he grasped it firmly. 'And now I really must go,' she said. 'John needs me.'

'I'll walk you to the boat,' Thomas offered, still keeping hold of her hand.

'Farewell, brother,' Katharine said. 'I hope that when we next meet you are in a more understanding frame of mind. And Thomas, know this: I will never vary in my feelings for you.'

As she approached Charterhouse Square, she was lost in thoughts of what Thomas had said to her as they hastened through the torchlit palace gardens. He meant to wed her. He loved her. Her heart was still singing. Then she saw that the door was open and the steward was standing there, holding a lantern.

'My lady!' he called. 'Thank God you've come. My lord has taken a bad turn. I took the liberty of summoning the priest from St Anne's.'

She flew upstairs. The priest was there, kneeling by the bed, praying. She looked at John. He was leaning sideways on the pillow, eyes closed, mouth open, which was how he usually slept these days. As always, she watched to see if he was breathing, and saw his shoulder rise and fall. Then he moved no more. She would always believe that he had waited for her.

* * *

216

The next days passed in a blur. She had all to do to comfort Margaret and the servants. That she was free at last meant little when balanced against the weight of guilt she now carried for having so blithely encouraged Thomas and made plans for her widowhood.

John had wished to be buried in his beloved Yorkshire, but the cost of conveying his body there was dear. Jack decided that his father should be buried in St Paul's Cathedral, where he had attended Mass frequently, and which was fittingly grand. The funeral, which took place on a cold day in early March, seemed to take place in a dream.

Afterwards, clad in widow's black for the second time in her life, and wearing a nun-like wimple with a chin barbe instead of her usual headdress, Katharine sat in the parlour with Jack and Margaret as John's lawyer read his will. Everything went to Jack, the new Lord Latimer, who was twenty-three now, well into man's estate. Katharine was to be eighteen-year-old Margaret's guardian, with the incomes from Stowe and other manors near York to support them until Margaret came of age at twenty-one.

John had bequeathed Katharine his best silver basin and ewer, two fine silver flagons and his New Testament, which she knew she would treasure always. She had been left comfortably off, with properties of her own and a good income. She was glad to be bringing so much to her marriage to Thomas. But she should not think about that now. She must wait a decent year. It was enough to know that he loved her and was waiting for her.

Jack surprised her. 'I am moving up to Snape,' he told her. 'It was tainted for my father by what happened there, but we Nevilles belong in the north. You are most welcome to stay on here, if you wish.' It was uncharacteristically kind of him and evidence that, deep down, he did respect her, and perhaps feel gratitude to her for having been a good stepmother, despite the difficulties he had created.

She stayed. She could have gone to live in one of her manor houses, but she wanted to be in London, near to the court, so that she could see Thomas once a respectable interval had elapsed.

Will ended up spending more time at Charterhouse Square than he did at court. He had come hastening to condole with her after John's death and their quarrel had been forgotten. By unspoken mutual agreement, they did not mention the King or Thomas.

Needing company, for she missed John more than she had anticipated, she took to hosting small gatherings at her house, serving good food and wine and inviting those she knew were of like mind to herself, most of them introduced to her by Will. Among them were Miles Coverdale, who had helped to translate the Bible into English, and Hugh Latimer, the radical chaplain of the Duchess of Suffolk, who was also a welcome guest at these gatherings. Latimer had been bishop of Worcester, but had suffered a brief imprisonment in the Tower for opposing the King's reforms as not being sufficiently progressive, and had been forced to resign his bishopric. He was a farmer's son who had made good, a learned man with deep convictions that tended, Katharine suspected, to Lutheranism, and he was happy to preach sermons to her guests.

No one admitted to being Protestant. They were all aware of the danger. The emphasis was purely on reform; even the King could not argue with that.

John had been dead for three weeks when Sir Thomas Seymour called. He swept off his feathered bonnet and bowed. 'I came to convey my condolences, my lady,' he declared, as he was shown into the parlour. No sooner had the door closed on the steward than he bounded forward and took her hands. 'How are you, Katharine?' It was the first time he had used her Christian name.

She should have sent him away. Both of them knew that this was not just a courtesy visit. But she was feeling so lonely and hated being shut up in this house of mourning. 'I am all the better for seeing you,' she said.

'And you are free,' he said, looking at her with undisguised desire. 'You can make your own choices now.'

'I've made my choice,' she said, and he took her into his arms.

A letter of condolence arrived from the King, all very correct and pious, except for the last line: *Written by the hand of him who would be a comfort to you.* She was in no doubt as to his true meaning.

This letter was followed, a week later, by another, in which he told her that he had been suffering pain in his legs and been confined to his chamber, but was better now. He had enclosed some verses he had composed in her honour. It was one of the worst poems she had ever read.

> Though that men do call it dotage,
> Who loveth not wanteth courage;
> And whosoever may love get,
> From Venus sure he must it fetch . . .

They were such tortuous lyrics that she couldn't even be quite sure of his meaning. He seemed to be saying that he would be a coward if he did not pursue her. He begged that she would come to see him, under cover of a visit to her brother.

Most reluctantly, she went. A page fetched her from Will's lodging and led her by a winding route through the palace until they came to a secret stair concealed behind panelling. She climbed the steps in some trepidation and was shown into a small, richly panelled room hung with an antique-style tapestry. The King sat in a velvet-upholstered chair by a crackling fire. The room was very hot.

'You will forgive me if I do not get up,' he said, as she rose from her curtsey. 'I am still a little indisposed. Come, sit with me.' He indicated the smaller chair opposite.

'Is your Majesty's leg much improved?' she asked.

'Somewhat,' he said. She noticed the silver-gilt walking stick propped against the wall near his chair. 'But, Lady Latimer, I am feeling out of sorts and not myself.' He lifted a book from the table next to him. 'I was going to read to you from this – it's about priestly celibacy – but my eyesight is troubling me. The words blur.' He reached for a reading glass and peered at the text.

'Your Grace needs gazings,' Katharine said. 'They are reading glasses set in a frame and hinged across your nose.'

'You think they will help?'

'Assuredly, Sir. My uncle has a pair.'

'Then I will order some.'

'Shall I read the passage for us?' she asked, and he nodded.

They discussed celibacy and other theological matters for an hour. Then the King fixed his gaze on her. 'I like you very much, Lady Latimer. I enjoy your company immensely and would be more to you than a friend.'

She was thrown. It had come so unexpectedly, out of the blue.

'Sir,' she stammered, 'you do me far too much honour. I fear I do not quite know what to say to you. My lord has not been dead a month and I am still in mourning. I have given little thought to my future. Might we talk about this another time?'

'Time is what I do not have,' the King said heavily. 'I am not a well man. But if you could give me cause to hope that you might one day allow me to be your servant, I know I would feel very much better.'

'I dare say I shall feel able to think about such matters in time.' Katharine smiled, hoping he could not detect her reluctance. 'In the meantime, I shall cherish your Majesty's friendship.'

'Well, I shall content myself with that.' He gave her a rueful grin.

She was surprised to receive a late letter of condolence from Ann, her sister-in-law. They had never been close, but Ann seemed genuinely grieved for her. As she read on, though, it appeared that Ann had an ulterior motive for sending the letter.

I know you have no reason to think kindly of me, she had written, *but I hope you can understand what it means to love someone so much that a life of poverty is infinitely preferable to living without them. We are happy together and our child flourishes. I will never make any claim on William, and both of us, I am certain, wish to put the past behind us, but there is a lady who hates me and stirs up trouble for me. Do not believe all that you hear of me. Farewell.*

It sounded unlike the Ann she had known, and she wondered again why her sister-in-law had been so cold towards Will. Had something bad happened between them of which she was unaware? Was *he* to blame for the failure of the marriage? Or was it that John Lyngfield was not the blaggardly seducer Will said he was and had been able to offer Ann true love? She wished she knew the answers to these questions, but it was best not to probe too deeply now. It was time to lay old scandals to rest.

In the middle of March, Thomas Seymour arrived at Charterhouse Square in a raging temper.

'Someone has talked!' he fumed, as soon as he and Katharine were alone.

'About what?' she asked, shocked to have him burst in on her like this, especially after she had told him again not to call on her.

'The King knows about us!'

'He can't! Has he said something?'

'No, but I am being sent on an embassy to Brussels. I am being got rid of!' He slammed his fist on the table.

'Oh, no!' she cried. 'When do you have to leave?'

'In May.'

'Thomas,' she said, relaxing a little and trying to be rational, 'if the King thought you were a rival and wanted to get rid of you, he would be sending you away now!'

He stared at her, breathing heavily.

'The only person who knows about us is my brother,' she went on, 'and he would never betray us.'

'No? He wants you to marry the King. He has every reason to see me off.'

'He wouldn't go that far. I know him. Thomas, be reasonable. You've been in England for two months. It's inevitable that you would be sent on another embassy at some stage. You are reading too much into this. The King has given me no hint that he suspects anything.'

'He wouldn't. He'd play a devious game. But maybe you are right. I just can't bear the thought of leaving you. If I am away, he will have the field to himself.'

'You're forgetting that I have a say in this!' she reproved him, and he hastened to her and kissed her hungrily, and it was glorious, and she melted into his arms. This time it was unbearably poignant, because soon they would be parted indefinitely and she did not know how she would endure it.

The next day, Will came to dinner in a strange mood.

'I am being admitted to the Privy Council,' he announced, and Katharine hugged him.

'It is a well-deserved honour! I am so proud of you. Dorothy must be delighted.'

'She *is* pleased,' he said, not seeming as jubilant himself as he should be. He followed her into the parlour where the table had been laid for just two, as Margaret was visiting a friend.

Over some very good spring lamb, they discussed his new responsibilities and how he was worthy of the trust the King had reposed in him. Among so many clamouring for preferment, he had done very well.

After dessert was served, Katharine asked him outright if he had said anything to the King about her and Thomas, but he denied it.

'Whatever I think of your marrying him, I would not break your confidence,' he assured her, cutting himself a piece of currant tart.

'I told Thomas as much,' she said, then paused. 'You have something on your mind.'

'You know me too well.' He made a face and laid down his spoon. 'It's Ann. She is now apparently bedding with all and sundry, and she has been telling people that her child is mine and should be named my heir. I will not have it!'

Katharine was about to interrupt, recalling what Ann had written to her, but Will gave her no chance. 'I intend to put an end to her mischief. I am going to divorce her and petition the King for all her property.'

'Divorce? It will cost you a fortune to obtain an Act of Parliament! And it will bring public shame on Ann. Think of the scandal! Remember the outcry when Lord Borough had his daughter-in-law's children declared bastards by Act of Parliament.'

Will regarded her severely. 'Adultery is a serious offence.'

She stood up, thoroughly agitated, and walked to the window. 'Who told you that Ann has taken other lovers?'

He hesitated for a moment. 'Dorothy told me.'

She rounded on him. 'Don't you think she might have an ulterior motive? If you divorced your wife for adultery, you could marry her.'

Will looked angry. 'It is my honour that is at stake, Kate, not what Dorothy wants. I will be writing my petition to the King this afternoon.'

'But have you asked Ann herself if it's true, or anyone else?' She knew, from Will's sullen, sheepish look, that he had not.

She wondered if she should tell him what Ann had written in her letter. She did not want him thinking that she was taking Ann's part, and he was in a foul enough mood already. She had little time for her sister-in-law, but Will's actions would leave her in worse penury than she was now. She decided that she would go to the King today, before Will got a chance to petition him.

She waited until the afternoon, an hour after he had left. The court was busy. She had changed into smart clothes so that she could be admitted to the great watching chamber. It was full of petitioners and she had to fight her way through the throng to get to the Gentlemen Pensioners who guarded the door to the presence chamber.

'Pray tell his Majesty that Lady Latimer begs to see him,' she said.

'So do a lot of other people,' one said, barely deigning to look at her.

'I think we should admit this lady,' his fellow told him. He beckoned to a page, who led Katharine through to the privy chamber and asked her to wait in a small, but sumptuously appointed, closet. He was back almost immediately.

'This way, please, my lady.'

The King received her in a small room lined with linenfold panelling, his bandaged leg resting on a stool, the satin upholstery shot with stains. A table and cupboard were piled with books and writing paper, and there was a small globe on the windowsill, with a set of virginals and a lute propped against it. As his Grace laid down his book and rose to greet her, she saw a pair of gold-and-silver gazings on the table. He had taken her advice!

'Your Majesty!' she said, kneeling before him.

'My Lady Latimer!' he exclaimed, beaming broadly. 'This is an unexpected pleasure. Please rise. What can I do for you?'

'I have a favour to beg, Sir.' She remained on her knees; she would not get up until he had granted her wish. She told him, concisely, what Will was intending. 'I beg of you, Sir,' she pleaded, 'to spare Lady Parr some means of existence.'

She had thought that he would leap to grant her least whim, but, when she looked up, she saw that he was frowning.

'Alas, Madam, the law provides that a woman of rank who so forgets herself shall receive nothing unless her husband pardons her.'

'Your Majesty is above the law,' she cried. 'You alone can grant my brother's petition.'

'If he petitions me for her whole estate, I am bound to grant it. In cases like this, the husband's will is paramount above the will of the King.'

'Then I will try to get my brother to forgive her,' she said, rising to her feet.

'If he can be content, I will grant your request,' he promised.

'I will go to him,' she said, 'with your leave.'

'And come back later, my lady,' he said, standing up. 'After five o'clock. I have a council meeting before then. You could sup with me if you wish.'

'Your Grace does me too much honour,' she said. 'I will return, as you please.' She owed him that much, for he did seem willing to help her.

She hastened to Will's lodging and caught him on his way to the meeting – his first appearance on the Privy Council.

'Walk with me,' he said, and she fell into step and related to him what Ann had said in her letter.

'The circumstances are not as you have been given to believe by Dorothy.'

'And you believe Ann?' he retorted.

'I know that there were issues on her side and I hope that you might show a little compassion and spare her some means of sustenance.'

'Why should I?'

'Will,' she panted, struggling to keep up, 'Dorothy may have lied. I'm not saying that Ann hasn't behaved badly, only that she should not be further defamed for someone else's gain. Slander is against the law. I am ready to use my influence with the King to have Dorothy questioned, and then, with God's help, we shall know the truth.'

Will came to a sudden halt. 'You've got me by the balls, Kate. We both know that the King will grant you anything in his power. Very well, you leave me no choice. I will show clemency. Take this and tear it up.' He thrust a rolled-up document into her hands. It was his petition to the King.

'You are a better man for doing this,' she told him.

'More a blackmailed one, I think.' But a hint of a smile was playing about his lips.

In the middle of April, Parliament granted Will's divorce, passing an Act establishing Ann's adultery in law and declaring her child and any future children born outside wedlock bastards and unfit to inherit her husband's estates. It was enacted that Will could retain all the properties of the earldom of Essex, while Ann would have a small income from them. There was little doubt that the earldom itself would be granted to him soon, but Parliament had stipulated that neither Will nor Ann could marry again while the other still lived. That was a blow, for a man, especially a landed peer, needed an heir to succeed him; yet there was nothing to be done about it.

When Katharine next visited Will's lodging, she surprised him at table with a beautiful young woman she had never seen before. He introduced her as Elizabeth Brooke, the daughter of Lord Cobham. She was young – at seventeen, nearly half Will's age – and exquisitely dressed, and when Katharine looked into her dancing eyes and saw her looking so adoringly at her brother, she knew that this was what Will needed. And she was glad to see the back of Dorothy Bray.

Chapter 16

1543

Katharine was still accustoming herself to widowhood, yet she was spending her days performing a delicate balancing act between her two suitors. The King continued to show himself warm and courteous, dropping heavy hints that he would like to be more to her than just a friend, but respecting the fact that she was in mourning. Thomas – he was Tom to her now – was becoming increasingly ardent, furious at the prospect of being parted from her, and demanding that she tell the King she was promised to him. She was finding it hard to placate him. He did not understand that she was frightened of making it clear to her sovereign that she did not want him in the way he wanted her, and scared to offend him when Will was desperate to be told that the earldom of Essex was his.

The King, of course, had the advantage. All the cards were in his hand. He could summon her whenever he wished, and he could afford to give her expensive gifts of jewellery. To please her, he had Will installed as a Knight of the Garter, the highest accolade of chivalry he could bestow.

'I call him my Integrity,' he told Katharine. 'He is a true and honest man and always tells me what he thinks I should hear, not what I necessarily want to hear.'

His Grace also created Will baron of Hart in Northamptonshire, then appointed him Lord Warden and Keeper of the Scottish Marches. These were inducements, Katharine knew; the King was making it plain how much he could do for her family if she showed favour to him. She was in little doubt now that he was thinking of marriage and was merely biding his time.

He had given no hint that he knew of her meetings with Tom. As the days went by, she was beginning to think that she should have come clean about that at the beginning. But it was too late now. He would be mortally offended if he found out that she was seeing another man. Yet Tom was becoming more and more restive and hard to contain. It would almost be a relief when he went abroad, although she knew she would miss him dreadfully.

Early in May, Will was sent north to take up his new post. The Scots had adamantly refused to let their little Queen marry Prince Edward, and King Henry was pressurising them with a show of military force. But Will saw little action, for operations had been delegated to Lord Hertford. In his letters from his base at Darlington, he grumbled that there wasn't even enough desk work, although the Duke of Suffolk had made him very welcome and was clearly aware of the King's interest in his sister. Doubtless the Duke thought that Will would soon be his Majesty's brother-in-law and should be treated accordingly. But he was also commandeering all contact with the Council in London, and Will felt slighted. He had even asked for Father Cuthbert's help in finding him something useful to do, but the Bishop had been unable to help and told Will he should be grateful for everything the King had done for him.

Anne and Herbert *were* grateful. The King's favour had extended to them in the form of grants of land in Wales. Katharine knew it was all because of her. She felt guilty because she did not want his attentions or his love, and yet she was happy for those dear to her to profit from it. She was a hypocrite and did not like herself for it.

There came the evening when, walking through the gardens of Whitehall after a supper with the King, escorted by one of the royal ushers, she saw Thomas walking towards her.

'My Lady Latimer!' He swept an elaborate bow. His eyes were full of desire. She was praying that the usher would not notice.

'Sir Thomas, it is a pleasure to see you,' she said briskly. 'If you will forgive me, I have to catch the tide.'

'Why, my lady? You have no sick husband who needs you, and I imagine that the servants will feed your dog.' She could smell the drink on his breath. He seemed always to be angry these days. 'You could spare me a few minutes. You're not usually this aloof.'

She could have brained him. The usher was looking at them curiously.

'I have a bad headache,' she lied, 'and wish to lie down.'

Instantly, his mood changed. 'Forgive me. I am so sorry, my lady. I will see you soon, I hope.'

She forced a smile and walked on. Had he not seen the usher's Tudor rose badge? Of course he had! He just enjoyed being provocative and his patience, of which he had little, was clearly running out.

She wondered if, in the wake of this encounter, she would receive another summons from the King. He would surely be angry with her for leading him on. A man of his pride would see it as an unforgivable betrayal, made worse by the fact that his rival was a much younger man with all the vigour and beauty that had once been his.

She waited in trepidation. She would be relieved if she didn't have to see the King again. It would solve her problem. She only cared that she was free to marry Tom and that Will got his earldom. But a week after that incident in the gardens, the King's messenger arrived at her house and asked if she would care to join his Majesty in his barge for a trip along the Thames. So he was not angry with her.

Seated in the plushly upholstered cabin with the leather curtains pulled back, a warm breeze caressing her and the minstrels playing at the bow of the boat, Katharine felt uncomfortable. The King had looked sad and pensive when she arrived and nothing she had said had seemed to cheer him. He sat beside her, letting her chatter away and sighing from time to time, until she began to wonder if he did know about Tom and was hurt. She fell silent, watching the scenery pass by and listening to the rhythmic splash of the oars as they propelled the barge forward towards Richmond.

She decided that she must tell the King what was in her heart. She genuinely had no desire to be queen of England; she loved her freedom too much. She was in love with Tom. Her mind was fully bent on marrying him.

'You must forgive me for being poor company tonight,' his Grace said suddenly, before she could speak. 'Bishop Gardiner has been particularly aggravating today.' She remembered Henry saying that he did not like the hawk-eyed Gardiner because he was too aggressive and troublesome.

She had never spoken to the Bishop of Winchester, but she had seen his tall, imposing figure from a distance and knew of him by reputation. Her friends derided him as a bigot, too firmly entrenched in the old ways, and too zealous against those who disagreed with him.

'May I ask what he has done?' she asked.

'He is pressing me, in his usual haranguing way, to make Parliament pass an Act for advancing true religion.'

That meant Gardiner's true religion, she thought, wondering what it would mean for those of her own persuasion.

'I would have sent him packing if I hadn't agreed with him,' the King growled. 'I don't like being dictated to!'

'On what point did your Grace agree with him?' she asked, trying to sound indifferent.

'Most of them!' he admitted, grimacing. 'We both think that only persons appointed by me should be authorised to read the Great Bible in English and that nobody else should take it upon themselves to read it openly to others in any church or assembly. The penalty for disobedience will be one hundred months in prison.'

Her heart sank. Gardiner really was turning back the clock and, in so doing, he would be depriving many of one of God's most precious gifts.

'You see, Lady Latimer,' the King went on, 'it has become clear that every man has his own opinion of the Scriptures and each thinks he knows best. I will not have ignorant persons interpreting the Word of God!'

He had a point. But she herself was not an ignorant person, nor were many others, of both sexes.

'I agree with the Bishop,' the King was saying, 'that the lower sort do not benefit from studying the Bible in English. They have not the education or the intellect to understand it. Therefore, I have decided that no women, craftsmen, servants, farmers, labourers or yeomen may henceforth read the Scriptures in church or in private.'

The words 'no women' stunned her. This was appalling. To have had this great privilege granted only a few years back, only to have it withdrawn now, was dreadful.

'No women?' she echoed, forgetting herself. 'But Sir, women like me read the Scriptures for the comfort they give and to afford us deeper insights into our faith.'

'And there lies the rub, my lady,' he reproved, but not too sternly. 'Women do not have the wit to understand these matters as men do. Some may place foolish interpretations on the Scriptures.'

'I defer, as always, to your Grace's wisdom, but some of us are educated and gain much pleasure from the Word of God. Must we be deprived of that consolation? Would you yourself wish to be deprived of it?'

She feared she had gone too far, but the King looked thoughtful, fingering his beard in the gathering dusk. 'You have a point, my lady. I will amend the draft to permit any noblewoman or gentlewoman to read the Bible. But – and I must stress this – they may not read it in public or to others. They may only read it for themselves.'

She knew better than to push further. 'Your Grace is at once wise and beneficent.'

'Would Gardiner were the same!' he snorted. 'He wishes to be rid of all of the reformist persuasion, especially those in office. I prefer to take a middle way, eradicating abuses within my Church but retaining the tenets of the Catholic faith. It is important to keep a balance between these factions that are warring with each other. When I marry again, I will choose a lady who represents that middle way.'

She froze. She realised that he was talking about her, the widow of a Catholic and sister and niece to reformists. It was time to change the subject!

'I have read your Grace's book defending the sacraments,' she said, as the pinnacles of Greenwich Palace appeared in the distance ahead.

He smiled. 'The Bishop of Rome awarded me the title Defender of the Faith for that. Hah! Little did he know how zealously I would be defending the faith that he and his ilk have disparaged. In truth, I know not why men think ill of my reforms. I will never subscribe to the doctrines of Luther. I hear Mass daily. I am a devout servant of God. I defend the Real Presence in the Mass. I believe that we attain Heaven by the good works we do in this world, and not through faith alone. All I seek is for men to live in unity in the love of Christ. Is that too much to ask, Lady Latimer?'

Well, for some people, it was, considering that he had closed down the monasteries, ordered the breaking-up of shrines and images, and swept away long-established religious traditions. Yet she supported him in all these measures. They had been necessary changes. 'There are not many who criticise your Grace,' she said. 'Most of your subjects applaud your reforms. There are only a few fools who speak out against them.'

'Dangerous fools!' he barked.

'Some are ignorant,' she said. 'Others are confused. People need to know where they stand. The changes have been so rapid – and rightly so, for they were needful. Take reading the English Bible, for example. One day it is legal, the next it is not. I am not criticising your Grace, but I think your people need greater clarity.'

'Well, they shall have it!' he declared. 'I am about to publish a book – the King's Book, it will be called – in which I have set forth the tenets of our reformed Church that all must observe. It should silence those who arrogantly presume a sinister understanding of Scripture. I am determined to crush dissent.'

They sat there in silence as the oarsmen turned the barge around for the journey back to Whitehall. She was thankful that she had been able to persuade his Grace not to take away her right to read the English Bible. What great luck that she had caught him at that opportune moment. She could hardly believe that she, humble Katharine Parr, had been able to influence him. She marvelled at it, thinking that it boded well for the future.

Yet her heart was heavy. She was certain that this new book, and the coming Act of Parliament, signalled the King's return to religious orthodoxy. Who was encouraging him? Bishop Gardiner! And who was there that the King listened to, in order to counteract that pernicious influence?

The answer suddenly came to her with blinding clarity.

It was herself.

On the balmy May night before he left England, Tom came to see her. She had supper served in the parlour, where they could be private, and wore her most becoming black gown, the one with a low square neck, and a simple strand of pearls. She had set aside her wimple and chin barbe in favour of a French hood. It was good to be free of their swathing folds.

Tom was in a volatile mood, alternately railing against being sent away and acting the ardent suitor.

'I don't know how I am going to live without you,' he declared, putting down his knife and leaving the choice food virtually untouched. 'I have no idea when I will be back and when I will see you again.'

Katharine felt like weeping. He wasn't making it any easier for her. She had resolved to be at her best for him tonight, to give him a warm memory to take with him.

'We will write to each other,' she said. 'We can write every day.'

'And, in the meantime, the King will be pursuing you and it will not be easy for you to resist him.' Tom was nearly beside himself.

'My dearest, it is you I wish to marry, you on whom my heart is set!' she protested.

'It is dangerous to flout the King's wishes,' he told her.

'Then I shall play for time, keep him dangling in hope. Anne Boleyn did it. How long did she hold him off? Six years? You'll be back by then.' She attempted a smile.

'He wouldn't wait that long nowadays. He hasn't got the time left to him.'

She looked around to check that the door was firmly shut. It was treason even to imagine the King's death. She lowered her voice. 'Then God may solve the problem for us. And, think, if I do marry him, I will soon be a rich widow and we will be in an even better position to wed.'

'Don't you think I've thought of that? But I can't bear the idea of your being married to him, bedding him. God!' Tom stood up and pulled her to her feet, crushing her in his arms. 'I don't want him there first. Lie with me, Kate! Be mine tonight – and for always!'

'Tom,' she gasped, after he had kissed her passionately. 'Tom, listen. I would sleep with you now, but I dare not risk a pregnancy. Think of the scandal!' It was unlikely, but it could happen.

'It would see off the King!' His eyes glinted dangerously.

'And what of my reputation? It would be in the dust! I could not show my face at court or in London.'

His arms tightened around her. 'I will be careful. Just be mine.'

'You would not respect me for it,' she said. 'If you love me, you must love the honour in me.'

He sighed, his lips nuzzling her hair. 'Oh, God, Kate, why must we be tortured like this?'

'God is testing our love.' She was savouring the closeness between them, committing it to memory for the separation that lay ahead. 'I have no doubt we will be the stronger for it.'

They spent the rest of the evening in each other's arms. She allowed Tom to kiss her breasts above the neckline of her gown, but nothing more, for all that she was longing to be fully his. She had known married love with two husbands, but she knew that it would be infinitely, blissfully different with Tom. She had never wanted a man so much.

The clock on the mantelpiece was showing eleven o'clock when they finally drew apart. She stood up, straightened her gown and retrieved her hood from the floor, where Tom had tossed it.

She poured some wine and they drank it in silence. She felt a creeping sense of dread. 'Well,' she said, 'this is farewell, my love. May God be with you.'

'Oh, Kate!' Tom groaned, and kissed her again. 'Stay true to me. I will hasten home to you as soon as I can.'

'Just go now,' she begged. 'Go now, while I have the strength to let you.'

Tom had not been gone for two days, and already the time was dragging painfully. He wouldn't even have reached Dover yet. It would be weeks, months even, before they were together again.

She made herself keep busy, supervising the spring-cleaning of the house. She barely heard the knock at the door and was still in her apron, with just a linen cap on her head, when the King's messenger was announced. His Majesty was asking if she would care to join him to watch a game of tennis and then have dinner with him.

She hastened upstairs to change her clothes, putting on one of the gowns he had given her. It was a little too grand for watching tennis, but not for dinner, and she should wear it to show her appreciation. Only when she was in the boat, out in the middle of the river, did she realise that he might see her wearing the dress as a sign of encouragement. But it was too late to go back and change.

She enjoyed the tennis, cheering along with the King when his champion won.

'You should have seen me in my day, Lady Latimer! I could knock them all out. Alas, these days I can only watch. But I have the advantage of watching in good company.' He gave her a sideways smile.

Dinner was laid out in another richly furnished closet. There were no servants and they helped themselves to an array of cold meats, fish, salads, fruit and jellies. During the meal, they chatted about the tennis and the archery contest the King had arranged for the afternoon, for which he hoped she would join him. 'Seeing how expert you are!' he grinned. Then he paused and his gaze grew more intent.

'My Lady Latimer,' he said, dabbing his napkin to his mouth, 'you must be aware that I think very highly of you. You are a very comely lady with many virtues and rare gifts of nature – all the things in which I most delight. You are a warm and stimulating companion. You exude goodwill.'

She felt herself flushing. 'Your Grace, you flatter me.' Dear God, where was this leading?

'I was never a flatterer,' he protested. 'I'm a plain man. I say what I think. And I think that you are a woman I can respect, and that you would be a perfect queen of England.' He reached across and took her hand as she sat there, barely able to breathe. 'Lady Latimer, I am asking you to marry me.'

She had been dreading this moment and, although it was half expected, she still did not know how to react. But she must respond.

'Sir, I am utterly amazed. I mean, I am not worthy. Your Grace does me too much honour.'

He squeezed her hand. His voice was gentle. 'You have every requisite quality, and we two get on well, do we not? I have had many disappointments in my marriages, and some ill-conditioned wives, but I know we would accord well together.'

'In truth, I do not know how to answer your Majesty. I am not long widowed. I was not looking to remarry so soon, if at all. And given your Grace's health, I thought you just appreciated some feminine companionship.'

'By God, my lady, I'm not looking for a nurse, but a queen to grace my court and a wife to give me more sons! I want a mature and intelligent woman with whom I can enjoy good conversation, someone I can trust. And I know I can trust you. I'm lonely. I want a wife in my bed and at my board. And there is about you a certain glow. You have feelings for me, I think.'

She wanted to shrink into the ground. Yes, she had feelings – but not for him. 'I do,' she said. 'I worship your Grace, not just as my sovereign, whom I am bound to love, but as a man. You have been so good to me and mine.'

'I hope you see me as more than just the fount of patronage?' he teased her.

'Of course! I would not have you think me mercenary, only grateful.'

Did she have a choice in the matter? If she refused him, she would not mind losing his favour, but would her family suffer? Was he that vindictive? She did not know, she had not the measure of him yet. But she loved Tom, above all. He was everything she wanted in a husband. Even his unpredictability excited her. Saying yes to her sovereign was not an option, she decided.

The King was watching her. 'You have doubts? I am offering you the world.'

'Sir, I am indeed sensible of that,' she faltered. 'You have taken me by surprise . . .'

'I love you, my lady,' he said, and he got up painfully, stooped down and kissed her gently on the lips. 'I would kneel to you if I could. I pray you will make me a happy man.'

'Your Majesty's favour means everything to me,' she said, feeling cornered. 'If you would grant me a little time to think and pray on the matter?'

His Grace resumed his seat, looking disappointed. 'Of course,' he said. 'But do not keep me waiting too long.'

She dared not tell Uncle William or write to Will. She knew what they would say. She sought guidance in prayer, all the time telling herself that there was no need, her mind was made up. She did not want to marry an old and ailing man who had had five wives already, however kind and attentive he was. She did not want to be at the mercy of his changeable nature, or at the centre of a court riddled with dangerous intrigue. She did not want to go to bed with a man with diseased legs that sometimes gave off a nasty smell, or lie suffocating under his vast bulk. Tom had awakened physical feelings in her she had not known she had, and she could not deny herself that fulfilment. The King could never, ever satisfy her in that way, whereas her knees felt weak at the prospect of Tom in her bed. She could not forsake him.

And yet . . . It was not the exalted status, the glory, the magnificent palaces, the gorgeous robes and jewels of a queen that drew her, or the power and riches her family would enjoy. These things weighed lightly in the balance against her love for Tom. But there was something else nagging at her, like a call to arms. The vengeful spectre of Bishop Gardiner haunted her dreams and her waking hours. He was the enemy of true religion and the faith she held dear. Had not Anne Boleyn influenced the King in favour of reform? Wasn't it true that no one had been burned for heresy in Anne's time? Was God calling her, Katharine, to lead the King to the path of righteousness?

Kneeling at the prayer desk in her bedchamber at Charterhouse Square, though, she begged Him not to lay that burden on her slender back. Why did she have to be chosen? Why not somebody else? Was He really expecting her to make the supreme sacrifice of relinquishing Tom so that true religion could be saved? No! He would have to think again.

For hours, every day, she knelt there wrestling with her conscience. Every time she made the decision to turn the King down, she hesitated, wondering if it was God's will that she be queen. How she resisted! She fended off the notion with all her might. Yet He withstood her objections, leading her every time back to the path He wanted her to take – or so it seemed. Each time she told herself she could not do it, He gave her the grace to see that she could. Finally, she accepted that He was asking her to renounce utterly her own will in the matter and follow His willingly. And she knew, in her heart, that she had it in her to win the King over for Christ. If she achieved that, she might bring thousands of souls to salvation. How could she pit her personal feelings against something so huge?

And yet, if she did the unthinkable, forsook Tom and embarked on this path, she would be putting herself in danger – there was no doubt of it. Gardiner was sniffing away in every corner of the court, seeking out heretics. The consequences of being exposed did not bear contemplating. And yet, and yet . . .

Her inner turmoil was so great that she could not sleep and was eating very little. She was aware that time was moving on and that the King would not wait for ever. He had written to her, sending another bad poem to his 'fair nymph', begging her to set her doubts aside and couple herself with him. She had to make a decision soon.

She kept her English Bible locked up in a cupboard with John's New Testament and the old Queen's baptismal cloth. It was her wont to let the Bible fall open at random, close her eyes and let God guide her finger to a verse. Often, when reading the passage she had touched, she had found inspiration, comfort and guidance. Today, after reading the King's letter, she took out her Bible, hoping for an answer to her dilemma. Closing her eyes, she opened it and pressed her finger to a page. Then she opened her eyes – and stared.

The Bible had fallen open at the Book of Esther, the Jewish queen of the Persian King Ahasuerus, a brave woman who had saved her people from the persecution of the King's evil minister, Haman. And Katharine's finger was resting on the text, 'Who knoweth whether thou art come to the kingdom for such a time as this?'

It was the sign she had been looking for. It could not have been clearer.

With a heavy heart and tears in her eyes, she sat down to write to Tom. It felt as if she was writing the fateful words of farewell in her own blood. She did not sign the letter, for fear it would be intercepted on its way to Brussels. But he would know it was from her, and she prayed that he would understand and forgive her.

She wrote telling Anne her decision; she did not feel that she could confide in anyone else. She begged her sister to come to London and stay with her, for she felt fragile and needed moral support. Already, it felt as if she was set apart from others and must play the queen. Anne dropped everything, left the children with her mother-in-law and hastened to Charterhouse Square, where she flung her arms around Katharine and told her how happy she was for her.

Katharine then braced herself to take the irrevocable step of telling the King that she would marry him. She had heard that the court was about to move to Greenwich and resolved to see him there. Gathering her courage, she wrote to ask if she could visit him. A summons came back the same morning: would she join him for supper?

She wore a black velvet gown with her pearls and a French hood of white satin. It was an understated ensemble compared to the usual court finery, but it looked elegant.

'It's perfect!' Anne pronounced. 'The King will love you in it.'

'Anne . . .' Katharine grasped her sister's hand. 'I *am* doing the right thing?'

Anne knew how hard it had been for her to renounce Tom.

'Yes, you are. I know it. Now go and slay him!'

It was a warm June evening with that golden haze that follows a hot day, but Katharine could take no pleasure in it. Her footsteps were leaden as she alighted from the boat and followed an usher to the King's lodging.

When she entered his closet, he came to her as fast as his bound leg would allow him and held out his hands. 'No, Lady Latimer, there is no need to curtsey. Pray sit down.' He indicated the chair on the other side of the hearth, on which a great vase of roses had been placed.

'What beautiful flowers!' she said, breathing in their scent, trying to steady herself. 'I trust your Majesty is well?'

'Aye, and I hope to be even better soon. Tell me, my lady, do you have something to say to me?' He was looking at her avidly.

Once the words were out, there would be no going back. She made herself smile at him. 'Yes, your Majesty. I should be deeply honoured to accept your gracious proposal.'

His face was transformed, lit up by joy. 'You have made me the happiest man in the world,' he said, his voice breaking, and she saw that there were tears in his eyes. 'Katharine, I have been hoping and praying for this.' It was the first time he had called her by her given name.

'God has brought me to you,' she said. 'May He bring us much happiness.'

The King pulled her into his arms. He kissed her, a proper kiss, filled with desire. 'I will make you happy,' he murmured. 'You shall have whatever you want, my darling.'

'I will try with all my heart to be a good wife, Sir, and a good queen.'

He chuckled. 'You don't have to call me "Sir" in private, Katharine, not now. Call me Henry, or Harry. And, if I may, I will call you Kate! Oh, my darling, I cannot wait to show you to the world. I never thought to know such joy again.'

She prayed he would never detect that she did not feel as he did. She responded to his kisses as enthusiastically as she could and acted as if this was the most wonderful thing that had happened to her. It came to her that, from now on, she would be living a lie. *Oh, Tom, oh, Tom, what have I done?*

Henry – for so she must now think of him – insisted on her meeting his daughters. They were arriving at Greenwich the following day. There would be no announcement of his coming marriage yet, for he wanted her to himself for now, but he wished Mary and Elizabeth to know that they were to have a new stepmother.

When Katharine returned to court, she brought Anne with her; it seemed fitting, and it gave her moral support. Henry himself escorted her to his privy garden where the princesses were waiting in the little banqueting house. They were not, legally speaking, princesses any more, for both had been declared bastards, but Katharine had always thought of them as such and, indeed, they were always spoken of with the same reverence as if they were the trueborn daughters of the King.

She was eager to meet them and hoping that they would like her. She had had good experience of being a stepmother and was ready to play her part again, feeling great compassion for these two young ladies, who had both lost their mothers in tragic circumstances.

Mary and Elizabeth rose at the coming of their father – Mary was holding her sister by the hand – and sank into billowing curtseys. She noticed that they had hair of the same shade of red as the King's, although his was threaded with grey. Mary, in her late twenties, was no beauty, being small and spare with a snub nose, a firm jaw, weak eyes and a nervous look on her plain face. Elizabeth, who would be ten in September, seemed more confident. She had sharp features, flashing, intelligent eyes and a winning manner.

Henry kissed his daughters. 'It does my heart good to see you both,' he told them, at which they visibly relaxed. 'I wish to present to you Lady Latimer, who is to be your new stepmother.'

Two pairs of eyes appraised her. Then, simultaneously, both princesses smiled.

'I am so pleased for you, Sir!' Mary said, in a deep, manly voice. 'Lady Latimer, I congratulate you. I have heard good things about you. And I remember your mother with affection. She served my mother well.'

'I am pleased to meet you, my lady,' Elizabeth greeted her. 'I hope that you and my father will be very happy.'

The pleasure Katharine felt was genuine. 'I will do my very best to be a good mother and friend to you both.'

Henry bade them all sit down and called for wine to be served in the banqueting house. It came with an assortment of sweetmeats.

'Gilded marchpane!' Elizabeth cried, helping herself to two pieces.

'She has my sweet tooth,' Henry smiled.

'Your reputation goes before you, my lady,' Mary said, turning to Katharine. 'I hear that you are very learned.'

'I cannot hope to match your Grace's own fame in that regard,' Katharine said, 'but I should very much like it if we could study together, and with my Lady Elizabeth, of course.'

'Alas, I am not often at court,' Elizabeth pouted.

'You are too young, and the court is not a healthy place for children,' the King said.

'That's why Edward hardly ever goes there,' Elizabeth told Katharine.

'I cannot take any risks with his health,' Henry declared. 'He is my only son.' His eyes met Katharine's; she knew what he was hoping for.

He rose. 'I will be back soon. Sit down, ladies. No ceremony.' He stumped off in the direction of the royal lodgings.

'I am so glad that we are to have another stepmother,' Elizabeth said, taking Katharine's hand. 'The last one was quite wicked.' She looked troubled.

'I never had a high opinion of her,' Mary said, 'so I was not as shocked as some by her fall.'

'I liked her,' Elizabeth said, 'although I didn't see her very often. It was horrible, what happened to her, like . . .' Her voice tailed off. *Like her own mother's fate.* How terrible to have to live with the knowledge that your father, however justified, had sent your mother to a violent, bloody death. It would colour all your memories of her. Not that Elizabeth could have had many, for she had not reached three when Anne Boleyn was executed.

'You must try to put her out of your mind,' Katharine said. 'But, if you ever want to talk, I am ready to listen.'

'I don't want to think about it,' Elizabeth said. 'And I'm never going to get married. Bad things happen if you get married.' Katharine was sorry to hear her speak thus, yet it stood to reason that she would feel like that, considering what had happened to her mother and stepmother.

'That's nonsense,' said Mary. 'I would love to be married. We will both have to obey our father's will in the matter.' She sounded wistful, as if she longed for a husband. There had long been talk of new matches for her, but nothing had come of it. How sad it was to see how both princesses had been damaged by the tragedies that had blighted their youth.

'Your mother was devoted to mine,' Mary was saying to Katharine. 'She eased the difficult times for her.' Elizabeth looked uncomfortable. It had been her mother who had caused those difficult times. Close as the sisters seemed, that would always lie between them.

'I have some things that were left to me and my mother by Queen Katharine,' Katharine told Mary. 'I will show them to you.'

Mary's face was transformed. 'I should like that. I have so few things that were hers. Elizabeth, stop stuffing yourself, and take your elbows off the table.' It was clear that Mary had grown used to mothering – or smothering – her half-sister. Elizabeth made a face. As soon as Mary had turned to greet their returning father, she sneaked a tartlet and crammed it in her mouth. Katharine stifled a smile.

By the King's command, Katharine was often at court after that. His intentions towards her seemed to be an open secret and she found herself being treated with a new deference. She had now confided her future plans to those close to her. Margaret was beside herself with excitement. Uncle William turned up at Charterhouse Square with a huge bunch of flowers and congratulated her, and Father Cuthbert sent his warm congratulations. Even Archbishop Cranmer called on her. His mild exterior concealed formidable learning and statesmanship, and he was a firebrand for reform.

'We are all delighted with the news, dear lady, absolutely delighted,' he declared, as she poured him some of her own strawberry cordial. By 'all', she knew that he meant the reformists at court. 'You are known to be very zealous towards the Gospel.'

He was giving her an opening, waiting for her to say more, but she knew she must be discreet. 'Like your Grace, I am a great admirer of his Majesty's reforms. He is like a second Solomon. More than that, he has delivered us out of a Babylonish captivity.' She hoped her words would convey more than she was able to say.

Cranmer looked pleased. 'Some of us are hoping that his Majesty will go a little further in religious policy. There are those who fear he is being cajoled into a reactionary stance. Maybe we are worrying unnecessarily. But you, Madam, are in a unique position to influence him. He will listen to you.'

She had not expected such a bald hint.

'I am but a woman, your Grace. It is divines like yourself whom his Majesty heeds. If God wishes me to be His instrument, He will make that plain. And I wish to do only what is right.'

He looked at her with respect. 'May God succour you in the task ahead of you.' He gave her his blessing and left.

The King had now forced the Scots to agree to a marriage between Prince Edward and their Queen, and court celebrated when the treaty was concluded at Greenwich early in July. Henry was in a buoyant mood because he was now free to declare war on France in support of the Emperor, who was engaged in hostilities with the King of France. He liked nothing better than trouncing the French, England's ancient enemy.

Katharine dared not think too much about Tom Seymour, who might be caught up in the coming conflict. She was consumed with guilt and regret. Had he received her letter? Did he hate her for abandoning him? Uncle William, who was entrusted with lots of confidential information in the privy chamber, had heard that Tom was in Brussels. Now, he said that he had been recalled.

Her heart managed to soar and plummet at the same time. She was longing to see him again, even though she must never betray what he still meant to her; yet she feared he would be cold to her, that he would hate her, and she knew she would not be able to bear it. Was it too late to tell the King she could not marry him after all? Or perhaps she and Tom could disappear together and live on the proceeds of their properties. They could flee to Europe, which Tom knew so well.

She was being ridiculous. Her wedding was just over a week away. It would be a quiet, almost secret affair with only a few select guests, for Henry hated big weddings and the fuss they entailed. She could not leave him now. The blow to his pride and his kingship would be devastating and humiliating, especially as he had shown her nothing but kindness. She had promised to marry him and she would honour that and do everything in her power to forget Tom.

The flimsiness of that resolve became clear when Uncle William told her that Tom was not coming home after all, but had been ordered to join an English force that was being sent to aid Imperial troops in France. She was desperately disappointed and had to fight back tears all the way through a fitting for her wedding gown.

On 10 July, with no fanfare, Archbishop Cranmer published the marriage banns. The King had moved to Hampton Court, where Katharine would be joining him the next day. It felt strange to be shutting up the house in Charterhouse Square. She would miss living there. It was her own space, something she would not enjoy in palaces, where there would be attendants at all times. She wandered through the familiar rooms, remembering John and all those who had graced her dinner table, the cosy evenings spent reading by the fire, the convivial gatherings. Margaret and some of the servants would be joining her household as queen; she would be keeping only a skeleton staff here until she could find a tenant; the rest were going to Jack at Snape.

When the time came to leave, she took a deep breath and closed the door on her old life.

Part Four

'Dangerous snares'

Chapter 17

1543

A small crowd of splendidly dressed people had gathered in the holyday closet behind the royal pew, that overlooked the nave of the Chapel Royal. Attired in crimson cloth of gold, Katharine stood with Henry under the all-encompassing gaze of the tall, handsome Bishop Gardiner, aware of what a momentous step she was taking. She had wondered why Cranmer had not been chosen to officiate; she would have preferred him any day to Gardiner, but Henry had told her that his middle way in religion required him to show favour to both sides in the religious debate, which was why he had asked Cranmer to publish the banns. And, he added mischievously, he wanted Gardiner to be seen to be approving the marriage. Gardiner, she knew, would be horrified if he knew he was uniting the King with a Protestant. She had smiled to herself at the thought.

Mary and Elizabeth were in attendance on Katharine, beautifully gowned. Carrying her train was the King's niece, Lady Margaret Douglas, a proud and vivacious redhead whom Henry had forgiven for carrying on an unsuitable love affair with Katheryn Howard's brother. The Herberts stood near the front with the Duchess of Suffolk, revelling in their new prominence. It was sad that Will hadn't been able to return for the wedding, and that Margaret was recovering from a megrim and was too unwell to attend. Among the lords and gentlemen, Katharine spied Hertford and his wife, which had given her a jolt. She wondered if the Earl knew that she had broken it off with his brother. He, of all people, should understand why, for ambition drove him, but family pride might make him despise her. His expression gave nothing away, but his wife had flashed her a malevolent glance as she entered.

Gardiner asked the King if he would take Katharine for his wedded wife.

'Yea!' Henry replied heartily, smiling at her.

'And will you, Katharine, take this man as your lawful wedded husband?'

'I will,' she answered.

The King took her right hand in his and recited his vows. Then it was her turn. Prompted by Gardiner, she spoke clearly: 'I, Katharine, take thee, Henry, to my wedded husband, to have and to hold from this day forward, for better for worse, for richer for poorer, in sickness and in health, to be debonair and buxom in bed and at board, till death us depart, and thereto I plight unto thee my troth.' She watched the King slide the ring on her finger and offer up gold and silver at the altar, and waited as he eased himself down gingerly to his knees, then sank beside him for the blessing.

When they rose, everyone clapped. It was done. She was queen of England.

As they left the holyday closet, a tall, angular-faced lady curtseyed low to them.

'Kate,' Henry said, 'this is the Lady Anna of Cleves.'

Katharine put on a charming smile and extended her hand to be kissed. 'It is a pleasure to meet you, my Lady Anna.'

'The pleasure is mine,' Anna answered, in a guttural voice that betrayed little warmth. 'Please accept my warmest congratulations. I am overjoyed for you both!'

Maybe, Katharine thought, as they moved on, Anna had not wanted to be divorced and resented her marrying the King. Well, they need not have much to do with each other – and, when they did meet, she would be all smiles and kindness.

Her imminent wedding night held few terrors for her. She had bedded with strangers twice before and emerged none the worse for it. And the King, who had been a most considerate suitor, would surely be a considerate lover – if he ever got that far. She would not let herself think of how different it would have been with Tom.

There was to be no bedding ceremony. Henry hated them. Yet she still found herself surrounded by the ladies and maids who had been appointed to her household, when she would have preferred to be alone to prepare for this most intimate of occasions. But this was to be her life from now on, so she must get used to it. At least Anne was with her, and Margaret, who was feeling better, and Lady Suffolk, whom she had grown to like, for all her stridency.

Katharine had resolved to be a good wife and queen and she would hold to that. She must give her bridegroom the welcome he deserved. She would not think of Tom.

She rose from her bath of milk, stood while her maids towelled her dry and perfumed her skin, and raised her arms so that they could put on the fine lawn chemise with the gold-embroidered neckline. She ordered wine and little savouries to be set out on the armoire in her bedchamber – the most magnificent bedchamber she had ever had – and donned her black satin night gown. Then she sent everyone away and sat in the chair to await Henry. She kept glancing at the great bed with its tester bearing the royal arms of England above the carved headboard, reminding her that this was to be no ordinary coupling. It was all about the getting of princes.

Resolutely, she put from her mind all thought of the women who might have occupied that bed before her. She was not going to end up like them. She would be the wife who triumphed and lived to tell the tale!

It was not long before she heard footsteps – it sounded like the tramp of marching feet. Suddenly, they stopped and she heard the pad of soft soles approaching. The door opened and there stood the King in a damask robe over a long white nightgown, with a nightcap on his head and slippers on his feet.

'Sweetheart!' he said and held out his arms. She rose and went into them, noticing a nasty sweet smell emanating from his unclothed leg. Trying not to breathe it in, she let him lead her to the bed and hand her up the step beside it. She climbed in and waited for him to heave his bulk into the space beside her. Then he turned and pulled her to him, kissing her tenderly.

'It will be easier if you mount me like a man does a horse,' he murmured. Relieved that she was not going to be crushed by the weight of him, she lifted her night-rail and climbed astride, guiding him into her.

'Oh, Kate!' he groaned. It was over before she knew it.

He was very sweet. He took her in his arms, pulled her down beside him and kissed her ardently.

'I love you, darling,' he whispered. Then he started snoring.

In the morning, she awoke to a bad smell. It was coming from Henry's leg. She turned away from him and tried to bury her nose in the sheet, but an arm snaked over her shoulder and she could feel something hard pressing into her lower back.

'Sweetheart!' the King said. There was no mistaking his intent. Hiding her reluctance, she turned to him.

After he had left, promising to dine with her, she got up. The bed stank, and it was going to be a hot day. Her first priority was to order perfumes of juniper and civet to freshen the chamber. She summoned Margaret, who sped away to find a still room.

'They are making them now for your Grace,' she said, when she returned.

'You don't have to call me that, sweetheart,' Katharine told her. 'Just go on calling me Mother, as you have always done.'

Margaret hugged her and hurried off to tell the other ladies that the Queen was awake now and ready for her uprising as a married woman.

Those first few days of her queenship were a revelation. Katharine found herself living in apartments of sumptuous splendour, surrounded by priceless tapestries, exquisite furniture, fabulous Turkey carpets and gilded ceilings. Henry's workmen had been busy. Her family's badge, the maiden's head, was everywhere, carved in wood and stone and embroidered on the very bedclothes. Yet she was not comfortable in the Queen's lodgings, aware that they had been refurbished for Anne Boleyn and then for Jane Seymour. And the privy kitchen was directly below; noise and the smell of cooking wafted up to her open windows, which she could not keep closed because the weather was so hot. She was relieved to hear Henry say that they would be departing on their summer progress soon.

She had written to Will with news of her coming wedding, telling him that it had pleased God to incline the King to take her as his wife, which was the greatest comfort that could have happened to her. *And you, brother, are the person who has most cause to rejoice. I pray you, let me know of your health, in as friendly a manner as if I had not been called to this honour.*

Will had written back promptly, in jubilant vein, and had the grace not to say I told you so. He told her that her marriage was the talk of the north; people were celebrating and praising her for her virtue. *Your news has revived my spirits and turned all my cares to rejoicing. This marriage will be a real and inestimable benefit and comfort to the whole realm.* She wished that he could be with her to share in her good fortune.

Everyone was hurrying to congratulate her. She held open court in her presence chamber, seated in a richly upholstered chair beneath a canopy of estate, and showed herself gracious and friendly to all. Many who came to see her were petitioners, seeking her influence and patronage. She received each request with a smile and promised to give it her urgent attention. She would be the gentle face of monarchy, approachable and kind. She tried to be dignified at all times, yet not too distant or proud. She wanted to win the people's respect – and their love.

She saw Henry frequently. They dined and supped together, slept together most nights and walked daily in his privy garden, sometimes taking their meals in the little banqueting house. She seized these occasions as opportunities to intercede for her petitioners, knowing that Henry could refuse her nothing.

'You'll have me giving away half my kingdom!' he said, having granted yet another request.

'But think how popular you will be,' she retorted, popping a comfit into his mouth.

He was easy company, she was finding, apart from when his leg pained him, but she was learning how to divert him with lively discussions about religion and with the music they both loved. At court, there was an Italian family of royal musicians called the Bassanos, whom she knew by sight as they lived near Charterhouse Square. They were virtuoso players and she and Henry spent many an afternoon enthralled by their music.

She loved being queen. She loved the glorious gowns, the sumptuous furs, the choice food and having her every whim deferred to. As far as Henry was concerned, nothing was too good for her. She had never owned so many jewels. On the day of her uprising, he gave her the casket containing the jewels of the queens of England, which had been handed down from consort to consort, and told her that she could keep them during his lifetime and then until his son was married.

Delighted as she was with such a wealth of exquisite and historical pieces, it caused her a pang because she had last seen this casket when Anne concealed it under her floorboards at the time of the last Queen's fall. She thought of the fair necks these pearls and necklaces had graced, two of them untimely severed, and shivered.

Looking through the jewels, she found a particular coronet-shaped brooch she especially liked, as well as an unusual pearl carcanet and an ouche pendant with a ruby. These she would enjoy wearing, along with the new jewels with which the King was showering her.

What she loved most was being able to indulge her love of books. She had been happy to buy them in any condition from the booksellers at St Paul's, but now she owned, or had access to, books that were beautiful objects in themselves, bound in velvet or fine leather. She was amassing quite a collection, from Petrarch to prayer books. With Henry's blessing, she had commissioned English and French New Testaments, which were being illuminated by her clerk of the closet and would be bound in purple and silver-gilt. Having the freedom to acquire books in unlimited quantities was one of the greatest advantages of being queen.

She had more wealth than she knew what to do with. Her receiver general had shown her a list of the dower properties that were now hers, and she had stared at it, realising that her lands were spread across nearly every county. She made a mental note to discover how well her estates were run and how much money they yielded. She also resolved to check and approve her household accounts.

It was heartening to see how much Henry loved her. She had ample evidence of it – his kindness, his generosity, his eagerness to please her and the way he openly kissed and caressed her. He was proud of her, she knew. He liked showing her off when they appeared in public. One day, as they were watching a game of bowls, he put his arm around her waist in front of all the courtiers and murmured in her ear, 'You look beautiful, Katharine, and you are doing so well. I could not have made a better choice. You have all the qualities most meet for a queen – virtue, wisdom and gentleness. I have never had a wife more agreeable to my heart. I pray God will grant us long life and much joy together.'

She blushed. People were staring at them. But she took his hand and squeezed it.

'I can't tell you how much that means to me,' she whispered, realising that, in a way, she was coming to love him. She enjoyed being with him. She found his air of authority irresistible; it tempered the sentimentality of his love for her. She had not realised that he could be so emotional. He wept easily, which she found strange in someone so autocratic. He could also be sanctimonious, peevish and irritable, and he always had to be right. It was going to be a hard task persuading him to embrace reform. She hadn't even started yet.

He had not mentioned her being crowned queen, and she did not expect it. None of his last three wives had been afforded a coronation. Either treasury funds were low, or the honour was dependent on the birth of a son. But she did not mind. She had never looked for that kind of glory.

She was relieved that people admired her for her virtue. She did not want to be thought another like poor Katheryn Howard. A queen should set a good example. Having chosen 'To be useful in all I do' for her motto, she sought for ways in which she could improve herself and the lives of others. She spent a lot of time reading, learning and at prayer. She encouraged scholars to visit her, taking care to welcome Catholics as well as reformists. She gave substantial sums of money to fund poor students. She ordered that the children of her tenants be given an education appropriate to their abilities. When Matthew Parker, one of the King's chaplains, warned her that the cost would be prohibitive, she rounded on him.

'It can never be too great for such a vital task! Besides, I am paying for it out of my own money.' Dr Parker subsided. He was a good man and a sound reformist, and took several of her poor scholars under his wing at the college of Stoke by Clare in Suffolk, of which he was dean; gladly, she consented to be its patron.

Francis Goldsmith, a cleric she admired and had appointed one of her chaplains, was a regular visitor to her privy chamber. He had looked approvingly at the flowers she had arranged herself in vases around the rooms, the tray of delicate sweetmeats served to him and the neat piles of devotional books on the court cupboard and beamed at her. 'You are a marvel, Madam. Your fame will excel that of Queen Esther! Your rare goodness has made every day like Sunday at court, which was never heard of, especially in a royal palace.'

'You are too kind, Dr Goldsmith,' she smiled, aware that he was flattering her.

'Madam, the kindness is yours. I cannot sufficiently express my thanks to you for admitting me to your household, and I pray God to feed you with manna from Heaven, that you may daily grow stronger in faith.'

Dr Goldsmith was not the only one with whom she enjoyed debating religion. Most of her ladies were educated women and there were many stimulating, and sometimes heated, discussions in her chamber. The Lady Mary, who now had her own apartments at court, was often present, blossoming in this relaxed ambience. Katharine encouraged men of learning to join them, which they did eagerly, and the courtiers came too. To her surprise, given that his father, Norfolk, was the leader of the Catholic faction, the lively Earl of Surrey spoke up enthusiastically for reform in the debates, as did his sister, the Duchess of Richmond, and his younger brother, Lord Thomas Howard. Sometimes Henry came, loving nothing better than an intellectual argument.

'Speak freely!' he exhorted those present, but, of course, there were limits, and Katharine took care to ensure that conversation that was tending towards anything controversial was steered in another direction. She was getting rather good at this.

Henry was most encouraging when she said she wanted to improve her language skills. He was fluent in many tongues and had recommended a tutor for Anne, who had agreed to be the patron of the celebrated scholar, Roger Ascham, but felt unworthy because her Latin was rusty after years of child-rearing. Henry himself helped Katharine to a greater understanding of Latin.

'I want to find something for the Lady Mary to do,' she told him one day when they were sitting at table with her well-thumbed copy of Cicero open before them. 'She is learned and she needs a project. I've been thinking that Erasmus's paraphrases of the Gospels should be translated into English and was wondering if she would like to be involved, if you think her Latin is good enough, and you approve.'

'I think it's a capital idea,' Henry beamed, 'and one that will appeal to her. Yes, I think she is proficient enough in Latin to do it. But it's a big task. Are you planning to undertake any of the translating yourself?'

'No, my role would be purely supervisory. I have too many royal duties to occupy me.'

Henry squeezed her hand. 'You will be setting a fine example as a patron of religious scholarship. I cannot but approve!'

She was touched by his praise. 'I want to help those who have an earnest zeal for their faith and hunger for the simple, plain knowledge of God's work. I don't mean to make them curious searchers of the high mysteries or troublesome, irreverent disputers of the Bible, but faithful followers of God's Word.'

'Erasmus would have been pleased. I met him once, when I was a child. He was the greatest scholar of his generation.'

Katharine agreed. 'I have always tried to follow his precept of learned piety. One can only applaud his desire to see the holy texts in their original languages, enabling us to achieve a greater understanding of them.'

Henry nodded. 'He cherished the ideal of peaceful cooperation in religious matters, but few were listening. It is something I have tried to achieve myself, and I have seen the difficulties he faced. But he was not interested in doctrine; he was all about faith and devotion. He would not get involved in the debate against Luther. Some said he had laid the egg, and Luther hatched it, but he refuted that.'

'If only he was alive now,' Katharine said.

'He'd have hated the way his precepts have been distorted and used as weapons in disputes about religion. But you will be extending the reach of his work, which is no mean thing.'

'I was thinking that I should bring in someone else to assist. Master Ascham recommended Dr Udall, who I believe was the headmaster of Eton. He has published a Latin textbook.' He was also, like Ascham, a reformist, which pleased her.

Henry frowned. 'Hmm. Udall has a poor reputation. He was made to leave Eton a couple of years ago after sodomising one of his pupils. He should have hanged, but his friends at court made frantic pleas to me to spare him on account of his scholarship, and I had the sentence commuted to imprisonment. He showed great remorse and became a different man. I had him freed after a year.'

Katharine was shocked. 'Master Ascham told my sister that Dr Udall was a grave and studious man who is in demand for his translating skills. Surely he knew of his conviction?'

'People can change,' Henry said, 'and, when a man has served his punishment, there must be forgiveness. As he likes little boys, I doubt he is a threat to you or Mary. He is a good scholar. And he is not likely to risk being caught a second time. There would be no reprieve then.'

'I read his translation of Erasmus's *Apophthegmata*,' she said. 'It's very impressive. If you agree, I will give him a chance – and keep an eye on him.'

'Mary will not need to see him very often. He is the best man for the job. Just be vigilant, Kate.'

Mary was delighted to be involved in the project and happy for Dr Udall to work on the translations. She was a very naïve young woman, and Katharine suspected that she had not heard of – or, if she had, had not understood – his fall from grace. She went pink with pleasure when Katharine asked her to work on St John, the most challenging of the Gospels.

'I know you will make a fine job of it,' Katharine said, pleased to have done something for her stepdaughter. She then made sure that Udall would only meet with Mary when she herself was present. She did not take to the man, and preferred not to have him near her, but, when she saw his work, she knew that Ascham and Henry had been right.

Katharine would have liked to have had Uncle William as her chamberlain, but he was often ailing these days and was spending less and less time at court. She missed his reassuring presence and his wise advice, and worried about his health. But Anne was with her, as chief lady of her privy chamber, serving alongside Margaret, Aunt Mary and Magdalen Lane, good friends and kinswomen all of them.

Sitting among her women as they sewed and read together, she thought herself fortunate to have the Duchess of Suffolk among her many ladies-in-waiting, and Lady Hoby, a learned woman whose husband, Sir Philip, was a respected diplomat. One she did not care for, though. Lady Hertford was strident to the point of being obnoxious and clearly had a low opinion of Katharine, who supposed she was angry that her husband's brother had been jilted. She would have liked to dismiss her, but the woman was so clever with her jibes that complaining about them would have sounded lame, and she did not want to injure the Seymours any further.

She was fond of the stolid Susanna Gilman, a Flemish artist who had given up her career to serve her as gentlewoman, but who undertook a few private commissions for her. Henry thought it a good idea for Katharine to have some portraits painted, anticipating a high demand for them, and promised to commission his painter, Hans Holbein, to take her likeness. Holbein had already sketched her sister and captured her brilliantly, but he was busy with other projects for Henry, so Katharine took pleasure in patronising a rotund and fussy artist called John Bettes and another Flemish artist, Levina Teerlinc, one of the King's painters; her appointment had been a unique honour for a woman. Privately, Katharine thought her talent inferior to Susanna's; all her sitters had stick-thin arms.

Today, she and her chief ladies had read aloud passages from Scripture to each other and a lively discussion had ensued. She was in little doubt that the majority of those who formed her inner circle were secret Protestants. It was the one matter on which she was in sympathy with Lady Hertford. They all took care not to be openly controversial. Even the outspoken Lady Suffolk remained circumspect, although she had no time for bishops and had christened her spaniel puppy Gardiner. 'Heel, Gardiner!' she would say, or 'In the corner, Gardiner!' amidst gales of laughter. Katharine smiled at that, but was at the same time chilled to think what the consequences would be if their secret beliefs were ever exposed. A nest of heretics, the real Gardiner would have called the Queen's chamber if he knew the truth. She was doing her best to avoid him.

Mindful of the King's middle way, she had been careful to ask for a traditional Catholic, the Bishop of Chichester, as her almoner; her chaplains, however, were reformists. Among them was her old friend, Miles Coverdale, who had translated the Bible. For all her circumspection, religious radicals came flocking to her little court to join the debates. One was a royal chaplain, Nicholas Ridley, who had lately evaded a charge of heresy. Another was Lady Suffolk's firebrand of a chaplain, Hugh Latimer; he brought his friend, Nicholas Shaxton, who had been banned from preaching. All three expounded freely at the Queen's gatherings. Katharine was concerned that Gardiner and the Catholic faction would see her as a focus for dissidence, so she took care to let those who attended her meetings know that any views expressed were to be entirely in keeping with the King's reforms. And, as Henry sometimes attended them, and she was winning golden opinions from so many, even Gardiner could not argue with that.

When Henry arrived in her chamber one warm summer evening, he waved her ladies away.

'God's bones, I am weary!' he said, sinking into the great chair that always stood ready for him. She rose and poured him some wine.

'Has Bishop Gardiner been bothering you again?' she asked.

He gave a great sigh and accepted the goblet gratefully. 'Yes. There is plague in London because of this heatwave and he thinks it's a visitation from God because there is an infestation of heresy in the realm.'

'Plague?' She had barely heard the rest. 'Oh, no.'

'Don't worry, Kate, you are quite safe here at Hampton Court. If I thought there was any danger, I would be on the move! But there has been great death in London and I have had it proclaimed that no one from the City is to come within seven miles of the court. I've also forbidden anyone here to go to London and return to court again.'

'I'm so relieved to hear that,' she said, kneeling at his feet. 'I have heard of these summer plagues and have always been glad to be far away.'

'You'll be safe with me,' he said, patting her shoulder.

'And Gardiner is blaming it on heresy?'

'Gardiner blames every ill on heresy.'

She gathered her courage. She had to start somewhere. 'Henry, why do you listen to that man? Anyone can see that he's dragging you backwards to a reconciliation with Rome.'

Henry withdrew his hand. There was a long pause. She dared not look up at him.

'I'm not a fool, Kate,' he said gently. 'I know what Gardiner would like. But he is destined to be disappointed. Even so, he is an able servant, and his thoughts chime with mine on many issues.'

'But there are those who might assist you along godlier paths.'

'Your gospellers? And Cranmer? Hah! They think I don't know their secrets.' His words struck fear into her.

'Their secrets?'

'Ah, Kate, you are too trusting. These people would have me go too far in the opposite direction, and there lies heresy. No, my middle way is best.'

She relaxed. 'If only Gardiner would see that. He is trying to undermine it. And he is an enemy of reform.'

'Some would say I have gone too far with my reforms. I have to consider that the souls of my people must be my first consideration.'

'Then be wary of Gardiner, I beg you.'

259

He raised her face to his. 'Kate, no one could question your sincerity in these matters, or your learning. But this is not just about religion; it is also about politics, for which women are not fitted. Never fear, I shall stick to my middle way, whatever Gardiner says.'

Ah, but was it really a middle way? She would have liked to challenge him, but feared she had said too much already. This was going to be a long game, but she was determined that Gardiner would not win it.

Katharine was standing in her bedchamber with her two stepdaughters, Mary and Margaret. A heap of newly delivered garments lay before them on the bed – gorgeous creations of cloth of gold and silver, damask, tissue, silk and velvet. In the outer chamber, her women were shrieking with laughter at the antics of her two jesters, Jane the Fool and the Dwarf, her parrot was squawking on its perch and her spaniel, Rig, a gift from Henry, was barking as if the hounds of Hell were baying at the door. She flung it open.

'Quiet, please!' she cried. The hubbub ceased; even the parrot looked subdued. Rig barked again, but she grabbed him by his velvet collar and wagged a finger. 'Naughty! Bad!'

She smiled at her ladies. 'Pray continue – just keep the noise down. I can't hear myself think.' She shut the door and grimaced.

Mary and Margaret were carefully looking through the garments.

'These are gorgeous!' Margaret said, awestruck.

'You will look every inch the Queen,' Mary told her. She too loved sumptuous clothing, although her tastes were more flamboyant – to make up, Katharine thought, for her plain looks. Or maybe she just wanted to attract male attention, poor girl.

'I like this one,' Mary said, touching an Italian gown in a rich shade of orange. Katharine was pleased to see that she was wearing the pair of bracelets set with rubies, emeralds and diamonds that she herself had given her. 'And this French kirtle is beautiful.' It was crimson, her favourite colour.

'These are exquisite,' Katharine said, peering into a box containing a set of six gold buttons in the form of Catherine wheels. 'And this.' She picked up a fan of ostrich feathers with a gold handle.

'Look at those shoes!' Margaret exclaimed. She pointed to the dozen pairs lined up on the floor, gold ones, velvet ones, leather ones and some with cork heels.

'Shoes are my weakness,' Katharine confessed. 'I was never able to indulge myself until now. But I'm feeling very selfish, having all this finery to myself. You must each choose a gown and I will have my tailor alter them to fit.' She had already sent a purple gown to Elizabeth.

Basking in their thanks, she waited until they had made their choices, then sent Margaret to join the other ladies. She wanted to have a private word with Mary, whom she led down the privy stair to the courtyard below and thence to her privy garden. It was another hot day, so they found a shaded bench beneath a tree.

'I cannot tell you what a pleasure it is to have you as a stepdaughter,' she told Mary. 'I am only four years older than you, but I hope you can think of me as a mother figure – and a friend.'

'You are already that, Madam,' Mary smiled.

'I have written to Prince Edward and the Lady Elizabeth, inviting them to come and visit me at court.'

'My father will never let Edward come just now, with the plague raging,' Mary said. 'Or Elizabeth, I suppose.'

'She replied to me,' Katharine told her. 'Her letters are very sophisticated; one would think she was a woman of forty!'

'She is very clever – and sharp.' Mary's gaze momentarily hardened. Of course, there must be some jealousy between the sisters – how could there not be? 'What did she say?'

'She thanked me for my kindness, which she said she did not deserve, and promised to come as soon as she was permitted. She said she would conduct herself in such a manner that I would never have cause for complaint, and that she would show me all due obedience and respect. She added that she was waiting with great impatience for the consent of the King.'

'That sounds like Elizabeth.' Mary was smiling again now. 'She was ever precocious.'

'When she does come, I am going to make you both my chief ladies-in-waiting.' Anne would not mind. She would understand that the

King's daughters must take precedence, and why Katharine felt the need to shower them with kindness.

'You have both had difficult times,' she said. 'I was touched to see how you look after Elizabeth.' They could easily have hated each other. Elizabeth was the living reminder of all that Mary and her mother had suffered as a result of Anne Boleyn's bewitchment of her father.

'She needs someone to guide her. Kate Champernowne, her lady mistress, is too soft with her. Elizabeth is too much like her mother. She loves flattery and her temper is changeable.'

Katharine took out her embroidery. 'She is young and perhaps defensive about her place in the world. As, I imagine, are you.'

Their eyes met, and Mary nodded. 'It has not been easy. When you have been an adored princess with the world at your feet and then . . . To have it all taken away and be declared a bastard – it was devastating. I am sure it is a barrier to finding a husband. And I do so long to marry and have children.'

Katharine leaned across and took her hand. 'I feel for you. It is good that you are lavishing all those maternal feelings on Elizabeth. She needs you. And I hear that Mistress Champernowne is a learned woman and a fine teacher, whatever her other faults.'

'Oh, yes,' Mary admitted, pulling off her hood and shaking free her long red hair. 'She has taught Elizabeth languages, at which she excels, and made her familiar with classical writers. She has also helped her to become proficient on the lute and virginals.'

'I'm sure you played no small part in that,' Katharine smiled. 'I hear that you are a talented musician yourself.'

Mary blushed with pleasure. 'I love music, like my father,' she said. 'It is in our blood.' She hesitated. 'I help Elizabeth because she is a winning child, not because we are tied by blood. In fact, we are not. She is not my father's daughter.'

Katharine stared at her.

'Her father was a musician called Mark Smeaton. He was one of that woman's lovers. She looks like him.'

Katharine gathered her wits. 'I can't believe what you are telling me. She looks like your father – that struck me when I met her.'

'But your Grace never met Mark Smeaton,' Mary pointed out. 'If you had, you would see the resemblance.'

Katharine was by no means convinced. She felt uncomfortable even talking about it, and somehow disloyal to Henry. Did he know what Mary believed? Should she tell him? No. A still tongue . . . It was time to change the subject.

She stood up. 'I am not qualified to comment. Shall we walk a little?'

Mary rose and put on her hood. 'As you wish.'

'I am longing to meet Prince Edward,' Katharine said, as they emerged into the palace gardens and made for the bowling alley, where a game was in progress. 'It would be a pleasure to me to have you all at court.'

'Edward rarely comes,' Mary said. 'My father is terrified he will catch something. He insists he is better off in the country where the air is healthy.'

'When the plague has passed, I will ask if he can visit. I would so like to have us all together as a family.'

'It would be lovely,' Mary replied, looking wistful. It *would* be lovely, Katharine thought, bringing these damaged girls and that lonely little boy under her wing and showing them that life had so many good things to offer. And, the more mercenary part of her thought, it would be advantageous to win the love and gratitude of the future King. But, until she could have him with her, she could pave the way by writing him affectionate letters, showing him kindness and sending him gifts; she had already dispatched two suits of crimson velvet and white satin.

'Edward will be six soon,' Mary was saying. 'My father is talking of engaging his chaplain, Dr Cox, as his tutor. That worries me. There is talk that Dr Cox was sent down from Oxford for spouting Lutheran views. I would not want such a man to be near my brother.'

'I doubt your father would have appointed him chaplain if the rumours were true,' Katharine said.

Mary frowned. It was as if she had not heard her. 'I hate these reformists; they're all Protestants underneath. It was a sorry day for England when my father broke with Rome.'

'Shh! Mind what you say!' Katharine hissed. They were approaching the bowling alley and might be overheard. Already, people were bowing and curtseying to them. She could not have anyone saying that Mary had spoken treason. People had died horrible deaths for less. She shuddered inwardly to think what this young woman, of whom she was becoming fond, would say if she knew that her stepmother held the very views she reviled. She did not want to lose Mary's affection or her respect, or add to her unhappiness.

The King came to her chamber that evening with a group of his gentlemen, and there was dancing. Henry did one turn with her on the floor and then retired to his chair, leaving Lord Hertford to partner her.

'I've received a letter from my brother, Madam,' Hertford said in that cold manner of his. 'He asks me to send you his congratulations on becoming queen.'

She realised that she was trembling. It took all her concentration to focus on the dance steps and keep her hands steady when she had to hold his. 'That is very kind,' she said. To her horror, she felt tears welling up. She blinked rapidly while executing an elegant twirl, then forced a smile. 'I trust he is faring well abroad?'

'He is being kept very busy, which is as well,' he replied.

She could sense the disapproval in his tone. He did know about her and Tom. If only she could tell him that she would have preferred his brother to the King any day.

She had arranged a programme of music for Henry's entertainment and was relieved when the dance was over and the Bassanos could play for the company. She was their patron now, and proud of them. They were followed by her Italian consort of viols. Katharine noticed that Master Tallis, the organist of the King's Chapel Royal, was standing at the back of the room. Both she and Henry greatly admired his musical talent and his compositions. His Masses and motets were sublime – it was as if angels were singing. She wished she had asked him to sing tonight, but that was something special that could wait for another occasion.

'A wonderful evening, darling,' Henry said as the final notes died, and began clapping loudly. The musicians bowed low and the guests stood to applaud.

'I will come to you tonight,' Henry murmured in Katharine's ear.

He joined her in bed most nights. Sometimes, he had not the vigour to thrust inside her, but they had coupled together often enough for her to wonder if she might be pregnant. She did not hold out much hope of that after two childless marriages – but what a wonderful thing it would be if she could bear Henry a son. She could conceive a child, she knew it, and she was not that old. She let herself imagine his joy when she told him she was pregnant, and herself holding the precious babe in her arms, showing him off triumphantly. If only . . .

When she was in her nightgown and Anne began brushing her hair, she waited for her other attendants to leave, then asked, 'Anne, did you ever see Mark Smeaton?'

She could see her sister's face in her mirror, the new one with sapphires, rubies and pearls, and it was obvious that the question had surprised her.

'Yes, several times. He used to haunt Queen Anne's chamber. I think he fancied her, not that I ever saw her reciprocate it. I never believed that she would have stooped so low as to commit adultery with him. Why do you ask?'

Katharine kept her voice low. 'The Lady Mary is convinced that he is Elizabeth's father. She says Elizabeth is the image of him.'

Anne thought about it. 'I don't think so. Anyone can see that she is the image of the King. Her hair, her nose. I'm sorry, Kate, but I think the Lady Mary is too willing to believe anything bad about Anne Boleyn.'

It did not bother Katharine when Henry rode over to Richmond to dine with Anne of Cleves. She had heard gossip that Anne had indeed hoped to be reinstated and had been upset that the King had chosen another, so she applauded him for breaking the ice. She knew she had no need to worry. He seemed genuinely fond of Anne, but in a brotherly way. Besides, who was she to talk? She was in love with another man.

When Henry returned, they departed on a summer progress, planning initially to lodge at the royal houses at Oatlands, Woodstock, Langley and Grafton, their route taking them further and further from

265

plague-stricken London. They made the journey in leisurely stages, hunting every day. Katharine would have liked to follow the chase on horseback, but felt obliged to remain with Henry on the new standings he had had built now that riding was a challenge when his leg was troubling him. The beaters would drive the quarry past the stand, where Henry and Katharine stood, taking aim. It was not nearly as exciting as the chase.

Gardiner, thank the good Lord, had remained behind, thinking no doubt that, with the King away, he had a free hand in sniffing out heresy. True to form, he was soon up to mischief – dangerous mischief.

One of the gentlemen of the King's privy chamber who frequented Katharine's chamber and joined in the scholarly debates was Thomas Cawarden, a man of parts in Surrey and Sussex, who acted as steward of Bletchingley, a palatial manner that had been given to Anne of Cleves as part of her divorce settlement. He was one of those restless men with a volatile temperament, overconfident and unpredictable – an explosion waiting to happen. He was good-looking in a sardonic way that did not appeal to Katharine, and she strongly suspected that he secretly shared her Protestant faith. And it was obvious, from disparaging remarks he had made in conversation, that he did not like Gardiner.

When Katharine returned to Oatlands from the hunt on a warm afternoon in late July, Cawarden was waiting for her in the antechamber to her apartments.

'Your Grace.' He bowed elaborately. 'May I crave a few words in private?'

The urgency in his tone disconcerted her.

'Of course, Mr Cawarden. Do come in.' She led him into her dining chamber, where the table was already laid for supper. 'What can I do for you?'

'Madam, you should know that five members of the King's Chapel Royal at Windsor have been arrested for heresy.'

'The Chapel Royal? Dear Heaven!'

'One of them is the Master of the Choristers, John Marbeck. They are all in the town gaol.'

'Is this Bishop Gardiner's doing?'

'Oh, yes.' His eyes narrowed. 'He is aiming his bow at the big deer, but to get to them he has to catch the little coneys first.'

'And why have you come to me?'

He fixed his dark eyes on her. 'Because, Madam, I believe that you too are a friend of the Gospel.'

She froze. If Cawarden could detect where her sympathies lay, others could too.

'I support the King's reforms,' she said firmly.

'Of course. But, Madam, if someone does not do something to stop Gardiner, men will burn.'

She shuddered.

'Two of those taken are good friends of mine,' he went on. 'One is close to Sir Philip Hoby, whose wife serves in your Grace's chamber.'

That struck too close to home. Katharine began trembling as she perceived that Gardiner had found a means of infiltrating her circle and discovering its secrets.

'What can I do?' she asked.

'Someone in the Chapel Royal got word to me that Mr Marbeck's house was searched by Gardiner's men. They found incriminating letters – sufficient evidence, I fear, to indict people in the court. A list of other suspects has been drawn up and is to be sent with the letters to Gardiner in London. Madam, I fear that my name may be on it because of my connections with the accused, and that people close to you may be incriminated too. I have to get my hands on that list.'

'How do you know about the list?'

'My friend at Windsor heard the Bishop's clerks discussing it. Madam, we need to get someone trustworthy down there to find out who is taking those documents to Winchester House. Once we know that, you can safely leave the rest to me. I cannot go. I am too well known and my opinions are already suspected. Hourly, I expect to be arrested.'

Katharine thought quickly. She had a groom, Fulke, who had been in her household since Snape days. A taciturn Yorkshireman, he was as loyal as a rock. He would do this for her without asking any questions, and she could rely on him never to talk.

'I know the very man,' she said. 'I will send for him now.'

* * *

Fulke got back to Oatlands the following afternoon and found her at her prayers. 'Something for your Grace,' he murmured, placing a folded piece of paper on the altar rail and vanishing.

She looked at it surreptitiously, mindful of her women praying nearby. Two words were written there: *Robert Ockham.*

She rose and left the chapel, then hurried to her privy chamber, where she found a page. 'Please find Mr Thomas Cawarden and bring him here,' she commanded. 'He will be either in his lodging or the King's privy chamber.'

Cawarden was with her in ten minutes. Aware that the page was behind him, she handed him the folded paper, her heart thumping. 'Ah, Mr Cawarden. Here are the details of the grant we were discussing.'

'Your Grace is most kind,' he replied and, with a quick bow, hastened away.

She returned to her prayers, beseeching God to speed him on his way. She did not know what he was planning to do, but somehow she trusted him to accomplish it. He was the kind of man who expected, and got, his way. The hours dragged as she waited to learn if his mission had been a success.

When the King joined her for supper the next evening, he was in an irritable mood.

'Has Gardiner angered you again?' she asked.

'You might say that,' he growled. 'He's gone too far this time. He has been rooting around in *my* Chapel Royal at Windsor and found a nest of heretics. What's more, he's had the effrontery to draw up a list of a great number of *my* true and faithful courtiers who are to be charged with heresy. Fortunately, some trusty person brought the list to the Council.'

Katharine was feeling faint with relief, but busied herself with buttering her manchet bread, which she was going to have to force herself to eat. 'But surely you are concerned to root out heresy wherever it is?'

'These people are not heretics! I know them. They are my true subjects and I will not have them persecuted. I have pardoned all those on the list, and Marbeck, for he is a great musician, and I have ordered that those who drew up that list be paraded around Windsor facing their horses' tails and wearing placards proclaiming their offences; then they shall stand in the pillory!' His face was puce with outrage.

'Thanks be to God that justice has been done,' Katharine said fervently. And thanks be to God that Thomas Cawarden, Sir Philip and Lady Hoby and all the rest were safe. But what of those four who were still in prison and doomed to die? Her heart bled for them, yet she dared not plead for their lives.

Cawarden came up to her the next day, as she and her ladies were taking turns at the archery butts. Several spectators had gathered, so no one would think there was anything amiss about his joining them.

'A fine day, your Grace.' He looked as if he had not a care in the world.

'You were happy with the grant, Mr Cawarden?' she asked. 'You were hoping for a good outcome.'

'More than satisfied, Madam. Everything is going well. But I was surprised to see my name and my wife's listed among the twelve named on the document.'

'Well, it is settled now,' she said, and moved closer to Lady Hertford, for she should not be seen talking to him for too long. 'Your turn next, I think, Nan.' Cawarden bowed and moved away.

Inwardly, Katharine had mixed feelings. Gardiner had been foiled of many of his victims, and she had been instrumental in that – and got away with it. She had probably saved the lives of twelve people, even if she had not saved everyone. Yet she knew that the Bishop and his friends would not be put off. They would fight back. Gardiner was like a cat with a mouse, determined to purge the realm of heresy. So far, she had not crossed swords with him personally, or even spoken to him beyond courtesies, and he could not know that she was his enemy, so she was safe – for the present, anyway.

After the progress ended, the court returned to Windsor. Henry and Katharine were there when the four Chapel Royal heretics were burned at the stake in the Great Park. Henry might have spared Marbeck, but he sent the others to their deaths to show that heresy would not be tolerated. Some of the men of her household went to watch the executions and came back sickened. She could not bear to hear their accounts of what they had seen or take pleasure in the plans for the new apartments Henry was having built for her at Hampton Court, or in her new barge.

Nan Hertford, whose husband received regular letters from his brother, seemed to enjoy telling her that Tom Seymour was still encamped with the army in France, in some peril, for the French were nearby.

It was hard to hide from Henry how troubled she was, and Katharine was glad to have Mary's company to divert her from dark thoughts. But, at the end of September, Mary fell ill with what she told Katharine were her usual autumn ailments and went home to her house in Essex. Not long after that, Nan informed Katharine that the army in France was running out of food and adequate clothing to keep out the cold. Katharine could have killed her.

The plague was still striking people dead in London, even though the weather was now autumnal. The King moved the court to Dunstable, where the old priory had just been converted into a luxurious palace. Katharine spared a thought for Henry's first wife, whose marriage had been dissolved here during the years of her exile. She had been confined nearby at Ampthill Castle, and Katharine could not but dwell on the fate of the tragic woman who had been denied a happy deliverance.

From Dunstable, Henry and Katharine rode over to Ashridge to visit Prince Edward on his sixth birthday. At last, she was to meet her stepson, and future king. She was pleased to find Elizabeth there too, and to be welcomed warmly by her.

As Edward was brought to meet his father, she took one look at the solemn, fair-haired little boy with the heart-shaped face and was overwhelmed by pity. Splendidly attired, still in long skirts, he looked so small in the sumptuous chambers of his palace. He was fussed over by his lady mistress, the redoubtable Lady Bryan, his nurse, Mother Jack, and his sister, and surrounded by an army of attendants.

'Most noble father and gracious king,' he greeted Henry, executing a perfect courtly bow. What precocity! How distant and formidable must this massive sire in his magnificent clothes and jewels appear to his son.

Henry patted him on the head. 'I have brought your new stepmother to meet you.'

'Your Majesty.' Edward bowed to her. She would have liked to hug and kiss him, but did not know how it would be received.

'I am overjoyed to meet your Grace,' she said. 'I have been looking forward to it for so long. I do hope that we are going to be friends and that you will allow me to be a mother to you, as I am to your sisters.'

The cool grey eyes, so like Henry's, regarded her directly, almost disconcertingly. 'I should like that very much, Madam.'

'I have brought you a jewel, Edward,' Henry said, removing a velvet pouch from the pocket of his gown. Edward drew from it a pendant enamelled with figures of St George and the Dragon and stared at it as if it were the Holy Grail. 'You must love me, your Majesty, to give me such a fine gift,' he said.

'Of course I love you,' Henry smiled. 'You are *my* most precious jewel.' Taking the boy by the hand, he led them through to the privy chamber and bade Edward sit beside him.

'He looks well, Lady Bryan.'

'He is, Sir. His Grace already knows his letters and his Catechism. He excels in his daily exercises in horsemanship. Above all, he strives to satisfy your Majesty's good expectations. We tell him every day that he must emulate his father. What is it I say to you, Prince Edward?'

'If I equal the deeds of my father, men can ask no more,' the child recited. Katharine could have wept for him, remembering the carefree days of her own childhood at Rye House, something he would never know. What a burden to place on his young shoulders. Could learning to emulate his father not wait until he was a little older?

'What do you like to play with, Edward?' she asked.

'I like my wooden horse and my spinning top,' he told her.

'You love your skittles too,' Elizabeth reminded him.

'What can I send you as a present?' Katharine asked. 'Do you like to play ball?'

271

'I would very much like a ball, thank you.' Was that the glimmer of a smile? She wondered how often this little boy laughed.

Henry was beaming at her approvingly.

'I will send you a ball,' she promised.

'I'll play with you,' Elizabeth offered. Edward was definitely smiling now.

'I imagine that you are very happy to be marrying the Queen of Scots,' Katharine said to him.

'Yes, Madam, but she is only a baby.'

'She will grow,' Henry said heartily, 'and you will be king of both Scotland and England. No more Scots raiding across the border! No more subversive Scottish treaties with France. Think yourself happy, my boy!'

'I am happy,' Edward declared, looking anything but. 'I cannot thank you enough, Sir, for securing me such a great princess.'

Henry looked his son up and down. 'You are a big boy now, too old to be brought up by women. It is time for you to be breeched and begin your education. Does that please you?'

'Yes, Sir.' Edward did look pleased, Katharine was glad to see. But how would he feel when Lady Bryan and Mother Jack had been replaced by tutors, as Henry intended? What would his life be like without those mother figures he had known from infancy?

'Dr Cox is to be your tutor,' the King told him. He and Katharine had discussed the matter and agreed that Dr Cox was perfect for this high responsibility. He was a learned fellow of King's College, Cambridge, and a stout reformist, but, more to the point, as far as Katharine was concerned, Edward knew him, for he was the boy's almoner and had heard all his infant confessions. Unlike most tutors, Dr Cox believed that learning should be an enjoyable experience, not reinforced by beatings, although he approved of them as a last resort.

'You will have friends about you to share your lessons,' Henry told his son. 'I have appointed fourteen noble boys to reside with you and be company for you. And your sister Elizabeth will join you in the classroom. You should take example from her, for she is good at her studies.' He smiled proudly at his daughter.

'Thank you, Sir.' Elizabeth looked inordinately pleased. 'I can help you with your lessons, Edward.'

'That is kind of you, sister.' The boy took her hand. There was clearly great affection between them.

They stayed for dinner, then rode back to Dunstable. Katharine felt sad leaving Edward to face the looming changes in his life alone, but at least he had Elizabeth to support him. She resolved to write to him regularly, to let him know that she was thinking of him.

Still the plague lingered and, in the autumn, claimed Hans Holbein, the King's gifted artist. He would never now paint Katharine's portrait; nor would she receive the cups and brooch she had commissioned from him. Yet he had delivered to her three roundel portraits of her step-children, and his work was to be seen everywhere in the royal palaces.

'He is irreplaceable,' Henry mourned, as they stood before a painting by the late master. 'We shall never see his like again. Your picture will have to be done by Master Hornebolte. He is good, but nowhere near as good as Holbein. And I've been recommended to patronise an artist newly arrived here from Antwerp, a Master Eworth. I've seen his work and it's impressive. I've been thinking that he can complete the pictures Holbein left unfinished.'

'Can he paint miniatures?'

'I believe so.'

'I would like matching miniatures of ourselves.'

'Then feel free to approach him. You may charge the cost to my privy purse.'

Katharine was sitting for Master Eworth early in December when the King came stumping into her presence chamber. 'Out! Out!' he commanded, and everyone fled, the artist dropping his brush in his haste to depart.

Seeing his face, and that dangerous flush, Katharine rose in alarm. 'What has happened?' Her first thought was that he had found out about Tom or was about to condemn her as a heretic. But she had been so careful . . .

'The Scots have revoked the Treaty of Greenwich!' he barked. 'The churls have renewed their old alliance with France. By God, they shall suffer for it!'

He slumped into her throne, his head in his hand, weeping tears of angry frustration. 'Gone! All my hopes of one united kingdom, gone! The Scots are virtually telling me that my heir is not good enough for their Queen. Well, they shall pay for that too.' He sat up, his eyes wet and blazing. 'This is war!'

'I am utterly shocked,' Katharine sympathised, laying a tender hand on his shoulder. 'You do not deserve this after all your careful diplomacy. It is dishonourable of the Scots to ratify the treaty and then flout it.'

'Aye, and they couldn't have done it at a worst time. I'm due to join the Emperor for the offensive against France next year but I cannot fight a war on two fronts. I have not the resources. I shall send Hertford north with an army to teach the Scots a lesson. He can set off right away! They will know what it means to defy me!'

When the plague had at last run its course, they returned to Whitehall. Henry was still in an angry mood, but he had calmed down by the time they arrived at Hampton Court, where they were to spend Christmas. Katharine was delighted with her spacious new lodgings in Clock Court. Her windows overlooked the gardens and the fishponds, and the River Thames beyond. She could find peace here. After the turbulent events and emotional upheavals of the past year, she needed it. Already, she was beginning to feel safer, and even thinking less of Tom. Maybe now she could allow herself to relax.

She had persuaded Henry that all three of his children should join them for Christmas. It was a joy to bring them together under one roof. Mary, who was quite recovered now, looked happier than Katharine had ever seen her; Elizabeth was throwing herself with gusto into the preparations, making mistletoe boughs and wrapping New Year's gifts; and Edward was as excited as any ordinary child.

Will was back at court, having completed his tour of duty, and Katharine's happiness was crowned when, after Mass, two days before Christmas, in an impressive ceremony in the presence chamber, Henry at last created him earl of Essex. Then Uncle William came forward, looking greyer at the temples, and was invested with the barony of Horton. Katharine, watching, had tears in her eyes. Afterwards, as her brother and her uncle, wearing their new robes and coronets of estate, strode off to dine with the lords in the council chamber, her heart was fit to burst with pride.

Chapter 18

1544

It had been a good dinner. Henry leaned back, satisfied, and wiped his mouth, while Katharine helped herself to another spoonful of syllabub. They were alone; they always dismissed the servants when they dined in private. Outside the window, she could hear a storm blowing, with the wind whistling around the towers and turrets of Whitehall. It was nearly February, and very cold, but not in her privy chamber, where a great fire burned.

It was now or never.

'Henry,' she said, 'I am sorry that we have not yet been blessed with a child.'

He frowned. 'It is God's will. I pray for it daily, though.'

'You must worry about the succession,' she said. 'Edward is a healthy boy, but it's clear that you fear for him.' She was thinking of the rigorous cleaning of the child's apartments, three times a day, the restrictions on those visiting him and Henry's obsession with Edward enjoying clean country air.

'I do,' he replied. 'So many children die young.'

'But you have two daughters, both intelligent and able ladies, who are quite capable, I am sure, of ruling this realm should anything befall Edward, which God forbid.'

Henry crossed himself. 'Amen to that. But, Kate, a woman cannot wield dominion over men.'

'Queen Isabella ruled over Castile and is today accounted a great ruler. There have been female regents in France who have governed ably, and you yourself have highly praised the Imperial princesses who have ruled the Netherlands. They have all wielded dominion over men.'

He shook his head. 'The English would not tolerate a female ruler. They saw off the Empress Matilda in the twelfth century because of her insufferable pride and lack of judgement. How can a woman be an infant in law and yet wield sovereign power?'

'Forgive me, Henry, but I think it is all down to personal ability – and Mary and Elizabeth have that in abundance. In your own realm, many women run estates and businesses. And think – if Edward's line fails, one of your blood would still sit on the throne.'

'Hmm.' Henry stroked his beard. 'Isabella was joint sovereign with her husband, King Ferdinand, but a queen regnant would face a problem when it came to choosing a husband, which she must do to ensure the succession. He would, in the natural order of things, rule in her name. Yet who should she choose? A foreign prince? England might end up as an outpost of the Empire or France. And remember, the English don't like foreigners. But if she took one of our noblemen, she might raise jealousies among the peers.'

She smiled at him. 'I understand. I was only thinking of your peace of mind. It was just an idea, but I defer to your better judgement.'

Henry sat there, pensive, for a while. 'I take your point,' he said at length. 'I can name anyone I please as my successor, and Parliament would ratify it. Bastardy need not be an issue. I would have named young Richmond my heir if he'd lived.'

She was halfway to winning the argument. 'You have valuable assets in your daughters. And think how overjoyed they will be to know that you place enough trust in them to restore them to the succession. They deserve that. Oh, Henry . . .' She slid to her knees before him. 'I pray you, think on it.'

'You shouldn't kneel to me, Kate,' Henry said, leaning forward and raising her by the elbows. 'I will think on it, I promise. But I won't have Mary and Elizabeth declared legitimate. That would be to acknowledge that my unions with their mothers were true marriages.'

'I do see that you couldn't do that,' she answered.

'Have you any more of that excellent wine?' he asked. She knew it was time to change the subject.

* * *

'I am giving my assent today,' Henry told Katharine when she came to sit with him in his closet. 'It's all decided – as you wanted. Mary and Elizabeth will be restored to the succession, after Edward. We may yet have children, darling, but you are right, I must make plans for all contingencies. Here is the draft Bill, if you would like to read it.'

He handed her a scroll and she looked over the new Act of Succession that Parliament would soon pass. Her eyes were brimming with joy at her achievement. The Act also provided that any issue she bore the King would come after Prince Edward in the order of succession. Failing that, the next in line would be any children the King might have by other queens. She drew in her breath.

'Other queens?' she faltered.

'Oh, darling,' Henry said, 'I have to consider all eventualities. I pray God that you will be spared to me for as long as I live, but, if He decrees otherwise, it will remain my duty to provide for the succession.'

She relaxed. She could not wait for Mary and Elizabeth to hear the happy news.

'I am commissioning a large painting to mark the Act,' he told her. 'It will show me and my heirs – the Tudor dynasty.'

'That's an excellent idea,' she said.

She would never forget how Mary's face lit up when Henry told her that she was to be restored to the succession. They were at dinner and Mary couldn't eat a morsel after that. When Henry had gone to bed, basking in her gratitude, she turned to Katharine and there were tears in her eyes.

'I know I have you to thank for this. My father would never have thought of it. I cannot tell you how happy I am. It was what my sainted mother fought for – that I should take my rightful place in the succession.' She hugged Katharine impulsively. 'I do not look for a crown; I hope that Edward thrives and grows up to have children. I only ever wanted my right to the throne acknowledged. How my mother will be rejoicing in Heaven this day!'

When Katharine rode over with Henry to Ashridge to tell Elizabeth the news, she rejoiced to see another stepdaughter so excited. Elizabeth could never have looked to see her mother rehabilitated, but this was the next best thing. She threw her arms around Henry and hugged him tightly. Katharine noticed that there were tears in his eyes.

She was not so elated when she saw the finished painting that Henry had commissioned. There was Henry, seated on his canopied throne in the presence chamber at Whitehall, with Edward at his knee and Mary and Elizabeth standing at either side, beyond the pillars representing legitimacy. And there, sitting beside the King, was not herself, but Jane Seymour.

She was a little shaken. She had thought that she would be appearing in the picture; after all, it had been she who had persuaded Henry to restore his daughters to the succession. She had been expecting a request for a sitting and was quite surprised when Henry told her that the painting was finished.

She stood before it. 'It is a fine work,' she said.

'You understand why I had to include Jane,' Henry told her. 'She gave me my heir. It is fitting that she is portrayed as the founding matriarch of my dynasty.'

Katharine did understand. She felt better. If only she too could give the King a son.

That February, the Emperor sent a special envoy, the Spanish Duke of Najera, to England to discuss strategies for the coming war with France. Will and the Earl of Surrey were deputed to dine with him at the Spanish embassy before escorting him to court.

Henry was waiting impatiently. He was full of going to France and winning glory there.

'From my youth,' he told Katharine, 'I have wanted to be a second Henry V. We trounced the French in 1513, and we shall do so again!' Yes, she thought, but in 1513 you were a young man, and fit; that was over thirty years ago. Yet she knew that nothing would deter him from his purpose. He was going to France and he was determined to lead his army.

'I only hope that Hertford thrashes the Scots and gets home before I leave,' he said. 'I'd rather not have a war on two fronts.'

'I will pray for his success,' Katharine murmured.

'I will receive the Duke first, and then he will visit you,' Henry told her. 'I want you to afford him an especially warm welcome, to demonstrate our friendship towards the Emperor.'

'Of course,' she assured him, and sincerely, because she would rather he was allied to the Emperor than to the King of France, that slippery old reprobate, any day.

'You look every inch the Queen,' Henry complimented her.

'I wish to do all honour to his Imperial Majesty,' she told him. She had chosen a kirtle of cloth of gold beneath a gown of brocade lined with crimson satin, with matching velvet sleeves and a long train. Around her waist was a gold girdle and hanging around her neck were two crosses and a jewel of magnificent diamonds. There were diamonds too in her French hood. She glittered, as did Mary, who was waiting with her, splendidly attired in cloth of gold and purple velvet. She was the Emperor's cousin, so her presence was fitting, and she spoke Spanish, which would make Katharine's task easier.

Henry left the Queen's apartments by the secret gallery that led to his bedchamber. He was becoming obsessed with privacy these days, wanting none to know his movements, anxious to conceal his increasing spells of poor health.

An hour later, the Duke of Najera arrived, escorted by Will, Surrey and the ageing Imperial ambassador, Messire Chapuys. At that precise moment, Katharine felt nauseous, yet she received her guest graciously, extending her hand to be kissed, and introduced him to Mary, who greeted him in Spanish, and to Margaret Douglas, who was also present.

'I trust you bring us good news of the Emperor, my lord,' Katharine asked, as Mary translated. The Duke assured her that his master was in perfect health.

'Pray send my humble recommendations when you next write to his Majesty,' she said to Chapuys. She had quickly warmed to the ambassador. He had been at the English court for fifteen years, knew everyone, and was the soul of courtesy. Henry called him an old rogue, but he enjoyed sparring with him and genuinely liked him.

'His Imperial Majesty is appreciative of the favour you have shown to the Princess,' Chapuys told her. She noticed that he gave Mary the title that had been taken from her.

'It has been my pleasure to help her,' she said, wishing she didn't feel so sick. But she must not give in to it. After drinks had been served, she led the Duke and his company into her privy chamber, where, at her signal, the musicians struck up and the dancing began. She took to the floor first with Will as her partner, while the Duke danced with Mary. Then Katharine and Mary danced together, their ladies whirling around them in silks of many colours and jewelled hoods. After that, they all stood at the side to watch a dextrous Venetian in the King's service dancing galliards with such extraordinary agility that he seemed to have wings on his feet.

The dancing and the music went on for at least two hours. Katharine felt fit to drop and feared that she might actually vomit. For the first time, it occurred to her that she might be pregnant. She was utterly relieved when the Duke came to kiss her hand in farewell and she could present the gifts she had brought for him. Then she retired gratefully to lie down, nursing her wildest hopes.

The sickness came again the next day, and the next. Then her courses arrived. It was a crushing disappointment.

Katharine stifled a sigh. The weight of Henry's leg on her lap was becoming uncomfortable and she did not think she could endure the stench for much longer. He was recovering, but it had been a worrying two days because he had become feverish and the doctors had begun shaking their heads. She had been so anxious that she had ordered her bed to be placed in the closet by his bedchamber and spent two sleepless nights listening to him moaning, and getting up to sponge his brow and make him take the liquorice pastilles and cinnamon comfits she had obtained from his apothecary. It had been a salutary reminder of his mortality; not for the first time, it had occurred to her that it might not be long before she was a widow once more – and free to marry where she pleased.

Henry shifted, arousing her from her reverie. He was happily absorbed in fiddling about with the gold clock salt that Sir Anthony

Denny, the head of his privy chamber, had given him at New Year. It had been one of the last things Holbein had designed before his death, and Henry was fascinated by it, for cunningly concealed inside it were an hour glass, two sundials and a compass.

But he had to set it aside to receive Chapuys, who had come to discuss preparations for the war with France, which were progressing well. Katharine, listening silently, saw that Henry was rejuvenated by their talk. But, when Chapuys had gone and he struggled to his feet to process to the Chapel Royal for Mass, he staggered and would have fallen had not the guards at the door hastened to steady him. Barely able to stand, he leaned on his stick and tottered out of the room.

If only he could lose some weight, Katharine thought; she was sure that his health would improve, and his legs. But he was over-fond of his food and leading such a sedentary life that she feared he would never reduce his bulk. It worried her deeply, not least because she had become very fond of him. That was her reward for her efforts to make her marriage work. They were easy together, and he had grown to rely on her. She was the first person he came to when he was angry or worried. He listened to her advice, but never allowed her to interfere in politics unless he himself had commanded her, as when he had asked her to show friendship to the Emperor. She was aware, through Chapuys and various Imperial envoys, that her friendship and support were valued in Imperial circles.

She supported Henry in his war with the Scots too, deploring the perfidy of the Scottish government. Hertford's army was wreaking havoc in the lowlands. She had seen the letter Henry had written to the Earl, commanding him to sack, burn and subvert Edinburgh and other towns, and put every man, woman and child to the sword. She had watched him working himself into yet another rage and had not dared to remonstrate with him.

'I will crush them,' he'd sworn. 'I will make them agree to the marriage!'

They were calling it the Rough Wooing. If anything, she thought, it would put the Scots off making an alliance with England ever again.

Despite herself, she could see why they were fighting back, having made their little Queen disappear to God knows where. They were a proud, stubborn people who cherished their independence. But they had been wrong to break the treaty, and England and Scotland *would* be better off united.

Anne, great with child once more, came hastening to Katharine's bedchamber, just as Katharine was about to call on the Prince, who was enjoying one of his rare visits to court.

'The King has granted Herbert Wilton Abbey, Ramsbury Abbey and Cardiff Castle!' she cried, beside herself. 'I can't believe it. We have not just one house of our own at last, but three!'

Katharine hugged her. 'I knew his Grace was going to make the grants. I am so pleased for you both.'

'This is all down to you, Kate! If you had not wed the King, we would not be riding so high.'

'That is one of the great pleasures of being queen. And these.' She indicated the bolts of purple velvet and satin lying on the bed. 'The mercer delivered them this morning.'

'They're beautiful,' Anne said, fingering them. 'You deserve them.'

They sat down by the fire.

'Herbert has great plans for Wilton,' Anne said. 'He's going to have the abbey demolished and build a fine house.'

'You will be quite the grand lady,' Katharine smiled.

At that moment, Will was announced. 'I knew you'd be here, sister,' he said to Anne. 'I've come to congratulate you.' He bent and kissed her. 'And Kate, I have some news for you.' The smile slipped. 'Sir Thomas Seymour has returned to court.'

Katharine felt as if she had been winded.

'He turned up in the privy chamber today, bragging about his adventures in France and as full of himself as ever.'

'I don't want to see him,' she said. 'I can't see him.'

'You ought to brace yourself. In reward for his services, he has received grants from the King and been appointed Master of the Ordnance and a man-at-arms to the Master of Horse.'

'He must have acquitted himself well in France,' Anne observed.

'Aye,' said Will. 'He's more insufferable than ever.'

'Don't say that,' Katharine reproved him.

'Kate, you should not think of him.'

'Don't you think I try not to?' she blurted out, getting to her feet. 'Excuse me, I have to see the Prince.'

'I'm only thinking of your safety,' Will protested as she swept past him.

'I think of it every day!' she retorted. 'Come, Anne!'

She sped through the galleries, Anne hurrying in her wake. They did not speak; there were too many people to hear them. Whitehall was a maze, a ramshackle old palace that had been added to and altered over the years. The Prince's lodging was near the river, overlooking the gardens. She had been visiting him every day, helping and encouraging him with his lessons under the benign gaze of Dr Cox, and getting down on the floor to play skittles with him. He did not seem to be missing Lady Bryan or Mother Jack. He was relaxed with Katharine now and even allowed himself to indulge in some childish high spirits. Dr Cox had told him off for telling her that she was his horse and trying to climb on her back.

'You don't treat the Queen of England with such disrespect!' he'd admonished.

'It's all right,' Katharine had replied, laughing. 'I'm enjoying myself.'

Today, she was in no mood for games; her heart was in turmoil. She did not know how she would act normally. But Edward was expecting her. She could not let him down. Hopefully, he was too young to detect that something was amiss.

She had not expected Henry to be there. She stopped in her tracks when she saw who was in attendance on him. It was Tom, with Thomas Cawarden, now Sir Thomas.

'Your Majesty,' she said, dropping a shaky curtsey.

'My lady!' he replied, beaming. He had Edward on his knee and a Latin primer in his hand.

She rose and made herself incline her head in acknowledgement of the two gentlemen, who resumed their conversation with Dr Cox as she sat down next to Henry. She did not dare look directly at Tom. She was unhappy about Sir Thomas being there too, for she did not want Henry to know of her connection with him either.

She did her best to ignore them both. She perused Edward's copybooks, praised his prowess at his studies and looked on as Henry taught him a simple tune on the lute. She had her back to Tom, but, all the while, she felt him looking at her. She longed to see him, to drink in the sight of him, but dared not even glance in his direction. Finally, when the strain was becoming unbearable, Henry rose, and she did too, most gratefully. They took their leave of the Prince and Henry led her out, her arm in his, with the two Sir Thomases following. When she got back to her apartments, she shut herself in her bedchamber, pleading a headache, and wept.

Pull yourself together! she told herself. It was best not to dwell on what could not be. She needed a distraction. She dried her eyes and went to the closet she used as a study. For some days, she had been planning a book, a translation of several stirring psalms that she felt particularly apt with the French war looming. They underlined the rightness of Henry's cause and called upon God to aid him.

It was her intention to have the book published, to whip up fervour for the war and inspire his subjects to pray for his success. To aid them, she was planning to compose additional prayers for the King himself and for men entering into battle.

She picked up her pen. She should begin with something to counteract the wickedness of the French. *Stand up, O Lord, and punish these naughty people!* she wrote. Already, she was feeling better.

In the afternoon, pleased to have made a start on her book, she walked in the gardens with Anne and Margaret for company, all of them wrapped in furs, for it was a cold day. Their route took them along the Low Gallery to the vast orchard that lay beyond the palace. The fruit trees were bare now, but soon they would be in blossom – a glorious sight. It was quiet here, for there were few people about. Margaret ran ahead, throwing sticks for her little lapdog to catch, with

Rig, Katharine's spaniel, bounding joyfully alongside.

'I hear that Sir Thomas Wriothesley has been appointed Lord Chancellor,' Anne said.

'What do you know of him?' Katharine asked.

'Herbert says he's a king's man through and through, but he has aligned himself with our friend Gardiner, which worries me.'

'That's what I heard,' Katharine said. 'It worries me too. We must be vigilant.'

'I was wondering if you should stop your religious debates and cease inviting reformist scholars to preach.'

'No!' Katharine protested. 'We are doing nothing wrong. It is not against the law to want the Church reformed.'

'Yes, but you know as well as I, Kate, that some of our visitors are also secretly of the Protestant persuasion. And I can tell you for a certainty that a few of your ladies have banned books locked away in their coffers. If Gardiner has the Lord Chancellor in his pocket, we ought to be careful.'

'I will not be intimidated by that man,' Katharine declared. 'If you know who has those books, tell them to get rid of them. But the gatherings shall continue.'

They were interrupted by a distant yapping. Two gentlemen were talking to Margaret, and the dogs were scrabbling at her skirts, wanting her to throw the stick again. Katharine halted as she recognised Tom Seymour, who was trying to restrain Rig.

'Let's go,' she said to Anne. 'I mustn't be seen with him.' She turned on her heel and began walking back the way they had come, but heard footsteps coming after her.

'Kate!' Tom said urgently.

'Is that how you address your Queen, Sir Thomas?' Anne reproved, as Katharine kept walking.

'I want just one word!' he said, catching up with her. 'Please – your Grace.'

Katharine paused and looked sideways at him, to find no rancour in his eyes. 'You know I should not be talking to you, Tom. Just say what you want to say and go.' Oh, how handsome he was, even more than she remembered. Every part of her longed for him – and she had thought to be over him by now!

'I just wanted to say that I understand. And that I will be waiting for you, when the time comes.'

'Hush!' she hissed, for he had spoken treason, imagining the death of the King. 'I am glad that you understand. And now it must be farewell.' She lowered her eyes from his gaze and walked on, fighting back tears.

One of the chief pleasures of queenship, Katharine had found, was the ability to help others. To her mind, it was the duty of a queen to assist those who came to her in need. Late that spring, she arranged for Anne to go to the royal manor of Hanworth for her lying-in and travelled with her to help her settle in. It took them all day to get there from Whitehall.

Henry had allowed Katharine the use of Hanworth, which had once been owned by Anne Boleyn, for whom he had extended the red-brick house in the Italian antique style, with terracotta roundels of goddesses flanking the outside doorways. While Anne's maids were stowing away her luggage, she and Katharine wandered across one of the bridges over the moat and walked in the glorious gardens, admiring the strawberry beds and the aviary, then sat by the fishpond because Anne needed to rest a while.

'It's so peaceful here,' Katharine said, inhaling the fragrant breeze. 'I don't get any sense of her, do you?'

'Who?'

'Anne Boleyn. All this was created for her.'

'I never thought about it.' Anne winced. 'Kate, I think we should go back to the house. I fear I'm having labour pains.'

'But you are only in your eighth month.' Their eyes met; Anne looked frightened.

'You must go back and lie down,' Katharine said. 'I'll fetch the midwife.' Mrs Jennings had already been engaged and had come to Hanworth with them.

They walked slowly back to the house. Anne's pains did not seem to be coming very frequently, but they were strong. The midwife came hastening to her and took her to her chamber, where she helped her undress and got her into bed.

'I shall be your gossip,' Katharine said, seating herself in the chair beside her.

But Anne was in no mood to talk. Already, her body's struggle to expel the child had begun in earnest. Soon, she was racked by severe pains, and all Katharine could do was mop her brow and hold her hand. It seemed to go on for hours.

'Pull on this,' Mrs Jennings said, attaching a length of linen to the bedhead. 'Now, one big push, my lady, and we're almost there.'

Anne dug her chin into her chest and bore down – and out slithered her baby, looking like a skinned rabbit. She sank back on her pillows, exhausted. The midwife began working on the child. At last, Katharine heard a faint mewl and her heart filled. She wished with all her might that she was the mother lying in the bed.

Mrs Jennings swaddled the infant, laid it in its cradle and made Anne comfortable. Leaving her to sleep, with the nurse on watch, she signed to Katharine that they should leave the room.

'Your Majesty,' she said, closing the door, 'Mrs Herbert is doing well, but the child is very weak, for it came too soon. It should be baptised right away.'

'I will send for the priest at the church,' Katharine said, her heart bleeding for Anne. 'And I will stand sponsor.'

She held the tiny babe in her arms as it was christened. It gave a little moan when the priest wetted its head and welcomed it to the Christian fold, then lay quiet. It was some minutes before she realised that it had died.

She had to go back to London almost immediately. Her presence was needed at a service that the King was attending at St Paul's Cathedral, where he would pray for victory in the coming war with France. The psalms she had translated had been published – anonymously, at her wish – and Thomas Tallis had now set them to music; she had worked on the project with him and they were to be performed during the

Mass. She had to be there. Anne, putting on a brave face, said that she must go and that, God be praised, she herself was recovering well.

Katharine's heart soared as the swell of voices singing Tallis's motets filled the vast church. It sounded like the celestial choir itself. Henry, seated on his throne next to her, had tears on his cheeks. God would give him the victory, she knew it, and her humble contribution, this stirring singing and her book, would aid his cause.

Afterwards, on her way back to Hanworth, she took a barge to Syon House, where Nan Hertford had also given birth. Her child, of course, was healthy. She bred like a rabbit, with irritating ease. Katharine would rather not have visited her, but Nan was her lady-in-waiting and she must be worried about Lord Hertford, who was still fighting in Scotland. But her pride was intolerable. She always had to be right! Katharine braced herself.

Today, however, Nan was in a friendly mood. Sitting up in bed, she showed off her baby with justifiable triumph, yet she did express what seemed like genuine sympathy for Anne. She had lost a child herself, she said. She knew what it felt like.

'My good gossip, the Lady Mary came,' she told Katharine. 'She was very kind. She adores babies and made much of this one. Poor soul, I know she longs for one of her own. Oh, I shall be glad to be out of here! Yet my lord has written to me, urging me to stay for the summer, as the country air will be good for the children. Will that be acceptable to your Majesty?'

'It will,' Katharine said, trying not to sound too pleased about it, and envying Nan her large brood.

'Madam, would you do something for me?' Nan asked, suddenly looking more vulnerable than Katharine had ever seen her. 'My lord is due home soon, but I fear that things are going hard for him in Scotland and that he may be required to stay. Would you kindly ask his Majesty if that is his intention? I hate the thought of my lord being in danger.'

'I can set your mind at rest now,' Katharine smiled. 'His Majesty said to me three days ago that Lord Hertford is to be recalled before he invades France.'

'That is such a relief,' Nan said. 'Thank you.'

'Well, I must go to Anne,' Katharine said, rising. 'I wish you well and will see you at court later in the year.'

She found Anne better in body, but not in spirits.

'My boy, my little boy!' she wept. 'Why did God take him from me?'

Katharine grasped her hand. 'That is easy to answer. He took him to be a partaker of everlasting joy, and we should all rejoice. But I know that it is hard for you, as a mother, to accept God's will.'

'I can't accept it!' Anne was beside herself. 'I want my baby!'

Katharine sat on the bed and drew her sister into her arms. 'Anne, you must not give in to excessive sorrow. You must not question what Our Lord has ordained. You must be happy that He has put your son in possession of the heavenly kingdom.'

'No! No!' Anne wailed. 'I just want my baby, my little boy! I ache for him. I can't believe he's gone.'

Katharine drew back and looked into her eyes. 'My dearest, to die is to waken to life again. It is foolish to bewail death. You do your son a great wrong with your lamentations, for this is the happiest thing that ever came to him, being in the hands of his Almighty Father.'

Anne sagged in her embrace. 'But he had his whole life before him! He was so perfect.'

'Which is why he was a pleasant sacrifice for Christ. Anne, give thanks for his life and his death, and be glad that it has pleased God to take him to His kingdom.'

Anne dabbed at her eyes, calmer now. 'You are right, dear sister. I am forgetting all my own precepts. But you have never been a mother. You cannot know how hard this is.'

'I do understand. And I'm sorry for preaching to you. I just wanted to bring you a little comfort. I will pray for you, I promise.'

When Katharine returned to court, her heart heavy for Anne, she told Henry about Nan's fears for Hertford.

'Where there is war, there is always danger,' he said, as they sat in the privacy of his privy garden. 'But we are bringing the Scots to heel, and our cause is aided by this new marriage treaty between my niece Margaret and the Earl of Lennox.'

It had been long in the making. Lennox was a slippery fox, yet he had at last been persuaded – with the hand of Margaret Douglas and the promise of great things to come – to betray his country and support the King of England.

Henry's satisfaction was evident. 'Lennox believes that Scotland should be united with England. He agrees with me that capturing the fortress of Dumbarton is the key to gaining the Scottish kingdom. As soon as this marriage is accomplished, I'm sending him north with an army to take it. And then our way will be clear. What with this and the French offensive, this is going to be our year, Kate!'

Katharine stood with Henry in the chapel of St James's Palace on a glorious June morning to see the Lady Margaret and the Earl of Lennox joined in wedlock. She needed something to cheer her, and it was a happy wedding, not just because of the alliance it represented, but also because the couple were clearly very taken with each other.

'This is turning out to be a love match,' Katharine murmured in Henry's ear as they sat with the clearly smitten newly-weds in the oriel window in the Holbein Gate watching the celebratory jousts that followed the wedding. Tom Seymour was among the challengers, but she was taking care to keep her eyes averted from him.

Henry nodded, looking pleased, and patted her hand. 'If they are as happy as we are, Kate, they will be lucky indeed.'

Behind her, she distinctly heard Lady Suffolk mutter that Margaret fell in love all too easily. But the King seemed oblivious. He bent to Katharine's ear. 'I want you to know that, in token of my appreciation of your many qualities, I am appointing you regent of England while I'm away in France.'

'Oh, my lord!' She was stunned. She knew that he respected and admired her, for he continually made it clear, but that he should consider her worthy of this high responsibility . . .

'I am deeply honoured,' she told him. 'I will strive to my utmost to live up to your good expectations.'

'I know that you will,' he said. 'I have ordered that you shall exercise sovereign authority in my name and have the advice and counsel of Archbishop Cranmer, Lord Chancellor Wriothesley, the Earl of Hertford, the Bishop of Westminster and Sir William Petre, my secretary of state. They will make up the Privy Council in my absence and at least two of them will be in attendance on you at all times. I have also arranged for Lord Parr, your uncle, to sit in on council meetings. Your brother, as you know, is coming to France with me as chief captain of the men-at-arms.'

'I shall certainly not lack for advice and support,' Katharine said, realising that, as ever, he had followed his middle way and appointed councillors of both factions. At least Gardiner was not one of them, although she would still have Wriothesley to contend with. She was glad, therefore, to have Cranmer. He had just published the Litany in English, for use in churches, a move she heartily applauded. He would be a bulwark against the conservatives. If she could just stay on the right side of Wriothesley, all would be well.

For the second time in a fortnight, she found herself consoling a bereaved mother. When Henry told her that Wriothesley's infant son Anthony had died, she wrote a letter to his wife, Jane, offering similar words of comfort to those she had given Anne, and exhorting her to be glad that her child was in a better place.

A day or so later, she came upon Wriothesley in a gallery, hurrying in the direction of the council chamber. He pulled off his cap and sketched a hasty bow.

'I am so sorry for your loss, my Lord Chancellor,' she commiserated.

'And I am sorrier still that your Majesty's letter so upset my wife,' he said, glaring at her.

Taken aback, she recoiled. 'I but meant to console her.'

'She's been weeping ever since she read it. There are some things that should never be said to a grieving mother.'

'I am heartily sorry to have added to her grief,' she said, knowing she must not antagonise him, for they had to work together, and he could prove a dangerous enemy.

'I will tell her, Madam,' he said, nodding stiffly and walking on.

'What did you say to her?' asked Lady Suffolk, who was in attendance.

'I urged her to give thanks, so that our Lord might think her most glad and contented to make Him a gift of her son. Maybe I rather laboured the point. But I meant to uplift her, not upset her. I feel bad about it.'

The Duchess shook her head. 'There's nothing you can do now, except be very nice to Wriothesley when you see him. You've apologised, so put it behind you. Gardiner, stop that, you naughty dog!' The animal ceased chasing around her skirts and whined petulantly.

'I wish we could control his namesake as easily,' his mistress said ruefully. Katharine had to smile.

Chapter 19

1544

Prince Edward's writing skills had come on apace and he and Katharine now exchanged letters regularly. He was pathetically grateful for her kindness to him and clearly relished her praise. She would have liked to see him more often, but Henry was always nervous about exposing him to the court, so she had to content herself with visiting him whenever proximity permitted, which was not often, since most of the nursery palaces were some way north of London. At least he had Elizabeth's company. With just four years between them, they were very close, but also highly competitive. It was partly due to wishing to excel over his sister that Edward had done so well in his studies.

Katharine felt that it was her greatest achievement as queen, so far, to have achieved some cohesion and harmony in the royal family and to have won the love and trust of her stepchildren. And Henry really appreciated it; he often told her so.

'None of their previous stepmothers made such an effort,' he said, 'but I suppose they did not have the chance.' His face clouded for a moment. 'It is good for my children to enjoy this stability. They needed a mother's love.'

They were in his closet, sitting at the table, which was covered with papers. Henry was making plans for his imminent absence in France.

'I'm sending Edward to Hampton Court with his household, and I'm appointing that renowned Cambridge man, Dr Cheke, to assist Dr Cox in the instruction of the Prince and the boys attending on him.'

'Dr Cheke has a fine reputation,' Katharine said. 'He is an excellent scholar, full of learning, and a great humanist.'

'I thought you would approve,' Henry smiled. 'He was recommended to me by my physician, Dr Butts, and Sir Anthony Denny. You might like to see this.' He handed her some papers covered in elegant handwriting. 'I asked Cheke to work with Cox in drawing up a new curriculum for Edward.'

Katharine took a few moments to peruse it. The chief thing that struck her was how demanding it was for a six-year-old. Scripture, theology, Latin, Greek, classics, philosophy, astronomy, mathematics, grammar, rhetoric . . . The list went on. She could only be grateful that Edward loved learning. And he would enjoy Cheke's instruction in horsemanship, military skills, archery, fencing, tennis, music and dancing. Yet would he ever have time for playing?

'I want him to be the best-educated and most accomplished king England has ever had,' Henry said. 'Cox says he is extremely advanced for his age and will do brilliantly.'

'I have no doubt of that,' she said, 'and I will continue to support him in his studies. And Elizabeth can only benefit from Cheke's coming. She is a prodigy of learning. Her fluency in Latin is remarkable.'

'And in other languages,' Henry added. 'That gentlewoman of her chamber, Blanche Parry, is even teaching her to speak Welsh.'

'I was impressed to hear that she is learning Italian too,' Katharine recalled. 'And she knows the classics as well as she does the Scriptures. You have much cause to be proud of her. She takes after you intellectually.'

'Her mother was learned too,' he said grudgingly, surprising her, because he never spoke of Anne Boleyn.

'I have heard that she was a great friend of the Gospel,' she said.

Henry nodded. 'She was. And very forceful in her views.' She didn't have Gardiner to contend with, Katharine thought. 'Yes, I am proud of Elizabeth,' the King went on, changing the subject. 'Never a day goes past without her reading or writing something for recreation. I try to do that too, when state affairs permit. Well, I think Edward will be happily occupied while I am away. Keep him safe for me.'

'You know I will,' she assured him. 'He is as precious to me as if he were my own son.'

* * *

In a short ceremony in the council chamber, Henry formally appointed Katharine regent and handed her the commission granting her sovereign power.

'Your chief task is to recruit men to defend the realm, should the French invade,' he told her. 'My justices of the peace will inform you how many able persons they can supply, and how well furnished with weapons they are. They are to be ready at one hour's warning to man the coast and light beacons to give notice of the enemy's approach. I have also commanded the justices to ensure that law and order are maintained in their jurisdictions. There must be no unlawful assemblies, riots or breaking of the peace. Once a month, they will certify to you and the Council the state of the country and their various proceedings.'

'I will do everything in my power to keep your Grace's realm safe and support my Lord Lennox when he ventures forth to the north,' she vowed.

'You may obtain money from the treasury as you please and, to augment your own income, I am granting you the manors of Wimbledon, Mortlake, Hanworth and Chelsea.'

'Your Majesty!' She could not hide her delight at the prospect of owning her beloved Hanworth and those other highly desirable properties, especially the palace at Chelsea. 'Your Majesty is most kind and gracious to me,' she said, curtseying, aware of the councillors' eyes on them. When she and Henry were in private, she would thank him properly. He had told her that, back in 1513, he had left the first Queen Katherine pregnant when he campaigned in France. How wonderful it would be if he could leave her with child this time.

'I have made my will,' Henry said, when they were lying in bed that night after a most successful coupling that gave Katharine cause to hope. She did not want to think about wills and death; she wanted to imagine herself as the mother of a prince. But Henry insisted on interrupting her fantasy. 'It mirrors the Act of Succession and outlines my plans for a regency if I die in battle.'

'God forbid!' she cried.

He drew her close. 'I have to plan for all eventualities, Kate, and I need to ensure that, if Edward comes to the throne before attaining his majority, he and this realm are governed by one who loves him and will put his interests, and those of the kingdom, before all else.' He gave her a meaningful look.

She was startled. Did he mean her? He knew she loved Edward and he had entrusted her with his realm while he was in France. 'Who did you have in mind?'

'I am still considering,' he said. She wondered if her regency was to be a test, for her to demonstrate how well she could govern when the time came.

In the middle of July, they rode at the head of a great cavalcade down to Dover, where the fleet was assembled. They were cheered on the way because the war was popular with the King's subjects high and low. Henry was in excellent spirits. His leg was better, he seemed to have regained some of his youthful vigour – which he had again proved in the bedchamber – and he had looked quite formidable when he tried on his armour. He was in his element, as eager as the young man he had once been to win glory in the field of battle.

Katharine had written a prayer beseeching God to keep him safe and award him the victory. He had been so pleased with it that he had ordered it to be read in all the churches while he was away. As they stood on the quayside in the shadow of the great warship that would convey him to France, Archbishop Cranmer declaimed her words to the multitudes assembled there. 'O Almighty King and Lord of Hosts, who doth minister both war and peace, our cause now being just, we most humbly beseech Thee to turn the hearts of our enemies to the desire of peace, so that no Christian blood be spilt. Or else grant, O Lord, that with small effusion of blood and little damage of innocents, we may to Thy glory obtain victory; and that, the wars being ended, we may all with one heart and mind knit together in concord and amity, laud and praise Thee, who livest and reignest, world without end, Amen.'

While Cranmer was invoking the Almighty, Katharine noticed Tom Seymour among the many gentlemen attendant on the King. So he was going to France too. She offered up a silent prayer, beseeching God to keep him safe.

Both she and Henry had tears in their eyes as the prayer ended. Then he took her hand, kissed it and bowed. 'God keep you, Madam. When we meet again, let us hope it will be in triumph.'

She did not want him to leave. Suddenly, she was fearful for him. She had grown to love him and did not want to lose him, even though she knew that, when she did, Tom would be waiting for her.

'May God bless and protect your Majesty,' she said, loud enough for the crowds to hear. 'Come home to us safely!'

When he had embarked, she stood on the quayside, watching the ships as they made their stately way across the Channel. It was a clear day, the sea was calm and blue, and she could see the French coast in the distance – hostile territory. She wondered if she would ever see Henry again.

Back at Whitehall, she found herself very busy with matters both great and small. It made her realise just how much Henry shouldered. She was glad to receive news of his safe arrival at Calais, but had little leisure in which to miss him as she was soon immersed in orders for provisioning and financing the army. She was profoundly grateful for the diligence and assistance of the councillors. Whatever their persuasion, they were working hard alongside her, deferring to her; everything was done at her pleasure.

She was conscious of her heavy responsibilities and sat in council every day, aware that she had to prove herself. At other times, she was receiving dispatches, ambassadors and envoys, and issuing proclamations. As the summer grew hotter, the plague returned and she had to put in place measures to contain it. There were a hundred different things to do as well as keeping England safe from a French invasion and monitoring the situation in Scotland, where the Earl of Shrewsbury was in command.

Each evening she sank gratefully into her bed, exhausted by the demands on her and grateful to have survived another day without any crises.

As July wore on, she joined Edward and Elizabeth at Hampton Court, taking Mary with her. With the plague raging in London, and people dying in their hundreds, they would all be safer there than at Whitehall. She had brought too Lady Lennox, Lady Suffolk and other great ladies of her household who had not craved leave to return to their homes.

Edward greeted Katharine in his usual solemn manner; it always took a while to coax him out of his innate reserve. But Elizabeth was deliriously happy to be reunited with her and, forgetting protocol, threw herself into her arms.

'I haven't seen you all year, dearest stepmother!' she cried. 'And yet I know that you have never stopped caring for me, and you know that I will always be bound to you and revere you with daughterly love.'

Katharine embraced her warmly. 'I would have seen you more often, but distance has prevented it. It was not through choice that I did not visit you.'

'How is my father? Have you had news?' Edward asked.

'He is well and raring to fight the French,' Katharine told him. Both children looked anxious.

'When you write to him, will your Highness crave his blessing for me and wish him the best success in gaining victory over his enemies, so that we may rejoice the sooner at his happy return?' Elizabeth asked.

'Of course I will,' Katharine promised. 'Now, let us go in to dinner.'

'I don't know how you do it,' Mary said, as Katharine started to fall asleep over supper that evening.

'It is a marvel to see a woman ruling England,' Elizabeth chimed in, her eyes full of admiration. 'It just goes to prove that it can be done.'

'Don't let our father hear you saying that,' Mary smiled. 'He doesn't approve of women ruling.' Katharine suppressed a smile; she knew better, she thought.

'Strange, then, that he made your stepmother regent,' pointed out Lady Suffolk.

'Ah, but I am to rely on the lords of the Council!' Katharine replied.

'It seems that they are relying on you!' her friend retorted. It pleased

Katharine to hear that. Hopefully, others were saying the same in their reports to Henry. She had decided that she did want, very much, to be regent for Edward when the time came. The boy was young and malleable, and God's work would be easier because of that. She was sure she could bend him to the right path in religion, and more certain than ever now that she had been called to this high destiny.

She was glad to receive news that Henry was in good health and spirits. All seemed to be going well on the other side of the Channel. As ever, he wanted more and more money, arms and provisions sent over, and she had all to do to get them for him. Somehow, she managed to find the time to send him regular news of his children and affairs at home and commend the diligence of his councillors.

Her greatest fear was that the Scots would take advantage of the King's absence to invade England, as they had in 1513, when Queen Katherine was regent. She had not the resources to fight another Flodden. To her continuing relief, the English military presence in the Scottish lowlands, where the Rough Wooing was to continue as soon as Lennox arrived, kept that threat at bay.

Anne had returned to court, putting on a cheerful face. She joined Katharine's other ladies in helping with correspondence and making banners for the army. This was how they spent their evenings now, while Katharine wrote her reports to Henry. She told him how much she was missing him, even though he was not that far away. *For want of your presence, so much beloved and desired by me, I cannot take pleasure in anything until I hear from your Majesty. Our time apart seems to me very long, and I have a great desire to know how your Highness is doing, for I desire your prosperity and health more than my own. And, while I know that your absence is necessary, love and affection compel me to desire your presence; but love obliges me in all things to set apart my own pleasure and to embrace most joyfully the will and pleasure of the man I love. God, who knows all secrets, can judge these words not only to be written in ink, but most truly impressed in the heart.*

Her courses had arrived, with their inexorable regularity, She was again conscious of having failed him in the one thing that mattered and felt bound to make him aware of that. *I have such confidence in your Majesty's gentleness*, she continued, *knowing myself never to have done my duty as were requisite and meet to such a noble prince, at whose hands I have found and received so much love and goodness that words cannot express it.* Concluding, she committed him to God, in the hope that he would long prosper on earth and enjoy the kingdom of the elect in Heaven.

It was only after the letter had been sent that she realised what she had written, almost without thinking. Recently, she had read *The Institutes of the Christian Religion*, a book by the Swiss reformer, John Calvin, which Lady Suffolk had lent her. God alone knew how she had come by it, for it was dangerous to have such a book in her possession. Henry hated Calvin as much as he hated Luther, and this particular book enshrined the tenets of the Protestant religion he abhorred. Katharine knew it was best to ask no questions.

Calvin had expounded on the theory of predestination, believing that God had chosen His elect before He created the world, and that they were the only souls who would attain Heaven, their sins alone meriting forgiveness. Those not of the elect would suffer divine justice unconditionally. It was an extreme Protestant view and a chilling one, and she was not sure that she subscribed to it. But would Henry, seeing those words, realise that she had been reading a forbidden text? She tried to think rationally. He had much on his mind. He might not notice. But what if he did? How would she explain it?

Wasting valuable time, for she had to decide the fate of a deserter in Scotland before she went to bed, she leafed frantically through the pages of her English Bible until she found what she wanted in the Book of Isaiah. *Behold my servant, whom I uphold; mine elect Chosen One, in whom my soul delighteth; I have put my spirit upon him: he shall bring forth judgment to the Gentiles.* It was perfect, apt for a king who had assumed the Royal Supremacy. If Henry questioned her, she had only to refer him to Isaiah. She was safe.

She waited, still in a little trepidation, for him to respond. Days passed, and there was no letter. She knew he was busy. His forces had laid siege to the city of Boulogne and were subjecting it to a furious bombardment. The ambassador Chapuys told her he had heard that the King seemed rejuvenated and was acquitting himself better than anyone had expected. She thanked him for sharing this with her. Will wrote, marvelling that the King could still mount a horse and harry the French. The Council with Henry sent regular letters containing his orders. Yet still there was no word from Henry himself.

She read again and again the missive in which the lords conveyed his thanks to the Council for their advancement of his affairs. Why had she not been thanked? She tried to rejoice when she learned that the King had seized six castles and hoped to take Boulogne within twenty days, for the walls had begun to tumble. He was short of men and munitions and looking to her to supply them. Yet still he had written no word to her and she was going out of her mind with worry. She thought she would scream when she received reports that the French were about to invade England. Immediately, she put the justices of the peace on the alert, and felt faint with relief when she was informed that the rumours were unfounded.

Of course, she had to inform Henry, in case he had been alarmed by them. She kept her letter formal, assuring him that England was quiet and in good order. She prayed fervently that he would respond. All kinds of horrible possibilities now filled her mind. God's plan for her might be frustrated even yet. She felt she had failed Him.

The Council with the King instructed her to send the Earl of Lennox north as his Majesty's lieutenant. It was time for Lennox to keep his part of the bargain. He had his royal bride; now he must take Dumbarton Castle and seize power in Scotland in Henry's name, toppling the Queen Regent, who was ruling for her daughter.

Margaret, who was already pregnant, did not want her husband to leave her so soon after their marriage, and pleaded with Katharine to delay his departure, but Katharine dared not disobey Henry. Lennox must go, but she assured Margaret that she was welcome to remain at court for as long as she wished and that she herself would visit her at her house at Stepney when the plague had abated.

She wrote again to Henry, telling him that the realm was in good order and that his children were well. Will briefly referred to Tom

Seymour in one of his letters home, from which she inferred that he was trying to tell her that Tom was all right, which was some comfort.

She was becoming concerned that the plague might spread to Hampton Court and thinking that it might be a good idea to take her stepchildren on progress to places further away. So they went to Enfield and then north to Oakham Castle in Rutland, where they were made very welcome by the Countess of Rutland, before returning south to Woking, Mortlake, Byfleet and Guildford, then back to Woking, where Katharine made time to go hunting. Before each move, she had the Lord Chamberlain send messengers ahead to check that there were no cases of plague in the area. Their reports worried her, for some areas were definitely unsafe, so she kept on the move, making brief visits to Beddington, Hampton Court, Eltham Palace, St James's Palace, Enfield and Nonsuch Palace, a beautiful hunting lodge Henry had built in Surrey, where she would have liked to have stayed longer. But it was not worth the risk.

As if she was not exhausted enough! All this dodging the plague was wearying, and alarming, and she was painfully aware of the necessity of keeping the Prince safe. She had thought of going down to Kent, but the pestilence had got there before her. The furthest she dared travel was to Archbishop Cranmer's great palace at Otford, but she only stayed two days before returning yet again to Woking. It was the place where she felt safest. Henry's grandmother, the Lady Margaret Beaufort, had once owned the house, and it had since been converted into a sumptuous palace. Katharine and her stepchildren liked to take the air in the cloister below the gallery, which overlooked the river, or test their skills in the bowling alley. On fine days, Katharine arranged for Edward and Elizabeth to take their lessons in the King's privy garden, and she and Mary sometimes joined them. Yet she could not be quiet in her mind, for she had still not heard from Henry.

There was news from Boulogne, though. Lord Hertford had reported to the Council that foul weather and a lack of powder were hampering the siege, although he remained optimistic for they had overrun the hill on which the castle stood, which he considered to be of great strategic importance. Then Katharine's heart leapt, for Hertford had asked that, as he had been about to dispatch the report, Henry had stayed him, commanding him to send her the good news. *Thanks be to God, his Highness is merry and in as good health as I have seen him at any time these seven years*, Hertford had added.

Henry could not be angry with her if he had sent that message specially for her. He must simply be too busy to write himself. Still, a loving letter would settle her mind.

'I wish his Majesty would write to me,' she confided to the councillors when next they met. 'I would give much to have news from him and hear that he is safe.'

'God will strengthen His own against the devil, Madam,' Wriothesley said kindly, 'therefore do not trouble yourself, for He shall turn all to the best, and we are sure that the King's Majesty is out of all danger.'

Somewhat reassured, Katharine wrote to Henry again, asking after his health and sending him a side of venison. She asked if she might appoint temporary replacements for some of her ladies who were absent through sickness, although the ones she had in mind were not of the calibre of those who were away. Henry had conferred sovereign authority on her, yet she thought it courteous to ask him.

And then, at last – at last – he replied. When she read the salutation, *Most dearly and most entirely beloved wife*, she could have wept.

He thanked her heartily for the venison. He would have written sooner, but he had been so heavily occupied that he had had no leisure to do anything else. He had detained her servant in the hope that he could send her news of the taking of Boulogne, but the gunpowder he needed had yet to arrive. Nevertheless, he had held on to the castle hill. King Francis had sued for peace, but Henry was waiting to hear what the Emperor thought about that. However, he was growing tired of the Emperor's extortionate demands for spoils when the French were conquered. She was to inform the Council of this. And yes, she could take on the new ladies if she thought fit. They could help her pass the time at leisure or accompany her for her recreation. What recreation? she wondered. Had he any idea what her life was like? Yet she willingly forgave him. He had not mentioned the word 'elect', and he had signed himself 'your loving husband'. He'd added a postscript too: *No more to you at this time, sweetheart, both for lack of time and great occupation of business, saving we pray you to give in our name our hearty blessings to all our children and recommendations to our cousin Margaret and the rest of the ladies and gentlewomen, and to our Council also.*

Late one night, when the palace was sleeping, there was a knock on Katharine's door and Anne awoke her, her eyes shining.

'Herbert is here, fresh from France!'

Katharine rose hurriedly from bed and received him in her night robe.

'Madam, I have come post-haste, at the King's command,' he told her, and handed her a letter bearing the royal seal.

Boulogne had fallen! Henry had never sounded so joyful and elated.

'God be praised!' she cried, her heart rejoicing. The commotion had brought her ladies running, and they were thrilled to hear the news. Anne, who had been staring at her husband as if he were a heavenly vision, threw her arms around him, mud-spattered as he was. He kissed her soundly, making them all laugh.

'I am Sir William Herbert now,' he told them. 'His Majesty knighted me for gallantry in the field.'

'That's wonderful news,' Anne breathed. She had not looked so cheerful in weeks. The women were hugging each other. Most of them had husbands, brothers or sons in the army.

Dead of night though it was, Katharine summoned the Council. When she read out Henry's letter, the lords burst into applause. *I have vowed to bring France to submission*, he had written, *and I am fulfilling that vow. I have been all my life a prince of honour and virtue, who never contravened my word, and I am too old to begin now, as the white hairs in my beard testify.* He wrote that he had sat on his horse for two hours in the pouring rain, watching the surrender. Katharine prayed he had not done himself a mischief.

I thank God for a prosperous beginning of your affairs, and I rejoice at the joyful news of your good health, she wrote to him.

In the morning, she commanded that all loyal subjects go in

procession to church in every town and village to give thanks for the King's victory.

The next they heard, he had entered Boulogne at the head of his army, with the sword of state borne before him and the trumpets sounding, and received the keys to the city. But the moment of his triumph had been sullied by news that, pleading financial hardship, his ally, the Emperor, had abandoned him and made peace with the King of France. Katharine could imagine how angry Henry was. He had intended to take Montreuil next, but now had to abandon his plans for further conquests.

Katharine was still at Woking when she received a list of those whose services were worthy of reward and saw Tom Seymour's name.

'Draw up a grant of these lands for Sir Thomas,' she told her clerk, handing him the deeds for two estates near Woking. 'Say it is by the Queen's command.' As it was one of so many issued in her name, Henry could never take objection. But Tom would see her hand in it.

She was still worried about the plague, which continued to scourge London and Westminster. She issued another proclamation, ordering that no person whose house was infected, or who had been in any place stricken by the pestilence, was to come to court or permit anyone at court to resort to his house.

Now that the war was over and Henry's return was expected within days, Katharine found that her workload was lighter. Mary, who was suffering her usual autumnal complaints, had retreated to Hunsdon to work on her translation of St John's Gospel, so Katharine took Edward and Elizabeth hunting at Hanworth, which they loved. There, she received a letter from Mary and was saddened to read that her step-daughter was too ill to continue with her work. Immediately, Katharine sent one of her own chaplains to assist her, and wrote to assure her that she must still take the credit for the translation. *All the world knows that you have toiled and laboured much in this business*, she wrote. *I do not see why you should repudiate the praise men justly confer on you.*

She laid down her pen. Beyond her window, in the Italian garden, Edward and Elizabeth were romping about with a ball, with Margaret looking on, cheering. It was good to see Edward behaving like a normal child, for once.

She shivered. It was growing unseasonably cold. She must send to the royal wardrobe for some warmer clothes before they returned to Woking. Hopefully, the colder weather would see off the plague. Still, she was resolved not to stay at Hanworth for long. You never knew when the pestilence might strike. After Woking, they were going to Eltham, where she would wait for news of the King. She prayed that he would have a safe crossing, unmolested by the French ships that were prowling in the Channel. She composed a prayer for his safety and repeated it fervently.

Henry was home! His ship had docked safely at Dover and he had sent to command her to go to Otford, where he would join her, and to leave his children at Eltham, for he was informed that there were no reports of plague there.

Absence had made her realise how much he meant to her. Her heart leapt when she saw him riding through the gatehouse of the vast palace at Otford. Apprised of his coming, she was waiting in the great courtyard. There was joy in his eyes as he dismounted.

'My lady! I have longed to be with you again.' He crushed her to him in a bear-like embrace. 'I hear that you have excelled yourself in my absence, darling.'

'Nowhere near as well as you have acquitted yourself in France,' she complimented him, buoyed up by his praise. 'And you are looking so well.' It was true. He looked rejuvenated, better than she had ever seen him, affording her a fleeting glimpse of the golden youth he had once been.

'I've never felt better!' he declared.

He took her hand and led her into the palace. After he had washed and rested, they supped together, and he told her all about his campaign and asked her to bring him up to date about affairs at home. She waited for him to say something about her being regent in the future, but he did not touch on the subject. For now, though, it was enough that he was pleased with her.

'Is the plague abating?' he asked.

'There are still some cases in London,' she told him, 'but the numbers are much reduced.'

'Then we will leave Edward and Elizabeth at Eltham and spend a few days at Leeds Castle,' he said. 'You'll love it there.'

She did. Set on two islands on a lake, it was a little paradise. She and Henry came together as never before, and his vigour did not fail him. It was like a second honeymoon. They were rowed out on the lake, went hunting in the surrounding park and entertained local worthies in the magnificent banqueting hall with its newly installed stained-glass windows. Katharine was really enjoying herself. She took pleasure in Henry's presence, marvelling that this autocratic man who wielded power over the lives and souls of millions should be so kind and gentle with her, and yet be so authoritative and strong. It was like having God on earth, although she reproached herself for the blasphemy because no mortal could be like God.

'Passion blinds you,' Henry said suddenly one evening when they were walking along the path by the lake. 'It renders you oblivious to every flaw, every warning.' She guessed that he was referring to Katheryn Howard, or even Anne Boleyn, and was surprised that he had opened up on the subject. 'What we have is much better,' he said, reaching for her hand, 'and it takes an old fool to realise it.'

For a moment, she wondered if he was right and this contentment was preferable to the exciting turmoil Tom had aroused in her. Yet, for some, she knew, the thrill lasted. Would it for her and Tom, if they ever married? Heavens, what an awful person she was, thinking of remarrying when she and Henry were enjoying this special private time!

Alas, it was all too short. With no new reports of plague, Henry could delay returning to Whitehall no longer and so, reluctantly, they concluded their pleasant idyll and removed to London.

He was still angry that the Emperor had deserted him.

'It was no less than I expected,' he said sagely, as he and Katharine rode out hunting in St James's Park. 'But nothing can detract from my victory.'

Katharine was pleased to see that his new lease of life extended to following the chase again. Even the onset of winter did not deter him. She stayed snug indoors by the fire, reading Mary's completed translation. It was excellent, and she wrote urging her to publish it. Mary replied that she would do so only under a pseudonym, but Katharine persuaded her that her work should go down to posterity under her own name and offered to pay for its publication. She was not surprised when her visiting scholars and clerics began extolling it to the skies. Even Gardiner, she heard, had been impressed.

From Will, she learned that Tom Seymour had been briefly in England but was now away on the high seas, harrying French shipping and getting provisions to the garrison in Boulogne. She imagined that he would be in his element, loving the sea as he did. She was glad that he was happily occupied. She tried not to think of him too much these days. She had worked hard to make her marriage a success and did not want to do anything to upset the harmony that was between her and Henry. Tom had been banished to the far recesses of her mind, and there he must stay until she was free again.

Yet she was not to be allowed to forget him. One evening, at supper, Henry was grouching about the cost of provisioning Boulogne.

'I could have done without Seymour making a fool of himself!' he said.

She had been half listening, but now she was alert, scanning Henry's face for any sign that he was testing her to see if she reacted to Tom's name.

She kept her voice steady, impartial. 'What has he done?'

'He put to sea twice in a gale, with no thought for the safety of the men on board. He lost several of my ships and two hundred and sixty hands were drowned. The man's too impulsive for his own good. Give me his brother any day.'

'I am truly sorry for those poor sailors, and for your losses,' she said.

'I've had the Council write to him to complain of his negligence,' Henry growled.

'I hope he can satisfy you,' she replied, not wanting to get into a discussion about Tom. It was Henry, thank goodness, who drifted to other matters.

Some days later, Katharine invited Henry to see a finished full-length portrait of herself that John Bettes had painted.

'It's very fine,' he said. 'It's you to the life. We are most obliged to you, Master Bettes. We shall have you paint the Lady Mary.' The artist bowed, his plump, homely face flushed with praise. Henry dismissed him and bade Katharine sit with him on the padded seat in the window embrasure.

'I hear that my niece Margaret has gone home to Stepney,' he said.

'She plans to be confined there,' she told him. 'I shall visit her when the babe is born. I rather think she wants you to be godfather.'

'I'll accept, with pleasure,' he smiled. 'By the way, Sir Thomas Seymour has cleared himself. He put to sea in haste because he was concerned about the lack of provisions at Boulogne and Calais. He assured me that he had done his best to deliver them.'

'I am pleased that the matter is resolved,' she said.

'I rather regret judging him harshly,' Henry reflected. It was not like him to admit to being in the wrong. 'I must reward him for the sterling work he is doing for me. I mind to grant him Hampton Place by Temple Bar. It's been sitting empty since the Earl of Southampton died.'

'That is a very generous reward. I'm sure he will be sensible of the honour.' If she knew Tom, he would be ecstatic. A lordly residence in London, neighbouring the houses of the nobility along the Strand? She wished she could see his face when he heard of his good fortune.

'He's earned it,' Henry replied. 'Well, I must be getting back to my lodgings. Chapuys has asked for an audience.' He rose stiffly.

Chapter 20

Katharine was seated at the table in her privy chamber, staring at her New Year's gift from Elizabeth. She was deeply touched by the trouble her stepdaughter had taken, for Elizabeth had translated into English a poem written by the French King's sister, Marguerite of Valois, 'The Mirror, or Glass, of the Sinful Soul' – all 117 pages of it – and had embroidered the binding herself, stitching Katharine's initials in silver thread. It must have taken her ages. Her command of French was impressive for an eleven-year-old, but Katharine could only feel dismay at her choice of a work that had been twice banned in France because of its strong reformist slant. As Elizabeth herself had described in her affectionate accompanying letter, the poem showed how one could do nothing to achieve salvation unless it was through the grace of God. It was her faith alone that would sustain her.

What had the tutors been teaching Elizabeth and Edward? And yet Henry had nodded approvingly when Katharine showed him the gift. Was he aware of the poem's content? Or could it be that he was leaning towards a purer faith at last? That would be the best New Year gift of all.

Katharine's troubled reverie was interrupted by the Duchess of Richmond. 'Madam, a messenger has come from my Lady Lennox.'

Margaret had borne a son, named Henry after the King, her uncle. Katharine and Mary braved the frosty weather to visit the new mother at Stepney, taking jewels for the baby. But Margaret, cradling him in the bed, looked worried.

'He is so small. He came too early. He takes very little nourishment.'

Mary took him into her arms. 'Who's a lovely boy?' She adored children.

'Does the nurse have a wholesome diet?' Katharine asked.

'Oh, yes.' Margaret took back the baby eagerly.

'You might try pap,' Katharine suggested. Mixing the milk with a little bread had helped one of Magdalen Lane's children to thrive, she remembered. Margaret said she would do that, but they left her with heavy hearts. The child was too small, too weak for them to have much hope for its survival.

Katharine was becoming increasingly concerned about her stepdaughter Margaret, who, at twenty, had grown into a beautiful, graceful young woman with fair tresses and blue eyes. But Margaret had developed a cough that would not go away. Nothing the doctors gave her made any difference and now, Katharine was sure, she was losing weight.

One morning in March, Margaret entered her bedchamber. It was still dark outside, too early to get up, and she was not due to attend Katharine anyway.

'Margaret? What's wrong?' The girl's face, lit by the candle she was carrying, looked distraught.

'Mother, I'm frightened.' Her voice shook. 'I've coughed up blood.' She held out a handkerchief stained bright red. Much shaken, Katharine struggled to hide her dismay.

'It's probably nothing to worry about,' she said. 'Have your gums been bleeding?'

'No, I coughed it up.'

'You must see Dr Wendy, my physician. He will be able to reassure you.' The words were spoken with more conviction than she felt. Inwardly, she was trembling. Margaret was very dear to her. She could not bear to think of anything bad happening to her.

After breakfast, she summoned Dr Wendy, who was a confident, experienced doctor with a calming manner who had endeared himself to Katharine with his enthusiasm for reform. He examined Margaret and bled her to balance the humours, as he explained.

'I will prescribe an infusion of lungwort,' he told her, 'and see you again in a week, Mistress Latimer.'

'But what is wrong with me, Dr Wendy?' Margaret asked.

'It is too early to say,' he told her. 'Let us see if this treatment works.'
It occurred to Katharine that he was being evasive. She hoped she was wrong.

A week passed and still Margaret was coughing blood. Dr Wendy looked grave.

'I fear it is consumption,' he declared, to Katharine's horror, evoking unbearable memories of John's sufferings. 'You must rest, Mistress Latimer, and conserve your strength. You can keep taking the lungwort, and I will give you some mercury, which is good for this condition. If you have breathing problems, burn some incense in your chamber.'

Margaret was staring straight ahead, as if into a future she did not have. Her face was very pale. 'It is what my father died of,' she faltered. 'Am I going to die?'

'We are all going to die,' Dr Wendy said. 'Only God knows when. This is a serious malady, but where there is life, there is hope.' He smiled at her kindly.

Margaret said nothing; she just sat there, shaking her head. Katharine hastened to embrace her. 'My dear lamb, we will do all we can for you.' Tears were stinging her eyes, but she blinked them away, knowing that she had to be strong for her stepdaughter.

'Madam, you would do well to keep your distance,' Dr Wendy warned. 'This disease is catching.'

So poor Margaret too was to be deprived of physical comfort. It seemed so cruel. How could God visit this tragedy on such a sweet soul? This would be the ultimate test of faith for the girl – and for herself. She did not know how she would bear it.

Once the initial shock was behind her, Margaret took it stoically. 'I may get better,' she said, as she rested on her bed, with Katharine sitting at a safe distance. 'If not, I will be reunited with my dear father and mother. I am glad that God has blessed me with time to prepare to die in a state of grace, and to make my will. You will be my heir, darling Mother. I can never render you sufficient thanks for my education and the tender love and goodness I have always found in you.'

Katharine struggled to retain her composure. She hated to hear

Margaret speak of dying. Dr Wendy had told her privately that it was likely, but by no means certain; he knew of cases where consumptive patients had recovered. Yet it seemed that Margaret was prepared for the worst. Would to God she herself could accept it so serenely.

When she finally left her stepdaughter, she wanted to be alone to cry out her grief, but found her bedchamber full of maids putting away her clean body linen, mending garments and cleaning her shoes. Her outer chambers were no quieter, so she escaped to the orchard, muffling herself in a hooded cloak. There was a cold wind blowing and the place was deserted.

She was leaning against a pear tree, her back to the palace, sobbing her heart out, when she heard a footfall. She swung around to find Tom Seymour staring at her.

'Kate!' He was clearly shocked.

'Tom.' She gathered her thoughts, dashing the tears from her eyes. 'Please go! We mustn't be seen together.'

'What's the matter?' he persisted, not budging.

'It's Margaret, my stepdaughter. She is dying of consumption and she is only twenty, and very precious to me.' She broke down afresh.

'Oh, my darling,' he said, and went to put his arms around her.

'No!' she cried, stepping back. 'Have you lost your senses?' She began walking away, casting her eyes about in all directions, terrified lest they had been seen.

'I meant to comfort you,' he called after her. She hurried on and did not answer. Mercifully, there was no one in sight.

She looked to seek comfort from Henry, but, when she arrived at his lodgings, Sir Anthony Denny informed her that his Grace was ill with a fever and would not see anyone.

'Not even me?' she asked.

Sir Anthony lowered his voice. 'Between ourselves, Madam, he hates to be seen in a state of weakness.'

'Is he very ill? What do the doctors say?'

'It's a burning fever. They suspect that his leg is infected.'

It was the last thing she needed, although she reminded herself that

Henry's suffering was worse. 'You will keep me informed? And send him my heartfelt wishes for a speedy recovery?'

'I will, Madam.'

Four times a day, for the next three days, she sent to enquire after him, and the answer was still the same: the fever had not broken. On the fourth day, Will came to see her.

'His Grace is in great pain. The doctors are worried.'

'I have to see him!' she cried.

'No, Kate, you must not make a fuss. He has given orders that his condition be kept secret. He will not have it said that he is losing his grip on affairs.'

'But surely he will see me?'

'He will see no one but his doctors and Will Somers.'

She gripped his hand. 'Tell me truly, is he dying?'

Will raised his finger to his lips. 'Shh. The physicians say nothing. Only Gardiner has made so bold as to say that his Grace will not live until my Lord Prince comes to man's estate. He was ordered out. He's been haunting the watching chamber every day, begging to be admitted.'

'He seeks to suborn the King while he is at a low ebb, no doubt,' Katharine muttered.

'Aye, he thinks it's his chance to stamp out heresy.'

'Then I must persuade the King to see me. If Gardiner has been whispering in one ear, I can whisper in the other.' And, most important of all, she must find out who Henry intended to rule England after his death.

She waited for one day, then made her way to Henry's apartments.

'For God's love, ask his Majesty to receive me,' she pleaded with Denny. A few minutes later, he came back, smiling. 'His Grace will see you. He is a little better today.'

The bedchamber smelt frowsty; there was an unpleasant whiff of decay. She found Henry sitting in his chair, his bandaged leg resting on the stained footstool. He was playing chess with Will Somers.

'Kate! It is good to see you!' he greeted her. 'I have not been well.' His tone was plaintive.

'I am so relieved to see you looking better.' She bent and kissed his cheek.

'Aww,' Will smiled.

'I'm still in some pain,' Henry said, glaring at him. 'And I have been disturbed by reports of heresy.'

Gardiner! He had got there before her.

'Has Bishop Gardiner been bothering you? Surely the Privy Council can deal with such matters?'

'He was so persistent that I agreed to see him last night. What he had to say alarmed me. I will not have heresy tainting my realm; I will root it out.' He was becoming angry.

'Of course,' she said, chilled to the bone.

'He brought me a list of names. More than twenty of them! All will be arrested today and examined.'

For a horrible moment, she wondered if her name was on that list. But Henry would never have welcomed her so kindly if it was. Yet others would soon know the same fear, men and women whose views she shared. Her heart wept for them. They were going to have to summon up almost inhuman courage.

'I pray they will see the error of their ways,' she said, hating herself for being such a coward. Yet she could be of more use to the Protestant cause by staying alive, she was convinced of it, although now was not the time to get to work on the King, not when he was in such a bad mood. She wished she could see that list, but dared not ask.

The matter of the regency would have to wait too. It was a subject she could not broach herself, for Henry was terrified of death and it was treason to speak of his leaving this world. All she could do, ever so tactfully, was steer the conversation in that direction and hope he would open up about his plans. But he did not take up any of the openings she gave him and, in the end, she was obliged to leave off, lest her motive become too obvious.

That same afternoon, the Duchess of Suffolk drew her into a window embrasure.

'Anne Askew has been arrested,' she whispered.

316

Katharine remembered the fanatical woman who had tried to enlist her help. She was glad now that she had refused, but horrified to hear the news because, whenever Anne came to mind, she remembered that dreadful nightmare. Yet Anne Askew must have brought this upon herself. She must know the penalty for heresy, yet it seemed she had never troubled to hide her beliefs; indeed, she had preached them openly. Even so, Katharine pitied her.

'Not here,' she murmured, aware of the other ladies in the room, who were playing cards or chatting. She led the Duchess into her closet. 'What happened?'

'Her husband betrayed her, and I fear she may betray me. Her sister is married to my attorney – Protestants both! And that could lead them to you, Madam, and the rest of our friends here.'

Katharine's blood turned to ice. 'But they can know nothing. We have all been so careful.' Their discussions of contentious topics had taken place in secret, in lowered voices. Their store of banned books was stashed away beneath two floorboards under a Turkey rug in her bedchamber, and no one, looking at the place, would see anything amiss. 'If you are questioned, deny everything,' she muttered, thinking of St Peter, who had denied Christ three times. 'And warn Magdalen, Nan, Anne and the others.'

So began the nightmare. Was it worse to face danger or not know if there was any danger? They had no idea at first where Anne Askew was being held, still less whether she had betrayed them. Each day was an agony of waiting, waiting for the tramp of marching feet, the hand holding a warrant. Katharine took to studying Henry obsessively, seeking for evidence in his words and gestures that he suspected her, but he was often in a bad mood these days. His rejuvenation of the previous year had given way to illness and pain, and often she would find him short-tempered and peevish, frustrated at being confined to his chair. It was hard to guess what he was thinking, for he was often of one mind in the morning and of quite another after dinner.

Nothing happened. Presently, Hertford told Nan that the Askew woman had been sent back to her husband in Lincolnshire, who had been ordered to keep her under control. At last, Katharine began to relax. Her equilibrium was further restored when Henry's recovery gathered pace and he took to playing bowls again or even riding with the hunt in Hyde Park. Yet both his legs were painful, and sometimes she wondered how he got about at all.

She was grateful that he wanted her company at this time. He could so easily have shut her out. He liked to hear of the conversations she had had with the divines and scholars who regularly visited her chamber, and she was happy to give him edited versions. He still sometimes came to listen to the preachers she engaged, nodding sagely when he agreed with some point of theology, or challenging ideas he didn't support, all quite amiably. Of course, everyone stayed just the right side of wholly embracing reform, although they did touch on abuses within the Church, even in the King's presence. And he approved.

Buoyed up by that, Katharine seized her moment. One suppertime, after they had listened to Hugh Latimer preaching against the infamy of Rome, and when only Anne and Lady Suffolk were in attendance, she dabbed at her mouth, filled up their goblets and took a long drink of wine to give her boldness.

'I'm glad you enjoyed the sermon,' she said.

Henry leaned back in his chair, replete with good food. 'Latimer's a sound man.'

If only you knew, she thought.

'Henry, it is thanks to you that we have such an enlightened approach to true religion in this realm,' she said, seeing him incline his head appreciatively. 'To the glory of God and your eternal fame, you have begun a good and godly work in banishing that monstrous idol of Rome. Many of your devout and loyal subjects are praying that you will thoroughly perfect and finish the same, and cleanse and purge your Church of England, in which there remains great superstition.'

'Hmm,' Henry grunted. 'And what would you have me do, Kate?'

She swallowed. 'Put a rein on Gardiner. Be as open to new ideas as you were ten years ago.' She had been about to mention Anne Boleyn, but realised that would be unwise.

She watched the telltale flush of anger creep up from Henry's collar.

'Gardiner is a pest, but he acts for me. Heresy is a canker in the body politic and I will have it out! Things were different ten years ago. Protestant ideas had not taken hold. Now the pendulum has swung too far. It sounds as if you would make a heretic of me, Kate!'

'Not at all!' She was hot to defend herself. 'You said you were following a middle road, yet it seems—'

'Enough!' Henry barked, thumping the table. He had never spoken to her so harshly. 'I'm in pain, Kate, and you go on at me. You're as bad as Gardiner. Just leave it alone.'

'Of course. I am so sorry. Forgive me.' She was so taken aback, it was easy to summon tears.

He reached across the table and took her hand. 'Oh, Kate. I'm an old bear. Forget it. Let's talk about something else.'

Limp with relief, she told him about the flowers that were beginning to bloom in her garden.

Lady Suffolk lingered after the other women had prepared Katharine for bed and left.

'Madam, I heard your conversation with the King and I should tell you that my lord of Suffolk warned me today that Gardiner and Wriothesley and their cronies see you as an enemy. They are working to avoid a reformist government when the Prince becomes king, whatever it takes.'

Katharine kept her face impassive. Let these factions battle all they liked. She was convinced that Henry meant *her* to be regent.

'It is no secret where your sympathies lie,' Lady Suffolk went on. 'Anyone who has embraced reform is suspect. Hence this campaign to root out heresy, for they believe that many who advocate reform are, in fact, secret Protestants. My lord says they dare not proceed against you because you have the King's love and favour.'

Their eyes locked, acknowledging their peril. Suffolk was one of Henry's oldest friends, like a brother to him. He was at the centre of affairs and had supported the King unfailingly through his political and matrimonial causes. His opinion counted. But Gardiner had only suspicion to go on; he could have no proof that she was guilty of heresy.

'It is not against the law to advocate reform,' Katharine said. 'And I won't be silenced. God led me to this throne for a purpose.'

After dinner the next day, at Henry's summons, she joined him by the fire in his library. Will Somers was idling behind his chair and some clerks and clerics were working in the room, sitting with their heads together at the desks, shuffling documents or scribbling rapidly.

'I trust I find your Grace better today,' she said, as he kissed her hand in welcome. Aware of the presence of others, she took care not to address him familiarly, as she did when they were in private.

'Worse, if anything, Madam,' he said peevishly. 'And these reports of new heresies don't help.' He sounded very ill done by.

'You should not be bothered with such things when you are unwell,' she said. 'And, if others took a more tolerant view of reform, there would be no need for them.' She realised she was teetering on the edge of dangerous ground, but she was indignant that he was being put under pressure by these conservatives.

'And what do you mean by a more tolerant view, Madam?'

'Ease the restrictions on reading the Bible. Let each man follow his conscience . . .'

'By God, Madam, we'd have religious anarchy – every man with his own opinion, and few qualified even to have one. No, it won't do. Now, forget about that. I wanted to show you this.' He opened a large book of architectural drawings with an Italian text. 'I fancy building a palace in the classical style.'

She was taken aback at how he had sidestepped further argument, but she gathered her wits and took the book. 'These are from Italy?'

'That is Bramante's Tempietto in Rome. And that is the Palazzo Farnese. What a wonder it would be to have buildings like that in England.'

'I say we don't want outlandish foreign buildings in England!' piped up Somers, only to get a playful cuff from his master in response.

'Go away!' Henry ordered, and Somers slunk off into a corner, where he picked up a book and pretended to read it, upside down.

Smothering giggles, Katharine debated with Henry whether he should build anew or alter an existing palace. It was good to see him so absorbed, and she thought that maybe she had been wrong to push him on religion when he was in pain. The time passed pleasantly until he said he was tired.

'Farewell, sweetheart,' he said. 'I would rest now.' He closed his eyes and she left him, hoping he would not be disturbed by the ever-busy clerks.

She was surprised, when she visited him a few days later, to hear him bring up the contentious subject of religion.

'I was in no fit state to listen to you before, sweetheart, so now, I pray you, speak your mind.' They were quite alone. Even the ubiquitous Will Somers was absent.

She could have kissed him. This was what she had been hoping for.

'You have worked marvels, Henry,' she said, 'but there are those who feel you would be a Papist without the Pope. It is as if you have put a stay on reform, and now there is this persecution. People should come to Christ through love, not fear.'

'But if they fall into heresy, they will not come to Him at all,' he said gently.

'Yet where is the line between reform and heresy?' she asked. 'How are we to know who is right?'

'Through reading the Scriptures, prayer and a good grounding in theology,' Henry said.

'But that is the same for Catholics and Protestants.'

'Kate, we are talking about salvation. Tell me, do you believe that it is predestined?'

That set her senses on alert. But it was months since she had called him one of God's elect.

'No,' she said emphatically. 'I believe we can achieve it through our faith in Christ.'

'Is that all?' He was regarding her closely. 'Do we not need to do good works in this world?'

'Of course we should.' She was equivocating, hoping he wouldn't notice.

He nodded, apparently satisfied.

321

* * *

Two evenings later, while she was sitting in Margaret's bedchamber, reading to her, Dr Wendy was announced.

'And how is my patient today?' he asked cheerfully.

Margaret smiled at him. 'Better than I was,' she said. 'I did not expect to see you so soon.'

'I just thought I would look in. Are you eating?'

'Yes. I still have an appetite.'

'Good, good.' He took her pulse and felt her forehead. 'Well, I will see you next week.' He turned to Katharine. 'Might I have a word, Madam? No, Mistress Margaret, it is not about you, so don't worry.'

Katharine went ahead into the antechamber. 'She is barely eating enough to keep a sparrow alive,' she said.

'Alas, it is to be expected,' Dr Wendy said. 'I wish I could do more for her. But I came about something else, Madam. You should see this.' He reached inside his gown, drew out a scroll and handed it to her. 'I found it lying on the floor in the gallery that leads from the council chamber. Someone must have dropped it.'

It was a bill of Articles, drawn up against the Queen of England and signed by the King himself. The words swam before her horrified eyes. *Authorised to investigate . . . heresies . . . subverting religion . . . dangerous conspiracies . . .* The hand of Gardiner was clear.

Terror welled up in her. It was real . . . it was really going to happen. She could see the guards coming for her, see the grim shadow of the Tower engulfing her, feel the chain going around her waist, see the faggots piled around her being lit . . . Suddenly, she was on her knees, screaming uncontrollably, filled with a deep atavistic fear, and Dr Wendy was kneeling beside her, beseeching her to calm down.

'Your Grace must go to the King now and confront him with this,' he urged, but all she could do was wail and shriek. If she did that for long enough, someone would surely help her – help her to escape the flames that would slowly and agonisingly engulf her. She was aware of people coming running, asking what the matter was, and of her ladies cradling her in their arms, begging her to calm down and tell them what was wrong. Even Margaret had come, but they sent her away. Katharine was beyond speech. All she knew was that she had to keep screaming; it was her only hope. All she could see in her mind's eye was Henry's signature on that document, and the flaming pyre, herself at the centre of it, burning agonisingly into an object of horror.

Dr Wendy was exhorting her to calm down. 'Listen to me!' he begged her. Yet still she knelt there, crying and wailing.

'She will do herself a mischief.' That was Anne's voice. 'Kate, what's happened?'

She shook her head. 'Help me!' she sobbed.

She was aware of other doctors kneeling down beside her. She knew them: they were Henry's senior physicians, Dr Chamber and Dr Butts, greybeards both of them, and very experienced.

'Your Grace, the King has sent us to you. He is concerned for you. If you carry on like this, you will be in peril of your life. Now, take a deep breath and tell us what has brought you to this extremity.'

Dr Butts had a vial in his hand. 'This is poppy juice. It will soothe you and distance you from your fears.' He handed it to her. 'Drink it, Madam.'

She pushed it away. 'There was a warrant . . .' She thought of the flames again and began screaming afresh.

'If you will leave that vial with me, I will give it to her Grace,' Dr Wendy said. 'Leave us now, please.'

She was aware of the antechamber emptying until there remained just her and Dr Wendy kneeling on the floor.

'Madam, you must take this for your own good and listen to me,' he said. 'All is not lost. I think I know what lies behind this.'

Something in his voice brought a glimmer of reassurance. Her cries subsided into sobs.

'Two nights ago, his Majesty summoned me,' the doctor related. 'He told me he needed to unburden himself to me, for he was worried that you were relapsing into heresy. He said he could no longer allow you to be such a doctress of religion as you have become, always dictating to him what he should do. This was for your own good, for he knew certain enemies were working against you.' He looked around

323

furtively. 'I should not be telling you this, for his Grace charged me, upon peril of my life, not to utter it to any creature living, but he insisted that he would not give way to their demands. His plan was to have you questioned, expecting you to clear yourself. If you did not, he would intervene and stop the examination, for he intends you no harm, only to bring home to you the danger you are risking.'

Katharine found that she was at last capable of rational thought. 'So, he did this to silence me and frustrate my enemies. Couldn't he just have warned them off?'

'Madam, it was ever the King's way to play off one party against the other. It was his way of warning you.'

'Well, it was cruel and unnecessary. He could have talked to me! And how did this happen? Who has poisoned the King's mind against me?' The panic was rising again.

'Never mind all that now,' Dr Wendy said firmly. 'My advice is, firstly, reveal nothing of what I have said and, secondly, frame and conform yourself to the King's mind. I have no doubt that, if you show your humble submission to him, you will find him gracious and favourable to you.'

'You think so? Not when he has signed this warrant!' And she burst out weeping again, sobbing her heart out.

Through her misery, and the doctor's remonstrances, she heard footsteps approaching outside. It was the guards, come to arrest her! She began screaming again.

'Kate! Kate!' It was the King's voice; he sounded very out of breath. 'Help me to that chair.' The two Gentlemen Pensioners on whom he was leaning heaved his bulk into it. She stared at him though her tears, shocked into silence by his appearance.

'Kate, what ails you?' His face was full of concern. 'I could hear you in my lodgings. I was worried for you.'

'Oh, Sir.' She knelt up and clasped his hands as if they were a lifeline. 'I feared that your Majesty was displeased with me and had utterly forsaken me.'

'And why did you think that?' His voice was gentle.

Trembling, she picked up the bill of Articles and gave it to him.

He read it, frowning. 'How did you get this?'

'I found it in a gallery, your Grace,' Wendy said.

'The fools!' Henry barked. 'I did not mean it to go this far. I just wanted to have my doubts resolved. Kate, tell me truly: are you a heretic?'

Never would she admit that to him, after suffering this terror. A lie would be infinitely preferable. 'No, Sir,' she said firmly.

'Well, we will talk anon about that.' He was regarding her closely. 'Now, darling, calm yourself. Nothing bad is going to happen to you. Be at ease now. Help me up, sirs!'

The two Gentlemen Pensioners sprang into action.

'Good night, darling,' Henry said, as he limped to the door, leaning heavily on them.

'Good night, Sir,' she said, still on her knees, tears of relief streaming down her face.

In the morning. Will came to see her and embraced her warmly.

'I heard what happened last night,' he said. 'Anne told me. And I think I know who to blame.'

'Gardiner,' she said, much more composed now.

He nodded. 'One of the King's clerks told me that the Bishop was present in the library when you disputed with the King over religion. He was working on a treatise. When you had gone, his Majesty complained that he disliked being lectured by his wife. Gardiner said he had had his suspicions about you and your ladies for some time, but had feared to investigate, seeing the favour in which the King held you, but, if his Grace would give him permission, he would discreetly inquire into the matter. And his Grace did.'

'I have some explaining to do,' she replied. 'I can't have this hanging over me. I will see the King today.'

As soon as Will left, she summoned Anne, Lady Suffolk, Nan Hertford, Magdalen Lane, Lady Tyrwhitt and her other ladies of the Protestant persuasion to her closet.

'Get rid of any inconvenient things that are cluttering up my chambers,' she instructed in a low voice, aware that it was imperative no eavesdropper heard her. She looked at each one pointedly. 'It would be wise.'

They nodded and quickly dispersed. Throughout the day, she saw them disappearing, one by one, and returning within an hour. She wondered how many prized devotional books had been thrown in the Thames or burned. She could not risk asking.

In the evening, with Magdalen going before her, carrying the candle, and Anne in attendance, she made her way to the King's bedchamber, where she found him chatting with his gentlemen.

'Madam!' he said, as he beheld her. 'This is a pleasant surprise. 'Do be seated.' Sir Anthony Denny hastily vacated the other chair by the fire and Katharine smiled at him as she took it. She had taken care to dress becomingly and noticed Henry eyeing her low-cut bodice and the pearls that lay on the creamy skin of her breasts. A woman's weapons, she knew, could be highly effective in a war of words.

Henry's narrow eyes were boring into her. 'So, Madam, have you come to talk about religion again? Are you going to resolve my doubts? For you have said things to me that are capable of more than one interpretation.'

Don't get agitated or protest too much, she told herself. *Be humble, if it kills you. Flatter him.*

'Sir, I did not intend for you to take my ignorant utterances that way!' she cried. 'Your Majesty knows as well as I do what great imperfection and weakness God allotted to us women at the Creation, and that we are ordained and appointed as inferior and subject to man as our head, from whom all our direction ought to proceed.' She paused, seeing that Henry was watching her and listening keenly, which gave her the courage to go on.

She lowered her eyes modestly. 'When God made man in His own likeness, with more special gifts of perfection, He made woman of man, by whom she is to be governed, commanded and directed. Her womanly weakness and natural imperfection ought to be tolerated and aided, so that, by man's wisdom, such things that are lacking in her may be supplied.'

She looked up to see Henry nodding with approval; his gentlemen were inclining their heads sagely. One whom he favoured, George Blagge, was smirking.

She smiled at her husband. 'Since God has appointed such a natural difference between man and woman, and your Majesty is endowed with such excellent gifts and ornaments of wisdom, and I am a silly poor woman so much inferior in all respects of nature, surely your Majesty does not need my poor judgement in religious matters? I would always defer to your Majesty's wisdom, as my only anchor, supreme head and governor here in earth, next under God.'

Henry frowned. 'By St Mary, you know very well that you have disputed with me. You have become a doctor, Kate, to instruct me, rather than being instructed or directed by me.'

She thought quickly. 'You have very much mistaken me, Sir, for I have always been of the opinion that it is unseemly and preposterous for a wife to take upon her the office of an instructor or teacher to her lord and husband. Rather, she should learn from her husband and be taught by him. And, where I have been so bold as to dispute with your Majesty, I have not done it so much to offer my opinions as to divert you with debate, so that you might be distracted from your pain and find some ease. And I hoped that, hearing your Majesty's learned discourse, I might receive some profit from it.'

Suddenly, Henry was beaming at her. 'Is that so, sweetheart? And tended your arguments to no worse an end? Then we are perfect friends again! Come here.'

She went to him and he hugged and kissed her, not caring that his gentlemen were looking on and hiding their smiles. He sighed deeply as he released her. 'It has done me more good to hear those word from your own mouth than if I had been told I was to be given a hundred thousand pounds. I will never again think ill of you in any way.' He kissed her hand.

She stayed with him until it was late, talking and playing cards, and went to bed feeling a lot happier. The only thing that niggled was the memory of having to abase herself and denigrate her sex, for she was certain that women's minds were just as capable as men's. But to say so would be a worse heresy than Luther's!

The following afternoon, it being a fine April day, Henry invited Katharine to join him in his privy garden, where the trees were a mass of blossoms. They sat in the banqueting house, chatting over a ewer of wine, while their attendants strolled along the gravelled paths beside the flower beds, which were just coming into bud.

Katharine was telling Henry how far she had got with compiling another book of prayers, taking care to ask his opinion about her selections, when she heard the tramp of marching feet.

She looked up in alarm as it came closer, immediately thinking she had been played for a fool, only to see that Henry was alert to it too, and was rising, flushed with fury.

The iron gate opposite was suddenly flung open as Lord Chancellor Wriothesley marched into the garden at the head of a large detachment of the King's guard – heavens, there must have been about forty of them!

Katharine sat there, frozen with fear. Had Henry lulled her into a false sense of security and sprung the cruellest trick on her? Had they come for her after all? She was shaking uncontrollably.

But the King strode over to Wriothesley, his face the picture of outrage.

'What do you think you are doing, my Lord Chancellor?'

Katharine watched as Wriothesley fell to his knees and the guards began looking at each other in a disconcerted fashion. She hardly dared breathe or meet the eyes of her ladies, who had gathered about her.

Wriothesley, very agitated, was saying something she could not hear. But Henry's response came across loud and clear.

'Knave! Arrant knave! Beast! Fool!' he thundered. 'Get out of my presence!'

It was a sight to see, the Lord Chancellor of England scuttling away with the guards running at his heels, as if the hounds of Hell were after them. Henry limped back to Katharine, still seething with anger, although he attempted a smile.

'You seem somewhat offended with my Lord Chancellor, Sir,' she said, still trembling, but aware that the danger had gone. 'I cannot think what just cause you have to be angry with him. I pray you most humbly to be lenient with him.'

'Ah, poor soul,' Henry said, shaking his head, 'you little know how evilly he deserves this grace at your hands. On my word, sweetheart, he has been an absolute knave to you. Let him be.'

'As it pleases your Grace,' she said, pouring another goblet of wine to steady herself. As they resumed their conversation, she was inwardly thanking God for her escape from the dangerous snares of her enemies. He must have preserved her because she was a friend to the Gospel. This would do the conservatives' cause no good. It would be a setback to their plans to rule England after Henry's death. And it had been she who had confounded them.

Later, alone with her trusted ladies, she could not stop talking about what had happened. 'I am still shaking inside,' she confessed. 'I cannot believe I have escaped the danger. I did not truly know I was safe until his Majesty berated the Chancellor. I have much to thank God for!'

Henry was in a lot of pain these days. Katharine could not believe how much he was spending on medicines. His bouts of agony were more frequent, and he would try anything to alleviate them. His temper was as uncertain as his health, and Katharine learned when it was time to retire, to avoid offending him or prompting a quarrel. She would leave him to Will Somers, who did his best to cheer his master with his jests and capers, and to his doctors, especially Dr Butts, a learned reformist with whom Henry liked to discourse on theology and humanism on his better days. Archbishop Cranmer was a frequent visitor. He had a way of bringing Henry out of a black mood. It was good to know that the King was so often in the company of these great reformists.

The war with Scotland was dragging on with no resolution. Lennox had accomplished little and retreated to England, to Henry's disgust, and Hertford was now devastating the border country, sacking abbeys and slaughtering everything in his path. Katharine feared that England's destructive policy would only drive the Scots to seek French aid. But, especially on the days the pain struck, Henry was bent on continuing with the destruction.

He was enjoying a warmer friendship with the Emperor, thanks to the skilful diplomacy of Chapuys, who must have had a rough ride over the past months, trying to pacify Henry's anger against his master. Katharine worried about the ambassador, for he had aged a lot in that time and become so lame that he had to be pushed about in a wheeled chair. Whenever she thought about Chapuys, she felt guilty, for even as she showed the smiling face of friendship, she was deceiving him. Henry also had sent her secretary, William Buckler, on a secret mission to wean the princes of Germany, who were subjects of the Emperor, into an alliance with England, in an attempt to undermine Imperial power.

Katharine hated the deception, but it had not been of her making. She hoped that Chapuys would never find out and blame her for it.

She was not surprised when Henry told her that the ambassador had asked the Emperor to recall him. 'I shall miss the old fox,' he said, his eyes misting over. 'We have often been at odds, but I have come to value him.'

'I am so sorry to hear that he is leaving us. When is he departing?'

'As soon as a replacement can be found.'

In May, Chapuys came to take formal leave of Henry. Katharine and Mary were to meet him in the Queen's privy garden afterwards to say goodbye. Mary was very distressed about his going.

'He has been such a friend to me,' she sobbed, as they put the last-minute touches to their attire in Katharine's bedchamber. 'He was a rock of strength to my dear mother and myself during our tribulations. He went a long way beyond the call of duty. There was a time . . .' Her fair, freckled face went pink. 'Well, I know little about these things, but I thought he had feelings for me. And, if he had been of higher rank, I would have let myself reciprocate, for I could not have found a better man. And now he is old and ill, and I shall never see him again.'

Katharine held her until her tears were spent, then bade her wash her face and straighten her hood. 'Let his last memory of you be a smiling one.'

They spent a few moments in Katharine's oratory, to give Mary time to compose herself. To any observer, it looked like a conventional

Catholic prayer closet, but a keener eye would have noticed that there were no statues of saints. This was as far as Katharine had dared go in the outward observance of her religion. It was what was in the heart that mattered, she told herself.

They waited in the garden until Chapuys arrived, wheeled in his chair by the new ambassador, who introduced himself as Francis van der Delft and seemed urbane and genial. Katharine gave them both her hand to kiss.

'My lord ambassador, I am sad that you are leaving us,' she said to Chapuys. 'His Majesty has told me that you have always performed your duties well, and I know he trusts you. But I doubt not that your health will be better on the other side of the sea, and that you can do more there to maintain the friendship between England and the Empire that you have done so much to promote.'

'You are very kind to say so, Madam,' the old man said.

Katharine took Mary by the hand. 'You must say farewell to my Lady Mary, whose friend you have been for so many years.

'Madam,' Chapuys said, 'I must express the Emperor's thanks, and my own, for *your* kindness to the Princess.' It did not escape her notice that he persisted in using Mary's forbidden title. He was still championing her, after all these years.

'I do not deserve so much courtesy,' she told him. 'What I do for the Lady Mary is less than I would like to do and is only my duty. I have always done my utmost to further the friendship between England and Spain. I hope that God will avert the slightest dissension.'

Chapuys's tired eyes regarded her with admiration. 'I am only sorry that I will not be here to enjoy your goodwill and friendship, but Messire van der Delft will be fortunate to have the advantage of it.'

Delft bowed. 'It will be my pleasure, Madam.'

The ambassadors turned to Mary and conveyed the Emperor's greetings. After more pleasantries, Katharine begged Chapuys to present to the Emperor her humble service. And that was the end of the interview. Mary looked as if she might throw her arms around Chapuys when he said farewell, and Katharine noticed that his eyes were misty. She was filled with pity for them both, knowing only too well what it was to have to hide a precious love.

With Henry laid so low and in such a mercurial frame of mind, it had been hard not to think about Tom, who was now in Dover, Will had told her, in command of the Cinque Ports. The longing she was feeling for him made her realise it was better that he was away from court.

She made herself keep busy, arranging for Margaret to be moved to Charterhouse Square. She had kept the house on. Will used it, and she stayed there from time to time when she wanted to get away from the continual scrutiny of the court. Accompanied only by Anne, or Lizzie Brooke, Will's paramour, she would don a hooded cloak, take an unmarked barge to Blackfriars Stairs, and walk from there to Charter-house, enjoying the freedom to browse among the book stalls at St Paul's on the way, as she used to do. It always gave her a little thrill to see her anonymous book of prayers on sale there.

Now, the house was to afford rest to Margaret. Katharine had prepared the big front bedchamber, with its views of the green lawn of the square; she had had pretty curtains put up at the windows and bought fresh linen for the bed. When Margaret was brought there in a litter on a warm May day, she was full of gratitude.

'I could not have wished for a nicer room,' she declared.

'I have engaged a nurse, who will lodge here,' Katharine told her. 'And Dr Wendy has promised to come every few days to see how you fare.'

'It won't be for very long,' Margaret said, almost apologetically.

'Nonsense!' Katharine said sharply. 'You'll live to trouble us for a long time yet!' But, looking at the slight girl with her golden hair spread out over the pillows and her fair, almost translucent skin, she knew she was sowing false hopes. Margaret looked like an angel already. God would summon her soon. Katharine prayed that it would be an easy passing.

With a heavy heart, she went downstairs, wishing that she could stay here with Margaret, even go back to her old life and the freedoms she had enjoyed. She loved Henry, but her life as queen was wearying, especially of late, and she could never relax.

The nurse had made some cordial. Katharine downed some, reached for her cloak and waited for Anne to return from the privy. Then there came a knock at the door. It was Will.

'I hoped I'd find you here, Kate,' he said, kissing her. 'How's the patient?'

'Sinking, I fear,' she murmured.

'Poor soul. I will pray for her.' He stood awkwardly for a moment. 'Are we quite alone?'

Anne appeared before she could answer. 'Will!'

Will hugged her. 'I have news. It's all right, Kate, Anne can hear it too. Let's go into the parlour.'

After he had shut the door, they all sat down.

'There's no easy way to tell you this,' Will began, and Katharine was filled with foreboding. 'The Duke of Norfolk has asked the King's permission for my lady of Richmond to marry Sir Thomas Seymour.'

Katharine was stunned. She had thought that match dead and buried. And it seemed strange that the Duke would want a Seymour marrying his daughter. He was England's foremost Catholic peer, one of the leaders of the conservative party – and Tom and his family were firmly in the reformist camp. As for the Duchess, she had never betrayed any interest in Tom, or, indeed, mentioned him.

'But why?' she asked.

'It's obvious. The Catholics have had setbacks lately, as you well know. They fear the increasing influence of the reformists, especially the Seymours. The Duke is afraid that his family will be ruined and seeks to ally himself with the Seymours. That way, I surmise, he hopes to cling on to power. The Earl of Surrey says that his sister doesn't want to marry Sir Thomas, but it's for the King to decide.'

Katharine was speechless. An alliance between the two great factions at court. It was like uniting York and Lancaster – and it might well appeal to Henry, who was weary of all the jostling for power. Would Tom have a say? What *would* he say? Would he fight for her? Would he defy the King? And how could she bear to have the Duchess in her household if the two of them were made to wed?

'What shall I do?' she asked her siblings, who were both studying her anxiously.

'Warn him?' Anne suggested.

'No! Too dangerous,' Will cautioned. 'Kate, there's nothing you *can* do. You might betray yourself if you are seen in any way to oppose the marriage. And what could you say against it?'

'You are right,' she said, feeling overwhelmed with everything – the recent brush with Gardiner, Margaret's illness, Henry's constant crises, and now this.

With the King's blessing, she spent the best part of the following weeks at Charterhouse Square, sitting for short spells – all Dr Wendy would allow – with Margaret, who was growing ever weaker and racked with that bloody cough. In between times, she finished writing her new book, *Prayers and Meditations*, in which she exhorted her readers to suffer patiently all afflictions, set at naught the vain prosperity of this world, as Margaret was doing, and always long for the everlasting felicity. It was published that June, under her own name, 'the most virtuous and gracious Princess Katharine, Queen of England'.

Henry was touchingly proud of her. He read the book as soon as a copy fresh off the press was in his hands and praised it to the skies. She was glad that she had written so warmly of his reforms, thanking God that He had sent England a devout and learned King who could be likened, in his triumph over the Pope, to Moses conquering Pharaoh. Henry liked that comparison very much.

'The hand of God was clearly visible on both occasions,' he declared.

She received so many congratulations on the book that she felt quite humbled. It sold fast and was soon reprinted . . . and reprinted, again and again. The universities of Oxford and Cambridge beseeched her to be their patron, which was a high honour indeed, and one she took the greatest pleasure in accepting.

The success of the book helped to carry her through this difficult time, but her celebrity was only the outer shell of her being. The real Katharine had to find a way to cope with constant sorrow and worry. Margaret was failing and Henry was in low spirits. Confined to his chair, his riding days apparently behind him, he would sit there bemoaning his lot. Often, she would arrive in the middle of the morning and find him still in his night clothes. He only bothered to dress if he was mobile enough to go to Mass or had to appear in public.

'Time is of all losses the most irrecuperable,' he said to her one day, 'for it can never be redeemed for any price nor prayer. What would I not give to have my youth again, to feel as if I could take on the world, to be able to play sports and joust and leave every man standing?'

'You will get better soon,' she said, taking his hand. 'Just rest for now, and allow your leg to heal.' It was the same kind of lie she told Margaret.

With all of this going on, she was glad when Henry roused himself and turned his attention to his children's education. At her suggestion, he appointed a young scholar called William Grindal to stretch Elizabeth, for Edward was not as advanced in his studies as she was. Grindal was also to teach Edward Greek, a demanding language for a seven-year-old who was already learning French and German. Henry also asked Roger Ascham, the Cambridge man whose reputation was far renowned, to mentor Elizabeth and recommend books to the young tutor.

Soon, Ascham was singing Elizabeth's praises. *I have dealt with many learned ladies,* he wrote to the King, *but the brightest star is my illustrious Lady Elizabeth.* That brought a rare smile to Henry's face. He smiled again when he read Ascham's high opinion of Kate Champernowne, now Mrs Ashley, who supervised Elizabeth when she was doing the work set by her tutors.

Katharine worried about Edward. The slender boy seemed over-burdened with learning, yet strove manfully to live up to his father's expectations. He was even being taught statecraft by the Clerk to the Council. Small wonder that he mischievously rebelled on occasion. Henry himself couldn't help laughing when Dr Cheke complained that his royal charge, egged on by his noble companions, had used a thunderous oath in class. Cheke had reprimanded him, and another boy had been beaten.

'For all his impudence, he is doing well,' Henry told her. 'He can already conjugate Latin verbs and is now ready to read Cato and the profitable fables of Aesop. Do you know, Katharine, every day, he reads some of Solomon's Proverbs, and delights in them? And he learns from them to beware of wanton women and to be thankful to those who tell him of his faults.' He was inordinately pleased with his son.

Katharine loved it that Edward wrote to her as his 'entirely beloved mother' and signed himself 'your loving son', though they were stilted little notes in which the child was at pains to demonstrate that he wished to please his father. You don't have to display your accomplishments to me, she thought. In her replies, she praised his progress and diligence and told him she would love to hear from him every day, but that she knew he was busy with his lessons. *Love toward your mother, on the one hand, and the desire for learning on the other entirely free you from any suspicion of negligence*, she wrote.

She smiled when Edward informed her that Dr Cox did not believe she had written a Latin essay she had sent the Prince until he saw her signature at the bottom. Edward said he had been surprised himself. *Literature conduces to virtuous conduct*, he informed her. *Everything that comes from God is good; learning comes from God, therefore learning is good.* His words took her aback. Goodness, what a little prig he was becoming! Already, he was so sure of his divinely appointed status. God grant that she would be the one to guide him when the time came.

On a glorious sunny afternoon in July, cradled in her stepmother's arms, Margaret departed this life as easily as she had lived it, slipping away in her sleep. Katharine mourned her loss deeply, and suddenly understood the pain of losing a child, which made her wish she had been kinder to Anne and Lady Wriothesley. Her stepdaughter had brought her as much love and happiness as if she had been her own flesh and blood. It was tragic that she would never know the love of a man or have children. She would have made a good wife and mother. But there would be rewards in Heaven, better than anything she could have been granted on earth.

Henry was kind, even though he was worried about French raids on the south coast. He joined Katharine for every meal and visited her chamber at night, even if it was only to hold her while she cried. And that was all he could do. Their couplings had become rare since his health started to decline; he had not the energy or agility to make her his.

He rode to Portsmouth to review the fleet that would trounce the French, who had been sighted off the Sussex coast. He was there when his great ship, the *Mary Rose*, suddenly keeled over and sank in the Solent before his horrified eyes.

'It was dreadful,' he told Katharine on his return, as they ate a late supper. 'More than six hundred men drowned. I could hear their screams from the battlements of Southsea Castle. I will never forget Lady Carew's cries. Her husband was vice admiral of the fleet and went down with the ship. She was watching with me as it sank. I did my best to comfort her. We were both stunned. The ship had fired off all her guns and then turned around; it looked as if she was capsized by a gust of wind. But it shouldn't have happened. Oh, my gentlemen! Oh, my gallant men!' He wiped away a tear.

Katharine reached for his hand across the table. 'I am more sorry than I can say. I will write to Lady Carew to express my condolences.'

'We beat the French and sent them scuttling off homewards,' Henry said. 'But I had rather have kept my good ship and all on board.'

There was more grief to come. While Katharine and Henry were staying at Guildford during their summer progress, the Duke of Suffolk, who was with them, died suddenly. Henry was inconsolable.

'He was my oldest friend,' he wept, as he and Katharine stood looking down at the grizzled old man on the bed. 'As long as he served me, I never knew him betray a friend or knowingly take unfair advantage of an enemy. None of my other councillors could say as much.'

Opposite them, the Duchess of Suffolk, wearing a hastily donned black veil over her riding clothes, stared bleakly at her dead husband. She was young to be a widow, just twenty-six, and would not lack for suitors were she disposed, in time, to wed again. Yet twelve years of contented marriage could not easily be forgotten.

'You need worry about nothing, my lady,' Henry told her. 'I will take care of everything. I'm arranging for Charles to be buried in St George's Chapel at Windsor, and I will defray the cost.'

'Your Grace is more than kind. He would have been honoured to know that he would be buried among kings.'

'It is no less than his due,' Henry said. 'I trust your boys will take it well. Your elder is now, what, ten?'

'Eleven, Sir.'

'He shall succeed his father as duke of Suffolk, and I will find a place for him in the Prince's household.'

Katharine put her arms around Lady Suffolk. 'I know you will wish to go to Lincolnshire and sort out the Duke's affairs. Take as long as you need.'

This was proving to be a horrible year. She had heard nothing more about Tom marrying Mary Howard, and had been worrying about it for weeks when, in September, Will informed her that Tom was at Portsmouth and that his ships were rife with plague. It was a heart-stopping moment.

'He hasn't got it?' she asked, clutching at Will's sleeve.

'He said in his letter that he was very ill at ease and had had a bad night. The King had commanded him to patrol the seas, but he doubted he would be ready for that.'

'God preserve him!' she breathed. 'Keep him safe!' As so often these days, she sought solace in prayer.

She endured more anxious weeks until, in October, she learned that the navy had sailed, and that Tom was still in command of it. That sent her winging to her closet to thank the Almighty.

She seemed constantly to be putting on mourning. That winter, death claimed Margaret Douglas's little son and Dr Butts. Then Henry had a seizure. She was not with him at the time, but hastened to the King's lodgings when they brought her the news and was waiting when Dr Wendy, who had replaced Butts, emerged from the bedchamber. Myriad thoughts had been churning in her head. Was this the end? Was Edward to be king at such a tender age? She felt faint when she saw Dr Wendy's face.

'Your Grace.' He bowed, as all the gentlemen crowded around. 'I would speak with the Queen alone,' he told them, whereupon they departed in silence, some looking sorrowful, others shaking their heads.

She sat down, bracing herself to hear the worst.

'His Majesty has stabilised,' Dr Wendy said. 'We don't know what it was, but he passed out and then started moaning. He is himself again now, but he is very unwell and suffering agonising pains in his legs, and I fear that, considering his age and weight, he might not survive further attacks. I'm telling you this, Madam, only so that you are prepared.'

She had envisaged Henry dying so many times; there had been so many alarms with his health. Yet it was still hard to believe he might be taken now. It affected her more than she could have imagined. He had been a good husband and loved her truly; she had no doubt of that, or that she would miss him. England would miss him. How would she deal with the court factions if they heard that she was to be regent? How long would Henry's authority survive his death? She might well have a fight on her hands, not only for power, but also for the soul of the nation.

'Is there anything you can do for the pain?' she asked.

Dr Wendy looked distressed. 'Madam, we have tried everything.'

'I understand,' she said.

Henry was still unwell on Christmas Eve, when he was to address Parliament. When Katharine paid him her regular morning visit, she was shocked to find him dressed in his ermine-lined robes of estate, with his imperial crown, glittering with jewels, sitting on the table beside his chair.

'Henry, you're not going to the Parliament House?' she cried. 'You're not well enough and it's freezing outside.'

He wagged his finger at her. 'I have to go, Kate. Some things are too important to delegate to others. Besides, it may be the last chance I'll ever have to speak to Parliament.' Their eyes met and she knew he was telling her that he was aware that his time on this earth might be short.

'I think you know my mind about the future,' he said. 'I would have an end to this faction-fighting. I want this realm, and my son, governed by one I can trust.' He took her hand. 'You understand me, Kate?'

'I do, Henry.' He could not have given a clearer indication of the trust he had in her, and she was deeply touched, and humbled. That she, Katharine Parr, would one day rule England – it seemed incredible.

'All will be put in place in good time,' he assured her, 'and I will have my senior officers swear an oath to support you. Now, I must make haste.'

'Please, Henry, I beg of you, stay here in the warm.' She wrung her hands. 'Could not the Lord Chancellor speak for you?'

'Kate, my Church is riven with dissension. I would have my loving subjects live in perfect love and concord, but that will not happen because charity and concord are not among them. How can they be when one calls the other heretic and is called in turn Papist or hypocrite, and preachers themselves sow debate and discord? God has appointed me His vicar and minister here, and I will see these divisions extinct! That is why I must go to Parliament, to stamp out the dissension that my liberality has created.'

'What do you mean?' she asked, worried now.

Henry regarded her magisterially. 'When I authorised the English Bible to be placed in churches for all to read, I did not think it would lead to such controversy. I licensed it only to inform men's own consciences, so that they could instruct their children.' His face grew stern. 'I did not license it so that any Tom, Dick or Harry could argue with priests and preachers. I am very sorry to hear how irreverently that most precious jewel, the Word of God, is now disputed, rhymed, sung and jangled in every alehouse and tavern. I will have my subjects live in charity with each other, like brothers, loving, dreading and serving God, which I, their sovereign lord, will require of them today.'

She sat there, aware of the profound conviction that underlay his words, and would have liked to applaud him, even though she thrived on the debate that so concerned him. His vision of a unified Church of England was so at one with hers, its tenets so basic and sincere, and she realised why he wanted to correct those who were blind to his true aims. That was his genius, that he knew how to get to the nub of the matter. Therein lay his greatness.

She protested no more about his going to Parliament. She knew now that it was necessary. Let him speak like that and he would have them in the palm of his hand.

And so it turned out.

'The King's speech,' Will told her later that day, 'was such a joy and marvellous comfort that I reckon this day one of the happiest of my life. He spoke in so kingly a manner, so fatherly, that a lot of people shed tears.' Of course they had. Anyone could see that Henry was not long for this world. Maybe those quarrelsome factions would now give him some peace in the time remaining to him.

Chapter 21

1546

On New Year's Day, Katharine sat in her bedchamber at Hampton Court and opened her presents. There was a generous sum of money from Henry. Elizabeth's gift was another of her translations. It was beautifully presented, but Katharine stared in dismay at the title: *The Institution of the Christian Life* by John Calvin, a book with which she was all too familiar. Henry would see red! She put it back in its wrapping and pushed it in a drawer. What was the girl thinking of? At twelve, she was old enough to know that her father would never approve.

When she joined Henry in the presence chamber for the public present-giving, she waited until all the courtiers had given him their gifts, which were displayed on trestle tables. He was in a genial mood, bestowing smiles on everyone.

'Look what Elizabeth gave me!' he said and handed her a book. It was a translation of Katharine's *Prayers and Meditations* into French, Latin and Italian. Katharine blushed as she read Elizabeth's praise for her work in the dedication.

'What did she give you?' Henry asked, as they walked through to the privy chamber.

She could not lie. 'A translation of Calvin's work,' she said. 'I do not think she understands its import.'

'By God, I hope not!' Henry barked.

'Don't be angry with her. She but thought to impress me with her scholarship.'

'You speak to her.' He eased himself into the chair in his closet and she knelt beside him, cradling his bad leg in her lap, as had become her habit.

'Are you going to read that book?' he asked.

'Only if you think it meet for me,' she replied.

'I thought you were familiar with it anyway,' he said, startling her. 'You once referred to me as one of God's elect. That's straight from the mouth of Calvin.'

So he *had* picked up on what she had written all those months ago.

'Did I?' It was best to feign a poor memory. 'I did not mean it in that sense; only that God has chosen you to lead our people out of bondage. That's how I think of you. I am no Calvinist!'

He caressed her cheek. 'Yes, but you do incline to the new religion.'

She froze. He knew!

'I am an advocate of reform. I have made no secret of it.'

'Aye, Kate. But you would have me go further, yes?'

'Only if, in your wisdom, you see fit.' She was trembling, adrift on a dangerous sea.

'Have you ever discussed Calvin with Elizabeth?'

'No, of course not.' It was true.

'Then I must keep an eye on Grindal. He and Cheke and Ascham, even Cox – reformists all!'

'And men you admire. You yourself chose them to teach your children.'

Henry nodded. 'I did. But, if you speak to them, remind them of my determination to follow a middle road. And Kate, hide that book. Take it to your house, anywhere. We don't want Gardiner finding it.' He raised her chin so that he was looking directly at her. 'You are very precious to me. But I am Supreme Head of the Church. I cannot be seen to be condoning heresy in my wife, or protecting her, when others are being punished for it. I pray you, be careful.'

She dared say nothing; she just kissed him and left him to have his nap. It seemed he was telling her that she might hold her views so long as she kept them secret. She had never realised that he cared so much for her.

Later that month, after Parliament had proposed the confiscation of colleges and chantries, Dr Smythe, the advocate of the University of

Cambridge, arrived at Greenwich and presented Katharine with a letter from the dons, begging her to save their colleges.

'Pray tell the Chancellor that I shall be honoured to maintain and cherish the schools of Cambridge,' she told Dr Smythe, gesturing for him to rise. 'I hear that all kinds of learning flourish among you, as they did among the Greeks at Athens long ago. As your patron, I desire you not to hunger for the profane learning of the ancients, but to embrace Christian learning, for the furtherance of Christ's most sacred doctrine, so that Cambridge may be accounted a university of divine philosophy.' She looked at him meaningfully, knowing that the university encouraged reform – and, no doubt, even more radical ideas.

'Madam, I am sure that my masters will concur with so godly an exhortation.'

She smiled. 'Never fear, I will ask the King's Majesty to spare the university. I know he would rather advance learning than confound your ancient institutions.'

She spoke to Henry at the earliest opportunity.

'Sir, you cannot be seen to be destroying our fine universities. Will you not do something for them?

He frowned. Maybe she had spoken too forcefully, but this was important.

'I will give it some thought,' he said, stroking his beard. She knew not to push him further. He liked to weigh matters in his mind and take advice before making a decision.

Not long afterwards, he summoned her to his closet. His table was littered with papers covered with his scribble.

'I have come up with a plan for the universities,' he told her, looking pleased with himself, but clearly in pain. 'I plan to re-found and endow Wolsey's college at Oxford and call it Christ Church. Dr Cox is to be dean and the curriculum is to include theology, Greek and Hebrew. At Cambridge, I am founding a new college dedicated to the Holy Trinity. What do you think, Kate?'

'I think these are excellent plans! You will be celebrated in Oxford and Cambridge for centuries to come.'

Henry flushed; there were beads of sweat on his brow. 'I'm glad to find you so enthusiastic – unlike my courtiers. They gape at my proposed endowments, wanting my bounty for themselves, but I have told them that I judge no land in England better bestowed than that which is given to our universities.'

He drew in his breath sharply.

'Is it your leg?' she asked, concerned for him.

'Aye.' He shifted in his chair.

She felt his brow. He was burning up. 'I'll fetch the doctors,' she said.

His fever persisted through February. Katharine spent her time either sitting with him or fretting about him, searching for any sign of improvement.

'I hate it when he is ill,' she told Lady Suffolk as they played cards one afternoon.

'I am sorry for him,' the Duchess said. 'The only thing one can say is that it gives the lie to the rumours that are going about.'

'What rumours?'

The Duchess hesitated. 'My maid said there was some talk at dinner in the great hall. People were saying that the King will take a new queen.'

It hit her like a blow. 'What?' She thought of the things Henry could use against her if he wanted to be rid of her and felt sick. He had been so loving to her lately. Surely even he would not dissemble thus far?

'It's nonsense, of course,' the Duchess said, 'especially as I'm the one he's alleged to be marrying! He hasn't spoken one word to me beyond courtesies in two years, and yet I'm supposed to be high in his favour!'

Katharine relaxed a little. It *was* just idle gossip, she told herself. But it was offensive and upsetting. 'If you hear any more of this, please refute it.'

'You may depend on it,' the Duchess said.

When next Katharine saw Henry, who was no longer bedridden but sitting by the fire, she watched him all through their talk and could detect no change in his manner to her. He was in no fit state to court a lady, still less the lively Duchess of Suffolk. He did not like outspoken women like that. No, she was worrying unnecessarily.

'We're going on progress soon,' he announced, surprising her. 'I want to visit the more distant parts of my realm. Do you know, I've never been further north than York or further west than Gloucestershire?'

Katharine felt some alarm at the prospect of his travelling far away – or travelling at all. 'Are you sure you're well enough?'

'Don't fuss, Kate. My leg remains slightly sore, but I'm strong.' His looks belied that: pain had scored lines on his face and he appeared tired and drained. But maybe, just maybe, a progress would do him good, if they took it in easy stages.

'Gardiner's been at me again,' he said, frowning. 'This new alliance with the Emperor looks as if it will come to fruition. But the Bishop insists that I must put a stop to my reforms, for the Emperor is a true son of Rome and at war with the Protestant princes of Germany.'

Irritation welled in Katharine. 'You were friends with the Emperor before, when you were promulgating your reforms.'

'Yes, but I am excommunicate now.' He said it without emotion. 'He is nervous of offering friendship if England seems to be veering into heresy. Kate, I know what Gardiner is doing. He would oust the reformists from the Council. He thinks that, with the backing of the Emperor, he can do that. But I tell you now, in confidence, that I will never again allow the Catholics to wield power here. I humour Gardiner to keep him sweet because he is useful to me. He has no idea what I really think of him. That's my method, Kate. Play off one against the other. Divide and rule, and keep your hand close. Believe me, if I thought my cap knew what I was thinking, I would throw it in the fire!' He smiled at her.

'Wise advice!' She beamed at him, but was dismayed to see his smile fade.

'I need to warn you,' he said. 'Gardiner and Wriothesley are planning another purge. They're targeting Cranmer now.'

'No!'

'Yes, I'm afraid so. They're hauling in people suspected of heresy for questioning, and most of them are connected to Cranmer in some way.

346

And they've arrested a woman who was preaching in London. Her name is Anne Askew. Have you heard of her?'

She must tell the truth now, to protect herself. 'Yes. Her family lived not far away when I was in Lincolnshire. We visited them once and she came to see me in London some years ago. I thought she was a little crazy with the ideas she was spouting forth. She seemed to have no sense of discretion or awareness that her views would be seen as heresy. I sent her away and have had nothing to do with her since.'

'Very wise,' Henry observed. 'They're trying to get her to recant.'

'I hope, for her sake, that she does,' she said. The alternative was unthinkable.

She left Henry, feeling a sense of foreboding, knowing that some of her ladies had gone to hear Anne Askew preach and some had even met with her in secret. Unlike herself, they had a high regard for her, admiring her courage in publicly declaring her faith. But what if Gardiner and his ilk, spoiled of their prey last year, used her ladies' connection with Anne to get at her, their true target? She would not put it past them. They must fear her influence with the King and the Prince, and they certainly knew her to be no friend to their faction. Anyone could see that Henry would not live to see his son come to manhood and she could already sense that the rival factions were poised for a battle for the regency. The conservatives would see her as an obstacle to their attaining power after Henry's death. They probably thought she was influencing him to choose Hertford, the Prince's uncle, who was so high in favour. She wished they knew that her role was to be far more significant than that – if she survived that long.

She waited uneasily to hear more about Anne Askew's examination, worried in case the woman had incriminated her or anyone close to her. She did not dare ask Henry for news. She checked the secret places in her apartments where forbidden books had been hidden, although all were now empty, and bade her ladies do the same in their lodgings.

She even asked Uncle William, who was more or less retired these days, to come back to court and be her ears and eyes in the privy chamber, as Will was so often up north. She had new locks fitted to her doors and ordered new strongboxes, smiling wickedly at the thought of Gardiner banging furiously at the door, demanding to be let in. She ordered her chaplains and visiting preachers to keep to strictly orthodox themes and was furious when the Earl of Surrey, listening to a Lenten sermon in her chamber, derided it as Catholic claptrap. For that, he was sternly censured by the Privy Council.

To bolster her position, Katharine surrounded herself with the highest ladies in the land. That spring, she had Mary and Elizabeth in attendance as well as the King's nieces, Margaret Douglas and Frances Brandon, Frances's sister Eleanor and even Anne of Cleves. Showing herself so firmly entrenched in the King's favour gave her confidence. Let Gardiner dare touch her!

Just as they sat down to supper one warm May evening, Henry told her that his favoured gentleman, George Blagge, had been arrested on Wriothesley's orders.

'I do fear for my Pig,' he said, using his affectionate nickname for Blagge. 'But the fool was overheard denying the Real Presence in the Mass, and I can't save him from that, Kate!' He was clearly agitated. 'They hid the warrant among others, but I noticed it. What could I do?'

'What will happen to him?'

'It will go to trial. I pray he acquits himself well.'

'You could show mercy.'

'In such a case? My Pig has attacked the very core of our faith, of which I am the defender.' He pushed his plate away. 'I don't want this. I'm not hungry.'

'Try to eat something, for your health,' she pleaded.

Henry took a mouthful. 'The woman Askew recanted and was released. At least she saw sense.'

'That's good news,' Katharine said, casting about in her mind for ways to lighten the mood despite her own growing anxiety. 'I had a letter from the Prince today, and I had to smile. He asked me to warn Mary that she is ruining her good reputation by her love of dancing and other frivolous entertainments. I am to tell her that the only real love is

348

the love of God, and that such pastimes do not become a Christian princess. He's eight! She's twenty-nine!'

A smile played on Henry's lips. 'His tutors can be overzealous! I wouldn't mention it to her.'

'I wasn't going to!'

In May, Anne Askew was arrested again. Nan Hertford heard the news from her husband, and Katharine hurriedly assembled her circle of ladies in her prayer closet.

'Tell us what you know,' she demanded of Nan.

'Dr Crome – you'll remember him preaching at court – gave a sermon in which he denied the Real Presence. He was arrested and examined, and named Mistress Askew as one of his Protestant friends. She has been brought before the Privy Council.' She said it almost triumphantly, as if she was perversely pleased to be discomfiting Katharine. But Katharine was too upset to care.

Will was now back at court, and he was a Privy Councillor. Breaking the meeting up, Katharine sent a page to fetch him and almost began dancing with frustration when he told her that his lordship was in council. By the afternoon, when Will did finally appear, she was convinced that Anne Askew's arrest was part of a new attempt to unseat herself.

'Thank God you've come!' she said. 'What's happening with Anne Askew?'

He gaped at her. 'How do you know she was here?'

'My lord of Hertford tells his wife everything. I know that she was questioned today.'

'Yes. I examined her, with Gardiner and Lord Lisle, who is of our persuasion. Gardiner pressed her to say that she believed the Sacrament to be the body of our Lord. We were praying that she would do so and save herself.' He paused. 'I think you are right about what Gardiner intends. He will use her to bring others down.'

Their eyes met. 'You mean me?'

'Possibly. I hope not.'

'Did she profess a belief in the Real Presence?'

349

'No.' There was a heavy silence. 'Gardiner cozened her, asked her to speak to him as a friend. She said that was what Judas did when he betrayed Christ. That riled Gardiner and he warned her she would go to the stake. She said she had searched all the Scriptures, but never found that Christ or His apostles put any creature to death.'

'Gardiner's a bully,' Katharine declared, appalled.

'But she didn't give in to his ploys,' Will said. 'We sent her to Newgate. We had no choice.'

Katharine could not sleep. She was convinced that Gardiner was out to destroy her and that he would first attack the ladies in her circle. It felt as if the walls were closing in on her, and she was, frankly, terrified.

That was not the only weight on her mind. That afternoon, she had heard the Duchess of Richmond mention to Magdalen that Norfolk was pestering the King to agree to her marriage to Sir Thomas Seymour.

'I don't want to marry him,' she'd said. 'I like the freedoms of widowhood. Besides, Sir Thomas has never shown the slightest interest in me.'

Katharine had been glad to hear that, having sometimes wondered if Tom would see the lovely Duchess, who was younger and prettier than her, and free to wed, as a better match. He was a man of property now, and men of property wanted heirs, which she was convinced she could not give him.

He was still at sea, guarding the Channel and getting up to all kinds of daring exploits, if the reports Uncle William described were to be believed. There was no way of knowing what he thought of this proposed marriage.

She had been fretting for a week when Surrey again joined the company in her chamber, sitting there restlessly while the Bassanos played. He was such an irritating man, brilliant but dangerously volatile, and often in trouble for brawling and rowdy behaviour. Norfolk must despair of him, she thought. For all her friendship with his sister, and the fact that Will liked him, she sensed that he was not to be trusted.

When the music had ceased and they all fell to talking, Surrey said,

'My beloved father wants to ally us to the Seymours and chose Mary here as the sacrificial lamb, to be offered up into the arms of that hothead, Sir Thomas.'

'Shut up, brother,' the Duchess snapped.

He ignored her. 'I wasn't having it. Those Seymours may be the uncles of the Prince, but they are new men and not fit to mate with Howards.'

'That's enough, my lord!' Katharine reprimanded him, angered by his implied slur on the Prince's parentage and his disparagement of Tom.

'I crave your Grace's bountiful pardon,' Surrey replied, with exaggerated courtesy. 'I just wanted to tell everyone that I saw the King today and told him that I would never consent to the marriage for I knew my sister's mind in the matter, that she desired never to wed again. And he said he would not be a party to the match.'

'Father will be furious,' Mary said.

'He'll get over it.'

Katharine hastily invited the musicians to resume. At least she had one fewer thing to worry about.

Anne Askew was in the Tower. Will murmured the news to Katharine as he joined her to watch a game of tennis. 'Can we go outside?'

Her heart was juddering as she led the way out to the garden that lay between the tennis play and the Prince's empty lodgings.

'Why was she moved there?' she asked, as they sat down on a stone bench.

'Gardiner had sent Dr Shaxton to make her recant.' Katharine knew about Shaxton. He had been bishop of Salisbury, but had resigned because the King's reforms were not radical enough for his liking; lately, he had been arrested for heresy, but had recanted, which was probably why he had been chosen. 'When he exhorted her to it, she told him it would have been good for him never to have been born. It was Master Rich who sent her to the Tower.'

That was bad news. Katharine knew Rich only by sight and did not want to know him better. He had clawed his way up the political ladder, destroying Thomas More and Thomas Cromwell on the way. He seemed to have no scruples at all.

'Her case has been referred to the King,' Will said. Katharine knew it was unlikely that Henry would be lenient. A heretic who recanted and then relapsed got no second chance.

Will returned that evening and saw her in private. 'The King has authorised the examination of Mistress Askew. Wriothesley is to question her.'

Katharine fought down the panic that was engulfing her. There was no doubt now that they were all in peril. Otherwise, why would the Lord Chancellor himself be interrogating Anne Askew? She was unimportant and quite obviously her own worst enemy. What did the soul of one more lapsed heretic matter to the likes of Wriothesley? No, this was all leading to her, Katharine.

She tried to be rational, tried to tell herself that they could not possibly have anything on her. It was years since she had seen Anne Askew, and she had sent her away with a warning. She had always been dismissive of what her ladies had told her about the woman. But there was such a thing as guilt by association. She could still be implicated.

Yet Henry knew the truth, knew she had never involved herself with Anne Askew.

She clung to that knowledge as she went about her daily round, putting on a smiling face, trying to eat, trying to sleep. After two days, she was at the point where she did not think she could take much more tension, when both her brother and Uncle William arrived, asking to see her in private. She knew, from their solemn faces, that they brought bad news.

'What has happened this day makes me ashamed to be an Englishman,' Uncle William said, as they sat down in her closet.

'What *has* happened?' Katharine asked, desperate to know.

'The Lord Chancellor himself racked Anne Askew,' Will told her, his face like stone. 'Rich helped.'

'They racked her?' She was shaking with outrage. 'They don't normally rack heretics, do they?'

'Not unless they can't get information out of them otherwise.'

'Kate, we are convinced now that they are trying to get her to incriminate you or those close to you,' Uncle William said, taking her hand as she sat there, numb with horror.

'That's been my view all along,' she faltered. 'They see me as a dangerous influence, one that must be removed. But that they would go this far is unbelievable. Tell me, did she talk?'

'No. She is a very brave woman.' Will grimaced. 'Her sufferings must have been great.'

Katharine felt tears welling. She knew what the rack was and could barely imagine how agonising it must be to have your arms and legs slowly pulled out of their sockets. 'Poor soul. It's horrible, horrible. I shall pray for her.' She paused, wringing her hands. 'You are sure she did not mention me or my ladies?'

'She did not. Wriothesley took great pleasure in telling me they had asked her if any gentlewomen gave her money. She said some had, but she knew not their names. They asked her if she knew anything about the beliefs of the ladies of your household, but she answered that she knew nothing. Wriothesley was smirking when he told me that, as if to imply that he knew it was a lie. He said that was when they decided to have her racked.'

Uncle William chimed in. 'She would not talk. When the Lieutenant of the Tower thought she was at the end of her endurance, he went to untie her. But Wriothesley was furious because she had given them nothing and ordered the Lieutenant to strain her on the rack again. He refused because she was so weak that he thought she might die.'

'Good for him!' Katharine applauded. Nothing like this would happen when *she* ruled England.

'Wriothesley threatened to report his disobedience to the King,' Will told her. 'Then he and Rich threw off their gowns and began to turn the rollers. She suffered their cruelty till her joints were almost pulled asunder, but they did not take her down until she was nearly dead. Then they laid her on the bare floor and continued to interrogate her.'

'When it was over,' Uncle William added, 'the Lieutenant came to

Whitehall in all haste to speak with the King before Wriothesley and Rich got to him.'

'Did his Grace know that Anne Askew was to be tortured?' Katharine wanted to know. 'Did he consent to it?'

'No, Kate,' Will told her. 'Torture can be inflicted with the assent of the Privy Council, and Wriothesley and Rich are both Privy Councillors. They should have consulted the rest of us and obtained a warrant, but they didn't because they knew they'd be opposed, so they acted against the law.'

'Does the King know what they did?'

'Oh, yes.' Uncle William's eyes gleamed. 'The Lieutenant told him, making no bones about his opinion of them, and his Majesty was not at all pleased. The Lieutenant told me afterwards that the King had said the woman had been handled too severely, and he had readily granted the Lieutenant his pardon for disobeying orders, and told him to go back and see to his prisoner.'

'Do you know if his Grace has reprimanded Wriothesley and Rich?' Katharine asked.

'He summoned them, and they were with him for some time, but I don't know what he said to them,' Will told her.

'Let us hope that he gave them a piece of his mind!' Katharine said vehemently. 'And that this is the last gasp of Gardiner's party.'

'That dog won't lie down and die,' Uncle William said grimly, 'but I pray he's been muzzled for a space.'

She was safe – for the moment. There would be no more questioning of Anne Askew. If the woman hadn't said anything under extreme torture, she wouldn't now. They must have realised this for they quickly sent her for trial, and she was condemned to be burned as a elapsed heretic.

Katharine had not discussed the case with Henry because she feared to appear too interested in Anne. His tolerance could only extend so far, as he had made clear to her, and she had not forgotten his warning that he might not be able to protect her. So she went against all her instincts and refrained from pleading for mercy for Anne Askew.

Against such courage, she knew herself to be a coward. She would never be brave enough to die so horribly for her faith, and she prayed constantly that she would never be tested.

When, early in July, the King issued a proclamation commanding that all heretical books be burned, Uncle William went to Charterhouse Square, removed Katharine's from behind the panelling in a spare bedchamber and took them away. 'No one will find them,' he promised her. 'Not even you.'

Days later, Katharine was shocked to hear from a distraught Lady Suffolk that Hugh Latimer had been arrested. Then Uncle William told her that Norfolk's youngest son, Lord Thomas Howard, had been hauled before the Council and asked to explain certain remarks he had made in her chamber.

'What remarks?' she asked, alarmed.

'I don't know, Kate. He was assured of the King's clemency if he would frankly confess what he said, and he did acknowledge his fault, but he would not confess any particulars and was remanded.'

'I hope I wasn't implicated!'

'Not that I've heard of. Just stay alert and do not give them any cause for suspicion.'

'I've covered my tracks,' she told him. 'Oh, Uncle William, what dread times we live in. I fear that no one is safe.'

Katharine was with Henry on the day of George Blagge's trial. He was tense, angry with himself for not being able to intervene.

'But I cannot subvert the rule of justice,' he sighed, as they played a desolate game of bowls in the otherwise deserted alley. He kept looking over his shoulder, expecting to see a messenger materialise with news, for he had commanded that he be kept informed without delay.

By eleven o'clock, when they returned to his lodgings for dinner, he was in a state of agitation and could eat little. Two hours later, when he was told that Blagge had been sentenced to burn and committed to Newgate, he collapsed with his head in his hands. 'Oh, my Pig, my poor Pig! The bastards! I knew they would do for him.'

Katharine was rigid with shock. That they had dared to strike so close to the King – and got away with it! It was horrifying. Her heart bled for George Blagge.

But others had heard the news too. Sir John Russell, the Lord Privy Seal, was announced not a half-hour later and, to Katharine's astonishment, sank to his knees before the King.

'Your Majesty,' he said, his tone urgent, 'on behalf of many of your Privy Council, I come to beg for mercy for Mr Blagge.'

'Am I to show mercy to a heretic?' Henry asked.

'He's no more a heretic than I am, Sir, and many in your court,' Sir John replied. 'His words have deliberately been misinterpreted by those who think only of their own ambitions.'

Katharine was inwardly applauding Sir John and watching Henry's face closely.

'Your Majesty can only gain in stature and reputation in exercising your prerogative of mercy,' Sir John declared, then waited, head bowed in supplication.

Henry nodded. He had been shown a way forward.

'You have done well to come to me,' he said. 'I will pardon him. Have the document drawn up now and bring it to me for signing and sealing. And Russell, thank you.'

The Lord Privy Seal rose, made his reverence and hurried away. It seemed only minutes before he was back with the pardon.

'Send for the Lord Chancellor,' Henry instructed an usher of his chamber.

Wriothesley came bustling in, smug-faced as ever, and knelt.

Henry handed him the pardon. 'Take this to the governor of Newgate and command him to release George Blagge.'

All the grief they had suffered was worth the look on Wriothesley's face. He could not conceal his outrage and fury.

'Your Majesty, I would just ask you to consider—'

'I *have* considered,' Henry interrupted, his voice like steel. 'Now go. I want Blagge back here directly.' Wriothesley's look might have felled an army, but not Henry, who glared at him until he withdrew.

Late that afternoon, Blagge presented himself in Henry's chamber and fell humbly to his knees. He was a rotund, likeable man, not unlike the animal that had inspired his nickname.

'Ah, my Pig!' Henry greeted him. 'I cannot say how pleased I am to see you.'

'I cannot thank your Majesty enough for extending your gracious mercy to me,' Blagge said, with tears in his eyes. 'If your Majesty had not been better to me than your bishops were, your Pig would have been roasted.'

'I'll never forgive those who did this to you,' Henry said.

On an impulse, Katharine dropped to her knees beside Blagge. 'Sir, might I humbly crave some favour for Mr Blagge as compensation for his ordeal?' The little man was staring at her in gratitude. She felt he was a kindred spirit, for they both had survived the malice of the conservative faction.

Henry beamed at her. 'A capital idea, Madam. I will find some lucrative office for my Pig.'

Blagge departed, stammering his thanks.

It was tragic that Anne Askew could not be saved so easily. She, poor soul, could not hope for mercy.

Four days before she was due to be executed, Katharine called to her closet those ladies who shared her convictions. Some had known Anne and were in deep distress, which they struggled to hide.

'Take heed,' she said. 'None of you are to go to Smithfield. You must not be seen to have any association or sympathy with the woman Askew. That is my command. Please do not disobey it.'

They agreed, some nodding in approval, others looking un-happy about it. She was confident that they would do her bidding. But, when the day came, she noticed that the Duchess of Suffolk was absent.

'Has anyone seen her?' she asked nervously.

No one had. Someone thought she had gone to Suffolk Place, her London residence, to see her sons. Katharine fervently hoped so.

She spent an hour on her knees in her closet around the time she judged they would be lighting the faggots, praying that God would give Anne Askew the strength to bear her terrible ordeal. Then she sat reading, trying to divert her mind from what was happening not two miles from Whitehall.

In the middle of the afternoon, she thought she might walk in her garden. As she descended the privy stair, she almost collided with Lady Suffolk.

'I beg pardon, your Grace!' the lady cried. She looked ashen.

'Are you ill?' Katharine asked, her suspicions mounting.

'Not ill, no,' the Duchess said, her face crumpling. 'I'm so sorry, Madam. I have disobeyed you this day and lived to regret it. No one recognised me, I swear. I wore a plain mourning gown and a thick veil over my face. But it wasn't enough to blank out that terrible sight . . .' She began weeping in earnest, great harsh sobs. 'Oh, it was dreadful.'

Katharine put an arm around her. 'It's all right. I'm not angry. Come and sit in the garden.' She led the way to her favourite stone seat, bracing herself against what she might be about to hear. 'Do you want to talk about it?'

'They carried her to Smithfield on a chair as she could not walk, because of the racking. They offered her the King's pardon at the last, but she refused. I have never seen such a singular example of Christian constancy. She was so brave.'

'Was it quick?'

'Yes, but it was ghastly. The executioner had hung a bag of gunpowder about her neck. When the flames reached her chest, she started screaming, but then it exploded. I have never seen anything so horrific. I had to look away. But it made a speedy end of her.'

Katharine felt sick, but she was brisk. 'I know it is hard, but try to put it from your mind and go on as normal. Nothing can hurt her now, and she is at peace, but we are all alive and in peril. I fear that our tormentors will not cease until they snare us, so we must never betray any sympathy for Mistress Askew. This time, you must heed me!'

Chapter 22

1546–7

Katharine was relieved to hear that Lord Hertford had returned to court after successfully completing a punitive expedition against the Scots and agreeing a peace that was only ever intended to be temporary. He was in higher favour with the King than ever. The reformers were riding high and, miraculously, it soon became very clear that Gardiner's party was being eclipsed. That was an enormous relief. It made things less complicated in the long run, and Katharine was confident that she could happily work with Hertford when the time came. They were of the same mind on religion, she was certain.

There were no more arrests for heresy, for which she was profoundly thankful. She would not relax her guard, though. It was always best to be on the alert for trouble.

She was delighted when Henry summoned Prince Edward to Whitehall, and took pleasure in seeing the boy do well at the archery butts and tossing the quintain in the tiltyard. Henry was pleased with his son's prowess.

'He'll make a fine king,' he observed.

'He will assuredly,' she said, clapping the Prince as he bowed in the saddle. 'But I pray it will be a long time before that day comes.'

'Bless you, Kate,' Henry said. He looked pensive, sad even. Edward was eight now; in seven years' time, he could be declared of age. But would Henry last that long?

The boy walked back to the palace with them. 'When is the Admiral coming from France?' he asked. The question gave Katharine a jolt. She was still aware of the need to seem indifferent to Tom. Then she realised that the Prince was referring to the French Admiral, who was coming to

England to ratify a new treaty with France, that with the Emperor having foundered.

'Soon, my son,' Henry said. 'You will be looking forward to playing your part in the ceremonies.'

'I am, Sir, and hoping to give your Grace cause to be pleased with me,' Edward replied. 'I hope my Latin is good enough for the welcome speech.'

'It certainly is,' Katharine smiled.

Edward skipped ahead, as blithe as any normal little boy.

Henry was making a great celebration of the French envoy's arrival. The nobility flocked to Hampton Court and Katharine ordered new finery.

'Aren't they lovely?' she said, as Mary and Elizabeth exclaimed over the gloves of Spanish leather, the collar of crimson velvet trimmed with gold lace, the ribbons and jewelled aglets that the Queen's milliner had just delivered. 'Should I wear the crimson gown or the tawny silk?'

'The crimson!' Elizabeth said. At nearly thirteen, she loved rich clothing as much as Mary and Katharine did.

'I'll wear that one then. It's my favourite colour. These shoes will match.' She held up a pair in crimson velvet studded with diamonds, then regarded her stepdaughters affectionately, thinking, as ever, of the stepdaughter who was missing. 'You both look very becoming.' She kissed them warmly. 'You will be the chief ornaments of the court this day.'

Will had gone to Greenwich to receive the Admiral and escort him to Hounslow, where Prince Edward would receive him on behalf of the King. Katharine had watched Edward ride out from Hampton Court, leading a retinue of eighty gentlemen, all dressed in gold, and eighty Yeomen of the Guard. The boy outshone them all, sitting proudly on his horse, his hand on his hip. He had the authority of a king about him already.

She was impressed by his self-assurance over the next ten days, as he stood in for his father, who, much to his chagrin, was chair-bound. Edward presided faultlessly over receptions and banquets, giving speeches in competent Latin and a virtuoso performance on the lute for the ambassador and his suite. She could see that the French Admiral was impressed.

Although Henry was unable to join in many of the festivities and hunting forays, he had spent lavishly. In the palace gardens, tents of cloth of gold and velvet housed the Admiral's retinue. Two temporary banqueting houses had been erected and hung with glittering tapestries. An impressive display of gold plate studded with gems gleamed from the court cupboards. Here, every day, Henry and Katharine dined with the Admiral, treating him with as much courtesy as if he had been the King of France himself. Anne of Cleves was present, sitting and chatting animatedly with the Lady Mary, but Katharine noticed that Mary looked unhappy. Of course, she would not relish this new alliance with France; Spain was where her heart lay.

In the evenings, decked with the new jewels Henry had given her, Katharine sat with their guest on the dais in the presence chamber, watching lavish masques such as the court had not seen in years. Everyone was saying how wonderful it all was. Old King Harry could still put on a splendid display. Katharine was pleased to see him enjoying himself, although she knew it grieved him not to be able to participate as he would have done when he was younger and fitter. She was quite sad when the Admiral departed, laden with gifts.

Edward went to Hunsdon, and she and Henry set off on their usual summer progress. He was too unfit to visit the north, as he had planned, so they did not stray far from London, but went first to Oatlands in Surrey. Henry's leg was better and he insisted on going hunting, but he had to use a ramp to mount his horse and he again brought down his quarry from a standing in the park. By the time they got to Chertsey, he was well enough to ride with the hounds, shooting with darts and spears. For three days, he was out from dawn till dusk. Katharine accompanied him in the mornings and, in the afternoons, when it was too hot to be out in the sun – she could not strip to her shirt like Henry – she took Spanish lessons, seated at her desk by an open window. It was pleasant being away from the stresses of the court.

Henry's burst of energy soon burned itself out. By the time they set off for Guildford, his legs were agony and he gave the command to return to Windsor. There, he took to his bed and it was given out that he had a cold. But Katharine knew better. His condition had rapidly deteriorated and he was in great danger.

'Madam, I am sorry, but we have given up all hope of recovery,' Dr Chamber told her gravely.

Her heart plummeted. Three years ago, she would have grieved for Henry yet rejoiced that she would soon be free to marry Tom. But she had grown close to her husband and realised now that theirs had been a good marriage. She would miss him when he was gone. She could not imagine a world without him. He had bestridden England like a colossus for more than thirty-seven years.

She was as amazed as his doctors when he suddenly rallied. In October, he was back on his horse, hunting and hawking, and attending to state affairs. Again, it did not last. When they moved to Whitehall, he shut himself up in his private apartments and rarely stirred out of his chamber. He would see only Katharine and his chief Privy Councillors. When the weather was fine, she was able to persuade him to walk with her in his privy garden, but he was in such pain that he was often perverse and intractable. More than once, she saw him lash out at his gentlemen and servants, and he even used harsh words to her. It was like tiptoeing around a sleeping dragon.

Everyone was under the strictest instructions to breathe no word about his state of health.

'I will not have any man think that I am losing my grip on affairs,' he said to Katharine one awful day when he could not get comfortable and nothing eased the pain. She looked at his drawn features, etched with lines of suffering, and wondered how much more he could endure. Neither she nor anyone else dared mention the possibility that he might die. It was high treason even to imagine the death of the King, let alone speak of it, and Henry himself never liked to talk about death. He had a horror of it.

After several days, the pain lessened, but he was still immobile. He could barely stand and stairs were beyond him. Yet he was in better spirits and determined to be up and out in the world.

'I am still king!' he said. 'I must be seen by my subjects.'

He ordered that two trams be made for him, to his own specifications. They were chairs upholstered in velvet and silk with poles attached so that he could be carried around the palace. Katharine watched anxiously as four strong Gentlemen Pensioners struggled with their heavy burden. Every time she looked at Henry, she worried anew about how fat he had become. She had never seen so big a man. It was sad to compare him as he was now with the portraits of his younger self that hung on the palace walls, a constant reminder of a youth and vigour long gone. If only he could lose some weight, he might recapture some of it – and be restored to health.

Uncle William had gone back to the country now, but she still saw Will daily.

'Kate, you know he cannot long endure,' he murmured, when they were alone in her garden.

'I know, and I am prepared,' she said sadly.

'The vultures are poised to descend,' he told her. 'Each party wants control of the Prince. Each fears the other, and all of them serve only their own interests. Of course, the reformists are going to succeed. They are by far the stronger party. Gardiner did the conservatives no favours when he tried to purge the court of heresy and accused George Blagge.'

'Will, I must tell you something in the greatest secrecy,' Katharine said. 'It must go no further, promise me!'

He stared at her. 'You know you can count on me, Kate. What is it?'

'Henry is naming *me* regent,' she confided.

'You, sister?' He took a few moments to digest the news. 'By God, that would put an end to the faction-fighting! He has actually told you that?'

'Yes. He said he would have his senior officials swear an oath to support me.'

'Well, I never. You are a dark horse, Kate, keeping this to yourself all this time, especially as Hertford thinks that power is within his grasp. His nose will be knocked out of joint. He *is* the Prince's uncle.'

'So is Tom. And I intend to give them both prominent roles on the regency council.'

Will gave her a sideways glance. 'Don't expect Hertford to take kindly to sharing power with Tom. He has little time for him, and his lady wife wants all the glory.'

Katharine had guessed that. Nan had been giving herself airs and graces of late, dressing like a queen. But she would never be a queen, and Katharine was determined not to let her forget who was.

There was an increasingly tense atmosphere at court, with barely concealed menace emanating from both factions. Men were suspicious of their colleagues. The word 'treason' hung in the air. She was glad that Tom was abroad. God willing, he would be back in time to assist her when she was called upon to rise to her great task. When the King appointed Tom deputy governor of Calais and entrusted him with drafting the peace treaty with France, she felt sure these were marks of Henry's trust; surely he would direct that Tom be given some high office in the future? If he didn't, she would, when she had the power.

'You will be my right-hand man,' she told Will. 'And I will put an end to these dissensions that riddle the court.'

'It will not be easy,' he warned.

'I never expected it to be,' she replied. 'But, when you have God on your side, you cannot fail.'

Katharine was with Henry one day in November when Gardiner was announced. She still felt a shiver of fear whenever she heard his name, but he was courteous enough to her, although those hawk-like eyes were cold.

'My lord Bishop,' Henry greeted him. 'I have summoned you to discuss that exchange of lands I mentioned last week. I've been informed that your lawyer has not as yet agreed it.'

Gardiner looked uncomfortable. 'Your Grace, those lands that you want from me are church lands, part of my diocese. I do not think I should alienate them.'

Henry flushed with anger. 'My lord Bishop, *I* am head of the Church! Do you not think I care for its welfare? The estates I offered you are profitable ones.'

Katharine was enjoying herself. It was gratifying to see Gardiner discomfited.

'With respect, your Grace, I am not prepared to let go lands that have been part of my diocese for hundreds of years.'

Henry was incandescent. 'You forget that the monasteries, some of which were older than your see, surrendered all their lands to me. Are you going to obey my command, or do I have to make you?'

'Sir, I fear I cannot give you those lands. They are a sacred trust.'

'Sacred trust be damned!' Henry shouted, flushed with fury. 'Get out! And don't come back!'

Gardiner glared at him and stamped out.

'The man's a fool!' Henry growled. 'I offered him a fair deal. From now on, I shall ban him from my privy chamber.'

'A very wise decision,' Katharine applauded.

Gardiner evidently regretted his folly. Over dinner the following week, Henry told Katharine that Sir William Paget, one of his most trusted councillors, had come to plead that the Bishop be forgiven.

'I said no,' Henry said, piling his plate high with roast meats, which made her want to scream at him to stop. 'He told me that Gardiner begged him to intercede with me, so that he might approach me and apologise. I said it was too late for that. By God, Kate, it will be a relief not to have that man nagging me.'

It would indeed be a relief to have Gardiner at a distance, she reflected. It amused her, in the days that followed, to see her old foe standing with other petitioners in the galleries of the palace, hoping for the King to pass. He was in for a long wait, she thought as she sailed by, not deigning to look at him, for Henry rarely came forth from his lodgings these days. Most petitions were made in writing. Gardiner had written, more than once, but Henry had torn up the letters.

'I asked Denny to send him a note to say I saw no cause why he should molest me further, and commanded him to arrange the exchange of property with my attorneys.'

Katharine suppressed a smile. Denny was an ardent reformist who would relish his task. Gardiner would be spitting venom to see his enemies colluding in – and doubtless gloating over – his fall from favour. She dared to think that she was at last safe from his machinations.

Henry was taking regular herbal baths, convinced that they helped his legs, and it did seem that there was some improvement. Early in December, he was much restored, and the court moved to Oatlands. There, Katharine was delighted to receive a letter from Margaret Douglas, informing her that she had given birth to a lusty boy.

'He is to be called after you,' she told Henry, 'and he will be known as Lord Darnley, as his father's heir. I am so pleased for Margaret. She did so feel the loss of her first son. She wants you to be godfather.'

'Tell her I heartily consent,' Henry smiled. 'I'll send the lad a gold cup for his christening.' He rose awkwardly to his feet. 'I'm off hunting. It's a fair day and I want to make the most of it.' He reached for his stick.

She could only admire his determination, even as she worried about him.

'Don't overdo it, I beg of you,' she pleaded.

He bent and kissed her. 'Stop fussing, woman.'

He looked exhausted when he returned, but he was in high spirits. It had been a good day and there was venison on the table that evening. But the following morning, he complained of feeling shivery. Katharine felt his forehead. It was hot.

She called the doctors, who helped him into bed. He lay there shivering, his face grey.

'Madam, you should leave,' Dr Chamber urged.

'No, I want to be with his Grace,' she protested.

'Go, Kate,' came a croak from the bed.

'If that is your wish, Sir, I will, and I hope to see you very soon,' she said, squeezing Henry's hand. He waved her away impatiently. He was often like this when he was ill. He hated her seeing him when he was really laid low.

Reluctantly, she made her way back to her lodgings, her mind in a turmoil. Every few hours, she sent her chamberlain to ask how the King was. Each time, he was told that the doctors were fighting to save his life.

She could not sleep. She shut herself in her bedchamber and kept pacing up and down, fraught with anxiety. She thought of young Edward, who was unaware that the heavy burden of kingship might soon fall on his slight shoulders, and wept for him. She wept too for his sisters, who loved and revered their father, despite all the unhappiness he had caused them in the past. They would grieve terribly to lose him. Elizabeth was at Ashridge with Edward, but Mary had remained at court. Katharine was tempted to tell her how ill Henry was, but knew that he would not want her to know.

For two nights she endured an agonised wait for news, while the doctors did everything in their power to save Henry. At any moment, she expected to be told the worst. But, when they came to her on the second morning, it was to inform her that his Grace had passed the crisis and was asking for her. She hastened to him and would have hugged him, had not the doctors been present.

'It does my heart good to see you looking better,' she said, kneeling by the bed and kissing his hand.

'Was I an old bear to you?' he asked, with a wry smile.

'You were, rather,' she told him. 'But you had every reason to be.'

The next day, he insisted on getting up, against his physicians' advice. When he summoned Katharine to sit with him in his closet, she was dismayed to see him still ill and weak. His face was ashen and he seemed to have lost weight. But he made light of his ordeal.

'It was just my leg playing up,' he told her. 'I am now, thanks be to God, rid of the pain, and I hope will be free of it for a long time – long enough to deal with the Howards.' His tone was vexed, and she looked up, questioningly.

'Kate, I think you know that they are not your friends.' How could she not? Norfolk was England's leading Catholic peer. He and his son Surrey made no secret of their hatred for jumped-up parvenus like the Seymours – and no doubt they resented the Parrs too.

'What have they done?' she asked.

Unusually, Henry hesitated. 'My Council has just uncovered a plot to replace you.'

She drew in her breath, shocked. 'What?'

'My Lord of Hertford found out that Surrey has been encouraging his sister to win my favour, that she might attain a crown.'

Katharine was dumbstruck. This was absurd. That Surrey should even think that Henry would contemplate taking another wife in his state of health, and when he was clearly happy with her, showed how little he knew his sovereign. And Mary Howard was Henry's daughter-in-law; any marriage between them would be incestuous and barred by canon law.

'I can't believe this!' she said, shaking her head.

Henry shifted in his chair and helped himself to a candied plum from a dish on his table. 'Fortunately, the Duchess, at least, has some sense. When questioned by the Council, she revealed the whole matter. She said she would cut her throat rather than be a party to such villainy. She was furious with Surrey.'

'She laid evidence against her brother?' Katharine was thinking that she could never do that to Will. But then Will would never be rash like Surrey.

'And her father,' Henry revealed. 'Norfolk was involved too. But there's more to this than outwardly appears, Kate. Surrey has always had ambitions. Apparently, he meant to be regent if I died before the Prince comes of age. That, as you can imagine, did not sit well with Hertford. And I think it significant that it was Hertford who laid evidence against the Duchess. He said he had overheard her discussing the plot with one of her friends.'

It chilled Katharine to hear how far Hertford was prepared to go to secure the regency for himself. It dawned on her that he would be a dangerous enemy if thwarted of his purpose.

'So was there really a plot – or did Hertford make it up?' she asked.

'Oh, yes, there was a plot, as I have described. Hertford just made certain that I knew about it. But the Duchess confessed more than he could ever have hoped for. By God, she had it in for Surrey! She revealed that he had replaced the coronet on his coat of arms with a crown and the initials H.R.. To imagine oneself a king, Kate, is high treason. The councillors had his house searched and found glass, paintings and plate with the arms of King Edward the Confessor, who is not among his ancestors. There is no doubt in my mind that he was plotting to depose me and usurp my throne. And Norfolk knew it and concealed it, to my peril.' His anger was rising.

'I am horrified,' Katharine said, 'just appalled. What will you do?'

'I have given the order for them to be arrested and taken to the Tower.'

'It is what they deserve,' she declared. Why should she feel sympathy for them? They would have brought her down too.

Back in her own apartments, she realised that the conservatives were a spent force and no longer a danger, which was the most profound relief to her after all the suffering they had caused, to her and many others. The way was clear for a reformist regency, which could only be a blessing for England. And she would head it, whatever Hertford intended.

The weather was fine, if cold, and Henry was determined to go on another short progress, to make up for having had to curtail the last one. Because his health was precarious, they moved in slow stages to Greenwich, planning to go from there to Whitehall for Christmas. In three days, the festivities would begin. Looking at the King, Katharine wondered if he would see another Christmas after this, for he was so infirm that any new attack would surely carry him off.

That evening, he sent for her. She found him in his presence chamber, which was empty, save for the guards at the door. He was seated on his throne beneath the canopy of estate bearing the royal arms of England, staring at nothing in particular.

'Kate!' He stirred, and she saw that there were tears in his eyes. 'I was just remembering how many great triumphs this room has witnessed in the past. All done with now. They are all gone.'

He looked so sad, as if he was seeing in his mind's eye a procession of those who had shone here, the wives and ministers and throngs of courtiers whose voices were now silenced. How sad it must be to know that your life was behind you, and how bittersweet to remember what it was like to be young and full of hope and vigour.

'I'm leaving for Whitehall tomorrow,' he said, his voice brisker now. 'I want you and Mary to stay here with the court. Whitehall will be closed to everyone except my Privy Councillors and a few of my gentlemen. I need to give my full attention to this matter of the Howards. My councillors have stayed their investigations for my return, and I want to be at hand to direct the examinations.'

Katharine was shocked. 'But you love Christmas! It will be so lonely and bleak spending it apart from the court. And I will miss you dreadfully.'

'Solitude is what I need right now, Kate,' he told her, quite kindly. 'I feel my strength ebbing and need to rest and recover.'

'But we have never been apart for such a special occasion.' She felt near to tears. If she was to lose him, she wanted happy memories of him to cherish, and she could not bear the thought of him keeping what might be his last Christmas alone.

'I am commanding you,' he said gently. 'I need you to do what I cannot do and preside over the festivities. Lead people to believe that I am well and detained only by these treasons. As soon as I can, I will send for you.'

There was no point in complaining further.

The next morning, she said farewell to Henry at the top of the stairs leading down to his private jetty. Wrapped in furs, he looked old and grey, but his embrace was firm and he kissed her heartily. 'Be of good cheer, darling. We shall see each other again soon.'

She curtseyed low. 'May God be with your Majesty.'

'And with you,' he said, raising her.

She watched as, supported by his Gentlemen Pensioners, he clambered into the barge, closely followed by Lord Hertford, whose assistance he declined.

'I'm not dead yet, Ned,' he muttered. As he entered the cabin, he turned to Katharine. 'A very merry Christmas!' he called. The boat rocked as he sat down, and she saw him close the leather curtains. Henry loved his privacy.

She watched, filled with foreboding, as the royal barge pulled out into the middle of the Thames, then glided along the magnificent sweep of the river and out of sight past the Isle of Dogs.

Would she ever see Henry again?

She spent a tense Christmas, aware of the undercurrents of gossip about the King's absence. He wrote to tell her that he was well and working hard, and that Hertford and the councillors were proving indefatigable, which hurt a little, as she herself would dearly have loved to be there, supporting him. He seemed to be unhealthily preoccupied with the treason of the Howards, and she realised what a jolt it must have given him.

She could take no pleasure in the feasting and dancing or the wondrous aroma of oranges and spices from the festive decorations. She went through the motions, playing her part, but her mind was at Whitehall.

Two days after Christmas, Henry's messenger stopped appearing, which worried her. She sent messengers of her own to Whitehall, but they were denied admittance to the royal apartments. Will was one of those who were with the King, so she wrote to him asking for news and was surprised when he appeared in her chamber. She could see from his face that it was not good tidings he brought and hurried him into her prayer closet.

'I'm not supposed to be here,' he said. 'Hertford and the others are not allowing anyone to see the King and are determined to release no details of his condition. That way, they think to secure the regency before anyone else realises what is going on.'

That alarmed her. 'If anyone should be securing the regency, it is I, and they will soon find out what the King has decreed. Hopefully, they will accept it. Henry said he would have his senior officers take an oath to support me.'

'And have they?'

'I assumed so.'

Will shook his head. 'So you have no idea if an oath was taken, or who swore it?'

'No,' she admitted, her heart sinking. 'But we could find out. We could ask the King's Chamberlain and Vice Chamberlain, and Sir Anthony Denny, since he heads the privy chamber.'

'It is best to be discreet for now,' Will advised. 'You don't want to give the game away too soon.'

'No,' she agreed. 'Tell me, how is his Grace?'

'He is very ill and in great danger,' Will said gently. 'That is why I came. I thought you had a right to know. His doctors are in despair, for they can do nothing to alleviate his pain or his fever. Kate, it will not be long now.' He folded his arms around her and she wept on his shoulder.

'I have been expecting the worst for some time,' she said, disentangling herself and reaching for her handkerchief. 'Has he asked for me?'

'He has spoken of you several times. He would not have you see him looking so weak and poorly.'

'It would not matter to me!'

'But it matters to him. He will not be seen as anything less than a king. He would deny his mortality, even now.'

'Tell him,' she said, 'tell him that I desire to see him more than anything else.'

'I will,' he promised.

He left, pulling the hood of his cloak down over his face and making his way to the waiting boat. Not two hours later, he was back.

'They denied me entry!' he snarled. 'They said they did not trust me. I think they guessed I had come to see you. Maybe they know the King's mind.'

'If they do, they might try to make him change it,' she fretted. 'And no one would be any the wiser.'

Will was as taut as a bowstring. 'Kate, as soon as we hear that the King has died, you must summon the court and the councillors who are here and have yourself proclaimed regent. I will hasten to secure the Prince. We will outwit them, never fear!'

The new year of 1547 came in with little fanfare. Katharine hosted the celebrations with a heavy heart. She had commissioned several portraits from John Bettes as gifts. The one of the Prince she sent to Whitehall, hoping that it would get to the King. A double portrait of herself and Henry went to Edward at Ashridge. It was important that the boy associate her with his father's wise rule.

She was becoming increasingly anxious. Will had heard rumours in London that the King was dead, but no word came from Whitehall, nor any acknowledgement of her gift. When the French ambassador complained to her that he had been refused permission to see his Majesty, she could only pacify him with false promises. Mary too was becoming agitated over the silence from her father. Again and again, Katharine sent messengers to enquire after Henry's health, but they were turned away. She wrote to Sir William Herbert, but he replied that he had no news of the King. He had said the same to Anne. Katharine thought of questioning Nan Hertford, whose husband must have confided to her something of what was going on, but found out that Nan had become unwell and left court – without a by-your-leave to the Queen. That sounded all kinds of alarums.

'I'm going to Whitehall myself,' Katharine declared to Mary, Will and Anne. 'They cannot deny me entry. I am the Queen.'

She ordered six of her servants to go ahead to make ready her lodgings and had her chests packed and sent on. When all was ready, she and Mary, with their closest attendants, took a barge upriver. The great palace seemed deserted; although it was a dull day, they could see no lights. A chain barred the entrance to the King's Privy Bridge, so Katharine had the bargemen pull in at the Court Bridge. A chill wind whipped about them as they made their way to the Queen's lodgings. No one stopped them; there was not a soul in sight. Katharine began to wonder if Henry was even here. Had Hertford and his friends spirited him away somewhere?

She threw her cloak on the bed, tidied her hood and resolutely made her way to the King's apartments. It was a relief to see the guards at the door, but not to see them crossing their halberds at her approach, blocking the entrance.

'Let me in, good sirs,' she commanded. 'I would see the King.'

'No one is to be allowed in,' said one, his face like stone.

'By order of the Privy Council,' said the other.

'Do you know who I am?' she asked, anger rising, for they had not even given her the courtesy of her title. 'I am your Queen, and I rank higher than the Privy Council. I insist on being admitted.' She glared at them.

'I'm sorry, your Grace. Orders are orders.'

'We daren't, Madam. We could lose our positions.'

'Or worse.' They eyed her nervously, leading her to think that, if she stood her ground, they would give way.

'I will take care of that,' she said. 'I have not seen his Majesty for three weeks and more and I am worried about his health. I pray you, let me go to him.'

'Sorry, your Grace, we dare not.'

'Who has given you these orders?'

The men did not answer.

'Whoever it was, I demand to see them.'

Again, they just stared straight past her. There was nothing for it but to walk away. Gathering her train, she turned. 'The King will hear of your intransigence,' she said, and returned along the gallery. Something was very wrong. She was certain now that Hertford was making sure of the regency. It was possible that Henry really was already dead.

She must stay in credit with the Prince, whose letter thanking her for her New Year gift was in her pocket. She wondered whether she ought to go to him at Ashridge and pre-empt Hertford. But what would be the point of that if Hertford had Henry's mandate to rule? Merciful Heaven, what skulduggery was going on behind those closed doors?

Trembling with agitation, she sat down and wrote a letter to Edward, urging him to keep that painted image of his father always before his eyes and meditate upon his distinguished deeds. With God's help, whenever Edward looked at the double portrait, he would think on her kindnesses to him and the love she had lavished on him, and realise that she was the one who should have the governance of him and his realm. He must have some say in that, surely?

When she read over the letter before sealing it, she was dismayed to find so many corrections – and her handwriting looked awful. She had to calm down.

Mary came to her, looking as if she had been weeping. 'You didn't see my father?' she asked.

'They wouldn't let me in,' Katharine told her, taking her hand. 'But they might let you see him.'

Mary sped away. When she returned, she was the picture of dejection and just shook her head. 'If he is dying, it is cruelty to keep us out,' she sobbed.

'Maybe he is not so ill then,' Katharine replied, with more confidence than she felt.

'Then why can't we go to him? He only bans visitors when he doesn't want people to see him looking weak and poorly.'

'I don't think it is your father who is keeping us out.' She confided to Mary her fears about Hertford and told her of Henry's plans for herself to become regent.

Mary looked startled. Of course, the news had come as a surprise. Katharine knew that the princess would prefer her to Hertford any day and was pleased for her.

'Well, God does move in mysterious ways,' Mary observed. 'If my father has determined on that, he will not let them suborn him.'

'If he is in a fit state to do so,' Katharine warned. 'We can do nothing but bide our time. Then I will move quickly.' She explained the plan Will had devised.

'I will pray for your success,' Mary wept, embracing her.

Clasping her thin back, Katharine wondered if this devout Catholic woman knew what she was praying for, and felt a pang for her. Deception was an ugly thing – but God's will must be done.

Katharine had still not managed to see Henry when Surrey's trial took place on 13 January. Will was one of the commissioners who sat in judgement.

'There was no way to save him,' he said when he returned from the Guildhall afterwards, his expression sombre. 'Norfolk had already confessed to concealing his treason. And if a man presumes to assume the royal arms, which he has no right to bear, what can it be but treason?' He went over to the window, staring out at the murky Thames under a leaden sky. 'We received a note from the King himself, posing that question and arguing that Surrey had had treason in his mind when he cozened his sister to become his Grace's harlot. The message was clear. We were to condemn Surrey to death, which we did.'

Katharine was aware of some lack of logic in the King's argument, but she was too relieved to hear that he was alive and active in state affairs to care.

'You should have seen Hertford's face,' Will said. 'He almost punched the air. And Surrey saw his triumph and shouted from the bar that the King would be rid of all the noble blood of the kingdom and employ none but lowly people.'

A chilling possibility had occurred to Katharine. 'Will, was the King's note in his own writing?'

'Yes, I'm sure it was. Why do you ask?'

She shook her head. 'I don't trust Hertford. Is Henry so weak that he can be manipulated? Were those really his orders?'

'I think they were. But I agree, Hertford is not to be trusted, and he is ruthless. We must stay watchful.'

Two days later, Will came again to Whitehall. 'I bring good news,' he smiled. 'I've just met the Spanish and French ambassadors, on their way from an audience with the King. They said he looked fairly well, although he had told them he had been severely ill for a long time. He discussed with them the affairs of Christendom and even touched on matters of warfare, just as normal. They assured me he was in good spirits.'

'I am so relieved to hear this,' Katharine cried. 'I must let Mary know. But, if he is better, why has he not sent for me?'

'I think he will now, Kate, and soon. Just hold yourself in patience.'

She tried, but she could not quell her anxiety. As the days passed with no summons, her fears increased, and she even began to wonder if she had offended Henry in some way. But he had not summoned Mary either, so it was unlikely to be that. She was beginning to feel aggrieved with him. After all that she was supposed to mean to him, why would he keep her from him at this time?

Then it dawned on her that, in his usual secretive way, he might be keeping her out of sight and out of mind in case Hertford guessed that she was to be regent and tried to prevent it. It was the only plausible positive reason she could think of for this separation, and she clung to it.

There seemed to be no point in remaining at Whitehall. She should get back to the court anyway. She would be better placed there to seize power when – if – the time came. So she sent for her barge and returned to Greenwich. As she passed the Tower, she thought of Surrey, who had been beheaded on Tower Hill two days ago. Norfolk was in the fortress now, a prisoner and a bereaved father who would soon follow his son to the block. How speedily the mighty could be brought low. She said a prayer for the Duke and for Mary Richmond, who surely could never have anticipated that her revelations would end in tragedy for her family. How must she be feeling now, knowing that her father was to die? He had been good to Katharine and John at the time of the Pilgrimage of Grace, even if he had become her enemy since, and Katharine would not forget that.

She waited anxiously at Greenwich for news, but there was none. She asked Will to go to Whitehall and see if he could find out anything. Fortunately, Will was resourceful.

'I went to the privy kitchen,' he told her when he returned and they were alone in her closet. 'They are still preparing meals for the King and they are being served with fanfares, as usual.'

'That's heartening to hear,' she said. 'But this silence is unendurable. I do not know what to think. I still fear that it augurs some evil.'

'I hate to say it, but I agree.' Will sat down wearily. 'It's not knowing what's going on that's the worst.'

'The court is full of wild speculation. Everyone is wondering why they have not seen the King in over a month.'

'There must be news of him soon,' Will sighed. 'On the way here, I sought out Messire van der Delft and asked him if he had heard anything. He said he had sent to ask after the King's health and been told that he was slightly indisposed but attending to business in private.'

'And so it goes on,' Katharine observed. 'I'm wearing my knees out, I've prayed so long just for a word from him, and that he might be restored to health.'

* * *

377

It was now late January. Katharine was sitting with her ladies, aware of Lady Richmond's absence and trying to concentrate on the debate in which she was supposed to be engaging, but it was impossible. She was in a constant state of high anxiety these days. Something was badly wrong, and short of storming Whitehall, she was powerless to do anything about it.

Just when she thought – not for the first time – that she might go out of her mind, the door opened and three gentlemen were announced, come to join the company. Her vice chamberlain, Sir Anthony Cope, entered with Hugh Latimer and behind them – her heart began juddering – was Tom Seymour. He bowed and, at her invitation, seated himself with the others and gave his attention to the discussion. Not having known that he had returned to court, she was absurdly pleased to see him looking so alive and well, and felt familiar feelings stir within her. It was a while before she could collect her thoughts, and only then did it occur to her that Tom might be just the man to find out what his brother was up to at Whitehall.

How she contained her patience through the afternoon, she did not know. When the circle finally broke up, she stayed Tom, tugging discreetly at his sleeve. 'I would have a word with you in private,' she murmured. She saw Anne, who was great with child, looking at her questioningly. 'It is about your brother Hertford,' she added.

'Hmm. My brother. Of course, Madam,' Tom said, following her into her study, where she sat down at the desk and gestured to him to take the chair opposite. She could barely take her eyes off him. Maturity suited him: he was more handsome than ever and his eyes held that familiar admiration. All her feelings for him, long suppressed, surged to the surface. Was this to be her reward for putting duty first and making a success of her marriage to Henry? She loved Henry, it was true, but she was in love with Tom. There was a world of difference between the two.

'What's going on, Kate?' he asked. 'You're here, the King is at Whitehall, and my beloved brother is keeping me firmly locked out.'

'I thought you could have helped me to find out,' she said, her heart sinking. Dare she trust him with the truth, that she was to be regent?

He might well share his brother's ambition for their family. Yet wouldn't he wield more influence with her in power, especially if she was his wife? Shocked, she pulled herself up; how could she be thinking about remarrying, when Henry wasn't even dead? It was awful of her. Yet she had to think of her future. She suppressed a sigh. It was not just love and support that she wanted; she longed for children and, if any man could get her with child, it was Tom. But she was thirty-four and time was running out. And she could not wed until she was out of mourning, so that would mean another year gone by . . .

'A penny for your thoughts,' Tom said. 'You wanted my help?'

'I was just thinking things through. If I cannot gain access to the King, and you can't either, there is nothing to be done.'

'Let me see if there is a way,' he said, rising to his feet. 'Don't worry, Kate. I'll go back to Whitehall now.'

Chapter 23

1547

On the last day of January, Katharine was startled to hear the distant boom of cannon fire coming from further upriver in the direction of the Tower. Then all the church bells started ringing. She and her ladies stared at each other in surprise and puzzlement.

'Has the King recovered?' she wondered. 'Is this a celebration?' If so, why had nobody told her? It was outrageous – and utterly cruel. Again, she wondered if she had somehow incurred Henry's displeasure and he had not thought fit to keep her informed about his health. That was a chilling thought.

There came the sound of running footsteps, then the door to her chamber burst open and Will stood there. 'The King is dead! The Prince has just been proclaimed King Edward VI.'

Katharine sank to her knees, her attendants and Will following suit. 'Of your charity, pray for the soul of our late sovereign lord,' she enjoined, tears beginning to fall. Her head was teeming with questions, but, for now, she must show respect for the passing of a soul. Henry was dead. *Henry was dead.* Even though she had been expecting it for a long time, she could not quite take it in. She would never see him again, never hear his voice or sit companionably with him. He had truly loved her, she knew, and she would miss that love.

At length, she rose and dismissed everyone save Will. 'When did he die?'

'Three days ago. Kate, you must—'

'*Three days ago?*' She was horrified. 'And no one thought to tell me? No one summoned me to be with him at the end. How heartless of them.' She made an effort to control her fury.

'Kate, you must move quickly,' Will urged. 'Hertford has had a good start on you.'

'I know. Where is the Prince?' She could not yet think of Edward as king.

'They have brought him to the Tower. It is customary for monarchs to stay there before they are crowned, but the Tower is also secure. If you went there, I doubt they would let you in. But I am commanded there this afternoon for a meeting of the Privy Council.'

'Will, can you get hold of a copy of King Henry's will before you go? I am sure you will find it set out in there that I am to be regent. Then you can show it to them . . .'

'I will try the records office in the Tower.'

'Bless you,' she said. 'That poor boy. My heart goes out to him. To be fatherless and burdened with a crown at such a young age. I should be with him. He needs me.'

'I will do my best,' Will said, and left.

Katharine remained there, wishing she could see Henry. Was his body still at Whitehall? And what state would it be in after three days? Still, she wanted to say goodbye, as any devoted wife would.

She recalled her ladies. 'I must put on mourning,' she told them, thinking that this would be the third time she had donned widow's weeds. Fortunately, she had long since earmarked a plain black silk gown with a stand-up collar and matching French hood, one with the new square shape.

'Bring me a black veil to wear over it,' she commanded. 'And send for my tailor. I need proper mourning headgear.' The tailor came hastening and sketched out a headdress like a nun's with a pleated chin barbe, a long white veil and two lappets hanging down to the knees, knotted at the ends. Beneath this, she was to wear a loose black robe and a mantle with a train.

Her heart sank. I shall look like a frump, she thought. And she would have to wear these clothes for a year. But the conventions must be observed. The tailor promised to bring the headdress to her on the morrow. Before he left, she ordered black material for her ladies.

381

Carpenters were already at work in her apartments, putting up black hangings and curtains. Thanks be to God that she was not a French royal widow; over there, queens had to stay in seclusion for weeks until it was certain that they were not pregnant.

She had two letters to sign, which her secretary had brought her. Her hand shook a little, reminding her that she was still suffering the effects of shock. But, mindful of her new status, she wrote her name as *Katharine the Queen Regent, KP*. If only Will would come back and tell her that her appointment had been agreed, although she feared that was not very likely and that she would have a fight on her hands. Should she go to the great hall now and summon all the courtiers, as originally planned? No, it was best to wait upon the Privy Council.

When Will did return, she could see that he brought bad news. 'They have stolen a march on you, Kate. Hertford is entrenched. By the time I got to the Tower, the Privy Councillors were lined up to swear homage to the King. I did so too. Then his Grace sat in council and signed a commission appointing Hertford Lord Protector.'

'No!' she protested, her hand to her mouth. 'That's not what King Henry wanted, or provided for in his will.'

'I could not find that will, Kate. I searched in the records, but it was not there.'

'They must have destroyed it!' She was beside herself.

'Very likely, although that is immaterial now. The late King made a new will after Christmas.'

'You mean, they made him!' she cried. 'They are so low, suborning him when he was ill. I know what he intended. He wanted me as regent. And what of those who swore to support me?'

'Kate, Kate, none of that matters! Hertford is firmly in the saddle. He has already ignored what the King intended in this new will. He provided for a regency council with no man holding ascendancy; there was no mention of Hertford becoming Lord Protector and heading it. So he has overridden all. Tomorrow he will be proclaimed Lord Protector and we can look forward to his ruling here until the King reaches his majority at eighteen.'

Katharine had to sit down and get her breath back. It galled her that she had completely underestimated Hertford. 'I won't let him get away with this. Henry would be furious to see his orders thus flouted.'

'Kate, it's a *fait accompli*. The new King has approved it.'

'If I could just speak to him. He will listen to me.'

'Dear sister, Hertford controls access to him and is keeping most people at a distance. Do you think he would let you near the King?'

She was fighting tears of frustration. 'Has he no heart? I am the only truly loving mother Edward has ever known.'

Will shrugged and dropped into the chair opposite. 'Hertford is a cold-hearted bastard. He wouldn't see it like that. To him, you are a rival for power. Oh, he was very nice, saying he was sorry that the late King had not summoned you, and that I was to tell you that the end was peaceful. He was quite magnanimous in victory.'

'I cannot believe that I have been ousted in this underhand way.' Katharine stared bleakly into the fire. 'There will be no place for me or any woman at court now, for the King is unwed. What am I to do with myself?'

'Hertford told me to say that you are welcome to stay on at Greenwich until you are ready to move to one of your dower houses. He said that his late Majesty left you three thousand pounds in plate, jewels and goods in his will, besides all the possessions you have already, and that you are to receive your dower and a thousand pounds besides. You are a rich woman, Kate.'

'At least I can be idle in comfort,' she said bitterly, thinking of all the good she could have done as regent. At least Hertford could be counted on to further true religion in the realm. She, however, would have handled matters, and cared for the young King, with a kindness that cold man lacked. Sometimes, God did move in strange ways.

'There's something Hertford especially wanted you to know,' Will said. 'King Henry ordered that, as queen dowager, you are to be accorded the respect due to a queen of England, as if he were still alive, on account of your chastity and wisdom and the devotion and obedience you unfailingly showed to him.'

So Henry had not been displeased with her. He had loved her to the last. And now the tears did come.

Will let her cry, patting her hand and looking uncomfortable. When she had composed herself, he brought her some wine. 'Drink this. There is a future for you, Kate. You're still a comely wench and rich widows attract suitors like flies. If I am not mistaken, there is one particular suitor who has been very patient and might, after a decent interval, come a-calling.'

'Thomas Seymour,' she said, her spirits lifting a little. 'You would approve this time?'

'Yes, I would. He is a member of the Privy Council now, close to the throne and a man of property. You could do a lot worse. And you've done your duty, Kate, by your family, your country and your faith. I know you didn't want to marry the King, but you did and you made an excellent queen. You should marry where you wish now.'

She should not be thinking about that, but it did help to look to a brighter future.

'What of the King's daughters? Did he make provision for them?' she asked.

'He did. He made them great landowners and confirmed their places in the succession. When they marry, each will get ten thousand pounds, provided that the Council approves the marriage. If they wed without that sanction, they will be struck from the succession as though they were dead.'

'They are both too canny to do that,' Katharine observed. 'Tell me one thing – Gardiner is not on the regency council?'

'Thank God, no! They're all reformists appointed by King Henry, who never forgave Gardiner for defying him. The one good thing that comes out of this is that they will carry on God's work as you were hoping to do yourself. I can see great changes coming.'

She closed her eyes. 'It is what I have prayed for, even though I am not to see these reforms through myself. Henry has made good provision for everything. It's as if he knew that change had to come. Maybe I accomplished more than I could ever have dreamed of.'

She spent a fitful night. It gnawed at her that she had been bested by Hertford, and that he had blithely contravened Henry's will. She could not let him get away with it. She must do something – but what?

In the morning, feeling deathly due to lack of sleep, she instructed her attorney general to find her two lawyers well versed in wills. They presented themselves later that day, eminent gentlemen with excellent reputations, and she explained the situation, dismayed to see them shaking their heads.

'Your Majesty has no chance of successfully contesting the will,' one told her. 'As to those who may have sworn to uphold your claim to the regency, we can do nothing until we know who they are and if these oaths were even sworn.'

'The Lord Protector is lawfully appointed by the new King,' the other said. 'You have no court party to help you contest that. My advice to your Grace would be to forget about all this and enjoy the benefits his late Majesty has provided for you.'

She rose, controlling her anger. 'Thank you, sirs.' She watched them leave, then sat down and wrote to the King. He was her last resort. She dropped a heavy hint that she might be of service to him, she who loved him, and who had served his father as regent. She wondered if her letter would ever reach him, and was surprised to receive a reply three days later.

Edward was clearly brooding on his loss. In his reply, addressed to his *dearest mother*, he thanked her for her letter and dwelt on their common grief for his father. *This, however, is our consolation*, he ended, *that he has gone out of this miserable world into happy and everlasting blessedness.* There was no response to the main thrust of her letter.

She was beginning to despair when Father Cuthbert arrived in London. Henry had appointed him one of the executors of his will and, as soon as his business at Whitehall was completed, he came to see her. He had aged since they had last met, but he still had that calm inner strength and wisdom and, as they sat by the fire in her closet, she opened her heart to him.

'I can't let Hertford get away with this.' She would not call him Lord Protector. 'I don't know what to do. I've tried everything in my power.'

He regarded her sympathetically. 'Then I think you must admit defeat. Evidently, it is not part of God's plan that you be regent. Katharine, I do not relish having Hertford in power either. He is known to be hot for reform and I fear he will push things too far.'

She said nothing. She too would have pushed things too far for Father Cuthbert's liking. He was a great traditionalist. The Royal Supremacy had been as much as he could stomach.

She paused to think. 'I suppose you are right,' she said reluctantly.

'Do you really want to engage in a fight that you cannot win? Think of the cost to yourself, when you could be enjoying a pleasant life. You are wealthy and you are young. The world is offering you so much. It is God's reward for doing His will when your inclinations were elsewhere. And how magnificently you have done it, Katharine. Now it is your time to do as you please.'

'Yes, dear friend, you are right,' she said, brightening. 'When you put it like that, I can see my way clear. Thank you.'

Part Five

'Many shrewd taunts'

Chapter 24

She made up her mind to put her disappointment and frustration behind her. She would leave Greenwich and live at her palace at Chelsea. She could not bear to see the insufferable Nan Hertford queening it over the court. Nan had always been jealous of her and had never shown the respect that was a queen's due. She had barely concealed her opinion that Katharine, for all her queenship, was no better than she was. Katharine suspected that, although she was still the first lady in the land, Nan would arrogate that role for herself. Well, she wouldn't be around to see it!

Because she was in mourning, she had ceased hosting the gatherings in her chamber. They were as much a thing of the past now, she reflected sadly, as the way of life she had grown used to over the past three and a half years. Death brought about huge adjustments, especially the death of a king. England felt so empty without Henry. The court would never be the same again.

It was no good dwelling on such gloomy thoughts. She grabbed her fur-lined cloak, waved her ladies away – for she would do as she pleased now – and went off by herself into the wintry gardens, walking along paths glittering with February frost. There was barely a soul about. Then a man came into view, walking towards her. It was Tom.

As he approached, she knew that he had come for her, and much sooner than she had expected. She could read it in his eyes. The future suddenly looked bright.

'Kate,' he said, rising from his bow, never taking his gaze from her. 'By God, it's good to see you!'

She smiled at him. 'Will you walk with me?'

'With pleasure,' he said. She was glad that he did not offer his arm; it would not have done for her to be seen leaning on it so soon after the King's death. 'How are you, Kate? This has been a difficult time for you.'

'It has, in so many ways. I had grown fond of the King, and I mourn him, but one must accept God's will and try to go forward. I was glad to hear that you had been preferred to the Privy Council.'

'At least my brother did *that* for me,' he said bitterly. 'The old King was against it, but Ned persuaded him. Not that he intends to allow me much influence. The power is to be all his. He governs everything, and he's always bloody right.' Katharine could understand the vehemence in his tone, having her own grievances against Hertford.

'Would you believe that he is going about with gilt maces carried before him?' Tom went on. 'He's acting as if he was king! And he's planning to build himself a palace in London. He's strict with young Edward and no one can get near the lad without my Lord Protector's sanction. God, I pity the poor boy. He's allowed no money and no freedom, and his nose is always bent to his books. At his age, I was out all hours, climbing trees and running mock tournaments.'

'This is all very worrying,' Katharine said. 'Things could have been very different.' Glancing about to see that no one was in earshot, she told him how his brother had thwarted Henry's plan to make her regent.

'God's blood!' Tom exploded. 'How much better things would be now if you were ruling England. But I'm not surprised that you were bested. Ned will stop at nothing to satisfy his ambitions.'

'I hate him,' Katharine said. 'For what he has done to me, and because he slights you. And I hate the way he treats that poor boy.'

'It's all Nan's fault, you know. Behind every successful man there is a nagging woman, and she's a devil. Her pride is monstrous and she has a violent temper. Ned's afraid of her, so he opts for the quiet life and does as she wants. Make no mistake, it's she who is the real ruler of this realm.'

'The Lady Mary likes her,' Katharine pointed out.

'She, my dear Kate, is an innocent. She sees good in everything. She'd find something to like in the Devil!'

They came to a halt by the gate that led to the river frontage of the palace.

'We should go back,' Katharine said. 'I'm getting cold.'

'What will you do now?' Tom asked, as they retraced their steps.

'I'm retiring to Chelsea,' she told him, 'and taking my stepdaughters with me. They will be company for me. Elizabeth needs a mother. She's at that difficult age between childhood and womanhood.'

Tom nodded, trudging along with his cloak drawn tightly about him. He did not seem his usual ebullient self. Of course, he was an angry man.

'Will you be going back to sea?' she asked.

'I doubt I'll be at sea much now that I'm a Privy Councillor,' he said, halting. 'Well, Kate, this is the turning for my lodging. It's been good to see you.' He took her hand and raised it to his lips.

'Farewell, Tom,' she said, and walked on, tears stinging her eyes. He had not said one word, not one little word, about having waited for her, or given any hint that he envisaged their having a future together. She had melted at the way he had looked at her when they met, and thought he felt the same. Maybe he looked at all women that way. Maybe she had grown too old for his fancy. Maybe he was just miserable about being pushed to the fringes of power. And maybe, said the voice of reason, he considers it too soon to approach you. But Tom didn't seem like a man who cared much about the conventions.

Now was not the time to be thinking about love, she admonished herself as she climbed the spiral stair to her lodging. She could wait. If it had ended between them, so be it. She would get over it, as she had got over so many other things. Resolutely, she banished Tom to the back of her mind. But he would not go away and, that night, she cried herself to sleep.

In the morning, she donned the mourning garments the tailor had delivered. Swathed in her loose gown, the voluminous wimple with its pleated chin barbe tickling her flesh, she took her barge to Whitehall to pay her respects to her dead husband. Hertford had very graciously acceded to her request.

The presence chamber was hung with black and very dark. Candles surrounded the bier in the centre of the room. On it lay Henry's vast coffin, covered with palls of cloth of gold and the crown he had had made for him. His chaplains and his gentlemen knelt around it, keeping vigil. There was a strong scent of incense.

Katharine fell to her knees and bent her head, trying to pray. He is in Heaven, she kept saying to herself. *You must be glad for him.* People were saying that he had been the greatest man in the world. She knew he had been exceptional and wondered if his son would ever command the same respect and obedience. She prayed that he would carry on his father's great work.

It had hurt a little when Will told her that Henry had chosen to be buried with Queen Jane, but she understood why. Jane had given him his heir. Katharine would not be accompanying the funeral procession to Windsor – queens did not mourn in public – and was glad to be spared that ordeal, but she would be able to watch the funeral from the closet above King Edward IV's chantry chapel, which overlooked the high altar and choir of St George's Chapel.

The committal took place on a freezing day in the middle of February. Clad in dark blue velvet, the colour of royal mourning, and wearing a gold *memento mori* ring with a skull, she watched from her discreet vantage point as sixteen burly Yeomen of the Guard carried the coffin into the chapel. Black cloth hung from the walls and over the windows, and candles illuminated the faces of the throng of nobles, officials and mourners, all in black, many hooded. On the coffin lay a lifelike wax effigy of Henry, dressed in crimson velvet and a crown glittering with gems. Behind came men carrying banners. Only two bore the arms of the King's wives, hers and Queen Jane's. Evidently, he had considered these two alone to be true marriages.

At the end of the procession came Bishop Gardiner with his crozier. Katharine stiffened. Henry would not have approved of Gardiner officiating at his burial. How the Bishop had wormed his way in was beyond her comprehension. It saddened her to think that Henry's wishes did not count any more.

She searched for Tom among the Privy Councillors. There he was, his head bowed. Her heart contracted. Was it really over between them? Did she have a future to look forward to?

The vault in the choir lay open. In its cavernous space, she could see a small coffin with a moulded head – Queen Jane's. The Yeomen of the Guard set aside the King's effigy and lowered his coffin down beside her, and the Mass began.

Afterwards, Gardiner mounted the pulpit. 'Blessed are the dead who die in the Lord,' he began. 'We have all, each man, high and low, suffered a great loss in the death of so good and gracious a King.' Tears came to Katharine's eyes. 'But there is no need to pray for him,' Gardiner continued, 'since he is surely in Heaven.'

She could not listen any more. She tried to remember Henry at his best, not the prematurely aged colossus riddled with disease. She thought of the companionable times they had shared, his wry humour, his kindness to her, and the glimpses she had had of his greatness. All the time, she was fighting back tears.

The sermon ended. The chief officers stepped forward to the vault and broke their white staves of office, signifying the termination of their allegiance to the dead King. Then they cast them into the vault. From all four corners of the chapel came the sound of sniffing and sobs as a herald's voice rang out: '*Le roi est mort! Vive le roi!*' and the trumpets sounded, reminding Katharine that the monarch never died. The King is dead; long live the King! Henry would live on in his son and royal rule would be unbroken.

Everyone returned to the castle. Katharine did not attend the reception in St George's Hall, but went straight to her apartments. She had a headache and needed some peace and quiet. Her ladies made her rest on her bed and brought damp cloths and cordial to soothe her. Presently, she slept. When she returned to her privy chamber, dusk had fallen. She found Will sitting by the fire, chatting to Anne and Lady Suffolk. The other ladies were sitting in a circle at the far end of the room, sewing. Will rose and smiled when he saw her.

'Are you feeling better, Kate?'

'Yes,' she nodded. 'It's good to see you. I thought the funeral went well.'

'Indeed, it did.'

'It was magnificent,' said the Duchess. 'Very moving.'

'I bring good news,' Will told her. 'I am to be created marquess of Northampton. My Lord Protector is grateful for my support and it appears that I will be playing a prominent role on the Council. Kate, you will have a friend in high places.'

She realised that her brother was now more important at court than she was. She felt a bit cross with him for throwing in his lot with Hertford, but she understood why he had done it. After all, they all shared the same aims, and Will had ever been a pragmatist.

'Congratulations!' she said warmly and squeezed his hand.

'I'm going to ask the King if I can ask Parliament to permit me to take another wife, so that I can marry Lizzie,' he told her. 'We've been waiting so long.'

'I do hope you are successful,' Katharine said, sitting down.

'You missed the ceremony,' Will told her. 'The King was knighted this afternoon.'

'I had not realised he was here at Windsor.' Kings did not attend the obsequies of their predecessors.

'My Lord Protector wanted him here to give authority to the patents of nobility he handed out today. He himself is to be duke of Somerset.'

'So he gives himself a dukedom, the richest plum of all!' Katharine raised her eyebrows. 'It's a royal dukedom!'

Will snorted. 'In his mind, he sees himself as royal. Power has gone to his head.'

'Or rather his wife has been feeding him delusions of grandeur,' Lady Suffolk observed. 'That dukedom must bring with it a huge income.'

'I'm sure he was mindful of that!' Katharine said, tart.

'Lord Lisle is to be earl of Warwick and Thomas Seymour will be made Baron Seymour of Sudeley,' Will told them. 'That title carries great estates with it. And he is appointed a Knight of the Garter and Lord High Admiral.'

Katharine was overjoyed for Tom. These honours would surely make him feel more appreciated, and he would be an even greater match for her – if he was still interested. She tried not to feel despondent.

'I doubt he'll get to see much action,' Will was saying. 'It looks as if the Protector will keep him busy in council. They don't get on, those two. I can see jealousies arising between them.'

'Herbert is to be one of the King's guardians,' Anne told her.

'I'm so pleased to hear that,' Katharine said. 'Through him, we can keep in touch with Edward and continue to support him.'

'You'll be lucky,' Will shrugged. 'Herbert's been given strict orders to screen all access.'

'There are ways of circumventing that,' Katharine smiled.

She was surprised when the door opened and the new Lord Seymour was announced. As he strode in, she felt the heat rising in her cheeks and hoped nobody noticed.

'Your Grace.' He swept her a bow and, again, she saw that look in his eyes.

'Do join us,' she said, indicating a space on the bench Will occupied.

'I'm glad I find you here,' Tom said to Will. 'You were at that council meeting. You saw how my brother treated me.' Katharine became aware that he was seething.

'Kate, I'm sorry to barge in like this, but your chamber is the only place in this court where one can find a bit of sanity,' he told her.

'What's happened?' she asked, inordinately pleased that he had come to her.

'Ned made it very clear that he will not share power with me. But I'm the King's uncle too! I have a right to a voice in government. I don't like what Ned is doing. He's made himself Lord Protector, when there should have been a ruling council. He's created himself a duke and me a mere baron with a third of his income. He needs to be stopped!'

'And who will do that?' Will asked.

'I will!' Tom countered. 'I'm going to do everything in my power to unseat him. And, if that proves impossible, I'm going to demand he share the protectorship. King Henry never intended that one man should rule both king and kingdom.'

'No,' said Katharine, 'he intended that one woman would rule – myself. If anyone should want to see the Duke toppled, it's me. But I will be content if power is shared, as my late lord subsequently intended. How will you go about it?'

Tom was vehement. 'I'm going to look up every book and record I can lay my hands on, to find out if there is a precedent for a shared regency, and I'm going to get the King on my side. I'm his favourite uncle. He hates Ned. And I've thought of a way to win his Grace's support.'

'And that is?' Will asked.

'Wait and see!' Tom replied, his eyes gleaming. 'I know you're sceptical. But this can't fail.'

When Tom left with Will that evening, he bowed formally to Katharine, leaving her wondering once more where she stood with him. Was he here only because he wanted her as a political ally?

He was back the next morning.

'Can I see your Grace in private?' he asked. Then, seeing that her ladies' eyes were on him – and no wonder, since he looked so devastatingly attractive – he added, 'On a matter concerning the King.'

Katharine led him into her study and sat down, her heart pounding. Tom took the seat opposite, as before.

'I wanted to tell you about my plan in confidence,' he said. 'They are still determined to marry the King to the Queen of Scots, but that can only prolong a war we can ill afford. The kingdom is bankrupt, Kate.' It was no surprise to her, for Henry had been a lavish spender. 'We should forget about the Scottish match. I've found a better one, with the King's cousin, Lady Jane Grey, who is most dear to him, in regard to both her religion and her learning.'

Lady Jane Grey? Katharine hardly knew anything about her. Her parents were the newly created Duke and Duchess of Suffolk, the Duchess being the daughter of the late Duke by his first wife, King Henry's sister Mary, Queen Dowager of France.

'It is a fit marriage for the King,' Tom stressed, probably noticing her hesitation. 'He's eager for reform, a whisper away from turning

Protestant. That's the way the country is going, Kate. Soon, people like us will be able to practise our religion openly.'

She drew in her breath. The Kingdom of God was at hand. Her prayers had been answered. 'That is the most wonderful news you could have given me.' Then she realised she had given herself away.

Tom smiled. 'It's been obvious where your sympathies lie, Kate. Don't worry, we're all coming out of the closet now. It's quite safe to do so. And Jane is a fervent Protestant, I am assured. She is fourth in the line of succession to the throne and near in age to the King. I'm sure that Edward will prefer her to a Catholic bride like the Queen of Scots. I know him well. I can pull it off for him, and he will be very grateful – and then we shall see that smug smile wiped off my brother's face.' He jumped up and strode over to the window, ever restless. 'I mean to make the Lady Jane my ward. Her father will not refuse. He's ambitious. He'll be overjoyed to see his daughter made a queen. I'm sending my man, John Harington, to see him today.'

Katharine strove to hide her doubts. Against the kingdom of Scotland, she could not see what Jane had to offer. And Edward had been brought up to think of the Queen of Scots as his bride. 'You will let me know what transpires?' she said, rising.

'I will,' he promised, then hesitated. 'Kate, it is good to see you and be able to talk with you at long last. Will said that you have been very upset by the King's death. Were you really happy with him?'

Was this why he had kept his distance?

'Yes. He was a good friend and a kind husband to me. I do miss him.'

He took a step closer. 'But you did not love him as a lover?'

To deny it would be disloyal to Henry, and yet all her instincts were telling her to do so. 'There was great kindness between us.'

Tom took her hand, his eyes ardent. 'There is more to love than kindness, Kate. Love is feeling a raging fire when the person you desire is near you.' His grip tightened. 'Love is waiting for that person to become yours. It has been so long – God, it's been long, and there's not been a day when I haven't thought of you.'

His words resonated with her. 'Oh, Tom, you think I haven't felt that way too?'

She went into his arms without hesitation, wanting him, needing him. His lips found hers and she was overwhelmed, wanting the moment to last for ever. Never had she felt like this with any man. She clung to Tom, desperate to be one with him, to capture this feeling for always. This was *being* in love, not just loving.

When they drew apart, it was like a little bereavement. They stared at each other, then broke into smiles.

'Well, I didn't think I'd be that welcome!' Tom grinned.

'You have no idea how my heart beats for you under these ghastly weeds,' she told him. 'You have just lifted me from misery to sheer joy.'

'And you have made me the happiest man in the world.' He bent and kissed her again. She would have gone back into his arms, but she was aware that they must not be too long alone together.

'You should go and find Mr Harington,' she said. 'Come back to me later.'

'I will be counting the minutes,' he said, and blew her a kiss as he left.

She sat down, trying to still her raging heart. This was what she had dreamed of, waited nearly four years for – and it was within her grasp. All she needed to do now was be patient until her period of mourning was over.

Tom came back in the afternoon and they walked in her privy garden, her ladies at a discreet distance. She dared not dismiss them. Two private meetings in one day would give rise to talk. And anyway, in contrast to his ebullient state of mind earlier, Tom was brooding. 'Suffolk was dismissive,' he growled. He asked if I was in any position to arrange the marriage and, if I was, who would look after Jane if she became my ward, since I lack a wife.' He gave her a sideways glance and she caught his eye, reading his meaning. He was telling her that things would go much easier if she married him. But it was too soon, too soon.

'I won't take no for an answer,' he said. 'I'm going to invite the Duke to discuss the matter. And I will tell him that Jane can live at Seymour Place with my mother. Unless . . .'

'Unless what?' she asked, guessing what was coming.

'No matter,' he said.

He won Suffolk round. Actually, he bought him.

'I offered to pay his debts,' he told Katharine as they walked in the palace gardens, her ladies again following at a distance. 'That did the trick. He sold me Jane's wardship. She'll be brought to Seymour Place next week.'

Katharine felt a pang for the poor child. She knew what it was to be removed from your family and the life you knew and sent to a strange place. 'You must bring her to visit me,' she said. 'I should like to meet her.'

'You will,' he promised. 'And I vow to be a loving and kind guardian. She will lack for nothing.'

Now all he had to do was persuade the King to marry her. Katharine was still wondering if it would ever happen.

Being in mourning, she could not attend King Edward's coronation, but some of her ladies and servants went to watch the procession pass through the City of London, and both Will and Tom, wearing their robes of estate, came to see her afterwards and described the crowning in Westminster Abbey. She could not take her eyes off Tom in his crimson velvet gown and mantle, his coronet tucked under his arm.

'The King looked magnificent in his robes of silver and white,' he told her. 'He had on so many jewels that he sparkled.'

'The people cried out that he was a new King Solomon, come to abolish idolatry,' Will added.

'He held up well throughout the long ceremony,' Tom recalled. 'It's a demanding service for a nine-year-old, but his Grace seems older than his years. When they placed in his hands the swords that symbolise his three kingdoms, England, Ireland and France, he asked for a fourth, the Bible, which he called the sword of the spirit, saying he preferred it before the other swords. I'll never forget the look of exaltation on his face when Archbishop Cranmer placed the crown on his head. Truly, he will be a great king.'

'And a great lover of the Gospel,' Will added. 'He is our Josiah, like the child king of Israel who brought true religion to his people. Katharine, we have cause to rejoice this day!'

'And now, sadly, we must leave to prepare for the jousts tomorrow, in which I am taking part,' Tom said. 'I hope I shall see your Grace before too long.' His eyes were saying everything she wanted to hear, and she had to look away lest she betray herself. But he did not seem to care. She loved that recklessness in him.

After the coronation, when the court moved to Whitehall, she stayed on at Greenwich with just her household for company. She relished the quietness that had descended on the palace and enjoyed wandering through the empty rooms and galleries, at peace with herself and glad to have leisure to plan her move. She had already ordered the palace at Chelsea to be made ready for her.

Tom could come and visit her here unobserved, entering through the private water gallery. The vast, empty palace became their trysting place and, in that week after the coronation, they enjoyed blissful moments in deserted courtier lodgings. When they were not in each other's arms, indulging their feelings for each other, they sat and talked for hours. No one questioned Katharine's long absences from her apartments. She had made it clear that she needed solitude.

Tom proved an ardent suitor. More than once, she had to restrain him when he lost control.

'But I'm mad for you!' he groaned, breathing heavily. That was his idea of an apology. But she could not be cross with him. Her need for physical union was urgent too.

One day, late in February, he suddenly dropped on one knee before her. 'Marry me, Kate! I love you, you have always known it. Be my wife!'

He was looking at her so winningly that she could not resist. All her resolve to hold him off until Henry had been dead for at least six months flew out of the window. She wanted him too much. She was prepared to wait for the fulfilment of their love, but she wanted there to be an understanding between them now.

'Yes!' she said. 'Of course I will marry you!' And she bent and kissed him on the mouth. 'Oh, my dearest!'

'Oh, thank God!' he cried, and crushed her to him. 'When can we be wed?' he asked, between kisses.

'When I am out of mourning,' she told him.

He drew back, aghast. 'But that won't be for a year, and I want you now!'

'Tom, the King has been dead for less than a month,' she protested. 'I cannot possibly contemplate remarrying so soon.'

'We could marry in secret,' he urged. 'Neither of us is getting any younger. I'm over forty now. Why should we wait? We have only ourselves to please, and you are under obligation to no one.'

'Except to common decency,' she persisted, warring against her baser instincts. 'Tom, we *must* wait. I cannot with honour marry you now. It would be disrespectful to Henry's memory.'

There was something else that was worrying her. What would people think of a queen marrying a mere baron? Would they say that she had lowered herself? It might make matters worse if she and Tom also defied convention and married before she was out of mourning.

Yet why should she care about that?

'Let me think about it,' she said.

'Don't keep me in suspense too long,' Tom begged, seeking her lips again. 'I am in torment, wanting you.'

'You will just have to wait,' she said playfully, kissing him back.

When darkness fell and it was time for him to leave, she walked with him through the deserted palace.

'The King has very heartily embraced the Protestant faith,' he told her.

'God be praised!' she said. 'It is what I have always prayed for. Maybe Henry realised what he was doing when he chose Edward's tutors.'

'Someone has influenced the boy in the right way. Maybe it was you.' He smiled at her.

'I like to think that I contributed,' she replied, reaching for his hand.

'It is not surprising that he upholds the Royal Supremacy,' he observed, 'but he is determined also to establish the new religion and wipe out abuses in the Church. England is set to become a Protestant haven. My esteemed brother, God bless him, and Archbishop Cranmer are establishing a Protestant government, and most of us support them, although I wish I had been the one to institute it.' His jealousy of Somerset was always simmering just below the surface.

'So do I! But these reforms are welcome, whoever is responsible for them. It will be a blessing to have the freedom to observe our faith openly.' She felt like weeping with joy. 'I shall be able to retrieve my books. My uncle hid them for me. Now I can read them without fear. Tom, you have no idea what it was like when Gardiner was having his purges. I lived in terror – and others went to the stake. I thank God that our young King and his ministers are so enlightened.'

'It's going to be a new world,' Tom said, stopping at the jetty to embrace her. 'And our marriage will crown our joy.'

Chapter 25

1547

Every night, she lay awake, asking herself why she should not seize her chance of happiness while she was young enough to make the most of it. Another year, and there might be no chance of a baby. More than that, she did not know how she could contain her longing for Tom that long – and she was certain that he couldn't. St Paul had had great insight. It *was* better to marry than to burn. And it was better to marry than cause a scandal. There would be a scandal anyway, but surely they could keep their marriage a secret for a while. No one would know. No one knew about their trysts, not even Anne or Will.

Whenever she was with Tom, she was overwhelmed by his charm and virile masculinity. They were both, in a sense, outcasts from the world they inhabited, superfluous to requirements. United, they could support each other, look out for each other.

In the end, temptation overcame her. All her piety, her learning and her innate good sense counted as nothing against the raging fire in her blood. So she seized her chance. When Tom next came to Greenwich and asked her, yet again, if she had reached a decision, this time she did not say that she was still thinking about it.

'I will wed you now,' she told him, her heart singing. He gave such a shout of joy that she had to put her hand over his mouth.

'These halls echo,' she warned. 'We don't want anyone thinking there is an intruder and discovering us.'

'Oh, Kate, my darling, my own,' Tom breathed, holding her to him. 'I did not think it was possible to be so happy.'

'Nor I,' she gasped. 'It is our reward for putting others first. But we *must* keep our marriage a secret for a decent period. It is only five weeks since Henry died, and I have never heard of a widow marrying so soon. There would be a terrible scandal, so we must be discreet.'

'Of course.' He looked a little crestfallen. 'I do see that.'

'It will be easier when I move to Chelsea. My household will be smaller and I can enjoy a high degree of privacy. But, Tom, how are we going to be married?'

'I've thought about that,' he said. 'There can be no question of having banns called. I could apply to Archbishop Cranmer for a special licence, but I doubt he would keep quiet about it. He's hand-in-glove with Ned.'

'So, what shall we do?' she asked, dismayed.

'It's easy,' Tom smiled. 'We plight our troth to each other, ideally before witnesses, I give you a token – a ring or a jewel – and we consummate our love. That adds up to a valid marriage.'

'But we should have the blessing of the Church.' She was aware that, for some people, especially those of the lower orders, what Tom had described was normal; but, for her sort, where money, property, titles or rank were involved, marriages took place in church or private chapels.

'It's quite lawful,' Tom answered. 'We can have a religious ceremony later, if that would please you. Kate, this is the only way. I promise you, our marriage would be legal.'

'I know that. It's just sad that we cannot have proper nuptials. Still, we have to remember what's important.' She smiled at him. 'The main thing is that we will be husband and wife. I can ask Will and Anne to be witnesses.'

'No, darling,' Tom said. 'They might feel bound to tell the Council. It's best to have someone who has no connection with the court. Leave it with me.'

Katharine could not help thinking that it all sounded a bit underhand. But what else could they do?

A few days later, Elizabeth joined Katharine at Greenwich to prepare for the move to Chelsea, bringing her tutor and her attendants. Mary stayed away, although she too was meant to be going with them.

Katharine guessed why. Mary had probably heard that her brother had turned Protestant, which must be anathema to her, for Mary had always clung to the faith instilled in her by her mother in childhood. If she had hated her father's reforms, she must be in grief now. Katharine felt sorry for her and hoped that Mary was not avoiding her. They had become such warm friends and she would hate to lose that. If Mary did come to Chelsea, she would need to handle the religious situation tactfully.

And not just that situation. She worried about her stepdaughters finding out about her and Tom. They would surely see her speedy remarriage as a great insult to their father's memory. Their presence at Chelsea would mean maintaining stricter secrecy. Sometimes, Katharine wondered if she should defer the wedding, but, standing on the brink of attaining Paradise, she could not wait any longer.

Elizabeth had come from the court and was in a miserable mood when she sat down to the special welcome dinner Katharine had ordered to be served in her privy chamber.

'It's bad enough that I have lost a most kind father,' she mourned, 'but it seems I have lost my brother too. Mother, he's not the same. He's so distant. And we were really close, right up until our father died. Would you believe that I had to go down on one knee five times yesterday as I approached the throne, and then I was relegated to a bench at the other end of the presence chamber. It was never like that in my father's day. He would come down from his throne and embrace me. But Edward – I don't know what's happened to him. I came away feeling I had no place at court any more.' Tears glistened in her eyes.

Katharine reached across the table and took her hand. She knew how dearly Elizabeth loved her brother; Edward had called her his 'sweet sister Temperance'. 'I think you should blame those around him, rather than Edward himself. They are probably reminding him every hour of every day that he is the King and what is expected of him. He's just a child and he must be struggling to do everything correctly. Give him time to settle into his new role.'

Elizabeth sniffed. 'I will.'

As they ate their meal, Katharine did her best to cheer her, telling her about Chelsea and the happy, carefree life she planned to live there. After a while, Elizabeth caught her enthusiasm and brightened up. It struck Katharine that she had grown since she had last seen her. At thirteen, she was developing the curves of womanhood and an impressive sense of fashion. Her gown of rose damask was simply cut, but elegant, and she had matched her jewellery perfectly. Her red hair was parted beneath a French hood, and Katharine noticed that she had a habit of displaying her long, slender hands in various poses, to good effect. She was a vain young thing, there was no doubt about it, yet she was no beauty; her face was pleasing, but marred by the Roman nose she had inherited from Henry. And those eyes – they must have come from Anne Boleyn. Already, Elizabeth knew how to use them to effect. The time would come when Katharine would have to keep a watchful eye on her stepdaughter!

Tom was much occupied with council business at Whitehall, and with the refurbishments he had ordered for Seymour Place. Nothing but the best would do for his bride, he told Katharine. With Elizabeth staying, and often wanting to be diverted, Katharine sometimes found it hard to slip away to see him. She was beginning to regret having asked her stepdaughter to live with her at Chelsea, but she could not retract her invitation now. Besides, she genuinely loved the child and wanted to look after her.

One evening in early March, Tom asked her to accompany him to Seymour Place the next day.

'Everything is arranged,' he said. 'We can be married there. My mother and her maid will act as witnesses. Don't worry, Kate. I have sworn them to secrecy, and I know they will keep silent. My lady mother, as you can imagine, is absolutely delighted.'

It had come, the moment she had longed for. She was filled with an excitement she had not known for years.

'We need not be away long,' Tom said, whirling her around. 'Your ladies will never know you have left the palace.'

'And Elizabeth is busy with some translations that Grindal opportunely set her,' she laughed.

The next morning, wrapped in her cloak, with the hood pulled down over her face, and having abandoned her mourning garments for an elegant black velvet gown and a feathered bonnet edged with pearls, just for the occasion, Katharine hastened to the jetty, where an unmarked barge awaited her.

'I hired it from one of the livery companies,' Tom revealed, as she stepped aboard and he handed her into the cabin. 'They use it for pageants. Fortunately, it's stripped of its decorations now.'

The oarsmen pulled out and soon they were skimming along the Thames, watching London grow ever closer, then passing the City and docking at a landing stage below the Temple. They walked through unkempt gardens, for which Tom said he had plans, to a large mansion. Inside, Katharine could smell new paint and there were ladders and dust sheets everywhere.

'My mother and Lady Jane live in the other wing,' Tom explained. 'Wait till you see the main apartments. But that is for another day, when they are finished.'

He led her upstairs and along a gallery to a chapel with biblical scenes painted on the walls and an altar that was bare save for a jewelled crucifix.

'I would be rid of that,' Tom said, 'but my mother insists on keeping it.'

'I don't feel strongly about it,' Katharine told him.

'Ned sees crucifixes as idolatrous,' he told her. 'One more good reason to keep it!'

She winced inwardly at his disrespect.

Just then, the door opened and a plump matron of around sixty entered, followed by a young woman. The Dowager Lady Seymour had a kind face and was dressed in a fashion well behind the times, with a bodice that ended at her waist instead of tapering to a point below it, and a gable hood. She curtseyed low to Katharine.

'Please, Lady Seymour,' Katharine cried, raising her up. 'It is I who should be doing honour to you, as my new mother.'

'Bless your Grace,' the old woman smiled. 'Let me embrace you.'

Katharine found herself pressed to an ample bosom that smelt of oil of roses.

'You are very welcome,' the older woman told her. 'Tom, you have made a wise choice. You are a lucky man!'

Tom looked embarrassed. 'Thank you, Mother. Shall we start?'

He took Katharine's hand and stood with her before the altar.

'I, Thomas, take thee, Katharine, to my wedded wife and thereunto I plight my troth.'

Katharine's eyes locked on his as she plighted her troth in turn. Then Tom slid a ring with a large ruby on her finger. She could not keep it there, of course. For the time being, she would have to wear it on a chain, inside her bodice.

'Now we are man and wife before God,' Tom said, his eyes warm and shining, infusing her with happiness. 'And we will have the blessing of the Church when the time is right.'

'Congratulations and blessings to you both, my children!' Lady Seymour said, as her maid looked on, smiling. 'May every happiness be yours.'

They sat and talked for a while, as it would have been churlish to leave Lady Seymour so soon, although Katharine was aware that she should not be gone for too long.

'How is my grandson, the King?' the old lady asked.

'He is well, I am assured,' Tom said.

'I never see him,' his mother said wistfully. 'If Jane had lived, things would have been different, I'm sure. She was a lovely girl, Madam, my little helpmeet – and the King adored her. Oh . . .' She flushed. 'I am so sorry, my dear. How tactless of me.'

Katharine smiled. 'It was quite clear to me what his Grace thought of her, and I never begrudged it.'

Tom asked after his sisters.

'They are well,' Lady Seymour told him, 'and I see them from time to time. But Ned never comes.'

'He is very busy,' Tom told her. 'But he should visit you. You are only across the river. I will speak to him.'

'Tom,' said his mother, staying him with her hand, 'I want him to

408

come of his own accord. He shouldn't need to be pressed to see me.' Her voice grew brisker. 'Will you stay to dinner? We have some good spring lamb.'

'I would love to, Lady Seymour, but I have to get back,' Katharine answered regretfully. 'Maybe I could call on you one day soon? Or you could visit me at Greenwich or Chelsea, and bring Lady Jane?'

Her mother-in-law's plump face lit up. 'I should like that, my dear. And please call me Mother.'

'I will – Mother,' she replied, 'if you will call me Kate.'

After a lot of hugging and kissing – Katharine had quite fallen in love with Lady Seymour – she and Tom left for Greenwich, holding hands as they sat in the cabin.

'I can't believe we've done it!' he said, kissing her soundly.

'If the news gets out, so be it,' she said, thinking she could not feel more joyful than she did at this moment. It did not matter that she had not had a traditional wedding with family and friends and the throwing of the stocking; it was the forging of the bond that mattered. And all the subterfuge merely added spice. 'If your brother and his wife don't like it, it will be of no consequence,' she told her new husband.

'He might be brought round easily, were it not for her,' Tom sniffed. 'She rules him. It will gall her to realise that the wife of his despised younger brother will take precedence over her.'

'She has never liked me either,' Katharine said. 'She thinks me a parvenu. In her eyes, I'm no better than she is.'

'In my eyes, you are infinitely better!' Tom said, and then she was in his arms, kissing him so passionately that her hood fell back. Thank goodness they had closed the doors and could not be seen by the oarsmen. She had taken such care not to be recognised.

'What do we do now?' she asked. She had thought that Tom would delay their plighting until she was at Chelsea, when he could the more easily come secretly to her at night. She had been surprised when he had sprung it on her yesterday, although she had been eager to seize the moment.

'Don't worry, sweetheart,' Tom said. 'I've appropriated a courtier lodging at Greenwich, one of the better sort. It's a long way from your lodgings and we can be private there. No one will find us.'

Her heart was leaping, her body eager. 'But I can't easily get away in the night. One of my women always sleeps in my room and another on a pallet bed outside the door.'

'Then we'll go there now,' he declared, his eyes dark pools of desire.

There were the usual two rooms and a privy. Tom had spread sheets and a counterpane – not very tidily – over the bare feather bed. There was no other furniture apart from a small cupboard and a couple of stools. The windows overlooked a deserted courtyard – so quiet you could have heard a pin drop. It was such a contrast to the luxurious apartment in which Henry had first bedded her, but it seemed like Paradise. And Paradise was where her new husband took her that noonday, awakening sensations she had never known and transporting her to some distant plane beyond this earthly life. The world had narrowed down to just the two of them in this small room; she was aware of nothing else.

There was no awkwardness, no holding back. They fitted and moved together as if they had been made for each other. She had never felt so alive – so complete.

'It's tragic that we have to live apart,' she said, as Tom helped her to dress, lacing her kirtle with practised hands. It did not matter that he was experienced with women. She could hardly have expected him not to be, at his age, and she too was not a novice, having had three husbands. Yet, until today, she had never experienced anything like his expertise as a lover. 'It will be safer for the present,' she added.

'Aye, although I wish it otherwise,' he said, nuzzling her neck.

She turned to face him, pulling on her cloak and thinking that she must change back into that hateful, shapeless black robe.

Tom came every day after that and they enjoyed blissful stolen hours in their humble trysting place. The rest of the time, Katharine walked in the budding palace gardens with her ladies, continued to set her affairs in order and sometimes called for her musicians to entertain her and her household. Mary joined her at Greenwich, but she was very distressed about the death of her father, and they talked long into the night, remembering him and looking to the future.

Mary wanted to come to Chelsea; she needed the company, she said, and she could help Elizabeth with her studies. Katharine hated herself for thinking that Mary was only creating extra problems for her. Her stepdaughter clearly needed support and comfort, but hers would be one more pair of eyes to see what should not be seen, and Elizabeth, quite the young lady now, was resentful of Mary's attempts to mother her.

'She grows more like Anne Boleyn every day,' Mary muttered, as they watched Elizabeth showing off her expertise in dancing to the ladies. 'Have you seen the coquettish way she looks at men?'

'She's just growing up,' Katharine murmured. 'Life has not been kind to her, so she boosts her confidence with vanities. I am keeping an eye on her, don't worry.'

'I just don't want her to be like her mother,' Mary said. 'I do love her, you know, even though she is not my true sister.'

Katharine sighed. 'Mary, anyone can see that she is,' she said gently.

'Well, I can't see it,' Mary retorted, looking hurt. 'And I will never believe it.'

Katharine shook her head. Against such conviction, there was nothing more she could say. And she did not want to make an enemy of Mary.

One fine spring day, she and her stepdaughters took a barge to Whitehall Palace, hoping to see the King. But, when they arrived, there was Sir William Paget, one of the councillors, barring their way.

'Oh, Madam, if only you had warned us of your coming! His Majesty is receiving ambassadors this afternoon. Might I suggest you return at this hour on Thursday?'

Katharine agreed, feeling vexed. She had feared to meet with an outright refusal if she gave notice of her arrival, which was why she had turned up unannounced.

But she could wait till Thursday. She and the princesses were longing to see Edward, and she wanted to satisfy herself that he was happy.

On Thursday, they returned to Whitehall, and there was Paget again. 'Your Majesty, I am so sorry. The King's Grace is detained with unexpected affairs of state. He will be in council all afternoon.'

She seethed inwardly. 'When can we see him?'

'Well, Madam, it is not always easy to predict what demands will be made on his Highness's time. Shall we leave it that I will send a messenger to let you know when he can grant you an audience?'

Which will be never, she thought, anger mounting again. 'Sir William, stepmothers and sisters do not normally need audiences. We are the King's kinswomen and he will be wanting to see us. King he may be, but he is still a boy who has lost his father and needs comforting.' Mary and Elizabeth were staring at her in admiration.

Sir William looked uncomfortable. 'I can assure you, Madam, that his Grace's every need is being met.'

'By men,' she said, 'who do not always understand emotional matters. A child his age needs a mother and the company of his sisters. We are quite happy to wait until his Majesty is free, if you will kindly show us where we can sit.'

'He will not be free today, Madam,' Paget said quickly. 'The business cannot wait. I assure you, I will send for you.'

What more could she do but cause a scene and make matters worse?

'Very well,' she said, 'but I expect to hear from you very soon, Sir William.' With that, she swept out.

She waited a week, but there was no messenger, no summons. She had not believed there would be. Angry and frustrated, she unburdened herself to Tom as they lay entwined together after some very energetic lovemaking.

'What did you expect?' he murmured. 'I told you, sweetheart, they guard him like a prisoner. No one who might influence him is allowed near him. And they won't want you putting the idea into his head that there might be a better alternative to Ned!'

'I had no intention of doing that,' she said. 'I just want to be a mother to him.'

'Alas, Kate, they won't see it that way. You think my lady of Somerset will allow you any influence with the King? Forget it, darling, it's a lost cause.' He pulled her to him again and began kissing her hungrily, and she forgot her frustrations and surrendered to the moment.

Towards the end of March, when all was ready, she and her stepdaughters said a tearful farewell to the great ladies who had attended them at court and moved to Chelsea. Anne went home, to bear her child at Baynard's Castle. This fine mansion on the Thames had been part of Katharine's dower, and she had recently presented it to the Herberts, who had been profusely grateful.

Katharine was sad to lose the daily company of her sister and friends, but it was expensive maintaining the full estate of a queen and she would not need so many attendants now. She was taking two hundred servants as it was; the princesses had their own and her gentlewomen were bringing their maids. Even with accommodation above the stables and in outbuildings and cottages, there would not be room at Chelsea for them all, so she had found rooms for some in local boarding houses, while two big chambers on the ground floor of the palace had been set aside as dormitories.

She was touched, on her departure, to receive a little note from the King. *Farewell, venerated Queen,* he had written. It was as if he was saying goodbye to her for good. She made a mental note to write to him every week.

Chelsea was a pretty little red-brick palace – more like a manor house, really – and nestled in a rural setting by the Thames. It had two storeys and two courtyards, having been extended by King Henry for Jane Seymour, whose initials and badge were everywhere – and there they would stay, Katharine resolved, as testimony to a great love. Lady Seymour would be pleased.

For its new mistress, Chelsea's chief attraction was the glorious gardens, which were just coming into bud. The walled Great Garden stood at the London end of the site, and her privy garden, to the west, was surrounded by privet hedges, banks of rosemary and borders of lavender. There were cherry, filbert, damson, peach and nut trees and a fishpond. In summer, when the hundreds of damask rose bushes were in bloom, it would be glorious. Her apartments overlooked the rose garden and the River Thames.

As their attendants unpacked their personal belongings, Katharine, Mary and Elizabeth ascended the grand staircase and went hurrying through the house, exploring the hall, the presence and privy chambers and closets, the summer and winter parlours, the bedrooms and the little chapel. Katharine was pleased to see that everything was in good order; her furniture had been arranged just as she had directed, and there were fresh flowers in every room. There was even running water, piped from a spring in the village of Kensington. It was sad that all the chambers had had to be shrouded in black, and would be for ten months yet, but she had no choice in the matter.

They all exclaimed at the sumptuously appointed summer bedchamber. Katharine had chosen this room for herself, loving its large oriel window and view of the garden and orchard on the north side of the house. Then they ran downstairs to explore the vaulted cellars.

'I can store wine barrels down here,' Katharine said.

'It's creepy,' Elizabeth faltered.

'Nonsense,' retorted Mary. 'You know what the Church teaches. There are no such things as ghosts.'

Elizabeth made a face. 'It's still creepy.'

Wishing to avoid an argument, Katharine hurried them back upstairs. Kate Ashley was waiting to take Elizabeth to the schoolroom, where Grindal was about to resume lessons. Katharine liked Mrs Ashley, a warm, learned woman who was devoted to her charge – and Elizabeth clearly adored her. Katharine knew she could depend on Mrs Ashley to do what was right.

As she acclimatised to her new home, she began to feel a comforting sense of peace and freedom. It was a joy to be able to live her life as she pleased and not have to conform to courtly etiquette. She was no longer on display all day and could opt for solitude if she so pleased. Once her marriage to Tom had been made public, life here would be idyllic.

That evening, she took a walk in the gardens. Tom had scouted around the walls a week earlier and told her that there was a postern gate. She found it easily and left it unlocked, as he had suggested. No one would come here at this time. The gardeners would be snug in their cottages or at the local inn, their work done for the day. And there were no guards at Chelsea. Once she was ready for bed, she told her gentle-women that, from now on, she wished to sleep alone. The ladies could keep to their chambers, the maids to the dorter.

'No one will molest me here,' she told them. 'I am of no importance now.'

A few looked a little askance at her, but there were no protests. They too valued their privacy, a thing that was rare in palaces.

Tom came just as the bells of the old church nearby were chiming midnight. His approach was so stealthy that she jumped when the bedchamber door opened.

'It was easy getting in,' he said, pulling off his gown as he hastened to the bed, looking around him at the luxurious room. 'Well, this is marvellous – but not as marvellous as you.'

He took her in his arms and entered her without even taking his clothes off. The stiff damask of his codpiece chafed her thigh, but she didn't care. She was in another world, this private Heaven she had created for them, and nothing else mattered.

It was not long before Katharine became aware of gossip in her house-hold. Tom alerted her.

'I met Mrs Ashley in St James's Park today,' he related, lying in bed sipping a post-coital goblet of wine.

'Oh?' she responded sleepily.

'She said she'd heard that we were married.'

Suddenly, she was wide awake. 'What did you tell her?'

'Nothing. I just smiled and went on my way.'

She lay back, thinking. 'Maybe we were observed at Greenwich or Seymour Place.'

'If we were, no one can prove anything.'

'No, but I have my reputation to consider. Tom, we must be circum-spect. I won't write to you so often.' They had been exchanging letters almost daily, even when they saw each other, using different messengers.

'I'll write no more than once a fortnight.'

Reluctantly, he agreed that would be wise.

The women made much of Anne's new baby. Edward was a winning infant, happy and contented from the first, and looked very sweet in the pretty shirt and the jacket of damask and velvet that Katharine had bought him. She knew she was lavishing on him all the love she would have bestowed on a child of her own. If she had two regrets, it was that she had never given Henry a son and that she was getting rather old to have children. But God was good and there might still be time. Heaven knew, Tom was indefatigable in his efforts to sire an heir!

Will had managed to gain access to the King. Jubilantly, he told Katharine that his Grace had seemed to look favourably on his request to petition Parliament to let him remarry, although he'd said he would have to consult his Council.

Katharine had been at Chelsea a week when Will paid her another visit. She saw his barge approaching when she happened to glance out of a window, and hurried down to the jetty to greet him, only to find him tense with anger. This was no social call.

'My Lord Protector has refused me leave to apply for a divorce,' he spluttered. 'He said he has to have regard for the sanctity of marriage.'

Anger flared in her as she linked her arm through his and walked him to the house. 'I know who is behind this,' she opined.

'The Duchess?'

'I'm sure it is. She hates us Parrs. She enjoys obstructing us.'

'I fear you are right,' he groaned.

When they entered her privy chamber, she poured wine for them both. 'Will, I mean to show my support for you. Send Lizzie to me. She can be one of my gentlewomen, and you can visit her here whenever you wish. I want the Protector to see that *I* approve of the marriage.' Not that I have much influence now, she thought, but, if it makes him uncomfortable and discountenances Nan, well and good!

'That's wonderful of you, Kate,' Will said, raising his goblet to her. 'I just want to make an honest woman of Lizzie. She's waited so long. I don't know how I'm going to break this news to her.'

'I'll do my best to cheer her. And keep pressing the King and the Council to grant your request. Make them see that you're not going away. Don't take this lying down, Will.'

'By God, I won't,' he vowed.

And so Lizzie Brooke came to live at Chelsea and Katharine made much of her, genuinely liking this dark-haired beauty with her sweet manner. Being barred from wedding the man she loved was not easy for Lizzie, but Katharine saw that she was supported and tried to give her hope for the future.

When he was not needed in council, which was increasingly often, Tom spent his days hunting – and his nights in Katharine's arms. Already, he was growing weary of all the subterfuge.

'We can't even dine together,' he complained.

'Then take me to an inn!' she giggled, cuddling up to him in their great bed. 'It would be an adventure.'

'You're a queen! Queens don't go to inns.'

'This one would. I could go in disguise.' She tickled the hairs on his chest.

'This close to London, you'd be recognised. Seriously, darling, we should think about how we will go about announcing our marriage. Ned, damn him, is all-powerful now. He's even decreed that he no longer has to heed the advice of the Privy Council if he so pleases. His power is absolute.'

'That is not what King Henry intended,' she said, her happy mood dissipating. Just over a decade ago, the Seymours had been country gentry – and now Ned was a duke who liked to play the king.

'Even so, we should ask his consent for our marriage, without telling him, of course, that we are already married,' Tom said.

'I don't think that Ned or the Council will approve it,' she said. 'We should wait a while, as we discussed. It is too soon.'

'But already there is gossip,' he reminded her. 'On my way here tonight, I met one of your brother's servants, who gave me a knowing look and said he had heard that I was often at Chelsea.' He was pensive for a few moments. 'There might be another way to broach the matter.

I know you don't like Nan, but it might be worth approaching her and appealing to her vanity.'

'What?' she exclaimed. 'She's the last person who will help us.'

'I know she's proud and bitchy to you, but I've always got on with her. I think she quite likes me.'

'She won't when she knows you're married to me.'

'It's worth trying. I'll ask her if she will meet with me and try charming her.' He gave a mischievous smile, looking like a satyr in the candlelight. 'If she approves our marriage, Ned assuredly will.'

At dawn the next morning, Katharine watched him leave with misgivings. He was going to Whitehall today to see Nan, and nothing she had said had deterred him.

She was not surprised to see him in a despondent mood when he returned that night. 'God, that woman's insufferable. She's queen in all but name. I asked if she would see you, and she said she would be away from court for a few days, but would grant you an audience on her return.'

'Grant me an audience?' Katharine echoed. 'Who does she think she is? *I* am the queen, not her.' She was vibrating with indignation.

Tom shook his head. 'I just left it. I doubt she will help us. I think I will have to talk to Ned, although I am worried about how to broach the matter and persuade him to speak up for me in council. I saw Herbert at court today and told him in confidence that I was hoping to marry you, although I had not yet asked you. He was somewhat amazed and advised me to get Ned's approval before approaching you. He said he would not tell your sister. So, darling, I must gird my loins and prepare to have my head bitten off. I'll go back to court tomorrow.'

Katharine was in turmoil. What if Ned said no? What if there was some law against a queen dowager remarrying without the consent of the Council? She began to fear that she and Tom had done something very rash.

The next morning was Easter Sunday. She joined Mary and Elizabeth for breakfast in the winter parlour, noticing that Mary looked troubled.

As Elizabeth extolled the delights of Plato, her sister was not responding.

'Are you all right?' Katharine asked Mary.

'I have been better,' Mary said, giving her a strange look. Katharine suspected that her stepdaughter was again having problems with her courses and did not want attention drawn to it. Every month, she was either irregular or in pain.

She smiled sympathetically at Mary and forked some cold beef onto her bread.

In the chapel that morning, when she gathered with her stepdaughters and her household for Mass, she watched Mary in trepidation, knowing that her chaplain had an important announcement to make. It was the best news for her, but the worst for Mary.

Sure enough, when Dr Parkhurst announced that, from now on, by order of the King, church services were to be in English, not Latin, and would conform to Protestant rites, Mary stood up, burst into tears and rushed out of the chapel.

Katharine hastened after her and caught up with her at the top of the stairs, noticing that Mary had donned her cloak.

'I'm sorry,' she said. 'I know how you must be feeling.'

'No, you don't!' Mary cried. 'This is just the last straw.'

'What do you mean?' Katharine asked, stunned.

'You should know!' Mary flung at her. 'I will not stay here to see my father's memory so dishonoured, or consort with heretics.'

Katharine's heart sank.

Mary glared at her. 'I am not blind to the fact that Sir Thomas Seymour has been visiting this house nightly. I've seen him from my window. I cannot believe that you would so far forget yourself as to entertain another man so soon after the King's death.'

'It's not what you think,' Katharine said. 'We are married.'

'Married?' Mary looked horrified. 'That's almost worse than fornication. Couldn't you have waited a decent interval?'

'Mary, I want children,' Katharine cried, stung by her vehemence. 'I can't afford to wait. I will be thirty-five in August. And I had promised myself to Sir Thomas before your father courted me. I was in love with him, but I chose a higher duty. And I did come to love your father. I miss him, believe me.'

'You have no excuse for your conduct,' Mary said, sweeping past her down the stairs and calling for her attendants and her barge master.

With tears in her eyes, Katharine followed her out and watched her striding down to the jetty, outrage in every angle of her posture. All those years of looking to her interests, of loving her and restoring her confidence – all undone. Could this friendship that had meant so much to them both ever be mended?

An hour after Mary had gone, Katharine was still pacing about the parlour, trying to compose herself and wishing that Tom were there to comfort her. But he would not come for hours yet. She made herself sit down at the table by the window. She would write to Mary, explain herself better and trust that, when her stepdaughter had calmed down, she would see things from a more sympathetic perspective. She dipped her quill in the inkpot – and then saw Lady Seymour's barge coming to a standstill at the jetty.

She flew down to greet her. 'My lady, is everything all right?' she asked, as they embraced.

'I think so, my dear,' her mother-in-law replied as she handed Katharine a basket covered with a cloth. 'Some quince tarts I made for you. Kate, Tom asked me to come and tell you that he has to go to sea. Some pirates have apparently entrenched themselves in the Scilly Isles and he's been ordered to get rid of them. His orders came this morning and he had to leave at once.'

First Mary, and now this. Just when she needed Tom. Goodness knew how long he would be away. And he had almost certainly not spoken to Ned. That matter would now have to wait. Katharine sighed. Maybe it was best to keep their marriage a secret for a while longer. As long as people didn't gossip . . .

She led her mother-in-law into the parlour and there, on an impulse, she unburdened herself to her.

'I'm sure the Lady Mary will come to understand,' Lady Seymour said.

'I pray she will. But now Tom is gone and cannot speak to Ned. Could *you* speak to him for us?'

The old lady looked flustered. 'He doesn't listen to me, dear. I never see him, and I never go to court. Jane once told me what it is like, with all the intrigue and backbiting, and I don't know how she – or you – bore it. No, Kate, it's best to wait until Tom gets back, and then decide what to do.'

Katharine sighed. She understood Lady Seymour's reluctance and secretly wondered if she was afraid of her eldest son.

That night, after sending a letter to Tom, hoping it would reach him at some point, she suddenly decided to take matters into her own hands and wrote to Ned herself, inviting him to come to Chelsea to discuss a matter that touched her closely. He replied fairly promptly to say that he would come the following week. When the week passed with no sign of him, she wrote again, but heard nothing. Was he just busy? Or was he dismissing her interests as carrying little weight beside affairs of state?

As soon as Anne heard that Mary had left Katharine's house – although Katharine had not told her why – she invited her sister to supper at Baynard's Castle. It was now May, and Katharine could not endure wearing her voluminous widow's weeds any longer, so she arrived at her sister's house wearing a black silk gown and a matching French hood.

Baynard's Castle rose like a sheer wall from the Thames. Having once been a royal palace, it was very large and very grand, but it was a happy home and Katharine loved being there. Anne had ordered a lavish supper in her honour and, after the children had been admired and sent to bed with the gifts Katharine had brought them, she sat down with the Herberts at a table gleaming with heavy silverware.

As the conversation grew lively, she became aware of Herbert watching her speculatively. 'They are saying at court that the Lord Admiral is going to marry the Duchess of Suffolk,' he said.

Katharine stiffened.

'Yes, Herbert, but it's just gossip, and we don't know if there's any truth in the tale,' Anne said quickly. 'You were thinking of marrying him once, weren't you, Katharine?'

'Yes,' she managed to say.

Herbert's voice was gentle. 'I happen to know it isn't true. Kate, the Admiral told me that he hopes to marry you. Has he approached you yet?'

'We have discussed it,' she said carefully, aware of Anne looking on with an eager expression.

'He's a very handsome man. What a fine husband he will make!'

'Yes, but it's far too soon to think of marriage,' Herbert averred. 'I advised the Admiral to obtain the Lord Protector's permission. Has he done so?'

'Not yet,' Katharine said, 'but I very much doubt that my lord will withhold his permission. If he does, I will make his folly manifest to the world. I am a queen, a good match for his brother, and I will not beg!'

The Herberts looked taken aback at her strident tone, but she had been thinking that she should not be a suitor to Edward Seymour. She was a private person now, and what she did was her business alone.

That night, she wrote again to Tom. *I am waiting for Ned to deign to visit me, and then I will ask permission for our marriage. I think it sufficient to ask only once and then cease. I will not be dictated to by one who is inferior in rank.*

Anne turned up at Chelsea the next day.

'I did not think to see you again so soon,' Katharine said, welcoming her.

'I had to come. I got a strong feeling last night that something was troubling you. Do you really want to marry the Admiral? Take time to think about it if you need to.'

Katharine took a deep breath. 'Anne, I am already married to him. We were wed two months ago.'

Anne stared at her in amazement. 'So soon after the King's death? But, my dear, I understand. You loved him before, I know. You had to seize your chance of happiness. I am so pleased for you.' She hugged Katharine tightly.

'I fear we have courted scandal,' Katharine said. 'When the news gets out . . .'

'You put duty first when you married the King. Now, it's time to put yourself first. Just keep it quiet and announce it later on.'

'But there is gossip already.'

'There's gossip about everything. It's not necessarily true. Only fools like to believe it.'

'I hope you're right. But you will keep this a secret, won't you, Anne? The fewer who know, the better.'

'My lips are sealed,' Anne declared.

Chapter 26

1547

After four weeks away, Tom returned in a blaze of victory, having got rid of the pirates. Stealing in at night, he crushed Katharine to him and kissed her soundly before hurrying her to bed.

'Even Ned had to congratulate me,' he said later. 'What he doesn't know is that I struck a bargain with their captain. I said, you leave the Scillies and do whatever you want to do on the high seas, and I'll leave you alone, provided you give me a share of any booty you receive.' She could sense him grinning in the dark.

'That's illegal,' she reproved him, only half in jest. 'I dread to think of the consequences if it were discovered.'

'It was expedient – and it worked. Both sides left happy.' He pulled her to him again and she gave up. He was incorrigible.

The next morning, as Tom dressed in the dawn light breaking through the window panes, she told him about Mary's fraught departure. She did not mention her conversation with Anne.

'Mary will forgive you,' Tom reassured her. 'She's very fond of you.'

'I do hope so. Tom, we must talk to Ned. I will write to him today and invite him to dinner again. It's best to get things out in the open. I'm weary of all this subterfuge.'

Tom agreed and departed for the court, hoping to get breakfast there before the council meeting he was to attend. Katharine wrote her letter and got a reply that same afternoon, by messenger. The Lord Protector would visit her on 18 May.

Katharine looked in on Elizabeth at her lessons, as she did every day.

She was pondering on what she would say if Elizabeth asked why Mary had left. But the girl said nothing. She was good at keeping her own counsel.

At dinner that evening, Katharine felt she finally had to say something, as Mary's place had long been glaringly empty.

'Your sister has gone down to Essex,' she said to Elizabeth.

'I know,' her stepdaughter replied. 'She said she had matters to attend to there. I hope she comes back soon.'

Katharine relaxed. Mary had been discreet. 'So do I,' she said. 'I miss her.'

Tom was in a quiet fury when he came to her that night. 'I'm beginning to think that I was sent to the Scillies just to get me out of the way,' he said, slinging his gown over the chair. 'While I was away, others have been busy, taking over my work, and Ned now listens only to men who worship him. But I'm not going to be ousted. I shall make my presence felt.'

'I'm sure you will,' she said, kissing him. 'Tell me, how are you managing at Seymour Place with all those works going on? I felt bad about your having to forage for breakfast at court.'

'Not well!' He gave her a rueful grin.

'I could ask my sister if you could stay with her at Baynard's Castle, which is nearer to here. I could say I had heard that you were greatly inconvenienced and needed temporary lodgings and could she and Herbert offer you one – it would put them in credit with the Protector, and so on. What do you think?'

He nodded. 'That would be perfect – or as perfect as things can be in the circumstances. Thank you, darling.'

'I will ask her then,' she said.

The Herberts readily agreed to Tom staying at Baynard's Castle, and he told Katharine that they had made him very welcome. By day, he was at Whitehall, doing battle in the council chamber, or hunting. Occasionally a red deer would arrive with his compliments to the Queen. He and Katharine still wrote each other letters to enliven the long hours apart, but separation only added to the bliss of their nights together. Katharine began to wonder if her household noticed

425

the dark circles under her eyes, or that she had taken to making up sleep in the afternoons.

The weather was warm now and she spent long hours in the gardens, tending to the flower beds and gathering blooms to fill her vases. Elizabeth and Grindal sat nearby, having lessons out of doors, and it was all very pleasant and peaceful. It wanted but the permanent presence of the master of the house to crown her contentment. But all would be resolved soon, she was sure.

'You've been talking to Anne,' Tom said, as he softly closed the door behind him that night.

'Have I?' she asked innocently.

'You know you have.' He sat down heavily on the bed and tickled her. 'You should have told me.'

'Stop it!' she giggled.

'It's your punishment!' He gave her a playful slap on the bottom. 'Anne gave me a scare at dinner tonight. She said she'd heard that I'd been visiting you here at night. Of course, I said no, it wasn't true, although I had passed the gardens on my way to dine with the Bishop of London at Fulham. But she kept shaking her head and smiling and, in the end, she said she knew I had a key to the postern gate – and only you could have told her that. So I confessed the truth, and they both said they were very happy for us. She's a cruel wench, your sister – but you're worse!' He went to slap her again, but she grabbed his hand, and, for a few moments, they wrestled until he covered her mouth with kisses. 'Seriously, I am grateful to you for asking your sister to have me stay with her. Her company will help shorten the weeks we are apart. And she urged me to seek Ned's goodwill.'

'He'll be here three days hence,' Katharine said, and then Tom took her in his arms and, suddenly, she had more pressing things on her mind.

But Ned did not come. He sent his apologies and wrote that he would not be free until the end of May.

Katharine flung down the note. What would it take to get him to Chelsea? She was convinced that Nan was responsible for the delay. Probably, if Nan had her way, he would not come at all.

When she told Tom that Ned had put off his visit, he swore under his breath.

'If he won't come, we must go to him. This situation cannot drag on. I'm fed up with all the furtiveness, but I do fear that Ned will not be accommodating.'

'Let's have the Church bless our marriage now,' she urged, 'and then go to see your brother.'

Thus it came about that they were married in the chapel at Chelsea with Dr Parkhurst officiating and Anne and Lady Seymour as witnesses. As far as the world would be concerned, this was their first and only wedding.

The next day, Katharine visited the court at St James's Palace, intent on seeing the King. She did not want to lose Edward's love through remarrying so soon, as she feared she had lost Mary's, and was hoping to obtain his blessing before she saw Ned. She thought she could bring the King to approve by using kindness and gentle persuasion.

Having sent ahead word of her coming, she arrived at the palace, only to be informed that the Lord Protector would receive her in his chamber. That sounded ominous, she thought, as she was conducted there by an usher. She was not pleased to see that Nan was present. The Duchess remained seated, clearly disdaining to curtsey, as Ned rose and greeted Katharine with a slight bow. He was tall and fair with a long beard, though not as handsome as Tom, she thought, and very much on his dignity.

'I had hoped to see his Majesty,' she said, seating herself without waiting to be asked.

'I am afraid he is at lessons,' Ned told her, 'but he will be happy to receive your Grace at three o'clock tomorrow afternoon. It would be helpful if you could give me some idea of your business with him, so that I can ensure he is prepared.'

'Of course,' she said, smiling. 'Your brother, my Lord Admiral, wishes to marry me, and we are seeking his Majesty's permission.'

Ned and Nan looked at each other; it was easy to tell who was the more horrified.

'This is preposterous!' Ned declared.

'Never!' Nan spat.

'May I ask why it is preposterous?' Katharine asked. 'We are both free to wed, and we are well matched. If there is any condescension, it is on my part, but love has overcome the difference in rank.' She smiled again, very sweetly.

'How dare you!' Nan spluttered, assimilating the insult.

'How can you contemplate a marriage between you?' Ned asked, white with fury.

'It would be Hell!' his wife added.

'To me, it would be Heaven, and I cannot see what possible objection you could make,' Katharine told them. 'I would have thought you'd be pleased, my lord, to see your brother marry a queen.'

'It is not fitting!' he retorted.

'But why?' She switched her gaze to the Duchess. 'Or is it that you don't want to see your younger brother married to someone who will outrank you all?'

Nan's look could have felled her, but, before she could respond, Ned spoke.

'You will give my brother ideas above his station, more than he already has.'

Katharine smiled, restraining the urge to go for him. 'So I am right – it is jealousy that is at the root of this.'

'Not at all! But I pray that this marriage never happens.'

'So do I!' Nan found her voice.

'Pray all you like, my lord. But the King is the highest arbiter of what is fitting and honourable in this realm, and I will rely on his God-given judgement. Try to influence him all you like – he loves me, and he loves his uncle. Good day to you both.'

With that, she rose, turned on her heel and walked out.

As soon as she got back to Chelsea, she dashed off a letter to Tom. *My lord*, she wrote, *your brother has this afternoon made me a little warm! It was fortunate there was a distance between us, or I would have bitten him!* She recounted the interview, omitting no detail, then ended: *Tomorrow, I will see the King, when I intend to utter all my anger against your brother.*

Tom's messenger was back almost within the hour. His relief that she had broached the matter of their marriage with his brother came across loud and clear in his note. *I thank God that we will no longer have to keep our secret.*

She shook her head at that, rather regretting now that she had deliberately provoked the Somersets. But she had been living too long with mounting frustration and listening to Tom's rants about his brother. It had afforded her a lot of satisfaction at the time to give vent to her resentment, but she should have restrained herself.

As she had anticipated, when she arrived at St James's Palace the following afternoon, she was informed that his Majesty could not see her. She had prepared for that eventuality and brought a letter, which she asked the Lord Chamberlain to give to the King. In it, she spoke of his father and how she had revered him. She complimented Edward on his great wisdom and reminded him how much she loved him and missed seeing him. She begged for just a word from him. There was nothing in the letter to which the ever-watchful Ned could object. But it was a start, a softening of the way.

She went home and waited for a response, fearing she would get none. But it was not long before a royal messenger arrived and presented her with a letter bearing the royal seal. As soon as he had gone, she broke it open and read: *Being moved by your request, I had to answer your letter full of kindness. Since you loved my father, I cannot but esteem you; since you love me, I cannot but love you in return; and since you love the Word of God, I do love and admire you with my whole heart. And if I may do you a kindness, either in word or deed, I will do it willingly.*

She smiled as she read those words. It was heartening to hear that Edward still loved her, and that he was ready to do her service.

To her surprise, a side of venison and a barrel of good wine arrived at Chelsea – gifts from the Duke and Duchess of Somerset. Peace offerings? Katharine wondered, as she wrote a warm letter of thanks. Perhaps they too felt they had behaved badly.

Tom cheered up considerably when he saw the presents.

'I shall strike while the iron is hot!' he declared, and hared off to St

James's the next morning to see his brother. But he came back that night dejected – Ned did not feel that he could sanction the marriage so soon after the late King's death.

'Never mind,' Tom said, as he and Katharine lay in bed talking in the small hours. 'I shall appeal to the King.'

'Ned won't allow that.'

'I did think of barging past the guards and storming the royal lodgings,' Tom grinned, 'but I have a friend in the privy chamber. Master Fowler is close to Edward; he sleeps in his bedchamber every night. I spoke with him today and he told me that his Grace hates Ned's severity. His tutors work him hard; he has no leisure and no money, even to reward his servants. He is utterly miserable. Now, what if his Uncle Thomas sends him money and defers to him as king? That, Kate, is the way to win his favour – and his heart.'

'And what the King wishes, Ned can hardly refuse. I see where this tends. Will Fowler act as go-between?'

'He will – for a consideration, of course. Tomorrow, he will give Edward forty pounds in earnest of my goodwill and tell him that I have enormous sympathy for his plight and am willing to ease his situation in any way I can. When the time is right, I will raise the matter of our marriage. By then, the King will be so grateful to me that he cannot refuse.'

Katharine felt uncomfortable that they were using this isolated child who loved her in his own strange fashion, but, God willing, she and Tom would be able to go on trying to make life better for him, long after he had sanctioned their marriage. She could never have him think they had been mercenary.

The following night, Tom reported that Edward had been pathetically grateful, and showed Katharine the touching letter of thanks he had received. Over the next week, he sent more pocket money and more messages of support, and Edward was soon letting him know how much cash he needed.

'Time now to get Fowler to bring up the subject of marriage!' Tom declared.

Two nights later, before they went to bed, he told Katharine that, on his instructions, Fowler had remarked to the King that he thought it strange that the Lord Admiral was not yet married, and did his Majesty think he should wed?

'He said yes, and when Fowler asked whom I should choose, he suggested Anne of Cleves!' Tom lay back and chuckled. 'As if I could fancy her! But then he thought about it some more and said he wished I would marry his sister Mary, to turn her religious opinions.'

Katharine was beginning to think that Tom's ploy might work, and was filled with a sense of well-being. 'At least he thinks you worthy of marrying someone royal.'

'He does, because I got Fowler to ask him if it would please him if I married you, and if he would write to you supporting my suit.'

'And what did he say?'

'I'm going to see him tomorrow. Fowler is lending me his spare livery and I'm going to shave off my beard, so that no one will recognise me. I'll look just like any usher. Don't look so worried, darling. Soon, we will be able to proclaim our love to the world.'

In the morning, a clean-shaven Tom kissed Katharine farewell. He looked younger, fresh-faced for all his forty years, and so unlike himself. He would grow the beard again, he assured her.

'You make the handsomest usher I've ever seen,' she told him. 'God be with you.'

She was amazed to see him turn up at Chelsea in the afternoon. Did it mean what she hoped it did?

'He said yes!' he told her, as soon as she had whisked him into the summer parlour. 'I persuaded him that our marriage was his own idea. He said he loves us both and wishes us happiness, and he even wrote me a letter formally granting his consent to us marrying, and one to you bidding you look kindly on my suit. Here, read it. In effect, Kate, he has commanded us to marry!' He picked her up and whirled her around.

'You did it! You did it, you marvellous man!' she cried, and then they were holding each other tightly and kissing.

Tom broke away. 'You must write to him, Kate, and tell him you will happily obey his wishes.'

'I'll do it right away,' she said, sitting down at the table and reaching for her writing box. 'Does Ned know?'

'Not yet. But I saw him at court and he has promised to come to dinner here tomorrow. Unfortunately, Nan is coming too, but neither of them can gainsay the King's wishes. We'll tell them we are wed and then we can announce it to the world.'

'We're almost there,' she said. But she did not relish the prospect of dinner with the Somersets.

She sat at the head of the polished table beneath the cloth of estate in her dining chamber, a very visible reminder of her queenship. Tom sat at the opposite end and Ned and Anne at either side. She waited for the dishes to be laid out on the table and the napkins draped across each shoulder, then waved the servitors away.

'We have some news for you,' she said, addressing Ned. 'The King has been pleased to sanction our marriage; indeed, he has commanded it. We were wed a week ago. We hope you are happy for us.' She smiled, not too triumphantly, she hoped.

She heard Nan's sharp intake of breath, saw her flush with fury.

Ned glared at Tom. 'You went behind my back. You have an evil nature.'

Tom just shrugged.

'You shall both be punished for this,' Nan hissed, her face a mask of outrage. 'Ned, you cannot let this pass. You should send them both to the Tower!'

'What, for obeying the King's command?' Katharine asked. 'Things *have* come to a pretty pass in England!'

'Her Grace is right, Nan,' Ned said through gritted teeth, 'although, strictly speaking, they should have my sanction too, since I act for the King. Yet his Grace has pre-empted me, cozened, no doubt, by my brother.'

Tom smiled. 'The King suggested several possible brides, all of them royal. I had my pick.'

Ned regarded him darkly. 'I don't object to your marrying the Queen; I am proud of that.'

Nan's expression said that she did object, very much. She was glowering malevolently at Ned, who had dared to gainsay her and would no doubt face her wrath on the journey home.

'What I dislike intensely,' Ned went on, 'is the deception. I should have been consulted and I am much offended and displeased that I was not. Had you married earlier and her Grace here had proved to be with child, there might have been doubt whether it was yours, brother, or the late King's, which would have had implications for the succession and posed a marvellous danger to the realm. Fortunately, however, it is too late for such concerns.'

'I did try to tell you, but you were always too busy to see me,' Katharine reminded him. 'And I am not with child.'

'That is as well,' Ned said severely. 'I shall have to inform the Council at the earliest opportunity tomorrow. In the circumstances, I think we should leave now, Nan. I am sorry to have inconvenienced your Grace, but I think our dinner should be deferred to a happier occasion.'

'I perfectly agree,' Katharine said.

There was no need now for Tom to hide away. When their guests had gone, the two of them remained at table and ate some of the food, although neither had much appetite for it.

'What do you think the Council will say?' Katharine asked nervously.

'What can they say? We have broken no law.'

'That's true. And Ned will not want a scandal that touches him and his family.'

'He certainly won't!' Tom agreed. 'Don't worry, darling, it will be all right.'

'You must spend the night in a guest chamber,' she warned. 'We must be circumspect until our marriage is announced.'

'Fair enough,' he said, his eyes glittering. 'Just give me the one along the gallery from yours.'

Circumspection had its limits, she realised, with excited anticipation.

* * *

433

After dinner the next day, Tom was summoned before the Council at St James's. Katharine watched with misgivings as his barge sailed away and spent a restless afternoon, but he was back in time for supper. She had been watching out for him and ran to the jetty to greet him.

'Well?'

'I've been censured, that's all,' he told her, then kissed her soundly on the lips, not caring who was watching. 'The King wrote to the Council, making his pleasure known. They couldn't go against that. Even Nan can't object. And I think Ned wants to avoid a family rift. He likes a quiet life. So he said that the Council had approved our marriage and that we are free to announce it. Let's summon the staff and do that right now, and I'll arrange for my belongings to be sent here. This is my home now!'

They walked, hand in hand, to the house, and Katharine felt as if her feet had wings.

The young King wrote to her, sending his congratulations and thanking her heartily for her loving obedience to his command. *You shall not need to fear any repercussions, and my Uncle Somerset is of so good a nature that he will not be troublesome to you.*

If only the Lady Mary had been as sympathetic. Tom had written to her when he had first written to the King, telling her that he had proposed to Katharine and praying her to urge Katharine to accept. His messenger had reported that Mary was very unhappy and anxious because the Protector was doing his best to persuade her to convert to the Protestant faith. Katharine had given up hope of a reply, but when it eventually came, it was stinging. Mary remained horrified that Katharine had even contemplated remarrying so soon after the King's death. How could she forget her great loss?

Tom wrote again, informing Mary that he and Katharine were married, and received a very cool reply. Katharine hoped that Mary would soften towards them in time, but she feared she had lost a friend, and felt sad that she could do nothing to help her stepdaughter in her plight. Relations between her and Ned were strained as it was.

At least King Edward had been wonderful about their marrying.

Katharine continued to write to him regularly, and he replied whenever he had leisure. A grateful Tom was still sending him pocket money, which he much appreciated.

Apprised of the marriage and the King's approval, Uncle William and Aunt Mary wrote to say how delighted they were for Katharine. Elizabeth too had accepted the situation cheerfully. She had blossomed at Chelsea, seeming very happy and relaxed, and she was making excellent progress with her studies, displaying remarkable ability. Katharine was pleased to see her getting on so well with Tom and calling him Father.

But the news of their marriage caused a great scandal at court – and in the country at large. People were openly gossiping at St James's, even in Tom's hearing, and Katharine was aware of undercurrents in her household. Will, who was pleased for her, warned her not to go abroad because people were saying she was a woman of easy virtue, a fool who had unthinkingly subverted the succession. She was especially upset to overhear one of her gentlewomen saying to another that Lady Suffolk had named a new stallion and mare Seymour and Parr. And to think that she had called that lady her friend!

Tom was angered by the malicious talk. 'If anyone dares speak evil of you, I will take my fist to them!' he swore, banging his hand on the dining table. 'I'll not have you slandered. I'll make the Council bring in a law to protect your good name.'

Katharine blinked back tears. She was dreadfully upset by the gossip and even more so when the King's letters arrived fewer and farther between and sounding ever more formal. Ned must have got at him, or Edward had heard what people were saying and was perhaps regretting helping her. She had lost him, she feared.

Elizabeth joined her one day as she sat brooding in the garden, staring into space, willing the storm to pass, which it would, she comforted herself, it would.

'Mother, Mary has sent me a horrible letter,' Elizabeth said, pushing it into her hands and looking indignant.

With a sick heart, Katharine read it. Mary had warned that Elizabeth would be morally at risk if she remained in the household of a woman ruled by lust. *Our interests being in common, the just grief we feel in seeing the scarcely cold body of the King our father so shamefully dishonoured by the Queen ought to be common to us also. Dearest sister, it is of urgent necessity that you leave there at once and come to live with me.*

She swallowed. 'It is for you to decide, Bess.' Her voice shook. 'You will have my blessing whether you go or stay. But I must say this. I may have married hastily, for I was worried that it might be too late for me to have children if I waited longer, but I have never behaved immorally. I loved your father and I mourn him still. But, in this life, we have too few chances of happiness to throw any away.'

Elizabeth knelt down beside her. 'I know. I'm happy here and I don't want to leave. I really don't want to go and live with Mary and be embroiled in her quarrels about the Mass. She'll try to make me attend, but I could not stomach it, for I am committed to the Protestant religion. Above all, I don't want to leave you.'

Katharine's heart filled. She could barely speak. 'Bless you, my dear.'

'I will write to Mary and tell her I think it best if I stay here,' Elizabeth said.

She never showed Katharine the letter, and Katharine wondered how she had justified her decision to Mary. But Mary did not write again.

Katharine's distress was greatly mitigated by the presence of Tom at Chelsea. He had taken effortlessly to the role of master of the house, swaggering through its chambers, greeting all the servants jovially and organising entertainments nearly every day. There were sports and suppers in the gardens, private concerts in the hall, evening barge trips along the Thames, even a masque in which Elizabeth played the role of Helen of Troy. Katharine held archery contests and games of human chess. She stayed out in the fresh air as much as possible, hunting or hawking with Tom or taking long walks with Elizabeth.

She was determined to show she was not cowed by the court gossips. She might have married a baron, but she was still served as a queen and entitled to the privileges that went with the office. She saw no reason why she should not defy her detractors and go to court to see the King. As a member of the Privy Council, Tom had a lodging there and could bring his wife.

She would need to look the part. She wrote to Ned, asking for the casket containing the Queen's jewels to be conveyed to her from the Jewel House in the Tower, where it was being held securely, and was astonished to receive a curt reply, saying that he was unable to return the jewels as he was keeping them against the King's marriage to the Queen of Scots.

'He can't do that!' Tom shouted, and stormed off to St James's, where, as he told Katharine later, he demanded that Ned give the Queen what was hers, only to be told that the jewels were not hers but state property.

'Of course, you know who's behind this,' he seethed. 'It's her, Nan. I met her in a gallery before the meeting and saw that she was wearing a brooch with a crown on it, which might be one that you described. So I told the councillors I had reason to believe that my lady of Somerset had appropriated jewels to which she had no legal right.'

'I would not put it past her,' Katharine fumed. 'She bears me such jealousy and hatred, and all because I take precedence over her. I fear we will have a struggle to get her to give up the jewels. Tom, the wedding ring King Henry gave me is in that casket, as are some of my own jewels – a cross and pendants that my mother gave me. They are indisputably mine.'

'They are all rightfully yours,' he growled, 'and I'll see that you get them!'

'Don't worry – I'll get them myself!' Katharine declared.

She was ready. After six months of widowhood, she had cast off her mourning and the oppressive black hangings had been pulled down. The gown she was wearing today was of crimson silk with gold and pearl buttons and a long train. Accompanied by Tom, she went by litter to St James's. They were to attend a reception for the French ambassador.

At the gatehouse, she was received by the Lord Chamberlain, who escorted her into the palace. There, she found waiting for her an unsmiling Ned, with Nan by his side, the Duchess being got up almost as royally as Katharine herself. It was as well that she was not wearing any of the Queen's jewels – even she wouldn't have dared be that provocative, not with the French to impress.

'My lady of Somerset,' Katharine said, 'I am so glad to see you for I had intended to accord you the honour of carrying my train.'

Nan flushed a dangerous red. 'Madam, it is not suitable for me to perform that service for the wife of my husband's younger brother. Come, let us walk together.' There was a shocked silence – then a buzz of murmuring broke out among the gawping courtiers who lined the gallery.

Katharine could not have felt more outraged. She went to walk ahead, but Nan kept abreast of her and when they came to a doorway, she thrust herself through it first.

'Do that again and I will pull you back myself,' Katharine muttered in her ear.

Nan turned to her husband, who was walking behind with Tom. Her voice rang out. 'My lord, did not King Henry marry Katharine Parr in his doting days, when he had brought himself so low by his lust and cruelty that no lady who stood on her honour would venture near him? And shall I now give place to her who was but Latimer's widow and has now cast herself on a younger brother? If Master Admiral teach his wife no better manners, I am she that will.'

Shaking with fury and embarrassment, Katharine opened her mouth to deliver a scathing reply, but Tom spoke first, in a low tone that did not carry.

'Brother, I recall that this is the lady who made you disinherit the sons of your first marriage. I would happily call in my lawyers to have them reinstated before her sons, to right a great wrong. Remember, I was there when you threw out your first wife. There is much I could tell.'

Katharine dared not look back at Ned's face, but she could sense him stiffening behind her. His silence was most eloquent. Tom had told her that, twenty years before, Ned had suspected their father of having sired his two eldest sons. Disgusted, he had banished his wife to a nunnery and banned her from ever seeing her children again. But Tom thought that at least one of them might have been Ned's, and that disinheriting them both had been unnecessarily harsh. Nan had made Ned do it, nagging and wheedling until he gave in. It was easy to see why Tom's implied threat – blackmail, whichever way you looked at it – had been enough to silence his brother.

'My lady,' Ned murmured in Nan's ear, 'out of courtesy, you might let her Grace walk before you.'

Nan gave him a look that would have felled dragons, but she did fall back and the reception proceeded without further incident.

The next day, however, a letter was delivered to Chelsea. It was from Ned. He could not see his way to delivering up the jewels to Katharine because they were Crown property and could not be alienated, even by a king's will. Enraged, she kicked a stool over, startling her ladies and sending Rig scuttling into a corner.

'How dare he!' she cried. 'How dare *she*!' She escaped to her walled garden and paced round and round it, not knowing how to contain her anger. That woman – that vixen – had bested her, and she would have strangled her had she been in reach. Never, *never* would she go to court again.

Tom was furious, shouting and stamping; the whole household must have heard him. 'This is an attack on me,' he raged. 'They think to belittle us, but they will not get away with it. One day, I will rule this realm as Protector!'

So that Katharine could prepare Lady Jane Grey for queenship, Tom brought his ward to live at Chelsea.

'She will be company for Elizabeth,' he said, as he got out of bed and put on his robe. He always rose early in the mornings, leaving Katharine to lie in a little longer, reading, before she herself got up.

Jane was a strange little thing, wary-eyed and very small and thin, even though she had a good appetite. She had long wavy red hair and pale skin with freckles. Even at eleven, she had staunch Protestant views and refused to wear any colour other than black or white.

'Sobriety becomes a good daughter of the Gospel,' she told Katharine, eyeing her crimson gown distastefully. It was like talking to your maiden aunt. Yet Katharine could not but admire Jane's piety and learning. She was formidable. One day, for all her primness, she would make a great queen.

Katharine soon gained the impression that Jane had been unhappy living with her parents, who were clearly ambitious for her and had driven her hard to shine at everything. Lady Seymour had confided to Katharine that, when Jane first came to Seymour Place, she had expressed surprise at not being beaten or reprimanded harshly if she did not excel at her lessons.

Katharine took care to be especially kind to the child and praise her, and Tom was wonderful with her, drawing her out of her shell and making her laugh and even romp in the gardens, playing tag or ball, with Elizabeth joining in. Unfortunately, Elizabeth sensed a rival in Jane, who, for all that she was three years younger, could compete with her at lessons, and she adopted a distinctly superior attitude. But Jane was so pleased to be able to study in peace and enjoy reading at leisure that it clearly did not matter. Katharine often sat in on their lessons, watching the two red heads bent over their books, making suggestions that took them in new directions, and influencing them with new ideas.

It was a peaceful, happy time. She had put Ned and Nan and the court firmly behind her and resolved to be grateful for the joys God had given her. And it was stirring to watch Jane blossoming under her care, and to be praised by the girls' tutors and the scholars with whom they corresponded. Nicholas Udall, for one, had written to her, expressing his admiration: *When I consider, most gracious Queen Katharine, the great number of noblewomen in England given to the study of human sciences and strange tongues, and also thoroughly expert in Holy Scriptures, I am overcome with thankfulness.* He clearly believed it was all down to her.

Her charges, he enthused, compared with the best writers in their godly treatises, which were fit to instruct and edify the whole realm in the knowledge of God. He praised their ability to translate books from Latin or Greek into English, *and it is now no news at all to see queens and ladies of the most high estate, instead of courtly dalliance, embrace reading, writing and earnest study, applying themselves to the acquiring of knowledge. I hear that these excellent princesses continually read psalms, homilies, devout meditations, or St Paul's Epistles or some book of Holy*

Scripture, and know them all in Greek, Latin, French or Italian. Your Grace's household is now famous as the place where it is common to see young virgins so trained in the study of good letters that they willingly set all other vain pastimes at naught for learning's sake.

Katharine hoped that her achievements in the field of learning would help to restore her good name. Time was passing, and the scandal occasioned by her marriage had surely died its natural death.

Chapter 27

1547

Kate Ashley was like a mother to Elizabeth and even shared her bedchamber, which was on the opposite side of the courtyard to Katharine's. The summer nights were hot and, even with the window open, the air was still and oppressive. When Ashley asked if she might sleep in another chamber nearby, Katharine was unhappy about Elizabeth sleeping unattended, but she agreed. What harm could the girl come to? The only people who had access to her bedchamber were Ashley, herself and Tom, who had had his own complete set of keys to all the rooms made when he moved in.

One sweltering hot day in July, when Katharine was sitting outdoors in the shade with Elizabeth and Jane, looking over their French translations, Ashley appeared, looking anxious.

'Your Grace, might I have a word in private?' she asked.

'Of course.' Katharine rose. 'Try looking again at that passage,' she told the girls, and led the way into the house, opening the door to the empty steward's office.

'How can I help you?' she asked, seating herself.

Ashley stood there, not meeting her eyes. 'It's about my Lord Admiral, Madam.' Again, she hesitated. 'I thought nothing of it at first, but are you aware that, almost since he moved in, he has come many mornings into my Lady Elizabeth's chamber, before she was dressed and ready, and sometimes before she has risen. If she's up, he bids her good morrow and asks how she is and . . .' She paused, looking distressed. 'He strikes her familiarly on the back or the buttocks, and then goes off to his lodgings; or he might go through to the maidens' dorter and play with them. If he finds my lady in bed, he opens the curtains and bids her good morrow, then makes as though he would come at her, and she will shrink further into the bed so that he cannot get to her.'

Katharine swallowed, having listened with mounting dismay. But Tom was such an ardent and attentive husband that she found it hard to believe that this was anything worse than innocent horseplay. He was forty; he could not possibly be interested in a girl not yet fourteen. And he had indulged in this horseplay openly, in front of Ashley. No, there could be nothing in it.

'It sounds like my lord's natural exuberance coming to the fore,' she said. 'He never knows when to stop.'

Ashley looked doubtful. 'Madam, that is not all. The Lord Admiral has sent both me and Elizabeth saucy notes. In one, he asked if my great buttocks had grown any slimmer or not. I was quite embarrassed. Heaven knows what he wrote to my lady.' She shook her head. 'She does not like his antics. She has taken to getting up very early in order to be dressed when he arrives. When she hears him unlocking her door, she jumps out of bed and summons her maids, getting them to hide with her behind the bed curtains, but my lord waits until they have left, having decided he is not coming. One morning, Madam, he tried to kiss my Lady Elizabeth as she lay in bed, right in front of me. I bade him go away for shame because, already, people are gossiping. Some of her chamberers have complained of his behaviour, and the servants are saying evil things about my lady; they think she is encouraging him.'

This was dreadful. Katharine felt clammy and sick, and her heart was racing. It could not be happening. Her Tom could not be pursuing Elizabeth. He was her guardian; he would not do anything so dishonourable.

'When I bade my lord go away,' Ashley was saying, 'he swore and said he meant no evil, and he would not leave off! He said the Lady Elizabeth was like a daughter to him and he threatened to tell my Lord Protector how he is being slandered. Madam, are you all right?'

Katharine was gripping the arms of her chair for fear she might faint.

'I am perfectly well,' she managed to say, aware that the words sounded hollow. 'I am sure there is nothing untoward in this.'

Ashley's voice was brisk. 'Nevertheless, Madam, I said to my Lord Admiral that I must always be present in the future when he comes to my Lady Elizabeth's chamber. But he is still coming, still playing his pranks.'

'And that is all they are,' Katharine said firmly, regaining her composure and shaking herself inwardly.

'Of course, Madam, I'm sure you're right, but—'

There was a tap on the window and they both looked up to see Elizabeth's face there, mouthing, 'What are you doing?' Katharine waved to her, putting on a smile, and holding up five fingers to indicate she would not be long.

Elizabeth disappeared. Ashley was still wringing her hands. 'Madam, it's not that my lord means any harm, but there's no doubt that my little lady is falling for him. My husband noticed it first. He told me that, if anyone mentions my Lord Admiral, my Lady Elizabeth is all ears. Whenever she speaks of him, she blushes. The signs are there for all to see. My husband warned me to take heed a week ago. He said he feared that my lady bore some affection for my Lord Admiral.'

Katharine was gathering her wits. She was Elizabeth's guardian and honour-bound to protect her from any scandal. No man might aspire to her, for her marriage was in the gift of the King – or, in effect, the Privy Council. Her reputation must be preserved, unblemished, against some future great match. Elizabeth could be a queen one day.

'This must be stopped,' she said. 'I'm not suggesting that anything unseemly has taken place. I'm sure that my lord sees Elizabeth as no more than a child and treats her accordingly.'

'He doesn't romp with my Lady Jane,' Ashley pointed out.

'He doesn't know her so well,' Katharine said quickly, wondering if Ashley was trying to tell her something else. Was there anything she had not dared say? 'I will speak to him and tell him that these morning visits must stop. And I will talk to Elizabeth too. They should be aware that any hint of impropriety could land us all in serious trouble. It might be accounted treason.'

And the penalty would be death. For a woman, that would mean burning at the stake, or, if the King and his Council were merciful, beheading – such mercy had been extended to Elizabeth's own mother.

'That's what my husband fears,' Ashley said, looking distressed. 'It's why I felt I had to come to you. I'm sure my lady means no harm. She's just a naïve girl.'

Katharine rather doubted that. Love her though she did, she knew that Elizabeth had been born clever. As for Tom – he was a great fool! Did he not realise how his familiarity would look? No wonder people were gossiping. It would have been bad enough if he had smacked or kissed one of her gentlewomen – but to do that to a king's daughter, who was living under his roof and his protection? Was he mad? Did he not realise that any scandal would rebound on his wife too, at a time when she could least afford to court scandal? Anger rose in her.

Tom could not be that blind. Elizabeth was budding into womanhood. Her courses had started earlier this year. She was her mother's daughter, susceptible to masculine attention. Katharine must do what any good mother would do and put a stop to this horseplay before things went any further.

'Leave this with me, Mrs Ashley,' she said, rising, and feeling a little light-headed. 'I will speak to them both.'

When she returned to the garden and rejoined her charges, she found herself looking at Elizabeth with new eyes, searching for any sign of interest in Tom. She deliberately brought up his name in conversation, testing the girl's reaction. There it was – the unwitting blush.

She would say nothing to Elizabeth now, she decided. It was Tom who needed to change his behaviour. If there was any blame in this, it belonged to him.

With difficulty, she contained her feelings until the evening, when she and Tom went for a stroll by the river, alone.

'Ashley complained of you today,' she said.

'Oh?' He did not seem too concerned.

'She said you have been going into Elizabeth's bedchamber in the mornings and indulging in horseplay.'

He shrugged, unperturbed. 'So what if I have? That woman is always complaining and casting aspersions. Elizabeth enjoys horseplay.'

She tucked her arm in his. 'Tom, *I'm* not casting aspersions, but you need to realise that she is not a child any more and that she may be getting romantic notions.'

'Ha!' he laughed. 'Then she is more her mother's daughter than I thought.'

'It's her age,' Katharine stressed, wishing he would take this seriously. 'Young girls can be susceptible to older men. And Elizabeth is not any young girl. No breath of scandal must touch her. If it did, you and I, as her guardians, would be in dire peril – and so would she. Already there is gossip.'

Tom's nostrils flared, a sure sign that he was angry. 'Evil minds dream up evil things! I mean no harm, and I will not stop. I won't be dictated to by those who see wrongdoing where there is none.'

'Tom—'

'Enough, Kate. Don't you start.'

'Then I will join you in the mornings. If I am there, tongues cannot wag.'

He shrugged and made no protest. That, in itself, was reassuring.

The next morning, and for several mornings after that, Katharine got up early and went with Tom to bid Elizabeth good morning. When she first went into the bedchamber, she did not miss the flash of anger in Elizabeth's eyes and knew she was not wanted there. It was as plain as day to her that her stepdaughter was infatuated – so why couldn't Tom see it?

Regardless of her presence, or Ashley's, he kissed Elizabeth on the lips in the customary way, tickled her, chased her around the room and tapped her on the bottom, as if to demonstrate that it was all good, harmless fun. Elizabeth kept protesting and tried to evade him, but it was clear to Katharine that it was an act, that she was enjoying the attention immensely and even, in subtle ways, encouraging it.

At the end of the week, she realised she was wasting her time.

'There's nothing in all this,' she assured Ashley. 'As long as you are here, there can be no scandal. I don't need to come any more.'

Ashley looked dubious. 'As you wish, Madam.'

'But I will speak to Elizabeth. She has to learn to be more circum-spect.'

She asked her stepdaughter to stay behind after breakfast. Tom had long gone out hunting, and Lady Jane had departed silently for the schoolroom.

Katharine smiled at Elizabeth. 'These morning visits of my lord's – you enjoy them, I see.'

'Not at all,' Elizabeth replied, instantly on the defensive. 'I do my best to avoid them, but he insists on coming. I get up earlier than usual. I make sure my maids are present. I cannot make him go away.'

'But you have not thought to complain to Mrs Ashley or me or even to the King or the Privy Council, so these visits couldn't have been that unwelcome to you. In fact, I don't think they have been unwelcome at all.'

'They have!' Elizabeth cried.

'You don't realise how much you betray yourself,' Katharine said gently. 'I understand that you are a little infatuated, but I assure you that my lord does not see you in that way. To him, you are a child.'

She saw the angry flush suffuse Elizabeth's fair skin, just as it had her father's, and it came to her that her stepdaughter was jealous of her – jealous because she was married to Tom.

'He didn't think of me as a child when he asked to marry me!' Elizabeth flung back. Her words hit Katharine like a punch in the stomach. 'Kate Ashley told me. She said it was me whom he wished to marry before all others, but the Council wouldn't let him. So he had to be content with you.'

Her words were no doubt spoken impulsively in the heat of the moment and Elizabeth could have had no idea of how cruelly they found their target.

'You are a wicked, ungrateful girl!' Katharine cried, getting up and opening the door. 'Go! I will decide later what to do with you.'

'No! I'm sorry – I'm so sorry, I didn't mean to say that!' Elizabeth wailed. 'Don't send me away, please – I'll never look at him again, I promise, I promise!' She grabbed Katharine's hands and wrung them. 'You've been so good to me, the best stepmother I've ever had . . .'

'All right, *all right*,' Katharine said, on the verge of tears herself and longing to be alone to assimilate the terrible thing Elizabeth had revealed. 'I won't send you away. But I think we both need time to calm down. Go to your lessons and I will see you later. And please be circumspect with my Lord Admiral. People are gossiping and you dare not risk that. Remember who you are!'

'Yes, Mother,' Elizabeth sniffed, and hurried away.

She had nipped the problem in the bud, she thought. When she sat that evening at a lavish dinner Tom hosted in the newly refurbished Seymour Place, and watched him being so loving and attentive to her, she found it hard to believe what Elizabeth had said. It was probably no more than Ashley's own assumption. And yet – there had been that time, after Henry's death, when she had thought that Tom would press his suit, and he hadn't. But, surely, he had been respecting the fact that she had just been widowed? It would have been grossly unseemly to have approached her in those early days. And he had then proved so ardent, so adoring. No, it was a nonsense and she would not think any more of it, or of the horseplay with Elizabeth. Innocent fun – that was all it had been. He loved *her*, she was in no doubt of that – and he had married her.

She put any unsettling thoughts firmly behind her during dinner and decided to enjoy herself. Afterwards, Tom showed her around and she admired the improvements he had made to the vast house and the ornate terraced gardens that descended below it on the river side. Everything screamed nobility and status.

But they were not to stay here yet. Tom hated London in the high summer and Katharine was fearful of plague, of which several cases had been reported. She had suggested that they remove to her palace at Hanworth, which was more spacious than Chelsea. She was aware that, for Elizabeth, the house would have mixed associations, for that exquisite Italianate fantasy had belonged to Anne Boleyn. The chimney pieces painted with classical scenes, and terracotta busts of Roman emperors could only remind Elizabeth of her father's passion for her mother. But, when the household moved there, Elizabeth loved it. She seemed fascinated by anything connected to her mother.

The gardens were what drew Katharine to Hanworth. They were beautiful just now and she spent her days out of doors, enjoying them. There were games of bowls, archery contests and even dancing practice on the grass. Local people had a right of way through the hunting park and they were soon bringing her humble gifts of strawberries or pies or home-churned butter. Life was quite idyllic and she felt that nothing bad could touch her here. If Tom was still larking about with Elizabeth, then let him. He meant no harm. Lots of fathers played the fool with their daughters.

She had resolved never again to go to court, but Tom persuaded her to come with him to Oatlands, assuring her that Nan was not there just now, and that there was a good chance that she would be able to see the King. She allowed herself to be persuaded, against her better judgement, but was angered to find that the King was surrounded by Nan's kinsfolk, who took the greatest pleasure in informing her that his Majesty was unable to see her.

But Ned – much friendlier than when she had last seen him – did invite her and Tom to dine privately with him in his sumptuous apartment. She caught Tom looking around it enviously.

She was amazed when Ned actually apologised for not being able to give her the Queen's jewels. 'To make up for it,' he said, 'I'm appointing Tom Captain General and Protector's Lieutenant in southern England, and I'm giving him Sudeley Castle in Gloucestershire. It's a stunning place, and you, Madam, will love the gardens. The late King's great-uncle, Jasper Tudor, did a lot of rebuilding there fifty-odd years ago and the castle is quite palatial.'

'I'm grateful,' Tom said. 'It will be good to have a country seat of my own – of our own, Kate. I'll ride down there next week and see if any works need to be put in place. Thank you, Ned.'

If only relations between the brothers could always be like this. It was Nan who had driven a wedge between them, Katharine was convinced of it. Ned was so much friendlier and more accommodating when she wasn't there.

Tom came back from Sudeley full of ideas. 'It's magnificent!' he declared. 'It's out of date and somewhat neglected, but I've put in hand a programme of building works. When it's finished, no house of Ned's will rival it in splendour!'

From Hanworth, trying to build bridges, Katharine wrote to Mary, asking if she had finished translating St John's Gospel, and was delighted to receive a reply couched in fairly warm terms. Mary had completed the work, but had had help and still felt that it should be published anonymously. *You must take the credit*, Katharine replied and, at length, persuaded Mary to have her name on the book. It was a step forward, and she hoped Mary would thaw further towards her as time went on.

Their lives never seemed to be free of strife. Ned sometimes seemed deliberately to provoke Tom. The Scots were still resisting English attempts to secure the hand of the young Queen Mary for Edward and, in September, Ned resolved on resorting to force. Tom was fired up about the naval role he would play in bringing the Scots to heel and was itching to be away on the high seas once more.

Then came the news. There would be no naval offensive, so his services were not needed. He huffed around the house for several hours before he calmed down and joined Katharine in the parlour.

'Of course, Ned will need someone to act as regent when he marches north. It's bound to be me. That's why he's told me to stay behind.'

But it wasn't him. 'I'm not even on the list of Privy Councillors!' he stormed. 'Nor even governor of the King's person! It should be me! I'm the King's uncle.' He was beside himself, inconsolable. 'God's teeth, is there no end to that woman's malice?'

'How dare they!' Katharine seethed. 'There is no one more fitted for the role of regent. It's an insult – and it's motivated by jealousy, I have no doubt. They don't want to see you excelling in the office – as you surely would – so they deny you the chance to prove yourself, lest others think you are better at it than Ned. You can see their game.'

'And, in the meantime, I'm made to look a fool and passed over. I won't have it!' Yet however much Tom stormed at the Council or bullied his brother, he was still told to stay behind.

'If we win this war, the Queen of Scots will be whisked down here in ten minutes and then it's goodbye to Lady Jane!' he ranted.

'Have you actually spoken to the King about marrying Jane?' Katharine asked, aware that he had not raised the subject in a long time.

'Yes,' he muttered.

'And?'

'Lukewarm,' he admitted. 'Wants a well-stuffed bride – stuffed with a kingdom. He covets Scotland, as his father did. But I warned him he would have trouble if he took a Catholic bride, one whose uncles ride high at the French court.'

'Tom, she's five years old and can be moulded to his will – or, rather, Ned's.'

'That doesn't take care of the uncles. They'd have something to say about it. No, Kate, I will keep working on him. He trusts my judgement far more than he trusts Ned's.'

'That's true.' But she was doubtful. Edward had been brought up thinking that he would one day rule Scotland. Tom was going to have to do a lot more persuading. At least Ned was away and Tom had greater access to the King.

'Darling,' she said, 'Edward is nearly ten and advanced for his years. I think you should instil into his head that he should take upon himself the government and management of his own affairs as soon as possible.'

'By God, you're right!' Tom roared. 'I'll do that, never fear!'

In the middle of September, a letter came from Horton Hall in Northamptonshire. It was from Aunt Mary, informing Katharine that her uncle had died.

She wept for a long time. Uncle William had been a stable force in her life for as long as she could remember. His wisdom and kindness had been her mainstays. She found it hard to imagine a world without him.

She regretted not having seen so much of him in recent years, but his health had been failing and he had rarely been in London or at court, preferring to stay at Horton or Rye House, where the air was more healthful. If only she had made more effort to visit him; if only she had not been so preoccupied with her own affairs.

She, Will and Anne made the journey to Horton by themselves. Aunt Mary had all the cousins visiting and did not need too many noble guests. They attended the interment in the parish church and then returned to the hall for the funeral meats. Will had to go back to court, and the others left too, but Katharine, Anne and Magdalen Lane stayed to keep Mary company in the early, difficult days of her widowhood and to help her go through their uncle's belongings, many of which she gave to the Church for charity.

Magdalen was staying on for a while, so the sisters travelled back south. Katharine was physically and emotionally exhausted when she reached Hanworth, but there was Tom, in a fury and impervious to her unhappiness.

'Ned has won a great victory,' he hissed.

'Where?' Wasn't that good news?

'At a place called Pinkie Cleugh, near Edinburgh. And I should have been there!' He punched the air with his fist.

'Of course, you should,' she said wearily, sinking into a chair.

There was rejoicing in England at the victory, but still the Scots refused to come to terms, and the fighting went on. Tom seized every opportunity to criticise his brother to the King.

'I said this war can never be won and that it's draining us of money we don't have,' he reported to Kate one day, after returning from Hampton Court. 'I also reminded him that Ned has appropriated or sold off many Crown lands. The King was not best pleased to hear that. I warned him of the dangers of being too bashful in dealing with Ned and urged him to bear rule, as other kings do. I said his uncle is old and that I trust he will not live long.'

Katharine reminded herself that it was his brother to whom Tom was referring. But there was no love there. Ned had killed it, bit by bit, leaving only jealousy and resentment.

'And what did his Grace say?' she asked, laying down her embroidery.

'He said, "It were better he should die." And then he said he would rule himself with the help of his favourite uncle. He said he approved my taking secret measures to oust Ned.' Tom smiled and picked up a stack of papers from the table. 'I'm looking through these documents for precedents. It helps that Sir Richard Page, the King's present governor, is a drunkard – I can see him off without a problem. And I've begun to enlist support among the councillors.'

'This all looks hopeful,' Katharine observed. 'I pray God you will see a happy outcome.' Tom would certainly be easier to live with if he did, and he would gain the recognition and status that was his due. People underestimated him. It was Ned's jealousy that had prevented him from playing his proper part in government – and the enmity of Ned's wife. With any luck, Nan would soon be smiling on the other side of her face.

Everyone had expected Ned to pursue the war until he achieved total victory, but suddenly he was back at court with the army disbanded. No one was more surprised than Tom.

'And the worst of it is that he's being very nice to me,' he said. 'I think he knows something.'

The niceness continued. Nan sent Katharine some marmalade she had made and a doe taken while hunting.

'She probably hopes you'll choke on it,' Tom muttered.

But others followed the Duke and Duchess's example. The scandal surrounding Katharine's marriage had thankfully been consigned to history and she was now receiving many callers and entertaining again. Her house had become a second court, frequented by nobles and councillors, and Tom delighted in showing himself an open-handed and lavish host. Some of their guests were his secret allies, fawning on one who might soon be in power; others came for the lively intellectual and religious discussions that Katharine initiated, presiding serenely at the head of the table, deferred to and served like the queen she was.

Even the Duchess of Suffolk came calling, as friendly as ever, and Katharine tried to forget the hurtful jibes she had made just weeks before. They sat in the summer parlour, drinking cordial, and were soon engrossed in one of the intellectual debates they had once loved, although now, with the Protestant faith the official religion of England, it did not have that edge to it, for the battle had been won.

'What crusaders we were back then,' the Duchess recalled.

'We courted a lot of danger,' Katharine reminded her. 'I nearly got arrested.'

'You were so clever, mollifying the King. And I think he knew your true beliefs and protected you.'

'He did. But, as Supreme Head of the Church, he could only go so far. And Gardiner was on a mission.'

'He's still on a mission. I hear that he has opposed every one of my Lord Protector's reforms. If he's not careful, he'll end up in prison.'

'He's a spent force,' Katharine said.

'And good riddance! Tell me, are you planning another book?' the Duchess asked.

'I've been thinking about it. I felt inspired by Marguerite of Navarre's *Mirror of a Sinful Soul* to write something along those lines – my own spiritual journey, from the Popery instilled in me as a child to my embracing the true faith. What do you think?'

'I think it might prove highly edifying. Your other books sold well. You should do it. You need a project.'

'I will!' Katharine agreed, resolved. 'I'll start this very evening.'

She was aware that Tom was growing increasingly resentful of being her inferior in rank. Whatever he did, he would never be royal. He made no secret about disliking sitting to the left of her canopy of estate when they entertained. He grumbled about giving precedence to her when, as her husband, he should have priority.

It grieved her. It had not mattered to him at first. Love had overcome all when they were in the first flush of passion. He still loved and lusted after her, but he was a proud man and very much felt the slights meted out to him, and his resentment and jealousy of Ned now sometimes rebounded on her. He would create scenes and shout, usually about trivial things. It took very little these days to provoke his temper.

She understood his frustrations. Ned was stifling him. His talents were under-used, if they were used at all. The outcome of his scheme to seize power and marry the King to Lady Jane was increasingly uncertain. He was in an impossible situation and he was not a man to take kindly to being passed over. He must play his role in the world, the role for which God had fitted him. So she withstood the storms, knowing they were not really meant for her, and showed sympathy and solidarity.

In October, though, Tom's ever-simmering anger began to express itself in a more disconcerting way. One night, they were lying in bed after a particularly enjoyable supper party, during which Katharine's kinsman, Nicholas Throckmorton, had engaged her in a long discussion about Ned's grandiose plans for Somerset House, the palatial mansion he was building on the Strand, a stone's throw from Seymour Place.

'He's pulling down his neighbours' houses around their ears, and his own. He makes little distinction between mine and thine,' he'd told her.

'Like he does as he pleases with Crown lands,' she'd observed.

The company were listening agog, knives and forks suspended.

Katharine was enjoying herself. 'Do you not marvel that, while his Majesty is at war with Scotland, and there is plague again in London, and the kingdom is well-nigh bankrupt, my Lord Protector is bringing in architects from Italy and designing such a palace as has never been seen in England?'

Tom had been looking at her darkly. She had thought him angry at his brother's extravagance. She was shocked when, lying beside her, but keeping his distance, he growled, 'What did you think you were doing, flirting with Throckmorton?'

'Flirting? Are you mad? I was just talking to him. He's my kinsman.'

'I was watching you. You were making eyes at him.'

'I was doing no such thing!' she countered, outraged. 'What would you have me do, sit silent at supper parties? I was not aware of you contributing much to the conversation!'

Tom gripped her hand, too tightly. 'I was too busy watching you making a spectacle of yourself. You were ignoring our other guests. You're a queen, Kate, and should take care not to be showing particular attention to any man apart from me.'

His attack was so unfair, and without foundation, that she was momentarily speechless. 'What's got into you, Tom?' she asked. 'This is me, Kate, you're talking to, and you know me better than that. It's an

455

appalling accusation to make, and you should apologise.'

'You're my wife and you'll do as I command,' he countered.

'Oh, stop being silly!' she retorted, turning her back to him. For answer, he bounded out of bed and went off in a huff to his own lodging. In the morning, she anticipated, he would be different again, and so it proved, for he greeted her at breakfast as if nothing had happened. But he did not apologise.

A week later, the weather turned colder and Katharine ordered a fire to be lit in the winter parlour. She had retreated there alone, with her books, to work on her Spanish. As she sat at the table, a groom knocked and entered with a basket of coals for the fire. She was glad when he left her to herself again, but no sooner had the door closed behind him than she heard a commotion outside.

'You should not have been alone with the Queen, you varlet!' Tom shouted.

'I beg pardon, my lord, I was just delivering coal,' the groom responded nervously.

'Just delivering coal? That's a novel excuse,' Tom sneered.

Katharine leapt up and opened the door. 'This man was here on my orders and has acted perfectly respectfully,' she said, glaring at her husband.

'Go, man!' he ordered the groom, then pushed her back into the parlour. 'What were you thinking of, being alone with him?' he roared.

'He's a servant! I was studying, for goodness' sake. And I don't have to explain my every action to you. Tom, you are being ridiculous.'

It was then that he raised his hand as if to strike her.

She grabbed it and fended him off. 'Tom! What are you doing? What is wrong with you? Can't you see that I have eyes for no man but you?'

His arm slackened and she let it drop as he looked at her, stricken. 'By God, darling, I am sorry.' He sat down heavily and covered his face with his hands. 'I just feel so angry all the time. I'm acting irrationally, I know, and I'm sorry.'

'You've had me quite worried.' She knelt beside him. 'Don't let the outside world come between us. I'm on your side, remember.'

He drew her into his arms. 'Will you forgive me? I'll try not to be such a devil.'

'Of course I will,' she replied, resting her head in the crook of his shoulder, relieved to be close to him again. 'But, if you ever raise your hand to me again, your baggage will be in the hall!' It was only half said in jest.

Outwardly, they were in harmony again and Tom was once more the attentive husband. But Katharine could not help feeling on edge. Now that she knew how volatile his temper could be, she was nervous of provoking it, and she was also uncomfortably aware of the need to keep proving her love and fidelity. She would study him constantly, wondering if he was watching her, testing her constancy. She knew he was withdrawing large amounts of gold from her coffers, because her worried treasurer had told her, but she dared not complain. She noticed, however, that they were living ever more lavishly, and guessed where the money had gone.

Others had noticed Tom's moodiness. The atmosphere at Hanworth, once so welcoming, was now oppressive at times as the master's wrathfulness permeated its walls. Always, he was ranting against his brother and the wrongs done him, and he was not a man to grumble quietly. No, he had to shout and rave, which sent the servants scurrying.

Mrs Ashley told her that Tom had once more taken to invading Elizabeth's chamber in the mornings. To appease her, Katharine accompanied him on a couple of occasions, and they tickled Elizabeth as she lay in bed, reducing her to hysterical laughter. She knew she should put a stop to these antics, as they were not seemly, but she did not wish to antagonise Tom in his present mood. She supposed that Ashley did not, either, and wondered if Elizabeth too was nervous of him. So she tried to divert him, inviting him to linger in bed in the mornings and indulge in the pleasures of wedlock. Some days, the ploy worked, but she was unhappy about their lovemaking being part of a strategy.

One fine October morning, they arose late after lying together and strolled arm in arm through the gardens. From a distance, they saw Elizabeth leaving the house.

'Why does she wear that same black dress all the time?' Tom asked testily.

'She is still in mourning for her father,' Katharine said, looking down at her own green gown and feeling a little guilty for coming out of mourning so soon.

'She should wear something else. It doesn't suit her.'

'I agree, but let her be.'

'No. It's not right that a girl her age should swathe herself in black. I'll make her change it, by God!' Before Katharine could protest, he went charging back towards the house. Elizabeth saw him and took another path through the gardens. He chased her and soon she was running, her footsteps crunching on the gravelled path.

'Help me!' she cried, racing towards Katharine, who was standing by the fountain, watching them, wondering if this was just Tom's usual idea of horseplay and if she should intervene. 'My lord is after me! He says he's going to make me change my dress.'

'Hold her!' Tom commanded, coming up behind. 'Kate, hold her!'

Fearful of arousing his temper, Katharine took Elizabeth by the shoulders. 'He won't hurt you,' she said. 'It's only a game.'

She could not believe her eyes when Tom picked up a pair of shears from an astonished gardener's tool basket and began snipping at Elizabeth's skirts as she struggled and protested.

'You're not wearing this hideous gown again!' he roared, laughing. Snip, snip, snip. He was cutting so furiously that Katharine, fearing Elizabeth would get hurt, held her still, hissing at Tom to stop, as the gardener gaped at them. Tom blithely ignored her and soon the skirts were in ribbons and there were numerous bits of black cloth strewn on the ground, stirred by the breeze.

'That's enough!' Katharine said, seeing that Elizabeth was in tears. 'For pity's sake, Tom, desist!'

Tom stood back, admiring his handiwork. 'That looks better,' he grinned.

Without a word, Elizabeth fled back to the house, her ruined dress and kirtle barely covering her under-smock.

'You shouldn't have done that,' Katharine cried.

'I didn't hurt her. She'll be all right.'

'You've wounded her pride – and frightened her. That's not the part of a good guardian. I'd better go and calm her.'

She walked away, unable to believe what Tom had just done. It had been inappropriate and excessive. He just didn't know when to stop – and everyone was too afraid to tell him. She wished she had been firmer.

On the stairs, she met Mrs Ashley, who was red-faced with indignation.

'I was just coming to find your Grace,' the woman said. 'I was shocked when I saw the state of my young lady. She has told me what happened and she said she could not get away because you were holding her. Really, Madam, my lord has gone too far this time!'

'I know, and I am sorry for it. I did not know what he was about to do; I thought he would tickle her. When he began cutting the dress and she was struggling, I held her because I feared she might get hurt. I feel dreadful about it.'

'Your Grace, I beg of you, speak to him!'

'I already have.'

Ashley looked a little mollified. 'I just wish he would treat my lady with the respect she is due. I understand that he is familiar with you, Madam; you are his wife, but Elizabeth is second in line to the throne.'

'I will remind him again of that,' Katharine said.

But Tom was unrepentant. He could not see any harm in what he had done, nor would he apologise. Yet, maybe, she had misjudged him, or so she thought when, a few days later, he came to her parlour in an angry mood, full of fatherly concern for Elizabeth.

'Kate, I've just seen something that worries me greatly. I was walking along the south gallery and passing that little window that gives on to the antechamber to the chapel when I noticed someone moving in there. I looked in and saw my lady Elizabeth with her arms around a man's neck. They were kissing.'

Katharine's hand flew to her mouth. 'What man? Who?'

'I did not see his face – her head was in the way. But we cannot let this pass, Kate. Too much is at stake, not least her reputation.' He was working himself up into a fury now and, for one disloyal moment, she wondered if jealousy was at the root of it, but dismissed that notion instantly.

'Where was that woman, Ashley?' Tom growled. 'Doesn't she supervise her charge? Does she just let her run wild? She should be more vigilant!'

'I will summon her now,' Katharine said, deeply worried. If word of this got back to the Council . . . It didn't bear thinking about. 'I'll see her alone.' She didn't want Tom intimidating Mrs Ashley by losing his temper. To her relief, he agreed.

Ashley was shocked. 'I know nothing of this, Madam, I swear.'

'But you should have known! It's your office to know where your charge is and what she is doing!' Katharine's tone was cold. She was furious with Mrs Ashley for letting this happen. The last thing she needed was another scandal.

'Madam,' the governess said testily, 'I believed she was in her chamber at her studies. That's where she always is at this time.'

'Then bring her here and we will question her.'

Elizabeth arrived, looking wary. Katharine spoke first.

'You were seen in a man's arms, kissing him, in the chapel antechamber not half an hour ago. What have you to say for yourself?'

Elizabeth burst into tears. 'What? I did no such thing. Who is saying this?'

'Someone who wishes you well. Elizabeth, are you telling me the Gospel truth?'

'I am, Mother, I am! You can ask my women. They have been with me all afternoon. It's a foul lie!'

Katharine bade her wait in the bedchamber and summoned the women who attended her, one by one. They all said the same thing: my lady had been hard at work; she had not left her desk, even to use the privy. Katharine felt sick. Had Tom made it up? If so, why?

She called Elizabeth back. 'I am sorry to have misjudged you, and you too, Mrs Ashley. I am in no doubt that it was not you in the gallery. But I could not let it pass, you must understand that.'

'I wish I knew who had spread such a calumny about me,' Elizabeth cried.

'I think they meant well, but were mistaken. Now, go back to your books and forget about this.'

Elizabeth left without another word, leaving Katharine aware that she must build bridges. A thoughtful gift should do the trick – a pretty brooch or some fine leather gloves. She would give it to her stepdaughter at supper and apologise again.

Mrs Ashley was still standing there, giving Katharine an old-fashioned look.

'What is it?' Katharine asked.

'*Was* there a man in the gallery, Madam?'

Katharine did not quite know what Ashley was hinting at – and did not want to know.

'I am certain that there was,' she said.

'But what man could it have been, Madam? There's only Grindal and my Lord Admiral, if you discount your officers and servants. I don't think for one minute that Grindal would attempt such familiarity.'

'Nor do I. He is too dedicated a scholar and lives like a monk. No, Mrs Ashley, the only explanation is that my lord mistook a servant for Elizabeth.'

'Yes, I suppose you are right, Madam,' the governess said. But Katharine sensed she did not accept that.

Later that month, Katharine and Tom moved to Seymour Place, so that he could attend Parliament. Relations with Elizabeth and Mrs Ashley had remained strained and Katharine left them at Hanworth with Lizzie, having decided that they all needed some time apart. Jane, how-ever, was accompanying her and Tom to London, where the delightful Lady Seymour would take charge of her. That was a relief, for Katharine had come to believe that Jane should be apart from Elizabeth. There were too many things happening around Elizabeth, things the eleven-year-old Jane had no business knowing. If she breathed a word of them in her dutiful letters to her parents, there could be consequences – serious ones.

Tom was hoping for great things from Parliament. He was deter-mined to be given control of the King. He had paid out inducements in many towns, shires and boroughs to ensure that his supporters were elected, and Katharine had done the same in her dower lands, with the result that a substantial majority of lords and MPs were his men. His friends on the Privy Council had warned that nothing but bad could come of his scheming, and that it could rebound on him.

'Warwick tells me I'll end up in the Tower,' he told Katharine. 'By God, if anyone tries to send me there, I shall thrust my dagger in him!'

'Even in Ned?' she asked.

'Even in Ned! By God's precious soul, I can better live without him than he without me.'

Her heart sank. She had a bad feeling about this coming Parliament. Tom was investing so much hope in it. She could not bear to think what he would be like to live with if his hopes were dashed.

Thanks to the constant encouragement of Lady Suffolk and Will, her book was finished. In it, she had paid a warm tribute to Henry, again comparing him to Moses, who had delivered his people out of captivity and bondage; she praised him for having lifted the veils and mists of errors and brought his subjects to the knowledge of the truth, by the light of God's Word. She had a few choice words to say too about the tyranny of Rome. There was more of her in this third book than in the others. Above all, she wanted to convey her simple zeal for her faith, her humble and earnest love of God.

She called it *The Lamentations of a Sinner*. It was published that November and there was much demand for copies. It won her high praise from scholars and theologians alike.

Tom was pleased for her, but preoccupied with his own affairs.

'God's teeth, the boy's an idiot!' he swore, crashing into the parlour just as Katharine was packing up a copy of her book to send to Magdalen Lane.

'Are you referring to his Grace the King?' she asked drily.

'Who else? He's just refused to sign that document I drew up for him, naming me and Ned his joint governors. But Parliament's in my pocket. I just wish I had young Edward living here in my house. Or I could simply steal him away.'

'Don't even think about it,' Katharine said, ignoring the look he gave her.

To her surprise, when Parliament sat, he did nothing. In fact, Ned had to reprimand him for not attending on Christmas Eve, when the session was prorogued.

'You're wasting your opportunities,' Katharine warned him, not for the first time, when he got home. 'You packed Parliament with your own men; why have you not capitalised on that?' She was exhausted and exasperated with him.

'My brother threatened me with the Tower,' he confided. 'Some had told me openly they thought I was mad to suborn Parliament. So I'm going to continue putting pressure on the King. Fowler is constantly singing my praises to him and showering him with pocket money, and I'm offering inducements to the gentlemen of his Grace's privy chamber to persuade him to think seriously about signing that document.'

'God willing, it will all bear fruit,' Katharine replied, feeling despondent and wondering if Tom had been marked for failure from the start.

They had been invited to Hampton Court for Christmas, and Elizabeth and Mary were joining them, even though Mary was out of favour for stubbornly keeping the observance of Mass. As the barge carried Katharine and Tom upriver on Christmas morning, Katharine was hoping that she would have a chance to talk to the King and use her powers of persuasion on him. It would not be difficult, she was sure. His letters had been more loving of late.

But there was no opportunity. She was shocked at the rigorous etiquette that now surrounded the ten-year-old King. He sat on his throne like some oriental potentate, staring out haughtily at his assembled courtiers. There was none of the levity and hilarity of Christmas that had been seen under his father. He received his sisters with great ceremony and talked with them awhile in a friendly fashion as they knelt before him. He welcomed Katharine and Tom graciously, and Katharine, by virtue of her rank, sat at his right hand at dinner. But Edward kept the conversation general. When she asked if she might have a private word with him, he said he would ask the Lord Protector, who was seated on his other side, but made no attempt to do so. And that was the last Katharine heard of it.

Elizabeth had been pleased to see her and, after an awkward few moments in which they both stuttered nervous pleasantries, Mary was friendly enough, although not as friendly as she had once been. But Tom, putting on the charm, soon had her laughing and blushing.

'You must visit us, my Lady Mary,' he invited. 'We keep a merry household.'

Katharine looked askance at him. It hadn't been very merry lately. But she knew he was trying to smooth the way between her and her stepdaughter, and was grateful.

'I should like that,' Mary said. 'Maybe in the spring.'

Chapter 28

1548

Snow was lying on the ground when Will called on Katharine at Hanworth in January. She invited him into the parlour to get warm and had them served hot spiced ale.

'Something is troubling you,' she said.

He sighed. 'My Lord Protector has again refused to sanction my applying to Parliament for a divorce. My wife is living in adultery with that priest and her bastard – how can that uphold the sanctity of marriage my lord bleats on about? And there's Lizzie waiting for me to make an honest woman of her.'

'She's been very patient. She loves you truly. She will go on waiting.'

'She shouldn't have to! Kate, I want to put an end to her anomalous position. I want her to be my wife.' He hesitated. 'Archbishop Cranmer has been sympathetic. My lady of Suffolk thinks I should marry Lizzie anyway, as it'll be only a matter of time before he sees his way to granting me an annulment. She reminded me that King Henry himself married Anne Boleyn before Cranmer declared his union with Katherine of Aragon invalid and confirmed his new marriage.'

'You think he will grant an annulment?' Katharine asked. 'On what grounds?'

'I don't know. He said there probably were grounds.'

'If he said that, you can rely on it. Cranmer's a sound man. Seize your chance of happiness, Will.'

'You mean you also think I should marry Lizzie now?'

'I do,' she smiled. 'Shall I summon her? Then I'll leave you two alone to make your plans.'

* * *

In the middle of January, Will and Lizzie were married in the chapel at Hanworth, in the presence of Katharine, Tom, Lady Suffolk, Lady Seymour and Elizabeth, who loved Lizzie and thought it was all wonderfully romantic. Lizzie remained with Katharine, but made frequent visits to Charterhouse Square to be with Will. They were known to be lovers, so Katharine did not think there was any danger of anyone finding out that they had anticipated the Archbishop's ruling.

William Grindal had gone home to his family at Christmas and had since written to inform Katharine that he was unwell and would not be returning yet. Soon after the wedding, she was saddened to receive a letter from his mother informing her that he had died of the plague. How cruel, she thought. Plague was a disease of hot weather, although outbreaks had been known to linger into the winter months. He had been a brilliant man and a wonderful tutor and he would be missed.

Elizabeth was devastated. She wept for hours and would not be consoled. Meanwhile, Katharine had to find her another tutor. The renowned Master Ascham offered himself for the post, but Katharine favoured her chaplain, Dr Goldsmith, the sound Cambridge man who had served her since her marriage to the King and helped teach her languages. He was devoted to her, touchingly calling her 'our Queen Esther' or 'the Queen of Sheba who rivalled Solomon in wisdom'. His command of Latin was admirable, and he would make an excellent tutor for Elizabeth.

But Elizabeth wanted Ascham, who had long been her mentor. She was going through a difficult phase. When the first anniversary of King Henry's death signalled the end of mourning, she disdained to put on colours and took to wearing black and white. Tom made a point of groaning whenever he saw her.

'I am a godly Protestant maiden,' she told him haughtily. 'You won't see me in cloth of gold and fancy headgear.'

'You look a frump in that silly little hood,' he told her.

'And you look like Satan's spawn in your silks and velvets!' she retorted.

Tom just grinned at her. He was used to her sharp repartee, even encouraged it, but he would never rise to the bait.

Katharine reasoned that the best course was not to make a big issue of Elizabeth's choice of dress. With her red hair, she looked striking in black and white, and she suspected that there was more of vanity than godliness behind her choice.

Without consulting Katharine or Tom, Elizabeth invited Master Ascham to Hanworth. He arrived with the air of a man who had won a prize and stayed for several days, with Elizabeth fawning all over him. Katharine could not but be hospitable, and she did like Ascham, who was witty and erudite company. But she remained adamant that Dr Goldsmith was better fitted for the post of tutor.

In private, Elizabeth argued and had fits of temper.

'I want Ascham!' she stormed, as Katharine watched her, arms folded, shaking her head.

'Your mother has said that you will have Dr Goldsmith, and that's an end to it!' bellowed Tom.

'By God, I will not!' Elizabeth swore.

Ascham came to see Katharine. 'Your Grace, I heard the shouting. I do not want to cause dissension. I know that you and my Lord Admiral are in favour of Dr Goldsmith and I have advised my Lady Elizabeth to comply with your recommendation. What is important is that she brings to maturity those talents awakened in her by Master Grindal's teaching.'

Katharine told Elizabeth what Ascham had said. 'The matter is settled,' she declared.

'But I should have a choice in this,' Elizabeth insisted.

'No arguments, please,' Katharine said. 'I'm not feeling too well today.' She thought she might be going down with an ague.

Two days later, when they moved back to Seymour Place, she began to see a pattern to her symptoms. She felt unwell and fatigued only in the mornings. It was a strange, heavy feeling that could only be alleviated by eating certain foods, especially meat and fish. She took to lying late abed until it had passed – and wondered if her hopes and prayers were being answered at last.

Tom continued to rise early. And there was Mrs Ashley, accosting Katharine as soon as she emerged from her bedchamber on a morning when she had suffered intense nausea. She just wanted to sit in her chair and be quiet, but she invited Ashley to sit with her, willing her to be brief.

'I'm sorry, Madam,' the governess said, looking distressed, 'but I could not let this pass without troubling you. My Lord Admiral has come every morning this week to my lady's chamber and today, when my Lady Elizabeth was at her book, he arrived bare-legged in his nightgown and slippers! He just looked in at the gallery door, bade her good morrow and went on his way, but, Madam, I had to go after him and tell him that it was an unseemly sight to see a man come in such a state of undress to a maiden's chamber. I fear I angered him, but he just walked away.'

Katharine sighed. She did not need this just now. She felt so drained that she hardly cared what Tom was doing. But she did raise the matter at dinner, reiterating what Mrs Ashley had said.

'I was quite decent!' he snapped. 'I was hardly naked! I just bade Elizabeth good morning. That Ashley woman is always seeing evil where none is intended and, frankly, I don't like what she's implying.'

'Maybe, just for the sake of peace, you could bid Elizabeth good morning after you are dressed. I'm not feeling well, Tom. I don't need this.'

Instantly, he was all concern. 'Have you still got that ague? Shall I summon Dr Huicke?'

'Tom, I'm not ill.' She paused. 'It's very early days yet, but I think I might be with child.' She could hardly believe it.

He got up, his features lit by a joyful smile, and folded her in his arms. 'By God, that's the best news I've had in years! A son! I've long wanted a son, especially since I became a man of property. Kate, darling, this is wonderful. You are so clever. Now, you must take care of yourself. Take advice from Dr Huicke. If there's anything you need or fancy, I'll see that you get it. By God, I can't wait to announce the news!'

'Whoa!' she said, laughing, happy to see him so jubilant. 'Let's keep this to ourselves for a little, until this sickness passes. I just want to stay quiet for now and rest.'

'Of course, darling.' He arranged cushions in her fireside chair, then dragged over a footstool. 'Come and make yourself comfortable. You sit here and I'll fetch you some books. Cicero, yes? You'd like that?'

'I'm happy with anything,' she said, catching his hand and suddenly feeling happy because everything really was all right between them. She had a loving, attentive husband, who might be a little eccentric and overpowering at times, but who was at heart a decent man.

Soon afterwards, Katharine received a message from Anne, inviting her, Tom and Elizabeth to dine at Baynard's Castle to discuss a private matter of some urgency.

What could it be? She hoped it was not bad news. Surely, if it was, Anne would not be hosting a dinner?

She could have done without dining out, because the sight and smell of food could bring on the nausea and her sense of taste was all over the place. But, tired as she felt, she allowed her maids to dress her in her finery and tried not to look at the choppy water of the Thames as the bargemen rowed them to the opposite shore. Thank Heaven it was only a short journey.

She found her family gathered in the dining parlour the Herberts used for intimate dinners. It was apparent at once that something was badly wrong. Will greeted her with a face like thunder and Lizzie had clearly been crying. Anne was the picture of indignation.

'Have I done something to offend anyone?' Katharine asked.

'Of course not, dear sister,' Will said. 'But you should know now that the Council have found out about my marriage to Lizzie and ordered me to put her away and never see her again, on pain of death.'

'They said he should remember that he has a wife still living,' Lizzie sniffed.

'That's utterly cruel!' Elizabeth cried, outraged.

'They wouldn't dare carry out such a threat,' Tom growled.

'Just let them try!' Herbert chimed in.

'I was so happy,' Lizzie wept. 'So happy. They won't even let us wait for Archbishop Cranmer's verdict.'

'And you think it will now be favourable – if it ever comes?' Will asked bitterly.

'I know who's behind this,' Katharine said, gratefully seating herself at the head of the table. 'Someone who hates us Parrs.'

'Nan!' they chorused, as one.

'Well, of course!' Tom spat, his face livid. 'This is an injury to Will and Lizzie, and an insult to my wife, and I shall demand satisfaction from Ned himself!'

'You'll get none,' Will warned him.

'Lizzie, you must stay in my household,' Katharine said, 'and Will can see you under cover of visiting me. If anyone gets suspicious, I shall lie in my teeth.'

'So shall I,' Elizabeth added.

'This tyranny has gone on long enough,' Tom growled. 'We must see off this Protector and his cronies, once and for all. I can take care of the councillors and the western parts of the realm. Will, you could leave court and set up house in Northamptonshire. It would be an ideal base from which to raise support in the shires.'

Will looked dubious. 'You mean, come out in open rebellion?'

'Not against the King, of course, but against those who abuse power in his name. We can undermine them by subtle means.'

Katharine wondered at that. Tom had never done a subtle thing in his life.

'I will think about it,' Will said. 'In the meantime, I think Kate's plan is the best course. It will mean we can still see each other, sweetheart.' He took Lizzie's hand and kissed it. There were tears in his eyes.

When Katharine left Baynard's Castle that night, after a somewhat gloomy dinner, she felt despondent. Last year, she had striven to keep her love for Tom a secret; this year, she would be shielding Will and Lizzie. But she could not just abandon them to an endless separation. And she was so furious with Ned that she would have helped them out of anger alone.

When they alighted from the barge, Elizabeth turned to her. 'Please, Mother, let me have Ascham for my tutor! I'll do all I can to help keep Lizzie's meetings with Will a secret, I promise.'

Katharine looked at her searchingly. 'And if I say no, will you still keep them a secret?'

'Of course,' Elizabeth replied hopefully. Satisfied that she was not being offered an ultimatum, Katharine gave up. It would be one fewer problem to deal with, and she was feeling very tired.

'Since you are so set on him, and I do admire him, I cannot but say yes,' she said, whereupon Elizabeth threw her arms around her and kissed her.

'Thank you!' she cried. 'You are the most wonderful stepmother!'

And so Ascham joined the household and it was not long before Katharine could see that her stepdaughter was flourishing under his tuition. Truly, she had made the right decision. She was even more convinced of that when she discovered that she and this learned York-shireman shared a love of Cicero, which led to stimulating discussions in the evenings. And she admired his approach to teaching, which had far more of the carrot in it than the stick.

By the time they moved to Hanworth in the spring, Katharine was in no doubt that she was pregnant. When she felt the child move in her – a fluttering, miraculous sensation – they announced the news, and were overwhelmed with good wishes and gifts.

Some wrote giving her advice she would rather have not received. She could have boxed Nicholas Throckmorton's ears for telling her that she was middle-aged and must take care. She *was* taking care, for this child was a gift from God, the most precious jewel she would ever own. But she was not well. Her female friends had told her that the nausea would go away once the babe began to move, but it didn't.

Dr Huicke assured her that some ladies did feel unwell throughout their pregnancies; it was nothing to worry about. She took his advice to eat well and go for long walks. The gardens at Hanworth were awakening to spring and looking particularly beautiful.

Tom continued to fuss around her like a mother hen.

'I'm not made of glass!' she laughed at him.

'You're not to exert yourself too much,' he ordered. 'You carry all our hopes in your belly.'

He had not been pleased when the doctor had warned that marital relations should cease for fear of harming the child, but he had grudgingly agreed. He still shared Katharine's bed, to be close to her, which was a great comfort. Yet she worried that he might look for satisfaction elsewhere; a lot of men did – she had heard their wives complaining. She knew he was still visiting Elizabeth in the mornings – he made no secret of it. But now, she started to worry. What was it people said about hiding something in plain sight?

She could not help watching them both, searching for any sign that there was more between them than there should be. Elizabeth did not appear so infatuated as she had once done, but, with her, it was hard to tell. She was good at dissembling. In truth, there was nothing to see, nothing untoward. Katharine told herself she was worrying about nothing.

Tom was still driven in his campaign to topple his brother, who in turn was angry with him. He had amassed a lot of treasure after making his deal with the pirates, and repeatedly refused to obey Ned's orders to return it to its lawful owners. Ned was growing increasingly irate.

'He says I'm the greatest pirate of all,' Tom chuckled, not caring.

He was still devising schemes to seize the King and the government. By now, Katharine had become convinced that they would never come to anything. Ned and his allies were too firmly entrenched to be dislodged, but Tom could not see it. She was thankful that he was channelling his prodigious energy into retrieving her jewels, the loss of which still rankled deeply. He had engaged lawyers, who had told him that, if proof could be found that the late King had given Katharine the jewels, she would stand a good chance of getting them back. Frustratingly, it was proving hard to find such evidence, and she suspected that Ned – or Nan, more likely – was proving obstructive. She had heard that Nan was now going about dripping with the jewels that were rightfully hers, and her anger burned.

By May, she was seething at the delay.

'They could at least return to me those pieces that are my personal property, especially the gift from my mother and Henry's wedding ring,' she protested.

472

Tom put an arm around her. 'You must not work yourself up about it, Kate. Think of the child and leave this with me. I will go to Whitehall to sort it out, once and for all!'

He was away for a week, attending council meetings and, presumably, hectoring Ned. He kept in touch by messenger, and sent her fair words, but it was clear that Ned was stalling. Finally, Tom admitted he was getting nowhere, but said he had asked his brother at least to return her personal jewels. *He gave me no definite answer*, he wrote.

Katharine lost her temper when she read that and dashed off a reply castigating Ned; after all, her plea was upright and just. *He won't concede that, because his wife is determined to keep the jewels.* That was at the nub of it. She was beginning to think that she would never get them back.

When Tom returned to Hanworth and found Katharine lazing in the garden, he looked worried. 'There are cases of plague in London,' he said. 'With this warm weather, it could get worse. For our safety, and that of the child, we should remove to Sudeley Castle. It's better to travel the distance now than wait until you are nearer your time.'

Katharine looked down at her swollen stomach. At nearly six months pregnant, she was very large, and the infant gave her no peace, bouncing and fidgeting, usually in the mornings and evenings, when she was trying to rest. If she balanced a book on her bump, the little knave kicked it away. With the constant fatigue and the debilitating nausea, she was feeling very drained. She did not relish the hundred-mile trek to Sudeley, but Tom was right. It was the safest place.

'I agree,' she said. 'And it is fitting that Lord Seymour of Sudeley's heir is born in his father's country seat. I will give orders for preparations to be made. We'll take Elizabeth and Jane with us.'

Tom returned to court to wind up his affairs there. Within a week, Hanworth had been largely stripped of its hangings, movable furniture and household goods, which were all packed and piled in the hall, awaiting the move.

Katharine's cousin, Mary Odell, Uncle William's granddaughter, came to stay with her. Mary had been one of her gentlewomen while she was at court, and Katharine had invited her to join the gossips who would keep her diverted during her confinement. She had a pallet bed set up in her chamber for Mary, for company at night while Tom was away. As they lay talking, late into the small hours, she guided Mary's hand to her belly to feel the babe squirming about, and Mary's eyes widened in wonder.

'That will make my lord some pastime when he returns!' Katharine said, smiling.

The next day, a letter arrived from Tom. The French had threatened war. The navy might have to be deployed to keep the Channel safe. It was all they needed right now.

Katharine replied, asking him to keep her informed of any news. *I shall not be quiet till I know*, she wrote. *I would that my sweetheart and loving husband fares better than I do myself.*

She gave the letter to Elizabeth to hand to the waiting messenger, who had been dispatched to the kitchen for refreshment. Then, having a letter to the King dashed off, she hastened downstairs, hoping to catch the man before he left. That done, she could go for her daily walk.

She caught up with the messenger as he was striding along the path to the stables.

'Your Grace!' he said, startled, and bowed.

'I have another letter for you to deliver,' she said. She saw that he was carrying hers to Tom and caught a glimpse of some handwriting next to the seal. It looked like Elizabeth's.

'May I see that, please?' she asked. He handed it to her, his face expressionless.

It *was* Elizabeth's hand. She had written, in Latin, *Thou, touch me not.* But that had been crossed out and, below it, were the words *Let him not touch me.*

'Thank you,' Katharine said, and gave both letters to the messenger. As she went on her way, she was uneasy in her mind, wondering what those words were meant to convey. Had Elizabeth been making it clear to Tom that his morning romps were unwelcome? But why strike out the sentence and then write the same thing as if it was intended for someone else? Tom's words about seeing her in the gallery with another man came to mind. Had there been such a man, after all?

She sat down on a stone bench and tried to think straight. Everything pointed to the obvious explanation, that Elizabeth did not want Tom coming to her bedchamber. The tiny, nagging sliver of doubt was dispelled when she read Tom's prompt reply to her letter, which he said had revived his spirits. He praised her patience when his little man, as he called the child, was busily shaking himself about. *I trust*, he wrote, *that, if God gives him a life as long as his father, he will revenge those wrongs that neither you nor I can at the present time. I pray that God will deliver us from this turmoil.*

He had spoken again with his brother and so confounded him, he related, that Ned was no longer so sure of his ground and had said that, if Katharine's legal ownership of the jewels was established, she would receive them – or some financial recompense. Tom was aware that that was not what she wanted to hear, but he had good news too. As far as he was concerned, the French threat would not be preventing him from travelling with her to Sudeley or from staying with her until the birth, and he had told Ned that he would be setting off for Gloucestershire on 13 June, come what may.

He had advised her to maintain her good diet and exercise. *You must keep our little knave so lean he will give you no trouble at his birth, but creep out, as if from a mouse-hole. Thus, I heartily wish my most dear and well-beloved wife to fare well.* He had signed himself '*your most faithful, loving husband*'.

She smiled at his words, all her doubts allayed. She thanked God for sending her such a lord. Only later, in the dark reaches of the night, did it occur to her to wonder why he had chosen to sign himself as a faithful husband. It was just a figure of speech, she told herself, turning over and settling herself for sleep.

Tom returned to Hanworth two days before they were due to leave for Sudeley. He kissed Katharine soundly and she experienced one of those wonderful moments of pure happiness. She was excited about the move and looking forward to seeing the castle and Tom's improvements. And, sometime in early September, less than three months hence, she would hold her child in her arms. Supper that night was a happy occasion. Even the solemn Lady Jane, recently arrived from Seymour

Place, was chattering away, eagerly anticipating life in their new residence.

Of late, Katharine had taken to spending her evenings in the parlour with her feet up on the footstool and Lizzie and Mary Odell for company. Elizabeth was absent, and Tom, whom Katharine had hoped would join them, was giving final instructions to the steward. It was a shame, for it was a lovely, balmy evening, just perfect for a stroll in the Italian garden. Well, she would go alone. She liked to sit by the dancing fountain and listen to the trickle of the water. There was something very calming about it.

She made her way there, wandering through a patchwork of delightful garden 'rooms', each enclosed by high box hedges. She was marvelling, as she often did lately, that she felt no fear about giving birth. She had heard horror stories from other mothers, but she felt so calm that she was sure nothing bad would happen to her.

A twig cracking in a nearby garden intruded on her thoughts. Was someone there? Then there came a girl's giggle. Servants, perhaps, enjoying a secret tryst, although only the gardeners were supposed to come here. Maybe it was one of the gardeners. Irritated at her peace being disturbed, she made her way through the arch in the hedge, ready to issue a reprimand.

When she saw them together, she thought her eyes were deceiving her. Elizabeth was in Tom's arms and he was kissing her. Katharine stood there, staring at them for a moment, then found her voice.

'What do you think you are doing?' she cried out, anger and hurt welling up in her.

They fell apart and turned to her, shocked.

'Go back to the house, Elizabeth,' Katharine ordered tersely.

'But, Mother . . .' Elizabeth looked terrified. Her cheeks were flaming.

'Don't "Mother" me. Just go. I would speak with *my husband* alone.'

Elizabeth fled.

Tom looked pleadingly at her, like a man who had been winded. 'Kate, I can explain . . .'

'Of course you can. Isn't that what men always say?'

She was beginning to feel the effects of the shock she had sustained. A wave of dizziness was engulfing her, and her legs felt as if they would buckle beneath her. She swayed, and Tom moved to steady her, but she pushed him away.

'Don't touch me. I don't want you touching me.' She stumbled through to the next garden, where there was a wooden seat, and sank into it, shaking, Tom at her heels.

'Kate, I'm sorry. I got carried away.'

'Your head will be carried away if you're not careful. Do you not understand who she is? She is second in line to the throne and compromising her virtue is probably high treason. We're *in loco parentis*, Tom, responsible for ensuring that her reputation is unblemished, not endangering it as you have done. Never mind the damage you have done to us!'

Grief welled in her, a deluge threatening to overwhelm her, and she began sobbing uncontrollably, not knowing what to do with herself in her misery.

Tom knelt beside her. 'Kate, calm yourself. Think of the baby.'

'You didn't when you were busy seducing our stepdaughter!' she hissed at him.

'Seducing? She's her mother's daughter, and she can be quite the coquette!'

She rounded on him. 'You are blaming a fourteen-year-old child for your vile behaviour?'

'She's no child, Kate. She's as old as the hills. She was born knowing.'

'Oh, be a man and take responsibility!' She burst into a fresh paroxysm of weeping. 'I was happy, so happy. How could you do this to us?'

'Kate, I'm sorry, I really am,' he said, putting his arms around her. She shook him off violently.

'It has never gone beyond kissing, and that only today,' he told her.

'And I'm expected to believe that?'

'Believe it or not, it's true. Kate, it will never happen again, I vow it.'

'You won't have the chance. I'll have to send her away. I don't know where, or how I shall explain it, but she cannot stay with us. Look what a position you've put me in!' She sobbed afresh.

'Calm down, darling, please. You really must think of the child. I am so sorry, so sorry.' There were tears in Tom's eyes and that brought her to earth. He was not a man who wept easily. He had once said he couldn't cry, had never cried as a child.

What choice did she have in this? She tried to think rationally. Separating from him would cause a great scandal and a husband's adultery was no grounds for divorce or annulment. She did not even know where she would stand financially if she left him. Henry had settled on her properties and income, and she had too the manors bequeathed by her former spouses, but a wife's possessions became her husband's on marriage. She could end up with nothing, and she would be alone. She might even lose her child – it was a father's right to determine what became of him.

Or she could dry her tears and get on with her life, blotting out this unpleasantness and learning to live with her bitter sense of betrayal. One day, perhaps, it would fade.

'Kate?' Tom said, pulling her to her feet. 'This thing with Elizabeth – it was a bit of tomfoolery that got out of hand, believe me. She was there and she was willing and, like a fool, I fell for it.' He made a wry face. 'You know I have felt very frustrated of late. I know that's no excuse, but please forgive me for a moment of madness.'

Was he telling the truth? Could she ever trust him again? Those romps with Elizabeth had been going on for months. He might be lying, for all she knew.

'Can you swear to me, on our child's life, that it *was* just a moment and that you have never kissed her like that before?' She looked directly into his eyes.

'I swear,' he said, without hesitation. She thought he was telling the truth and relaxed a little. Maybe things weren't so bad after all. Other husbands she had heard of did far worse things than kissing.

'Very well,' she said, drying her eyes, 'we will put this behind us and I will try to forget it happened.'

'I'll make it up to you,' Tom promised, catching up with her as she walked back to the house.

She sent for Mrs Ashley, angry that the woman should have been so lax. Ashley was almost as much to blame as Tom and Elizabeth – her job was to be vigilant and, clearly, she had not been.

'What has happened, Madam?' Mrs Ashley asked anxiously. 'My lady is in floods of tears.'

'As well she might be,' Katharine retorted. 'I just found her in the gardens in my husband's arms, kissing him. I'm sure I don't need to spell out to you the possible consequences of such misconduct. And you, Mrs Ashley, must bear some of the blame. You have failed in your duty to your charge. Where were you when she was running loose like a hoyden?'

The governess bristled. 'Madam, I cannot be with her all the time. She said she would be at her books in the garden. And, with respect, my Lord Admiral must bear the greatest share of blame. A man of his age and a child – he should know better.'

'Indeed, he should, and you may be sure I have spoken strongly to him. But I relied on *you* to be vigilant with Elizabeth.'

Mrs Ashley flushed. 'Madam, I have been. I've warned you more than once about what was going on in the mornings. You came with my lord a few times, and then no more.'

'Because I believed it to be harmless.' Suddenly, Katharine's anger left her. Maybe she was being too hard on Mrs Ashley; maybe she herself had been remiss.

'The important thing now,' she said, 'is to decide what to do with Elizabeth. She cannot stay with me, but I must avoid a scandal. If I can find some place for her to go, we can say that she prefers not to join us at Sudeley as it is so far from the court. I'd have sent her back to Seymour Place, but my Lady Seymour has gone to Wiltshire because of the plague and the house is shut up.'

'My sister Joan might have her,' Mrs Ashley said. Joan, an attractive woman who had once served Katharine, was married to Sir Anthony Denny, who had been the head of King Henry's privy chamber, and Mrs Ashley often spoke about their lovely house at Cheshunt, north of London. 'I'll write to her, if you wish.'

'That would be most suitable,' Katharine said. 'Thank you.' She knew she could rest easy if Elizabeth was with the Dennys, a most upright and learned couple. She could only pray that her servants had no inkling of what had happened and would not gossip.

She felt so ill that she had to lie down for a while before facing up to confronting Elizabeth. When she finally emerged into the hall, Elizabeth was waiting for her, walking up and down, still distraught. When she saw Katharine, she ran to her.

'Mother, I am so sorry, so sorry!'

'And so you should be,' Katharine said. 'Your conduct has been disgraceful – especially after all the kindness I've shown you. And I cannot credit that you have so far forgotten yourself and what you are. Did you not realise that your behaviour might be seen as treason? You, of all people, should have known that.'

'No!' Elizabeth wailed. 'No – it was only a kiss.'

'So I am told. But a princess of the blood is forbidden even that, unless it is sanctioned by the King and the Council. And I am responsible for you. Your behaviour could rebound on me.' She paused to let that sink in. 'Now, I have made a decision about what is to be done with you.'

'Please don't send me away,' Elizabeth pleaded.

'I must, for your own good. I am worried that there is talk here among the servants already. We cannot risk more. You are to go to Sir Anthony and Lady Denny at Cheshunt, if they are agreeable, the reason being that you wish to stay near London and the court, rather than go to Sudeley.'

'No, please,' Elizabeth moaned, tears streaming down her face.

'I'm sorry, but this is for the best,' Katharine declared. In fact, she could not wait for the girl to leave. Looking at her, so young, vital and slender, she could not but compare her pregnant self, ageing, cumbersome and careworn. No wonder Tom had fallen under Elizabeth's spell.

'Go and order your maids to pack,' she said. 'And get a groom to sort out your things from that pile over there.' It was the baggage pile for Sudeley.

* * *

That evening, as they were at table, trying to eat and make conversation, a messenger arrived from Cheshunt. Sir Anthony and Lady Denny would be delighted to host the Lady Elizabeth and would be ready to receive her on the morrow.

When she heard that, Elizabeth burst into tears and ran from the room. Katharine and Mrs Ashley spent ages with her, calming her and helping her to prepare for the move. In the end, Katharine was so wrung out that she had to go to bed. She did feel sorry for Elizabeth, who was very young and had been foolish, but she would be glad when she had gone.

The next morning, Elizabeth came to breakfast with reddened eyes and said very little. Afterwards, as she embraced Katharine in the porch, she wept again.

'I am full of sorrow having to depart from you,' she sobbed.

'You will like it at Cheshunt,' Katharine said briskly. 'No tears, now.'

'If there is any gossip about me, you will warn me, won't you?' Elizabeth asked, dabbing at her eyes.

'I will,' Katharine assured her, 'but I do not think there will be because I have dealt with things very discreetly.' She stood back and regarded her stepdaughter. 'God has given you great qualities. Cultivate them always, and labour to improve them, for I believe you are destined by Heaven for greatness.'

She watched the litter carrying Elizabeth and Mrs Ashley disappear through the gatehouse, with Tom following on horseback; he was ready to escort them to Cheshunt. As she walked back into the house, she felt both sadness and relief. With luck, she had avoided a scandal, and she had managed to part with Elizabeth on good terms. Now all she had to do was mend her marriage.

Chapter 29

1548

The next day, they departed for Sudeley. Anne went with them, to be with Katharine for the birth, as did Mary Odell. Lady Jane Grey was also of the company and looking forward to this new adventure. Lizzie was absent. Not wanting to be parted from Will, she had taken lodgings by the Barbican, not far from Charterhouse Square.

Katharine's retinue was headed by Sir Robert Tyrwhitt, her comptroller, and his wife, who was a good friend to her. She had many ladies and gentlemen with her, a contingent of the Yeomen of the Guard, Master Coverdale, who had recently been appointed her new almoner, Dr Parkhurst, her chaplain, and Dr Huicke.

As they rode west, lodging by night at inns or the great houses of the nobility, Katharine's heart felt as heavy as the burden she carried in her belly. She was in turmoil, striving desperately to feel the same about Tom and fearing that things would never be the same. He was being exceptionally loving and attentive, yet she could take little pleasure in it. All she could think of was that moment when she had seen him kissing Elizabeth in the garden, and Elizabeth saying that Tom had wanted to marry her before anyone else. She had always known that he was ambitious. But she was carrying his child; he would not forsake her now, of a certainty. She was fretting unnecessarily. Maybe things would be better when the child arrived. She fervently prayed so.

Sudeley took her breath away. It was beautiful, a castle out of a fairy tale, nestling in a lush green park and surrounded by glorious gardens. The castle was built of the golden stone common to the parts roundabouts, and the new state apartments were truly regal. Tom had spared no expense on making them fit for a queen. He looked on, grinning, as Katharine walked through them, admiring the great windows with their ornate carvings and the sumptuous furnishings, and followed her upstairs to the presence chamber, which was two storeys high and looked out over the glorious gardens. From there, a door led to her private chambers and chapel. He was like a dog seeking its mistress's approval, clearly hoping that this beautiful home he had created for her would banish her unhappiness and make them whole again.

Leaving the castle, they walked along a covered cloister that led to a door at the side of a graceful chapel. When Katharine entered its cool, fragrant gloom, she found herself in a little oratory with a squint affording a view of the altar.

'For your private devotions,' Tom said, behind her.

'You have thought of everything,' she said. He squeezed her hand then let it go as she sank clumsily to her knees and bent her head in prayer, giving thanks for their safe arrival and beseeching God to help her find a way back to her husband.

Later that day, they sat in the privy garden with Anne and Mary, sipping cordial and watching Lady Jane, her red hair streaming free, picking flowers. It was so peaceful here. Maybe God had brought her to this place to be healed. She looked across at Tom and smiled at him.

She had not been at Sudeley for a week when a letter arrived from Elizabeth, saying how sad she had been to leave Katharine's household and acknowledging what a good friend her dear mother had been. She had signed herself 'your Highness's humble daughter'. There was a letter for Tom, too, which he showed Katharine, who saw nothing in it to which anyone could object. Elizabeth was making it clear that all she had to offer him was friendship.

Katharine asked him to send on some jewellery that she had kept for Elizabeth, but he kept forgetting, despite her reminding him. When he did send it, with an apology for the delay, Elizabeth assured him that it did not matter. *I am a friend not won or lost with trifles*, she declared, and concluded with her humble commendations to the Queen's Highness.

A short note from the King arrived, in which he asked to be remembered to Katharine. And then came the news, from Fowler, that Nan had borne Ned a fourth son, a lusty babe named after his Majesty.

'Well, I trust we shall have another!' Tom declared. He was very excited about the coming birth. The child's rooms were ready, the tapestries hung, the gold cradle lined with crimson velvet awaiting its occupant, the midwife, nursery maids and rockers installed. Nothing was too good for his son.

Katharine could not wait to hold her child in her arms and longed for her confinement to be safely over. She remembered Nan once saying that childbirth was easy, like shelling peas. She hoped it would be like that for her too and prayed that she would have a son, so as not to be bested by Nan. It rankled with her – and she knew it did with Tom – that Ned had not bothered to inform him of his happy news, a sure indication that he was still feeling sour towards his brother.

Elizabeth's letters kept coming. Katharine sent friendly replies until the day her thumb swelled up and writing became painful, and she had to ask Anne to pen a note for her.

'I feel so drained,' she told her sister. 'It's not just my thumb. I fear I am unwell. Everything's an effort. Did you feel like that when you were pregnant?'

Anne patted her hand. 'Everyone's different. Have you told Dr Huicke how you feel?'

'Yes, he said I'm not to worry.' She picked up the tiny cap she had been embroidering for the child and began stitching. 'If only Tom would allow me to rest.'

He had been dancing attendance on her and there was no doubt that things were better between them. Yet he had insisted on keeping open house, inviting all the local nobility and gentry to visit and even friends from London, and extending lavish hospitality. He was doing it to please her, she knew, and she was glad to hear their guests speak of Sudeley as the second court in the land.

'I know, he never stops,' Anne said. 'You must feel as if you are always on display. It's not right for a woman in your condition. Have you told him how you feel?'

Katharine rested her head back against the chair. 'I've tried, but he wants to show off Sudeley and get even with Ned. He planned this castle to outrival Somerset House.'

'I'll speak to him,' Anne insisted. 'He needs to understand that, if he wants a healthy son, you need to rest.'

'You're a good friend to me, sister,' Katharine smiled, barely able to keep awake.

Whatever Anne said to Tom, he paid heed. The guests departed, the entertaining ceased, and they were blissfully alone. Katharine spent her days walking in the gardens, praying in her private chapel or just sitting in the shade of an ancient oak tree, enjoying the warm August weather.

One afternoon, Lady Jane brought her another letter from Elizabeth, in which her stepdaughter expressed concern about her injured hand. *My Lord Admiral wrote that his naughty child is very busy in your womb. If I were at his birth, no doubt I would see him beaten for the trouble he has put you to.* Katharine had to smile at that; she had always loved Elizabeth's ready wit. And she was pleased to read that Sir Anthony and Lady Denny, and Mrs Ashley, had all sent their prayers and good wishes for her safe delivery. It wanted but a month till that happy day. Enveloped in her idyll and a strange yet comforting sense that everything would be all right, she could no longer feel rancour towards Elizabeth, or even Tom. What had happened at Hanworth seemed long ago and far away.

Tom joined her under the oak tree, setting down a goblet of wine before her. 'I've heard from our lawyers,' he said. 'The plague is bad in London, so they've had to defer pursuing the matter of your jewels. They will write again when they think it safe to meet with their colleagues in the Temple who are advising them on the matter. I'm sorry, darling. We will get the jewels back.'

'It doesn't matter,' she said. And, truly, it didn't. Like her other cares, it had receded.

Tom handed her a letter. 'It's from Will. He's at Rye House and I think he's taking my advice. We shall see. You'll be glad to hear that

Gardiner is in the Tower. He's preached once too often against the government's religious reforms.'

'That will keep him out of mischief,' Katharine smiled, marvelling how Fortune's wheel could turn. Gardiner would have had her burned if he could. She felt no pity for him.

'Good riddance, I say!' Tom grinned.

Katharine was overjoyed when, in the middle of August, Will arrived at Sudeley.

'I thought you were at Rye House?' she cried, struggling to her feet to embrace him as he was shown into her privy chamber.

'I had to come,' he said, kissing her. 'Something told me that a very important little person will soon be arriving. My, Kate, you do have a great belly!'

They all laughed and, when Anne had been hugged, and Mary and Jane, and Tom had shaken hands warmly with Will, they all adjourned to the garden, where the steward brought a flagon of wine.

'I have a letter for you.' Will handed it to Katharine. 'I saw the Lady Mary at Newhall last week.'

'I'm delighted to hear from her,' Katharine said and read the letter. Mary hoped to hear good news from her very soon and asked to be commended to Tom. Seeing that she had signed herself 'your Highness's humble and loving daughter', Katharine felt grateful tears spring to her eyes. Mary was her friend again. The world was righting itself, and soon her happiness would be crowned with a child.

Days after Will arrived, she took to her chamber, going into seclusion with her ladies to await the birth. Until she was churched after her lying-in, no men might be admitted to her apartments, apart from Tom, her chaplain and Dr Huicke, and none were permitted to be present at the birth; the midwife, a calm, motherly lady called Mrs Gotobed, would be in charge. Katharine felt safe with her.

She spent her days resting on her bed or helping Lady Jane with her lessons or making a layette for the baby. She was eating well, but suffering from the heat because the midwife had ordered all her chamber windows save one to be covered with hangings and kept closed. As soon as the woman had left the room, Katharine would open that one window wide, but it made little difference. The air was hot and still.

The weather broke on 30 August. Katharine awoke to the sound of thunder and the rain rattling against the windows. Now and then, there was a flash of lightning.

She became aware of a nagging pain like trapped wind. She twisted and turned in the bed, but still felt uncomfortable. Only when she got up to go to the privy did she realise that the pains were coming every few minutes.

It could not be, surely? The child wasn't due for another week or so.

She called Mrs Gotobed, who felt her belly and confirmed that her travail had begun. 'We must get your Grace on the pallet bed,' she said. But, as Katharine walked towards it, she felt a mighty convulsion.

'Help me!' she gasped, clutching her stomach.

Mrs Gotobed caught her and helped her to lie down, then parted her legs and examined her. 'Your Grace is ready to give birth!'

'I thought it would take hours,' Katharine breathed.

'One can never predict these things. Now, Madam, lie on your side and, when the urge comes, push!'

As Katharine lay there labouring, having found to her relief that pushing made it less painful, the midwife summoned Anne, Mary and the other gentlewomen. Anne took Katharine's hand and murmured gentle words of encouragement. Mary was rather more bracing. 'Push, Madam, push!'

'Oh, this is hard,' Katharine groaned. 'Bring me my cramp rings.' The King had blessed them for her at Easter and she had great faith in their power to ease pain. No sooner had she put them on than she felt the child moving downwards.

'I can see the head!' Mrs Gotobed cried. 'Now, bear down, Madam. He'll soon be here.'

Katharine gathered her strength for a final push and suddenly felt the infant slither out of her. She lay there panting, and heard it cry lustily. 'Oh, my baby!' she cried. 'What is it?'

There was a short silence. 'A fair young lady, Madam,' the midwife said.

For a moment, all she could feel was dismay. How was she going to tell Tom? He had never, for one second, entertained the idea that their baby might be a girl. He was all fired up at the prospect of having a son. But, when Anne laid her daughter in her arms and she looked at the little face and tiny, star-like hands, she felt an overpowering wave of love, and nothing else mattered.

She lay there, euphoric, cradling her child until the nursemaid took it away to be cleaned and swaddled; the wet nurse would then come to feed it. The midwife gave Katharine a wash, dressed her in a clean night-rail and combed her hair. She was bleeding a lot down below, and suffering stomach cramps. Mrs Gotobed wadded some towels between her legs and went away to consult Dr Huicke. When she came back, she told Katharine that the bleeding and the pains would ease soon; there was no cause for concern. Then the child was brought back to her and Tom was summoned.

Katharine took one look at his face and knew they had told him he had a daughter. Disappointment was writ there large. But, when she held out the baby to him, she saw his expression change. Gazing down at his perfect little girl, he broke into a smile. 'God bless you, little one,' he murmured, looking on her with love. Then he glanced up at Katharine. 'You have done well, darling. She is beautiful. It'll be a son next time, eh?'

She smiled weakly. She could not even begin to think about a next time, after what she had just gone through. She'd been saying to herself, *never again* – and had been amazed when the midwife had said it was an easy labour. She knew women who had gone through this ten or twelve times, and was suddenly filled with admiration for them.

'I'm relieved to see you looking so well,' Tom said, laying the child in her arms. 'I'm told it was a quick travail.'

'So they say. It was painful and hard work,' she said, kissing the infant's head, 'but well worth it, wasn't it, little darling?'

'What shall we name her?' Tom asked.

'I'd like Mary, after the Lady Mary. She would be so pleased.'

Tom nodded. 'Yes, I like Mary too. Mary Seymour. It sounds right, and it suits the little one.'

Katharine smiled and handed Mary back to him. 'Lay her in her cradle, please. I need to sleep.'

Just as she gave him the swaddled bundle, she felt a large clot come away from her womb.

'Tom, fetch the midwife,' she said, panicking. 'I'm bleeding quite heavily.'

He put the baby in the cradle and hurried out, returning with Mrs Gotobed, who shooed him away then inspected the clot.

'Quite normal,' she said. 'You probably won't lose much more. It's all come away at once.' As she spoke, Katharine lost another clot. 'It'll settle down,' the midwife said, and went away.

Tom returned. 'Mrs Gotobed said you're not to worry,' he told her.

'Darling, I am worried,' Katharine told him, gripping his hand. 'Please get Dr Huicke. I want him to see what I'm losing.'

Tom gaped at her, clearly shocked. 'I'm not having a doctor examine you. It's not seemly. Mrs Gotobed says that everything's all right, and I have confidence in her. Now get some sleep. I'm sure the problem will clear up.'

'I pray it does,' Katharine said, not convinced, 'but I'd really rather speak to Dr Huicke. I don't care if it's seemly or not.'

'No,' Tom said firmly. 'It would be most improper.'

She did sleep, but, when she awoke that evening and lifted the bedclothes, she was shocked to see a large scarlet stain. Mrs Gotobed, when summoned, examined it closely then smiled.

'No clots. Some women do bleed heavily immediately after childbirth. Not to worry.'

Tom came to see her and found her fretting.

'Calm down, Kate. All will be well. I hear that our Mary's got good lungs. She's been roaring for her milk. The wet nurse is feeding her now. I've written to all our friends and sent a letter by fast courier to Ned, to announce her birth.'

Ned. Nan. Inwardly, she groaned. Nan would be gloating, having

489

borne a son. But why should Katharine care? No child could ever be as wonderful and as loved as Mary.

The bleeding did not stop. When, two days later, Tom came to show her Ned's letter, she was beginning to feel light-headed and a little odd. It was a kind letter. Ned had said how pleased he was that she had escaped the dangers of childbirth and had made Tom the father of so pretty a daughter. Then he spoiled it by saying that it would have been to both him and Nan – and to Tom, he supposed – a greater joy and comfort if this firstborn had been a son; yet, to compensate, this successful confinement brought with it the promise of many happy sons in the future. He asked Tom to give her his hearty commendations and congratulations.

By that evening, Katharine was feverish and had a crushing headache. At midnight, she began to suffer cold sweats that left her shuddering. Mrs Gotobed and her women heaped the bedclothes over her, even though she was burning up and it was a warm night. They made her drink, sip after sip of ale or cooled boiled water.

In the morning, she awoke with a raging thirst and dreadful stomach cramps. Almost insensible with the fever, she was vaguely aware of figures clustered around her bed.

Someone gripped her hand. 'Kate, can you hear me? Kate! Kate!' That was Tom. She nodded at him weakly, then felt hands on her belly.

'Her Grace's stomach is swollen,' the midwife said, sounding concerned. 'I'm sending for Dr Huicke, my lord, by your leave.'

'Yes, all right.' There was reluctance in Tom's voice. Katharine drifted off again, conscious of waves of heat engulfing her and that constant cramping in her stomach.

She came to once more to find Dr Huicke taking her pulse.

'Much too fast,' he said. 'This is childbed fever, there's no doubt of it, and she's not putting up any resistance, just lying there listlessly. Mrs Gotobed, are you certain that the placenta came away completely?'

There was a pause. 'I think so,' the midwife said.

'I do hope so, for if it didn't, there can be complications. We need to watch for any sudden remission, because that is a dangerous sign.'

'Is she going to die?' she heard Tom whisper.

'With God's help, no, but we must be vigilant.'

The voices faded and she was left to sleep. In her fitful dreams, she was playing with her baby in the garden, the two of them sitting on a rug on the grass. She had a little rattle on a ribbon and the child was laughing at it and waving her hands, trying to grab it.

She awoke with terrible griping pains that gave way to a looseness of the bowels. Time after time, the midwife and her chamberers seemed to be heaving her out of bed, like a rag doll, and onto the close stool. Then she began to vomit. She had never felt so ill in all her life. When the purging finally ceased, she was so weak that she thought she would die. In fact, death would be a merciful release. She lay there, mechanically reciting a prayer she had been composing when her labour began. 'All my hope, most pitiful Lord, have I cast on Thee. Let me be no more, I pray Thee . . .'

She lost track of the days and the nights. But she knew it was night-time when she came to herself at last and became aware of Anne and Mary departing to their bedchambers, taking their candles with them. She slept then, on and off, although she could not get comfortable because of the pain in her belly. The towel between her legs felt sodden and she was aware of the sickly metallic smell of blood. How long had she been like this?

She awoke hours later and watched as Lady Tyrwhitt entered the bedchamber and went to open the window. Sunlight flooded the room.

'Lady Tyrwhitt,' she said weakly, 'what day is it?'

'Monday, your Grace.' Lady Tyrwhitt hastened to the bed and smiled. 'It's good to hear you sounding like yourself again.'

'I feel so ill. I fear I am so sick that I cannot live.'

'Nonsense, Madam,' Lady Tyrwhitt replied, rather too sharply. 'I can see no likelihood of death in you. Let's get you changed.'

Katharine dozed again, letting her maids wash her and change her night-rail. Then Tom came in and she could almost feel Lady Tyrwhitt bristling; she had never liked or approved of him.

Tom was standing over her. She watched him as if through water. He was laughing, grinning at her. He had hurt her, but she could not remember how, and he was taunting her, making a mockery of the hurt he had caused, and somehow it was all bound up with the cramping in her stomach. That was his fault!

He took her hand.

'She was lucid earlier, my lord,' Lady Tyrwhitt said. 'She seems to have relapsed.'

'I am perfectly well,' Katharine replied, 'but I am not well handled, for those about me do not care for me, but stand laughing at my grief.'

'Why, sweetheart! I wish you no hurt!' Tom cried.

Katharine gripped his hand and pulled him closer. 'No, my lord,' she said in his ear, 'but you have given me many shrewd taunts.'

'What did she say?' Tom asked. She was aware of him and Lady Tyrwhitt moving away and of a low murmur of conversation. Then Tom came back, lay down on the bed and took her in his arms.

'Darling, get well for me,' he begged, kissing her. 'I need you. You mean everything to me.'

Dimly, she was aware that this illness was all his fault. And then she remembered why and suddenly she was wide awake.

'My lord,' she told him, 'I would have given a thousand marks to have talked to Dr Huicke the first day I was delivered, but I dared not, for fear of displeasing you.' And then the floodgates opened, and all her hurt and anger poured out, about Elizabeth and how he had put them all at risk in dallying with her, without any thought for her or their marriage. She berated him for having set his cap at Elizabeth before her and treating her as second best, for all that they had meant to each other.

'Well, you can make your bid for her soon!' she cried, surprised that she had the strength for such vehemence. 'For I shall be dead. It would not surprise me if you had helped me on my way!'

'Darling, no, no!' Tom kept protesting. 'Be still, you are not well. You must conserve your strength. I don't want to lose you – I have been praying and praying for you to get better! You must believe me.'

She wept then and, once she had started, she could not stop. Still Tom lay with her, holding her and assuring her how much he loved her. 'This is not my Kate speaking,' he said. 'My Kate knows that I will never hurt her again. We have everything to live for, darling. Rest now, and live, for me, and for Mary!'

A great calm came over her, and an irresistible urge to sleep. She had been upset and angry about something, but she could not remember what it was, and it didn't matter now. She had got it off her chest, and that was an end to it. She slept.

When she woke, she was still in Tom's arms. Her mind seemed to be working normally, but her body felt drained and wrung out. She could still feel the blood seeping intermittently from her womb and the pain in her stomach. But she was getting better, she was sure of it.

Tom stirred and sat up. 'You're back with us,' he said, looking down at her anxiously. 'I'll fetch Dr Huicke.' As he left, she heard him murmur to Lady Tyrwhitt, 'I think she's in remission.'

The doctor checked her vital signs and regarded her gravely. 'Madam, I would be failing in my duty if I did not advise you to prepare your soul for death. You may yet recover, but I can do nothing more for you.'

Katharine could not quite take in what he was saying. Tom was staring at him in alarm. 'But she could still get better?'

'With God, all things are possible,' Dr Huicke said. 'But it will not be easy for her to get better.'

As soon as the doctor had gone, Tom turned to Katharine. 'Don't listen to him. All you need is rest and sleep and some heartening food, and you'll soon be well.' She could hear the fear in his voice and was surprised at how calm she herself felt. She was in God's hands and He would decide what was best for her.

'All the same, Tom, I should make my will, with your permission.'

He looked at her, crestfallen.

'It's best to be prepared, just in case,' she said. 'Then I can rest easy and concentrate on recovering.'

'Very well, I give you my consent,' Tom said.

At her request, he summoned her secretary to write the will and Dr Huicke and Dr Parkhurst to witness it.

'I will be brief,' Katharine told them. 'Write that, with all my heart and desire, I freely give, will and bequeath to my husband, Lord

493

Seymour, Lord High Admiral of England, all my worldly goods, wishing them to be a thousand times more in value than they are.' She smiled at Tom as she said it.

'I make no mention of Mary,' she told him. 'I know that you will do what is best for her.'

'But you will be here for her,' he said, raising her so that she could sign her name.

'That is my constant prayer,' she said.

They left her to sleep. When she woke up, Anne tried to get her to take a little broth, but she could only sip some wine. She felt light-headed again, as if everything was unreal. Sometimes, in her mind, she was playing in the gardens at Rye House, or facing up to Red Hair at Snape, or watching Henry see off the Lord Chancellor . . .

She was vaguely aware of Dr Parkhurst praying by her bed, intoning the prayers for the sick, and of his hands anointing her, preparing her for her final journey. There would be no Catholic last rites for her. She had seen God's great work accomplished and could now, like Simeon in the Bible, depart in peace.

It was dark when Tom brought Mary to her.

'Kate,' he said gently, and she knew he was weeping. 'Our daughter is here. Are you able to give her your blessing?'

He lifted her hand and laid it on the little head.

'Bless you, my darling one,' she mouthed.

The voices faded, as did the light. But there was a greater light beckoning ahead and, as she went towards it, full of joy and hope, she could just hear, faintly, far behind her, a voice crying, 'Of your charity, pray for the soul of Katharine, sometime Queen of England . . .'

Author's Note

The views on religion expressed in this book are those of the sixteenth century and the historical figures of the day. They are essential to our understanding of Katharine Parr's story.

When I came to write this novel, I had not researched Katharine Parr for thirty years, during which time new perspectives on her have emerged. I have consulted many sources, but I owe a huge debt of gratitude in particular to the work of Linda Porter, Susan James and Elizabeth Norton.

I have followed the historical record throughout the novel, although in places I have telescoped events slightly, so as not to create unnecessary small scenes that do not move the narrative along, and I have occasionally put quotes by historical figures into the mouths of other characters.

There is no evidence that Edward Burgh was homosexual, although some writers have put forward the theory to account for the fact that he and Katharine had no children. Katharine's views on homosexuality reflect those of her own time, not ours.

The titles 'your Grace', 'your Highness' and 'your Majesty' were all used when addressing the King. Likewise, the names Burgh and Borough are interchangeable. I have used Burgh for the surname and Borough for the title.

There is no doubt that Lord Borough was an overbearing and unpleasant character. The scene in which he beats his wife is fictional, but I based it on an Elizabethan woodcut showing a man doing just that, with his children looking on for their edification. It was a husband's right to beat his wife if she displeased him.

The historical evidence shows that Henry VIII and, probably, Thomas Seymour, showed an interest in Katharine Parr during the lifetime of her husband Lord Latimer. Henry's first recorded gifts to her were paid for on 16 February 1543; Latimer died at the end of that month. Four years later, in a letter to Seymour, Katharine wrote: *My mind was fully bent the other time I was at liberty to marry you before any man I know. Howbeit, God withstood my will therein most vehemently for a time.* This suggests that Seymour's courtship pre-dated the King's.

In regard to the storyline surrounding Katharine Parr's connection with the Windsor martyrs, eagle-eyed readers may have noticed that this episode occurs earlier chronologically in *Anna of Kleve: Queen of Secrets* than it does in this book. When researching *Anna of Kleve*, I found very little on the subject of Cawarden's involvement and resolved to research it in greater depth for Katharine Parr, but I did not realise that the dating was incorrect. That only became apparent when I began to work the tale into Katharine's narrative and had to delve further to make it fit historically.

In 1543, William Parr applied to Parliament for a divorce on the grounds of his wife's adultery. The unreliable 'Spanish Chronicle' of the reign of Henry VIII claimed that he pressed the King to authorise the death penalty (which a peer of the realm was entitled to demand if he found his wife to be unfaithful) and that Katharine Parr successfully petitioned the King to spare her. I can find no other evidence to substantiate this, but that same account suggests that Katharine knew something of the true circumstances of Lady Parr's adultery, which were not as her brother had been given to believe by false witnesses. It is this that gave me my storyline, and I apologise to the shade of Dorothy Bray for having maligned her.

Katharine's words of consolation after her sister Anne's baby had died are based on a letter she wrote to Lady Wriothesley. I have toned down her exhortations, as they seem harsh to modern sensibilities, yet they are evidence of her firm faith in attaining Heaven.

I have put my own interpretation on the much-debated events of Katharine's life. Most historians (myself included) have dated John Foxe's account of the plot to arrest Katharine for heresy to 1546, but Foxe places it in 1545, the year after the siege of Boulogne, which fits well with the conservatives' purge of heretics at that time. I don't believe that Katharine had much to do with Anne Askew, but I do think that they were connected in some way, although there is no record of the visits described in the novel. The details of Anne's torture in the Tower come from her own account.

It is said that Henry VIII did not know that Sir George Blagge was to be tried for heresy until after he was condemned, but it's hardly likely that he would have ignored the prolonged absence of a favoured gentleman of his privy chamber and not discovered the truth well before Blagge's trial.

Henry's conversation with Katharine on the morning he went to address Parliament for the last time is based on his celebrated speech to Parliament.

Katharine's wedding to Thomas Seymour was solemnised with such secrecy that the date is unrecorded. Gregorio Leti, a late and often unreliable source, states that they were married on 3 March 1547. Other sources suggest that they waited until the second half of May, but that date is at variance with other evidence, including Katharine's letters. This fourth marriage made Katharine Parr England's most married queen. There is nothing to say that she and Tom were married at Seymour Place, but it would have afforded them the privacy they needed. For the reasons outlined in the novel, their wedding must have presented logistical problems. Without banns, they may indeed have made vows according to widespread custom; such vows, followed by sexual intercourse, constituted a valid marriage. I have imagined their obtaining the Church's blessing in late May, when some sources state they were married.

It is not known who built the impressive state apartments at Sudeley Castle. Some suggest that it was Richard III, although there is no evidence that he ever visited, and he spent only a small sum on improvements. Jasper Tudor, uncle of Henry VII, lived for some years at Sudeley, and could have improved it, but the likeliest builder was Thomas Seymour, who paid out large sums for building works and installed as overseer Sir William Sharington, who had recently transformed Lacock Abbey into a palatial residence.

I have long pondered on why Katharine wished to consult Dr Huicke after her child was born, and why Thomas forbade it. She must, surely, have been worried about certain symptoms she was experiencing. Given that the evidence suggests that she died of puerperal fever, I wondered if it was caused by an infection arising from a partially retained placenta, which can cause the symptoms I have described in the novel. It was then taboo for doctors to attend women in childbed, which was probably why Seymour did not want Huicke to examine his wife.

I have hugely enjoyed writing the Six Tudor Queens series and feel sad that it is now finished. I should like to express my gratitude to my editors, Mari Evans at Headline and Susanna Porter at Ballantine, for commissioning the six books and for their great enthusiasm for the project; to Flora Rees, for her creative and sensitive editing; to Frankie Edwards, Kim Hovey, Emily Hartley, Jo Liddiard, Caitlin Raynor, Siobhan Hooper, Jane Selley, Katie Sunley, Emily Patience and all the unsung heroes and heroines in the production teams in London, Canada, New York, Australia and elsewhere. You have all given me warm and professional support *par excellence*, and I am hugely grateful.

I would also like to thank the amazingly talented Balbusso Twins for their fabulous, award-winning artwork for the book jackets and end-papers, which have given the series a rich and unique look of its own. As ever, I owe a great debt of gratitude to my agent, Julian Alexander, for all his support. I shall never forget how his face lit up when I first suggested the series to him back in 2014.

Lastly, but never least, my loving thanks go to Rankin, my husband, who has been my mainstay throughout the past six years; without him, these books would not have been written.

Dramatis Personae

(In order of appearance or first mention. Names in italics are fictional.)

Katharine Parr, daughter of Sir Thomas Parr and Maud Green
Maud Green, Lady Parr, Katharine's mother
Henry VIII, King of England
Katherine of Aragon, Queen of England, first wife of Henry VIII
William Parr (later Lord Parr and Earl of Essex), Katharine's brother
Dr Melton, chaplain to the Parr family
Anne Parr (later Lady Herbert), Katharine's sister
Sir Thomas Parr, Katharine's father
Sir William Parr (later Lord Parr) of Horton, Katharine's uncle
Cuthbert Tunstall (later Bishop of Durham)
Agnes, Katharine's nurse
Mary Salisbury, Lady Parr of Horton, Katharine's aunt
Magdalen Parr (later Lady Lane), Katharine's cousin, daughter of Sir
    William Parr
Anne (Nan) Parr, Katharine's cousin, daughter of Sir William Parr
Elizabeth Parr, Katharine's cousin, daughter of Sir William Parr
Mary Parr, Katharine's cousin, daughter of Sir William Parr
Margery Parr, Katharine's cousin, daughter of Sir William Parr
Elizabeth Cheyney (later Lady Vaux), Katharine's cousin, daughter of
    Sir Thomas Cheyney
Sir Thomas More (later Lord Chancellor), celebrated humanist scholar
Princess (Lady) Mary (later Mary I), daughter of Henry VIII and
    Katharine of Aragon
Dr Clarke, Sir William Parr's household chaplain
Thomas (later Lord) Vaux, husband of Elizabeth Cheyney
Nicholas, Lord Vaux of Harrowden, father of Thomas Vaux
Sir Ralph Lane, husband of Magdalen Parr
Henry, Lord Scrope of Bolton

Thomas Fiennes, Lord Dacre, his father-in-law

Henry Scrope, son of Henry, Lord Scrope of Bolton

Henry Fitzroy, Duke of Richmond and Somerset, bastard son of Henry VIII

Laetitia (Lettice), daughter of Sir Ralph Lane and Magdalen Dacre

Cardinal Thomas Wolsey, Lord Chancellor

Henry Bourchier, Earl of Essex

Ann Bourchier, wife of William Parr, Katharine's brother

Mary Say, Countess of Essex

Anne Boleyn (later Queen of England and second wife of Henry VIII)

Pope Clement VII

Charles V, Holy Roman Emperor

Edward Burgh, Katharine's first husband

Sir Thomas Burgh (later Lord Borough of Gainsborough), his father

Edward, Lord Borough of Gainsborough, Edward's grandfather

Agnes Tyrwhitt, late first wife of Sir Thomas Burgh

Alice London, second wife of Sir Thomas Burgh

Richard III, King of England

Thomas Burgh, Edward's brother

William Burgh, Edward's brother

Henry Burgh, Edward's brother

Eleanor Burgh, Edward's sister

Agnes Burgh, Edward's sister

Elinor, Katharine's maid

Groom to the Burghs

Sir Edward Seymour (later Earl of Hertford, Duke of Somerset and Lord Protector of England), brother of Queen Jane Seymour

Cardinal Lorenzo Campeggio, Papal legate

Dr Allgood, chaplain to the Burghs

Steward to the Burghs

Annie Burgh, Edward's sister

Marget Burgh, Edward's sister

Sir William Askew

Anne Askew, his daughter

A physician from Scunthorpe

Elizabeth Owen, wife of Thomas Burgh, Edward's brother

Katherine (Kat) Neville, Lady Strickland, Katharine's kinswoman

Sir Walter Strickland, her late first husband

Henry Burgh, her late second husband
Mr Darcy, her late third husband
Walter Strickland, her son
Thomas Strickland, her son
Roger Strickland, her son
Elizabeth Strickland, her daughter
Anne Strickland, her daughter
Mary Strickland, her daughter
Agnes Strickland, her daughter
Anne Burgh, her daughter
Frances Darcy, her daughter
Sir William Parr, Katharine's grandfather
John Neville, Lord Latimer, Katharine's second husband
The Holy Maid of Leominster
The Prior of Leominster
Dorothy de Vere, Lord Latimer's late first wife
John (Jack) Neville (later Lord Latimer), Lord Latimer's son
Margaret Neville, Lord Latimer's daughter
Elizabeth Musgrave, Lord Latimer's late second wife
Walter Rawlinson, Lord Latimer's steward
Bess Rawlinson, his wife
Marmaduke Neville, Lord Latimer's brother
Princess (Lady) Elizabeth (later Elizabeth I), daughter of Henry VIII
    and Anne Boleyn
William Neville, Lord Latimer's brother
George Neville, Lord Latimer's brother
Christopher Neville, Lord Latimer's brother
John Leland, the King's Antiquary
Sir William FitzWilliam (later Earl of Southampton)
Sir Thomas Cromwell (later Earl of Essex), Henry VIII's chief minister
Ralph Bigod, Margaret Neville's betrothed
Sir Francis Bigod, his father
William Knyvett, fourth husband of Katherine (Kat) Neville, Lady
    Strickland
John Fisher, Bishop of Rochester
Martin Luther, German reformer, founder of the Protestant religion
Jane Seymour (later Queen of England and Henry VIII's third wife)
Lord Redmayne of Harewood Castle

Charles Brandon, Duke of Suffolk
The Abbot of Jervaulx
A monk of Jervaulx
Robert Aske, a leader of the Pilgrimage of Grace
Martha Askew, daughter of Sir William Askew
Thomas Kyme, husband of Anne Askew
Sir William Ingleby of Ripley Castle
A rebel leader and his band
Lord Darcy, a leader of the Pilgrimage of Grace
Thomas Howard, Duke of Norfolk
Edward Lee, Archbishop of York
Red Hair, a rebel leader, and his band
Henry VII, King of England
The Skeleton, Red Hair's associate
A sentry at Bootham Bar, York
Sir Robert Constable, a leader of the Pilgrimage of Grace
Sir Thomas Wyatt
Henry Howard, Earl of Surrey, son of Thomas Howard, Duke of Norfolk
Sir Henry Wyatt, Sir Thomas Wyatt's father
Sir Richard Page
John, Lord Russell
William the Conqueror, King of England
Prince Edward (later Edward VI), son of Henry VIII and Jane Seymour
Sir William Herbert, husband of Anne Parr
Edward the Confessor, King of England
William Herbert, Earl of Pembroke
Sir Richard Herbert, his bastard son, father of Sir William Herbert
Margaret Cradock, Lady Herbert, mother of Sir William Herbert
Sir Roger, a priest at Ewyas Harold
William Tyndale, translator of the Bible into English
Henry Herbert, son of Sir William Herbert and Anne Parr
Anne of Cleves (Anna of Kleve), Queen of England and fourth wife of Henry VIII
Catherine Willoughby, Duchess of Suffolk, second wife of Charles Brandon, Duke of Suffolk
Mary Tudor, Queen of France and Duchess of Suffolk, sister of Henry VIII and late first wife of Charles Brandon, Duke of Suffolk

Stephen Gardiner, Bishop of Winchester
Sir Thomas Malory
Thomas Cranmer, Archbishop of Canterbury
Katheryn Howard, Queen of England and fifth wife of Henry VIII
John Lyngfield, Prior of Tandridge, lover of Anne Bourchier
Dorothy Bray, William Parr's mistress
Hans Holbein, the King's Painter
St Thomas Aquinas
Francis Dereham and Thomas Culpeper, Katheryn Howard's lovers
The ambassador of Cleves
Master Parr, Ann Bourchier's bastard son by John Lyngfield
A London physician
James V, King of Scots
Mary, Queen of Scots, his daughter
Marie de Guise, Queen Regent of Scotland, her mother, widow of James V
Sir Thomas Seymour (later Lord Seymour of Sudeley), fourth husband of Katharine Parr
Mary Howard, Duchess of Richmond, daughter of Thomas Howard, Duke of Norfolk, and widow of Henry Fitzroy, Duke of Richmond and Somerset
Sir John Seymour, late father of Jane Seymour, Edward Seymour and Thomas Seymour
Gregory, Steward
Margaret Wentworth, Lady Seymour, Sir John Seymour's widow
Adam, Katharine's cook
Will Somers, the King's Fool
A priest of St Anne's Church, Blackfriars
Miles Coverdale, translator of the Bible into English
Hugh Latimer, former Bishop of Worcester
Elizabeth Brooke, second wife of William Parr
George Brooke, Lord Cobham, her father
A royal usher
Lady Margaret Douglas, niece of Henry VIII
Charles Howard, brother of Katheryn Howard, Queen of England
Anne (Nan) Stanhope, Countess of Hertford (later Duchess of Somerset), wife of Edward Seymour, Earl of Hertford (later Duke of Somerset and Lord Protector)

The Bassanos, court musicians
Matthew Parker, chaplain to Henry VIII
Francis Goldsmith, Katharine's chaplain
Lord Thomas Howard, younger son of Thomas Howard, Duke of Norfolk
Roger Ascham, celebrated scholar
Desiderius Erasmus, celebrated humanist scholar
Nicholas Udall, former headmaster of Eton
Elizabeth, Lady Hoby
Sir Philip Hoby, diplomat, her husband
Susanna Gilman, Flemish artist
John Bettes, painter to Henry VIII
Levina Teerlinc, Flemish artist
Gardiner, Lady Suffolk's dog
John Christopherson, Bishop of Chichester, Katharine's almoner
Nicholas Ridley, chaplain to Henry VIII
Nicholas Shaxton, Bishop of Salisbury
Jane the Fool, Katharine's jester
The Dwarf, Katharine's fool
Rig, Katharine's dog
Katherine Champernowne (later Mrs Ashley), governess to the Lady Elizabeth
Mark Smeaton, musician
Dr Richard Cox, tutor to Prince Edward
Thomas Tallis, composer, organist of the Chapel Royal
Sir Thomas Cawarden, Master of the Revels and Tents
John Marbeck, Master of the Choristers of the Chapel Royal at Windsor
Fulke, Katharine's groom
Robert Ockham, Sir Thomas Cawarden's man
Lady Bryan, lady mistress to Prince Edward
Mother Jack, nurse to Prince Edward
Lucas Hornebolte, painter to Henry VIII
Hans Eworth, painter to Henry VIII
Isabella, Queen of Castile, mother of Katharine of Aragon
Empress Matilda, twelfth-century claimant to the English throne
The Duke of Najera, Spanish envoy
Eustache Chapuys, Imperial ambassador
Sir Anthony Denny, head of Henry VIII's Privy Chamber

Sir Thomas Wriothesley, Lord Chancellor
Mrs Jennings, midwife
Short-lived infant son of Sir William Herbert and Anne Parr
Infant child of Edward Seymour, Earl of Hertford, and Anne Stanhope
Matthew Stewart, Earl of Lennox, husband of Lady Margaret Douglas
Thomas Thirlby, Bishop of Westminster
Sir William Petre, Secretary of State
Anthony, infant son of Sir Thomas Wriothesley
Jane Cheyney, Lady Wriothesley
Dr John Cheke, tutor to Prince Edward
Sir William Butts, physician to Henry VIII
Blanche Parry, gentlewoman to the Lady Elizabeth
Francis Talbot, Earl of Shrewsbury
John Calvin, Swiss religious reformer
Eleanor Paston, Countess of Rutland
Margaret Beaufort, Countess of Richmond and Derby, Henry VIII's
    grandmother
Francis I, King of France
Marguerite of Valois, sister of Francis I, King of France
Henry Stewart, Lord Darnley, eldest son of Matthew Stewart, Earl of
    Lennox, and Lady Margaret Douglas
Dr Thomas Wendy, royal physician
Dr John Chamber, physician to Henry VIII
Elizabeth, Lady Tyrwhitt
George Blagge, Gentleman of Henry VIII's Privy Chamber
William Buckler, Katharine's secretary
Francis van der Delft, Imperial ambassador
William Grindal, tutor to the Lady Elizabeth
Mary Norris, Lady Carew
Sir George Carew, Vice Admiral of the *Mary Rose*, her husband
Henry Brandon, Duke of Suffolk, son of Charles Brandon, Duke of
    Suffolk, and Catherine Willoughby
Charles Brandon (later Duke of Suffolk), son of Charles Brandon,
    Duke of Suffolk, and Catherine Willoughby
Dr Smythe, advocate of the University of Cambridge
Frances Brandon, Marchioness of Dorset (later Duchess of Suffolk),
    daughter of Charles Brandon, Duke of Suffolk, and Mary Tudor,
    niece of Henry VIII

Eleanor Brandon, Countess of Cumberland, her sister
Dr Edward Crome, preacher
John Dudley, Lord Lisle (later Earl of Warwick)
Sir Richard Rich, Chancellor of the Court of Augmentations
Sir Edmund Walsingham, Lieutenant of the Tower
Claude d'Annebaut, Admiral of France, French ambassador
Sir William Paget, royal councillor
Henry Stewart, Lord Darnley, second son of Matthew Stewart, Earl of Lennox, and Lady Margaret Douglas
Henry Fitzalan, Earl of Arundel, Lord Chamberlain of the King's Household
Sir Anthony Wingfield, Vice Chamberlain of the King's Household
Two guards at Whitehall Palace
Sir Anthony Cope, Katharine's vice chamberlain
Lady Jane Grey, daughter of Henry Grey, Duke of Suffolk, and Frances Brandon
Henry Grey, Duke of Suffolk, husband of Frances Brandon
John Harington, servant to Thomas, Lord Seymour
Margaret Wentworth, Lady Seymour, mother of Jane, Edward and Thomas Seymour
Edward Herbert, son of Sir William Herbert and Anne Parr
John Parkhurst, Katharine's chaplain
A pirate captain
Edmund Bonner, Bishop of London
John Fowler, Gentleman of Edward VI's Privy Chamber
Nicholas Throckmorton, Katharine's kinsman
A groom at Hanworth
Dr Robert Huicke, Katharine's physician
Mary Odell, granddaughter of William, Lord Parr of Horton
Joan Champernowne, Lady Denny, wife of Sir Anthony Denny
Edward, son of Edward Seymour, Duke of Somerset, and Anne Stanhope
Mrs Gotobed, Katharine's midwife
Mary Seymour, Katharine's daughter

Timeline

1491

– Birth of Henry VIII

1509

– Accession of Henry VIII

– Marriage and coronation of Henry VIII and Katherine of Aragon

1512

– Birth of Katharine Parr

1513

– Birth of William Parr, Katharine's brother

1515

– Birth of Anne Parr, Katharine's sister

1516

– Birth of the Princess Mary, daughter of Henry VIII and Katherine of Aragon

1517

– Death of Sir Thomas Parr, Katharine's father

1527

– Marriage of William Parr and Anne Bourchier

1529

– Marriage of Katharine Parr and Edward Burgh

1531

– Death of Maud Green, Lady Parr, Katharine's mother

1533

– Death of Edward Burgh

– Marriage of Henry VIII and Anne Boleyn

– Birth of the Princess Elizabeth, daughter of Henry VIII and Anne Boleyn

1534

– Marriage of Katharine Parr and John Neville, Lord Latimer

– Parliament passes the Act of Supremacy, making Henry VIII Supreme Head of the Church of England, and the Act of Succession, naming the children of Queen Anne the King's lawful heirs

1536

- Death of Katherine of Aragon
- Execution of Anne Boleyn
- Marriage of Henry VIII and Jane Seymour
- Parliament passes a new Act of Succession, settling the succession on Jane's children by the King
- Death of Henry Fitzroy
- Pilgrimage of Grace (1536–7)

1537

- Birth of Prince Edward, son of Henry VIII and Jane Seymour
- Death of Jane Seymour

1538

- Marriage of Anne Parr and Sir William Herbert

1540

- Marriage of Henry VIII and Anna of Kleve
- Anna's marriage formally annulled by Act of Parliament
- Execution of Thomas Cromwell
- Marriage of Henry VIII and Katheryn Howard

1542

- Execution of Katheryn Howard

1543

- Death of John Neville, Lord Latimer
- Annulment of the marriage of William Parr and Anne Bourchier
- Marriage of Henry VIII and Katharine Parr
- William Parr created Earl of Essex

1547

- Death of Henry VIII; accession of Edward VI
- William Parr created Marquess of Northampton
- Marriage of Katharine Parr and Thomas, Lord Seymour
- Death of William Parr, Lord Horton, Katharine's uncle

1548

- Marriage of William Parr and Elizabeth Brooke
- Birth of Mary Seymour, daughter of Katharine Parr and Thomas, Lord Seymour
- Death of Katharine Parr

Reading Group Questions

- *They were a happy group, the eight of them, fair and auburn heads bent over their books, with the sun streaming in through the latticed window.* Despite her father's early death and her mother spending much of her time at court, Katharine's childhood at Rye House is never overshadowed by loss. What were your impressions of the freedom and education that Katharine, her siblings and cousins are afforded? How does this intellectual stimulation from powerful female role models influence her approach to adult life?

- Alison Weir brings to life Katharine's circles of friends and family, showing Maud Parr's intransigent confidence, the Duchess of Suffolk's charismatic wit and the quietly persuasive Anne Parr, alongside Kat Strickland's comforting friendship, Nan Hertford's vicious rivalry and of course her stepdaughters, the future queens Elizabeth and Mary. All are seen only through Katharine's point of view, yet each has a personality that leaps from the page. Which characters did you find particularly engaging or interesting? Who would you like to learn more about, and which relationships were the most intriguing? If you've read the previous Six Tudor Queens novels, who did you most enjoy rediscovering in *The Sixth Wife*?

- Within the period of *The Sixth Wife*, we see the sweating sickness regularly sweeping through the community, the intricacies of blended families and the dangers of uncontrolled power. Which of these or other elements of the novel most resonated with you as a mirror held up to modern times? Given this, what could we learn today from the characters' responses to these experiences?

- Katharine sees her mother as a paragon of wisdom, warmth and dignity. We first met the teenaged Maud Parr in Katherine of Aragon's story *The True Queen*, and it's startling to realise that Maud was widowed aged just twenty-five. Katharine herself lost her second husband at thirty, and would die just five years later. What are your reflections on the extreme youth of so many characters in both this and all the Six Tudor Queens novels, including those in crucial leadership roles with parental, religious and moral authority? How do you think this impacted on Tudor society, both positively and negatively?

- Carefully researched historical novels offer both entertainment and the opportunity to explore different periods of time. What are your impressions of the Tudor society created by Alison Weir? How does Katharine's life in Yorkshire, far outside the court, where Henry's reforms are deeply resented, offer a new perspective? What changes for her and for the country when she finally comes to court, and how is its dynamic portrayed?

- *Who was encouraging him? Bishop Gardiner! And who was there that the King listened to, in order to counteract that pernicious influence? The answer suddenly came to her with blinding clarity. It was herself.*
Katharine finds she is caught between personal happiness and moral duty when she captures the romantic attention of both Thomas Seymour and Henry VIII. While her family sees the advantage a royal marriage could bring, Katharine struggles to set Thomas aside. Ultimately it is her faith, which she knows would be unacceptable to the King, that sways her. Do you think she made the right decision, and is it only the belief she could save souls that leads her to becoming queen? Did she in fact have any choice, once Henry's eye was on her?

- *Katharine was chilled to think what the consequences would be if their secret beliefs were ever exposed. A nest of heretics, the real Gardiner would have called the Queen's chamber if he knew the truth.*

Though raised a Catholic, Katharine desires to read the Bible in English, and is encouraged to think for herself and view women as intellectually equal to men. Do you think it inevitable that she begins to question the received wisdom about religion and how it is controlled? What are the key moments and influences leading her towards Protestantism, despite its inherent dangers, and are these mainly intellectual or emotional?

- Over the course of four marriages, Katharine learns a great deal about compromise, courage and pragmatism as well as about love and respect. How would you characterise each of her relationships? Three of her husbands betray her in some way as she faces deceit and dangerous suspicion, and even John, through his actions during the rebellion of the North, puts her at risk. How does her character mature as she navigates her way through these events? When did you find the tension strongest, and when does she manage to increase her own power? Do you think Henry was really fooled by her protestations of innocence following his accusation of heresy, or was he just looking for a way to forgive her?

- *'You've done your duty, Kate, by your family, your country and your faith. I know you didn't want to marry the King, but you did and you made an excellent queen. You should marry where you wish now.'*
  Katharine's reunion with Thomas Seymour seems to be her reward for making responsible and sensible choices throughout her life, yet her happiness is cut tragically short. We first meet Tom long before Katharine does, in *The Haunted Queen*, where his antagonism towards his older brother Ned develops from their turbulent childhood onwards. Do you find Thomas charming or entitled — and does he deserve the power he so deeply craves? What is your take on his motives and ambitions? Do you think Elizabeth was the original target for his bride?

- This is the final Six Tudor Queens novel, drawing the ambitiously crafted series to a close. History has placed Katharine as the wife who 'survived' Henry VIII, though her life weaves through all five others, either directly or at a distance. While each queen influenced the society she lived in, who do you feel most affected Katharine's outlook, first as Henry's subject and then as his Queen? What overall insights have you gained from the rich sixteenth-century universe that Alison Weir has created through these books and their accompanying short stories? What has most moved you, most surprised you and most entertained you?